IT'S LIKE THIS, CAT

Emily Cheney Neville

HarperTrophy
A Division of HarperCollins*Publishers*

To

Midnight,

"Mayor" of Gramercy Park

1954–1962

 Printed in the United States of America. For information address HarperCollins Children's Books, a division of HarperCollins Publishers, 10 East 53rd Street, New York, NY 10022. Typography by Darcy Soper. Library of Congress Catalog Card Number: 62-21292 ISBN 0-06-024390-2 ISBN 0-06-024391-0 (lib. bdg.)
ISBN 0-06-440073-5 (pbk.)

CONTENTS

1	Cat and Kate	1
2	Cat and the Underworld	9
3	Cat and Coney	22
4	Fight	31
5	Around Manhattan	41
6	And Brooklyn	50
7	Survival	63
8	West Side Story	72
9	Fathers	79
10	Cat and the Parkway	85
11	Rosh Hashanah at the Fulton Fish Market	94
12	The Red Eft	106
13	The Left Bank of Coney Island	117
14	Expedition by Ferry	128
15	Dollars and Cats	137
16	Fortune	145
17	Telephone Numbers	156
18	"Here's to Cat!"	163

1
Cat and Kate

My father is always talking about how a dog can be very educational for a boy. This is one reason I got a cat.

My father talks a lot anyway. Maybe being a lawyer he gets in the habit. Also, he's a small guy with very little gray curly hair, so maybe he thinks he's got to roar a lot to make up for not being a big hairy tough guy. Mom is thin and quiet, and when anything upsets her, she gets asthma. In the apartment—we live right in the middle of New York City—we don't have any heavy drapes or rugs, and Mom never fries any food because the doctors figure dust and smoke make her asthma worse. I don't think it's dust; I think it's Pop's roaring.

The big hassle that led to me getting Cat came when I earned some extra money baby-sitting for a little boy around the corner on Gramercy Park. I spent the money on a Belafonte record. This record has one piece about a father telling his son about the birds and the bees. I think it's funny. Pop blows his stack.

"You're not going to play that stuff in this house!" he roars. "Why aren't you outdoors, anyway? Baby-sitting! Baby-talk records! When I was your age, I made money on a newspaper-delivery route, and my dog Jeff and I used to go ten miles chasing rabbits on a good Saturday."

"Pop," I say patiently, "there are no rabbits out on Third Avenue. Honest, there aren't."

"Don't get fresh!" Pop jerks the plug out of the record player so hard the needle skips, which probably wrecks my record. So I get mad and start yelling too. Between rounds we both hear Mom in the kitchen starting to wheeze.

Pop hisses, "Now, see—you've gone and upset your mother!"

I slam the record player shut, grab a stick and ball, and run down the three flights of stairs to the street.

This isn't the first time Pop and I have played this scene, and there gets to be a pattern: When I slam out of our house mad, I go along over to my Aunt Kate's. She's not really my aunt. The kids around here call her Crazy Kate the Cat Woman because she walks along the street in funny old clothes and sneakers talking to herself, and she sometimes has half a dozen or more stray cats living with her. I guess she does sound a little looney, but it's just because she does things her own way, and she doesn't give a hoot what people think. She's sane, all right. In fact she makes a lot better sense than my pop.

It was three or four years ago, when I was a little kid, and I came tearing down our stairs crying mad after some fight with Pop, that I first met Kate. I plunged out of our door and into the street without looking. At the same moment I heard brakes scream and felt someone yank me back by the scruff of my neck. I got dropped in a heap on the sidewalk.

I looked up, and there was a shiny black car with M.D. plates and Kate waving her umbrella at the driver and shouting: "Listen, Dr. Big Shot, whose life are you saving? Can't you even watch out for a sniveling little kid crossing the street?"

The doctor looked pretty sheepish, and so did I. A few people on the sidewalk stopped to watch and snicker at us. Our janitor Butch was there, shaking his finger at me. Kate nodded to him and told him she was taking me home to mop me up.

"Yes ma'am," said Butch. He says "Yes ma'am" to all ladies.

Kate dragged me along by the hand to her apartment. She didn't say anything when we got there, just dumped me in a chair with a couple of kittens. Then she got me a cup of tea and a bowl of cottage cheese.

That stopped me snuffling to ask, "What do I put the cottage cheese on?"

"Don't put it on anything. Just eat it. Eat a bowl of it every day. Here, have an orange, too. But no cookies or candy, none of that sweet, starchy stuff. And no string beans. They're not good for you."

My eyes must have popped, but I guess I knew right that first day that you don't argue with Kate. I ate the cottage cheese—it doesn't really have any taste anyway—and I sure have always agreed with her about the string beans.

Off and on since then I've seen quite a lot of Kate. I'd pass her on the street, chirruping to some mangy old stray cat hiding under a car, and he'd always come out to be stroked. Sometimes there'd be a bunch of little kids dancing around jeering at her and calling her a witch. It made me feel real good and important to run them off.

Quite often I went with her to the A & P and helped her carry home the cat food and cottage cheese and fruit. She talks to herself all the time in the store, and if she thinks the peaches or melons don't look good that day, she shouts clear across the store to the manager. He comes across and picks her out an extra good one, just to keep the peace.

I introduced Kate to Mom, and they got along real well. Kate's leery of most people, afraid they'll make fun of her, I guess; my mom's not leery of people, but she's shy, and what with asthma and worrying about keeping me and Pop calmed down, she doesn't go out much or make dates with people. She and Kate would chat together in the stores or sitting on the stoop on a sunny day. Kate shook her head over Mom's asthma and said she'd get over it if she ate cottage cheese every day. Mom ate it for a while, but she put mayonnaise on it, which Kate says is just like poison.

The day of the fight with Pop about the Belafonte record it's cold and windy out and there are no kids in sight. I slam my ball back and forth against the wall where it says "No Ball Playing," just to limber up and let off a little spite, and then I go over to see Kate.

Kate has a permanent cat named Susan and however many kittens Susan happens to have just had. It varies. Usually there are a few other temporary stray kittens in the apartment, but I never saw any father cat there before. Today Susan and her kittens are under the stove, and Susan keeps hissing at a big tiger-striped tomcat crouching under the sofa. He turns his head away from her and looks like he never intended to get mixed up with family life. For a stray cat he's sleek and healthy-looking. Every time he moves a whisker, Susan hisses again, warningly. She believes in no visiting rights for fathers.

Kate pours me some tea and asks what's doing.

"My pop is full of hot air, as usual," I say.

"Takes one to know one," Kate says, catching me off base. I change the subject.

"How come the kittens' pop is around the house? I never saw a full-grown tom here before."

"He saw me buying some cans of cat food, so he

followed me home. Susan isn't admitting she ever knew him or ever wants to. I'll give him another feed and send him on his way, I guess. He's a handsome young fellow." Kate strokes him between the ears, and he rotates his head. Susan hisses.

He starts to pull back farther under the sofa. Without stopping to think myself, or giving him time to, I pick him up. Susan arches up and spits. I can feel the muscles in his body tense up as he gets ready to spring out of my lap. Then he changes his mind and decides to take advantage of the lap. He narrows his eyes and gives Susan a bored look and turns his head to take me in. After he's sized me up, he pretends he only turned around to lick his back.

"Cat," I say to him, "how about coming home with me?"

"Hah!" Kate laughs. "Your pop will throw him out faster than you can say 'good old Jeff.'"

"Yeah-h?" I say it slowly and do some thinking. Taking Cat home had been just a passing thought, but right now I decide I'll really go to the mat with Pop about this. He can have his memories of good old Jeff and rabbit hunts, but I'm going to have me a tiger.

Aunt Kate gives me a can of cat food and a box of litter, so Cat can stay in my room, because I remember Mom probably gets asthma from animals, too. Cat and I go home.

Pop does a lot of shouting and sputtering when we get home, but I just put Cat down in my room, and I try not to argue with him, so I won't lose my temper. I promise I'll keep him in my room and sweep up the cat hairs so Mom won't have to.

As a final blast Pop says, "I suppose you'll get your exercise mouse hunting now. What are you going to name the noble animal?"

"Look, Pop," I explain, "I know he's a cat, he knows he's a cat, and his name is Cat. And even if you call him Admiral John Paul Jones, he won't come when you call, and he won't lick your hand, see?"

"He'd better not! And it's not my hand that's going to get licked around here in a minute," Pop snaps.

"All right, all right."

Actually, my pop sometimes jaws so long it'd be a relief if he did haul off and hit me, but he never does.

We call it a draw for that day, and I have Cat.

2

Cat and the Underworld

Cat makes himself at home in my room pretty easily. Mostly he likes to be up on top of something, so I put an old sweater on the bureau beside my bed, and he sleeps up there. When he wants me to wake up in the morning, he jumps and lands in the middle of my stomach. Believe me, cats don't always land lightly—only when they want to. Anything a cat does, he does only when he wants to. I like that.

When I'm combing my hair in the morning, sometimes he sits up there and looks down his nose at my reflection in the mirror. He appears to be taking inventory: "Hmm, buckteeth; sandy hair, smooth in front, cowlick in back; brown eyes, can't see in the dark worth a nickel; hickeys on the chin. Too bad."

I look back at him in the mirror and say, "O.K., black face, yellow eyes, and one white whisker. Where'd you get that one white whisker?"

He catches sight of himself in the mirror, and his tail twitches momentarily. He seems to know it's not really another cat, but his claws come out and he taps the mirror softly, just to make sure.

When I'm lying on the bed reading, sometimes he will curl up between my knees and the book. But after a few days I can see he's getting more and more restless. It gets so I can't listen to a record, for the noise of him scratching on the rug. I can't let him loose in the apartment, at least until we make sure Mom doesn't get asthma, so I figure I better reintroduce him to the great outdoors in the city. One nice Sunday morning in April we go down and sit on the stoop.

Cat sits down, very tall and neat and pear-shaped, and closes his eyes about halfway. He glances at the street like it isn't good enough for him. After a while, condescending, he eases down the steps and lies on a sunny, dusty spot in the middle of the sidewalk. People walking have to step around him, and he squints at them.

Then he gets up, quick, looks over his shoulder at nothing, and shoots down the stairs to the cellar. I take a look to see where he's going, and he is pacing slowly toward the backyard, head down, a tiger on the prowl. I figure I'll sit in the sun and finish my science-fiction magazine before I go after him.

When I do, he's not in sight, and the janitor tells me he jumped up on the wall and probably down into one of the other yards. I look around a while and call, but he's not in sight, and I go up to lunch. Along toward evening Cat scratches at the door and comes in, as if he'd done it all his life.

This gets to be a routine. Sometimes he doesn't even come home at night, and he's sitting on the doormat when I get the milk in the morning, looking offended.

"Is it my fault you stayed out all night?" I ask him.

He sticks his tail straight up and marches down the hall to the kitchen, where he waits for me to open the milk and dish out the cat food. Then he goes to bed.

One morning he's not there when I open the door, and he still hasn't showed up when I get back from school. I get worried and go down to talk to Butch.

"Wa-a-l," says Butch, "sometimes that cat sit and talk to me a little, but most times he go on over to Twenty-first Street, where he sit and talk to his lady friend. Turned cold last night, lot of buildings put on heat and closed up their basements. Maybe he got locked in somewheres."

"Which building's his friend live in?" I ask.

"Forty-six, the big one. His friend's a little black-and-white cat, sort of belongs to the night man over there. He feeds her."

I go around to Twenty-first Street and case Forty-six, which is a pretty fair-looking building with a striped awning and a doorman who saunters out front and looks around every few minutes.

While I'm watching, a grocery boy comes along pushing his cart and goes down some stairs into the basement with his carton of groceries. This gives me an idea. I'll give the boy time to get started up in the elevator, and then I'll go down in the basement and hunt for Cat. If someone comes along and gets sore, I can always play dumb.

I go down, and the coast is clear. The elevator's gone up, and I walk softly past and through a big room where the tenants leave their baby carriages and bicycles. After this the cellar stretches off into several corridors, lit by twenty-watt bulbs dangling from the ceiling. You can hardly see anything. The corridors go between wire storage cages, where the tenants keep stuff like trunks and old cribs and parakeet cages. They're all locked.

"Me-ow, meow, meow!" Unmistakably Cat, and angry.

The sound comes from the end of one corridor, and I fumble along, peering into each cage to try to see a tiger cat in a shadowy hole. Fortunately his eyes glow and he opens his mouth for another meow, and I see him locked inside one of the cages before I come to the end of the corridor. I don't know how he got in or how I'm going to get him out.

While I'm thinking, Cat's eyes flick away from me to the right, then back to me. Cat's not making any noise, and neither am I, but something is. It's just a tiny rustle, or a breath, but I have a creepy feeling someone is standing near us. Way down at the end of the cellar a shadow moves a little, and I can see it has a white splotch—a face. It's a man, and he comes toward me.

I don't know why any of the building men would be way back there, but that's who I figure it is, so I start explaining.

"I was just hunting for my cat . . . I mean, he's got locked in one of these cages. I just want to get him out."

The guy lets his breath out, slow, as if he's been holding it quite a while. I realize he doesn't belong in that cellar either, and he's been scared of me.

He moves forward, saying "Sh-h-h" very quietly. He's taller than I am, and I can't see what he really looks like, but I'm sure he's sort of a kid, maybe eighteen or so.

He looks at the padlock on the cage and says, "Huh, cheap!" He takes a paper clip out of his pocket and opens it out, and I think maybe he has a penknife, too, and next thing I know the padlock is open.

"Gee, how'd you do that?"

"Sh-h-h. A guy showed me how. You better get your cat and scram."

Golly, I wonder, maybe the guy is a burglar, and that gives me another creepy feeling. But would a burglar be taking time out to get a kid's cat free?

"Well, thanks for the cat. See you around," I say.

"Sh-h-h. I don't live around here. Hurry up, before we both get caught."

Maybe he's a real burglar with a gun, even, I think, and by the time I dodge past the elevators and get out in the cold April wind, the sweat down my back is freezing. I give Cat a long lecture on staying out of basements. After all, I can't count on having a burglar handy to get him out every time.

Back home we put some nice jailhouse blues on the record player, and we both stretch out on the bed to think. The guy didn't really *look* like a burglar. And he didn't talk "dese and dose." Maybe real burglars don't all talk that way—only the ones on TV. Still, he sure picked that lock fast, and he was sure down in that cellar for some reason of his own.

Maybe I ought to let someone know. I figure I'll test Pop out, just casual like. "Some queer-looking types hanging around this neighborhood," I say at dinner. "I saw a tough-looking guy hanging around Number Forty-six this afternoon. Might have been a burglar, even."

I figure Pop'll at least ask me what he was

doing, and maybe I'll tell him the whole thing—about Cat and the cage. But Pop says, "In case you didn't know it, burglars do not all look like Humphrey Bogart, and they don't wear signs."

"Thanks for the news," I say and go on eating my dinner. Even if Pop does make me sore, I'm not going to pass up steak and onions, which we don't have very often.

However, the next day I'm walking along Twenty-first Street and I see the super of Forty-six standing by the back entrance, so I figure I'll try again. I say to him, "Us kids were playing ball here yesterday, and we saw a strange-looking guy sneak into your cellar. It wasn't a delivery boy."

"Yeah? You sure it wasn't you or one of your juvenile pals trying to swipe a bike? How come you have to play ball right here?"

"I don't swipe bikes. I got one of my own. New. A Raleigh. Better than any junk you got in there."

"What d'you know about what I got in there, wise guy?"

"Aw, forget it." I realize he's just getting suspicious of me. That's what comes of trying to be a big public-spirited citizen. I decide my burglar, whoever he is, is a lot nicer than the super, and I hope he got a fat haul.

Next day it looks like maybe he did just that. The local paper, *Town and Village*, has a headline: "Gramercy Park Cellar Robbed." I read down the article:

"The superintendent, Fred Snood, checked the cellar storage cages, after a passing youth hinted to him that there had been a robbery. He found one cage open and a suitcase missing. Police theorize that the youth may have been the burglar, or an accomplice with a guilty conscience or a grudge, and they are hunting him for questioning. Mr. Snood described him as about sixteen years of age, medium height, with a long 'ducktail' haircut, and wearing a heavy black sweater. They are also checking second-hand stores for the stolen suitcase."

The burglar stole a suitcase with valuable papers and some silver and jewelry in it. But the guy they were hunting for—I read the paragraph over and feel green. That's me. I get up and look in the mirror. In other circumstances I'd like being taken for sixteen instead of fourteen, which I am. I smooth my hair and squint at the back of it. The ducktail is fine.

Slowly I peel off my black sweater, which I wear practically all the time, and stuff it in my bottom drawer, under my bathing suit. But if I want to walk around the street without worrying about every cop, I'll have to do more than that. I put on a shirt and necktie and suit jacket and stick a cap on my head. I head uptown on the subway. At Sixty-eighth Street I get off and find a barbershop.

"Butch cut," I tell the guy.

"That's right. I'll trim you nice and neat. Get rid of all this stuff."

And while he chatters on like an idiot, I have to watch three months' work go snip, snip on the floor. Then I have to pay for it. At home I get the same routine. Pop looks at my Ivy League disguise and says, "Why, you may look positively human some day!"

Two days later I find out I could've kept my hair. *Town and Village* has a new story: "Nab Cellar Thief Returning Loot. 'Just A Bet,' He Says."

The story is pretty interesting. The guy I met in the cellar is named Tom Ransom, and he is nineteen and just sort of floating around in the city. He doesn't seem to have any family. The police kept a detective watching Number Forty-six, and pretty soon they see Tom walking along with the stolen suitcase. He drops it inside the delivery entrance and walks on, but the cop collars him. I suppose if it hadn't been for me shooting my big mouth off to the super, the police wouldn't have been watching the neighborhood. I feel sort of responsible.

The story in the paper goes on to say this guy was broke and hunting for a job, and some other guy dares him to snatch something out of a cellar and finally bets him ten dollars, so he does it. He gets out and finds the suitcase has a lot of stocks and legal papers and table silver in it, and he's scared stiff. So he figures to drop it back where it came from. The paper says he's held over to appear before some magistrate in Adolescent Court.

I wonder, would they send a guy to jail for that? Or if they turn him loose, what does he do? It must be lousy to be in this city without any family or friends.

At that point I get the idea I'll write him a letter. After all, Cat and I sort of got him into the soup. So I look up the name of the magistrate and spend about half an hour poring through the phone book, under "New York, City of," to get an address. I wonder whether to address him as "Tom" or "Mr. Ransom." Finally I write:

Dear Tom Ransom:

I am the kid you met in the cellar at Number Forty-six Gramercy, and I certainly thank you for unlocking that cage and getting my cat out. Cat is fine. I am sorry you got in trouble with the police. It sounds to me like you were only trying to return the stuff and do right. My father is a lawyer, if you would like one. I guess he's pretty good. Or if you would like to write me anyway, here is my address: 150 East 22 St. I read in the paper that your family don't live in New York, which is why I thought you might like someone to write to.

Yours sincerely,
Dave Mitchell

Now that I'm a free citizen again, I dig out my black sweater, look disgustedly at the butch hair-cut, and go out to mail my letter.

Later on I get into a stickball game again on Twenty-first Street. Cat comes along and sits up high on a stoop across the street, where he can watch the ball game and the tame dogs being led by on their leashes. That big brain, the super of Forty-six, is standing by the delivery entrance, looking sour as usual.

"Got any burglars in your basement these

days?" I yell to him while I'm jogging around the bases on a long hit.

He looks at me and my short haircut and scratches his own bald egg. "Where'd I see you?" he asks suspiciously.

"Oh—Cat and I, we get around," I say.

3

Cat and Coney

Nick and I have been friends pretty much since I can remember. Our mothers used to trade turns fetching us from kindergarten. Nick lives around the corner on Third Avenue, upstairs over the grocery store his old man runs. If anyone asked me *how come* we're friends, I couldn't exactly say. We're just together most of the time.

Neither of us is a real whiz at sports, but we used to roller-skate and play a little king and stickball and ride our bikes around exploring. One time when we were about ten, we rode way over to Twelfth Avenue at the Hudson River. where the *Queen Mary* docks. This is about the only time I remember my mom getting really angry. She said Pop ought to take my bike away from me, and he did, but only for about a week. Nick and I still ride bikes a lot. Otherwise we sit and do our homework or play chess and listen to records.

Another reason we're friends is because of this creepy little kid who lived down toward the corner, between me and Nick. He always tagged along, wanting to play with us, and of course in the end he always fouled up the game or fell down and started to cry. Then his big brother came rushing out, usually with another big guy along, and they figured they were entitled to beat us up for hurting little Joey.

After a while it looked to me as if Joey just worked as a lookout, and the minute me or Nick showed up on the block, one of the big guys came to run us off. They did little things like throwing sticks into our bike spokes and pretending it was just a joke. Nick and I used to plot all kinds of ways to get even with them, but in the end we mostly decided it was easier to walk around the block the long way to get to each other's houses.

I'm not much on fighting, and neither is Nick—'specially not with guys bigger than us.

Summers, up in the country, the kids seem to be all the time wrestling and punching, half for fun and half not. If I walk past some strange kid my age up there, he almost always tries to get me into a fight. I don't get it. Maybe it's because sidewalks are uncomfortable for fighting, but we just don't do much scrapping for fun. The only couple of fights I ever had, I was real mad.

Come spring, Nick and I got restless hanging around the street, with nothing to do but stickball and baiting the super at Forty-six. It was so easy to get him sore, it wasn't even fun. Cat stayed out of that basement, but I wanted to get him really out in the open, where he could chase squirrels or something.

One day we rode our bikes up to Central Park. I put Cat in a wicker hamper and tied it on the back of my bike. He meowed a lot, and people on the street would look at me and then do a double take when they heard him.

We got up to Central Park and into a place they call The Horseshoe, because the parking area is that shape. I opened the lid a crack to look at Cat. He hissed at me, the first time he ever did. I looked around and thought, Gee, if I let him loose, he could go anywhere, even over into the woods, and I might never catch him. There were a lot of hoody looking kids around, and I could see if I ever left my bike a second to chase Cat, they'd snatch the bike. So I didn't let Cat out, and I wolfed my sandwich and we went home. Nick was pretty disgusted.

Then we hit a hot Saturday, the first one in May, and I got an idea. I find Nick and say, "Let's put Cat and some sandwiches in the basket and hop the subway out to Coney."

Nick says, "Why bring Cat? He wrecked the last expedition."

"I like to take him places, and this won't be like Central Park. No one's at Coney this time of year. He can chase around on the beach and hunt sand crabs."

"Why do I have to have a nut for a friend?" Nick moans. "Well, anyway, I'm keeping my sandwich in my pocket, not in any old cat basket."

"Who cares where you keep your crumby sandwich?"

So we went. Lots of people might think Coney Island is ugly, with all the junky-looking booths and billboards. But when you turn your back on them and look out at the ocean, it's the same ocean as on a deserted beach. I kick off my shoes and stand with my feet in the ice water and the sun hot on my chest. Looking out at the horizon with its few ships and some sea gulls and planes overhead, I think: It's mine, all mine. I could go anywhere in the world, I could. Maybe I will.

Nick throws water down my neck. He only understands infinity on math papers. I let Cat out of the basket and strip off my splashed shirt and chase Nick along the edge of the water. No need to worry about Cat. He chases right along with us, and every time a wave catches his feet he hisses and hightails it up the beach. Then he rolls himself in the hot, dry sand and gets up and shakes. There are a few other groups of people dotted along the beach. A big mutt dog comes and sniffs Cat and gets a right and a left scratch to the nose. He yelps and runs for home. Cat discovers sand crabs. Nick and I roll around in the sand and wrestle, and after a while we get hungry, so we go back where we left the basket. Cat is content to let me carry him.

Three girls are having a picnic right near our basket. One yells to the others, "Hey, look! The guy went swimming with his cat!"

Cat jumps down, turns his back on them, and humps himself around on my sweater until he is settled for a nap. I turn my back on the girls, too, and look out at the ocean.

Still, it's not the same as it would have been a year ago. Then Nick and I would either have moved away from the girls or thrown sand at them.

We just sit and eat our sandwiches. Nick looks over at them pretty often and whispers to me how old do I think they are. I can't tell about girls. Some of the ones in our class at school look about twenty-five, but then you see mothers pushing baby carriages on the street who look about fifteen.

One of the girls catches Nick's eye and giggles. "Hi, there, whatcha watching?"

"I'm a bird watcher," says Nick. "Seen any birds?"

The girls drift over our way. The one that spoke first is a redhead. The one who seems to be the leader is a big blonde in a real short skirt and hair piled up high in a bird's nest. Maybe that's what started Nick bird-watching. The third girl is sort of quiet-looking, with brown hair, I guess.

"You want a couple of cupcakes? You can have

mine. I'm going on a diet," says the blonde.

"Thanks," says Nick. "I was thinking of going after some Cokes."

"Why waste time thinking? You might hurt your head," says the redhead.

The third girl bends down and strokes Cat between the ears very gently. She says, "What's his name?"

I explain to her about why Cat is Cat. She sits down and picks up a piece of seaweed to dangle over his nose. Cat makes a couple of sleepy swipes at it and then stretches luxuriously while she strokes him. The other kids get to talking, and we tell each other our names and where we go to school and all that stuff.

Then Nick gets back on the subject of going for Cokes. I don't really want to stay there alone with the girls, so I say I'll go. I tell Nick to watch Cat, and the girl who is petting him says, "Don't worry, I won't let him run away."

It's a good thing she's there, because by the time I get back with the Cokes, which no one offers to pay me back for, Nick and the other two girls are halfway down the beach. Mary—that's her name—says, "I never saw a cat at the beach before, but he seems to like it. Where'd you get him?"

"He's a stray. I got him from an old lady who's sort of a nut about cats. Come on, I'll see if I can get him to chase waves for you. He was doing it earlier."

We are running along in the waves when the other kids come back. The big blonde kicks up water at me and yells, "Race you!"

So I chase, and just as I'm going to catch up, she stops short so I crash into her and we both fall down. This seems to be what she had in mind, but I bet the other kids are watching and I feel silly. I roll away and get up and go back to Cat.

While we drink Cokes the blonde and the redhead say they want to go to the movies.

"What's on?" Nick asks.

"There's a Sinatra thing at the neighborhood," the blonde tells him, and he looks interested.

"I can't," I say. "I've got Cat. Besides, it's too late. Mom'd think I'd fallen into the subway."

"I told you that cat was a mistake," says Nick.

"Put him in the basket and call your mother and tell her your watch stopped," says the redhead. She comes over and trickles sand down my neck. "Come on, it'd be fun. We don't have to sit in the kids' section. We all look sixteen."

"Nah, I can't." I get up and shake the sand out.

Nick looks disgusted, but he doesn't want to stay alone. He says to the blonde, "Write me down your phone number, and we'll do it another day when this nut hasn't got his cat along."

She writes down the phone number, and the redhead pouts because I'm not asking for hers. The girls get ready to leave, and Mary pats Cat good-bye and waves to me. She says, "Bring him again. He's nice."

We get on the subway and Cat meows crossly at being shut in his basket. Nick pokes the basket with his toes.

"Shut up, nuisance," he says.

4
Fight

I actually get a letter back from Tom Ransom. It says: "Thanks for your letter. The Youth Board got me a room in the Y on Twenty-third Street. Maybe I'll come say Hello some day. They're going to help me get a job this summer, so I don't need a lawyer. Thanks anyway. Meow to Cat. Best, Tom."

I go over to Nick's house to show him the letter. I'd told him about Tom getting Cat out of the cellar and getting arrested, but Nick always acted like he didn't really believe it. So when he sees the letter, he has to admit Cat and I really got into something. Not everyone gets letters from guys who have been arrested.

One thing about Nick sort of gripes me. He has to think up all the plans. Anything I've done that he doesn't know about, he downgrades. Also, I always have to go to *his* house. He never comes to mine, except once in a coon's age when I have a new record I won't bring to his house because his machine stinks and he never buys a new needle.

It's not that I don't like his house. His mom is pretty nice, and boy, can she cook! Just an ordinary Saturday for lunch she makes pizza or real good spaghetti, and she has homemade cookies and nut cake sitting around after school. She also talks and waves her arms and shouts orders at us kids, but all good-natured-like, so we just kid her along and go on with what we're doing.

She's about the opposite of my mom. Pop does the shouting in our house, and except for the one hassle about bike-riding on Twelfth Avenue, Mom doesn't even tell me what to do much. She's quiet, and pretty often she doesn't feel good, so maybe I think more than most kids that I ought to do things her way without being told.

Also, my mom is always home and always ready to listen if you got something griping you, like when a teacher blames you for something you didn't do. Some kids I know, they have to phone a string of places to find their mother, and then she scolds them for interrupting her.

Mom likes to cook, and she gets up some good meals for holidays, but she doesn't go at it all the time, the way Nick's mother does. So maybe Nick doesn't come to my house because we haven't got all that good stuff sitting around. I don't think that's it, really, though. He just likes to be boss.

One day, a couple of weeks after we went to Coney, he does come along with me. We pick up a couple of Cokes and pears at his pop's store.

Cat is sitting on my front stoop, and he jumps down and rubs between my legs and goes up the stairs ahead of us.

"See? He knows when school gets out then it's time to eat. That's why I like to come home," I tell Nick.

We say "Hi" to Mom, and I get out the cat food while Nick opens his Coke. "You know those girls we ran into over on Coney Island?" he says.

"Yeah."

"Well, I got the blonde's phone number, so Sunday when I was hacking around with nothing to do, I called her up."

"Yeah? What for?"

"You stupid or something? To talk. So she yacked away a good while, and finally I asked her why didn't she come over next Saturday, we could go to a movie or something."

"Yeah." I was working on my pear, a very juicy one.

"That all you can say? So she says, well, she might, if she can get her girl friend to come too, but she doesn't want to come alone, and her mother wouldn't let her anyway."

"Which one?"

"Which one what?"

"Which girl friend?"

"Oh. You remember, the other one we were kidding around with at the beach, the redhead. So I said, O.K., I'd see if I could get you to come too. I said I'd call her back."

"Hmp. I don't know."

"What d'you mean, you don't know?"

"How do I know if I like that girl? I hardly even *talked* to her. Anyway, it sounds like a date. I don't want a date. If they just happen to come over, I guess it's all right."

"So shall I tell them it's O.K. for Saturday?"

"Hmm."

"It's nice you learned a new word."

"Do I have to pay for the girl at the movies?"

"Cheapskate. Maybe if you just stand around saying 'Hmm,' she'll buy her own. O.K.?"

"O.K. But this whole thing is your idea, and if it stinks it's going to be your fault."

"Boy, what an enthusiast! Come on, let's play a record and do the math."

Nick is better at math than I am, so I agree.

Saturday morning at ten o'clock Nick turns up at my house in a white shirt and slicked-down hair. Pop whistles. "On Saturday, yet! You got a girl or something?"

"Yessir!" says Nick, and he gives my T-shirt a dirty look. I go put a sweater over it and run a comb through my hair, but I'm hanged if I'll go out looking like this is a big deal.

"We're going to a movie down at the Academy," I tell my family.

"What's there?" Pop asks.

"A new horror show," says Nick. "And an old Disney."

"Is it really a new horror show?" I ask Nick, because I think I've seen every one that's been in town.

"Yup. Just opened. *The Gold Bug*. Some guy

wrote it—I mean in a book once—but it's supposed to be great. Make the girls squeal anyway. I love that."

"Hmm." I just like horror shows anyway, whether girls squeal or not.

"You'll be the life of the party with that 'Hmm' routine."

"It's *your* party." I shrug.

"Well, you could at least *try*."

We hang around the subway kiosk on Fourteenth Street, where Nick said he'd meet them. After half an hour they finally show up.

It's nice and sunny, and we see a crowd bunched up over in Union Square, so we wander over. A shaggy-haired, bearded character is making a speech all about "They," the bad guys. A lot of sleepy bums are sitting around letting the speech roll off their ears.

"What is he, a nut or something?" the blonde asks.

"A Commie, maybe," I say. "They're always giving speeches down here. Willie Sutton, the bank robber, used to sit down here and listen, too. That's where somebody put the finger on him."

The girls look at each other and laugh like crazy, as if I'd said something real funny. I catch

Nick's eye and glare. O.K., *I tried.* After this I'll stick to "Hmm."

A beard who is listening to the speech turns and glares at us and says, "Shush!"

"Aw, go shave yourself!" says Nick, and the girls go off in more hoots. Nick starts herding them toward Fourteenth Street, and I follow along.

At the Academy Nick goes up to the ticket window, and the girls immediately fade out to go read the posters and snicker together. I can see they're not figuring to pay for any tickets, so I cough up for two.

Nick and I try to saunter up to the balcony the way we always do, but the girls are giggling and dropping their popcorn, so the matron spots us and motions. "Down here!" She flashes her light in our eyes, and I feel like a convict while we get packed in with all the kids in the under-sixteen section.

Nick goes in first, then the blonde, then the redhead and me. The minute things start getting scary, she tries to grab me, but I stick my hands in my pockets and say, "Aw, it's just a picture." She looks disgusted.

The next scary bit, she tries to hang onto her

girl friend, but the blonde is already glued onto Nick. Redhead lets out a loud sigh, and I wish I hadn't ever got into this deal. I can't even enjoy the picture.

We suffer through the two pictures. The little kids make such a racket you can hardly hear, and the matron keeps shining the light in your eyes so you can't see. She shines it on the blonde, who is practically sitting in Nick's lap, and hisses at her to get back. I'm not going to do this again, ever.

We go out and Nick says, "Let's have a Coke." He's walking along with the blonde, and instead of walking beside me the redhead tries to catch hold of his other arm. This sort of burns me up. I mean, I don't really *like* her, but I paid for her and everything.

Nick shakes her off and calls over his shoulder to me, "Come on, chicken, pull your own weight!"

The girls laugh, on cue as usual, and I begin getting really sore. Nick got me into this. The least he can do is shut up.

We walk into a soda bar, and I slap down thirty cents and say, "Two Cokes, please."

"Hey, hey! The last of the big spenders!" says Nick. More laughter. I'd just as soon sock him right now, but I pick up my money and say, "O.K., wise guy, treat's on you." Nick shrugs and tosses down a buck as if he had hundreds of them.

The two girls drink their Cokes and talk across Nick. I finish mine in two or three gulps, and finally we can walk them to the subway. Nick is gabbing away about how he'll come out to Coney one weekend, and I'm standing there with my hands in my pockets.

"Goo'bye, Bashful!" coos the redhead to me, and the two of them disappear, cackling, down the steps. I start across Fourteenth Street as soon as the light changes, without bothering to look if Nick is coming. He can go rot.

Along Union Square he's beside me, acting as if everything is peachy fine dandy. "That was a great show. Pretty good fun, huh?"

I just keep walking.

"You sore or something?" he asks, as if he didn't know. I keep on walking.

"O.K., be sore!" he snaps. Then he breaks into a falsetto: "Goo'bye, Bashful!"

I let him have it before he's hardly got his mouth closed. He hits me back in the stomach and hooks one of his ankles around mine so we both fall down. It goes from bad to worse. He gets me by the hair and bangs my head on the sidewalk, so I twist and bite his hand. We're gouging and scratching and biting and kicking, because we're both so mad we can hardly see, and anyway no one ever taught us those Queensberry rules. There's no point in going into all the gory details. Finally two guys haul us apart. I have hold of Nick's shirt and it rips. Good. He's half crying, and he twists away from the guy that grabbed him and screams some things at me before darting across the avenue.

I'm standing panting and sobbing, and the guy holding me says, "You oughta be ashamed. Now go on home."

"Aw, you and your big mouth," I say, still mad enough to feel reckless. He throws a fake punch, but he's not really interested. He goes his way, and I go mine.

I must look pretty bad because a lot of people on the street shake their heads at me. I walk in the door at home, expecting the worst, but fortunately Mom is out. Pop just whistles through his teeth.

"That must have been quite a horror picture!" he says.

5

Around Manhattan

By the next weekend I no longer look like a fugitive from a riot. All week in school Nick and I get asked whether we got hit by a swinging door; then the fellows notice the two of us aren't speaking to each other, and they sort of sheer off the subject. Come Saturday, I sit on the stoop and wonder, what now? There are plenty of other kids in school I like, but they mostly live over in the project—Stuyvesant Town, that is. I've never bothered to hunt them up weekends because Nick's so much nearer.

Summer is coming on, though, and I've got to have someone to hang around with. This is the last Saturday before Memorial Day. Getting time for beaches and stuff. I suppose Nick and I might get together again, but not if he's going to be nuts about girls all the time.

A guy stops in front of the stoop, and Cat half opens his eyes in the sun and squints at him. The guy says, "You Dave Mitchell?"

"Huh? Yeah." I look up, surprised. I don't exactly recognize the guy, never having seen him in a clear light before. But from the voice I know it's Tom.

"Oh, hi!" I say. "Here's Cat. He's pretty handsome in daylight."

"Yeah, he looks all right, but what happened to you?"

"Me and a friend of mine got in a fight."

"With some other guys or what?"

"Nah. We had a fight with each other."

"Um, that's bad." Tom sits down and has sense enough to see there isn't anymore to say on that subject. "I start work Memorial Day, when the beaches open. Working in a filling station on the Belt Parkway in Brooklyn."

"Gee, that's a long way off. You going to live over there?"

"Yeah, they're going to get me a room in a Y in Brooklyn." Tom stretches restlessly and goes on: "I suppose you get sick of school and all, but it's rotten having nothing to do. I'd be ready to go nuts if I didn't get a job. I can't wait to start."

I think of asking him doesn't he have a home or something to go back to, but somehow I don't like to.

"Like today," Tom says. "I'd like to go somewhere. Do something. Got any ideas?"

"Um. I was sort of trying to think up something myself. Movies?"

Tom shakes himself. "No. I want to walk, or run, or throw something."

"There's a big park—sort of a woods—up near the Bronx. A kid told me about it. He said he found an Indian arrowhead there, but I bet he didn't. Inwood Park, it's called."

"How do you get there?"

"Subway, I guess."

"Let's go!" Tom stands up and wriggles his shoulders like he's Superman ready to take off.

"O.K. Wait a minute. I'll go tell Mom. Should I get some sandwiches?"

Tom looks surprised. "Sure, fine, if she doesn't mind."

I'm not worried about getting Mom to make sandwiches because she always likes to fix a little food for me. The thing is, ever since my fight with Nick, she's been clucking around me like the mother hen. Maybe she figures I got in some gang fight, so she keeps asking me where I'm going and who with. Also, I guess she noticed I don't go to Nick's after school anymore. I come right home. So she asks me do I feel all right. You can't win. Right now, I can see she's going to begin asking who is Tom and where did I meet him. It occurs to me there's an easy way to take care of this.

I turn around to Tom again. "Say, how about you come up and I'll introduce you to Mom? Then she won't start asking me a lot of questions."

"You mean I *look* respectable, at least?"

"Sure."

We go up to the apartment, and Mom asks if we'd like some cold drinks or something. I tell her I ran into Tom when he helped me hunt for Cat around Gramercy Park, which is almost true, and that he sometimes plays stickball with us, which isn't really true but it could be. Mom gets us some orangeade. She usually keeps something like that in the icebox in summer, because she thinks Cokes are bad for you.

"Do you live around here?" she asks Tom.

"No, ma'am," says Tom firmly. "I live at the Y. I've got a summer job in a filling station over in Brooklyn, starting right after Memorial Day."

"That's fine," Mom says. "I wish Davey could get a job. He gets so restless with nothing to do in the summer."

"Aw, Mom, forget it! You got to fill in about six-hundred working papers if you're under sixteen.

"Listen, Mom, what I came up for—we thought we'd make some sandwiches and go up to Inwood Park."

"Inwood? Where's that?" So I explain to her about the Indian arrowheads, and we get out the classified phone book and look at the subway map, which shows there's an IND train that goes right to it.

"I get sort of restless myself, with nothing to do," says Tom. "We just figured we'd do a little exploring around in the woods and get some exercise."

"Why, yes, that seems like a good idea." Mom looks at him and nods. She seems to have decided he's reliable, as well as respectable.

I see there's some leftover cold spaghetti in the icebox, and I ask Mom to put it in sandwiches.

She thinks I'm cracked, but I did this once before, and it's good, 'specially if there's plenty of meat and sauce on the spaghetti. We take along a bag of cherries, too.

"Thanks, Mom. Bye. I'll be back before supper."

"Take care," she says. "No fights."

"Don't worry. We'll stay out of fights," says Tom quite seriously.

We go down the stairs, and Tom says, "Your mother is really nice."

I'm sort of surprised—kids don't usually say much about each other's parents. "Yeah, Mom's O.K. I guess she worries about me and Pop a lot."

"It must be pretty nice to have your mother at home," he says.

That kind of jolts me, too. I wonder where his mother and father are, whether they're dead or something; but again, I don't quite want to ask. Tom isn't an easy guy to ask questions. He's sort of like an island, by himself in the ocean.

We walk down to Fourteenth Street and over to Eighth Avenue, about twelve blocks; after all, exercise is what we want. The IND trains are fast, and it only takes about half an hour to get up to Inwood, at 206th Street. The park is right close, and it is real woods, although there are paved walks around through it. We push uphill and get in a grassy meadow, where you can see out over the Hudson River to the Palisades in Jersey. It's good and hot, and we flop in the sun. There aren't many other people around, which is rare in New York.

"Let's eat lunch," says Tom. "Then we can go hunting arrowheads and not have to carry it."

He agrees the spaghetti sandwich is a great invention.

I wish the weather would stay like this more of the year—good and sweaty hot in the middle of the day, so you feel like going swimming, but cool enough to sleep at night. We lie in the sun awhile after lunch and agree that it's too bad there isn't an ocean within jumping-in distance. But there isn't, and flies are biting the backs of our necks, so we get up and start exploring.

We find a few places that you might conceivably call caves, but they've been well picked over for arrowheads, if there ever were any. That's the trouble in the city: anytime you have an idea, you find out a million other people had the same idea first. Along in mid-afternoon, we drift down toward the subway and get Cokes and ice cream before we start back.

I don't really feel like going home yet, so I think a minute and study the subway map inside the car. "Hey, as long as we're on the subway anyway, we could go on down to Cortlandt Street to the Army-Navy surplus store. I got to get a knapsack before summer."

"O.K." Tom shrugs. He's staring out the window and doesn't seem to care where he goes.

"I got a great first-aid survival kit there. Disinfectant and burn ointment and bug dope and bandages, in a khaki metal box that's waterproof, and it was only sixty-five cents."

"Hmm. Just what I need for survival on the sidewalks of New York," says Tom. I guess he's kidding, in a sour sort of way. If you haven't got a family around, though, survival must take more than a sixty-five-cent kit.

The store is a little way from the nearest subway stop, and we walk along not saying much. Tom looks alive when he gets into the store, though, because it really is a great place. They've got arctic explorers' suits and old hand grenades and shells and all kinds of rifles, as well as some really cheap, useful clothing. They don't mind how long you mosey around. In the end I buy a belt pack and canteen, and Tom picks up some skivvy shirts and socks that are only ten cents each. They're secondhand, I guess, but they look all right.

We walk over to the East Side subway, which is only a few blocks away down here because the island gets so narrow. Tom says he's never seen Wall Street, where all the tycoons grind their money machines. The place is practically deserted now, being late Saturday afternoon, and it's like walking through an empty cathedral. You can make echoes.

We take the subway, and Tom walks along home with me. It seems too bad the day's over. It was a pretty good day, after all.

"So long, kid," Tom says. "I'll send you a card from Beautiful Brooklyn!"

"So long." I wave, and he starts off. I wish he didn't have to go live in Brooklyn.

6
And Brooklyn

You can't really stay sore at a guy you've known all your life, especially if he lives right around the corner and goes to the same school. Anyhow, one hot Saturday morning Nick turns up at my house as if nothing had ever happened and says do I want to go swimming, because the Twenty-third Street pool's open weekends now.

After that we go back to playing ball on the street in the evenings and swimming sometimes on weekends. One Saturday his mother tells me he went to Coney Island. He didn't ask me to go along, which is just as well, because I wouldn't have. I don't hang around his house after school much anymore, either. School lets out, and there's the Fourth of July weekend, when we go up to Connecticut, and pretty soon after that Nick goes off to a camp his church runs. Pop asks me if I want to go to a camp a few weeks, but I don't. Life is pretty slow at home, but I don't feel like all that organization.

I think Tom must have forgotten about me and found a gang his own age when I get a postcard from him: "Dear Dave, The guy I work for is a creep, and all the guys who buy gas from him are creeps, so it's great to be alive in Beautiful Brooklyn! Wish you were here, but you're lucky you're not. Best, Tom."

It's hard to figure what he means when he says a thing. However, I got nothing to do, so I might as well go see. He said he was going to work in a filling station on the Belt Parkway, and there can't be a million of them.

I don't say anything too exact to Mom about where I'm going, because she gets worried about me going too far, and besides I don't really know where I'm going.

Brooklyn, what a layout. It's not like Manhattan,

which runs pretty regularly north and south, with decent square blocks. You could lose a million friends in Brooklyn, with the streets all running in circles and angles, and the people all giving you cockeyed directions. What with no bikes allowed on parkways, and skirting around crumby looking neighborhoods, it takes me at least a week of expeditions to find the right part of the Belt Parkway to start checking the filling stations.

I wheel my bike across the parkway, but even so some cop yells at me. You'd think a cop could find a crime to get busy with.

On a real sticky day in July I wheel across to a station at Thirty-fourth Street, and nobody yells at me, and I go over to the air pump and fiddle with my tires. A car pulls out after it gets gas, and there's Tom.

"Hi!" I say.

Tom half frowns and quick looks over his shoulder to see if his boss is around, I guess, and then comes over to the air pump.

"How'd you get way out here?" he says.

"On the bike. I got your postcard, and I figured I could find the filling station."

He relaxes and grins. I feel better. He says, "You're a crazy kid. How's Cat?"

But just then the boss has to come steaming up. "What d'ya want, kid? No bikes allowed on the parkway."

I start to say I'm just getting air, but Tom speaks up. "It's all right. I know him."

"Yeah? I told you, keep kids out of here!" The guy manages to suggest that kids Tom knows are probably worse than any other kind. He motions me off like a stray dog. I don't want to get Tom in any trouble, so I get going. At the edge of the parkway I wave. "So long. Write me another postcard."

Tom raises a hand briefly, but his face looks closed, like nothing was going to get in or out.

I pedal slowly and hotly back through the tangle of Brooklyn and figure, well, that's a week's research wasted. I still don't know where Tom lives, so I don't know how I can get a hold of him again. Anyway, how do I know he wants to be bothered with me? He looked pretty fed up with everything.

So long as I got nothing else to do, the next week I figure I'll get public-spirited at home. I paint the kitchen for Mom, which isn't so bad, but moving all those silly dishes and pots and scrumy little spice cans can drive you wild. I only break one good vase and a bottle of salad oil. Salad oil and broken glass are great. In the afternoons I go to the swimming pool and learn to do a jackknife and a backflip, so Pop will think I am growing up to be a Real American Boy. Also, you practically have to learn to dive so you can use the diving pool, because the swimming pool is so jam-packed with screaming sardines you can't move in it.

Evenings Cat and I play records, or we go to see Aunt Kate and drink iced tea. One weekend my real aunt comes to visit and sleeps in my room, so I go to stay with Aunt Kate, and I pretty near turn into cottage cheese.

I've about settled into this dull routine when Mom surprises me by handing me a postcard one morning. It's from Tom: "Day off next Tuesday. If you feel like it, meet me near the aquarium at Coney Island about nine in the morning, before it's crowded."

So that week drags by till Tuesday, and there I am at Coney Island bright and early. Tom is easy enough to find, pacing up and down the boardwalk like a tiger. We say "Hi" and so forth, and I'm all ready to take a run for the water, but he keeps snapping his fingers and looking up and down the boardwalk.

Finally he says, "There's a girl I used to know pretty well. I didn't see her for a while till last week, and we got in an argument, and I guess she's mad. I wrote and asked her to come swimming today, but maybe she's not coming."

I figure it out that I'm there as insurance against the girl not showing up, but I don't mind. Anyhow, she does show up. It can't have been too much of an argument they had, because she acts pretty friendly.

Tom introduces us. Her name is Hilda and a last name that'd be hard to spell—Swedish maybe—and she's got a wide, laughing kind of mouth and a big coil of yellow hair in a bun on top of her head, and a mighty good figure. She asks me where I ran into Tom, and we tell her all about Cat and the cellar at Number Forty-six, and I tell them both about my Ivy-League haircut, which I had never explained to anyone before. They get a laugh out of that, and then she asks him about the filling-station job, and he says it stinks.

I figure they could get along without me for a while, so I go for a swim and wander down the beach a ways and eat a hot dog and swim some more. When I come back, I see Tom and Hilda just coming out of the water, so I join them. Hilda says, "Come have a Coke. Tom says he's got to try swimming to France just once more."

I don't know just what she means, but we go get Cokes and come back and stretch out in the sun. She asks me do I want a smoke, and I say No. It's nice to be asked, though. We watch Tom, who is swimming out past all the other people. I wish I'd gone with him. I say, "Lifeguard's going to whistle him in pretty soon. He's out past all the others."

Hilda lets out a breath and snorts, "He'll always go till they blow the whistle. Always got to go farther than anyone else."

I don't know what to say to that, so I don't say anything.

Hilda goes on: "I used to wait tables in a restaurant down near Washington Square. Tom and a lot of the boys from NYU came in there. Sometimes the day before an exam he'd be sitting around for hours, buying people Cokes and acting as if he hadn't a care in the world. Some other times, for no reason anyone could tell, he'd sit in a corner and stir his coffee like he was going to make a hole in the cup."

"Tom was at NYU?" I ask. I don't know where I thought he'd been before he turned up in the cellar. I guess I never thought.

"Sure," Hilda says. "He was in the Washington Square College for about a year and a half. He lived in a dormitory uptown, but I used to see him in the restaurant, and then fairly often we had dates after I got off work. He has people out in the Midwest somewhere—a father and a stepmother. He was always sour and close-mouthed about them, even before he got thrown out of NYU. Now he won't even write them."

This is a lot of information to take in all at once and leaves a lot of questions unanswered. The first one that comes into my head is this: "How come he got thrown out of NYU?"

"Well, it makes Tom so sore, he's never really told me a plain, straight story. It's all mixed up with his father. I think his father wrote him not to come home at Christmas vacation, for some reason. Tom and a couple of other boys who were left in the dormitory over the holidays got horsing around and had a water fight. The college got huffy and wrote the parents, telling them to pay up for damages. The other parents were pretty angry, but they stuck behind their kids and paid up. Tom just never heard from his father. Not a line.

"That was when Tom began coming into the restaurant looking like thunder. The college began needling him for the water-fight damages, as well as second-semester tuition. He took his first exam, physics, and got an A on it. He's pretty smart.

"He still didn't hear anything from home. He took the second exam, French, and thought he flunked it. That same afternoon he went into the office and told the dean he was quitting, and he packed his stuff and left. I didn't see him again till a week ago. I didn't know if he'd got sick of me, or left town, or what.

"He says he wrote his father that he had a good job, and they could forget about him. Then he broke into that cellar on a dare or for kicks.

"So here we are. What do we do next?"

Hilda looks at me—me, age fourteen—as if I might actually know, and it's kind of unnerving. Everyone I know, their life goes along in set periods: grade school, junior high, high school, college, and maybe getting married. They don't really have to think what comes next.

I say cautiously, "My pop says a kid's got to go to college now to get anywhere. Maybe he ought to go back to school."

"You're so right, Grandpa," she says, and I would have felt silly, but she has a nice friendly laugh. "I wish I could persuade him to go back.

But it's not so easy. I guess he's got to get a job and go to night school, if they'll accept him. He won't ask his father for money."

"You two got my life figured out?" Tom has come up behind us while we were lying in the sand on our stomachs. "I just hope that sour grape at the filling station gives me a good recommendation so I can get another job. The way he watches his cash register, you'd think I was Al Capone."

We talk a bit, and then Hilda gets up and says she's going to the ladies' room. She doesn't act coy about it, the way most girls do when they're sitting with guys. She just leaves.

"How do you like Hilda?" Tom asks, and again I'm sort of surprised, because he acts like he really wants my opinion. "She's nice," I say.

"Yeah." Tom suddenly glowers, as if I'd said I *didn't* like her. "I don't know why she wastes her time on me. I'll never be any use to her. When her family hears about me, I'll get the boot."

"I could ask my pop. You know, I told you he's a lawyer. Maybe he'd know how you go about getting back into college or getting a job or something."

Tom laughs, an unamused bark. "Maybe he'll tell you to quit hanging around with jerks that get in trouble with the cops."

This is a point, all right. Come to think, I don't know why I said I'd ask Pop anyway. I usually make a point of not letting his nose into my personal affairs, because I figure he'll just start bossing me around. However, I certainly can't do anything for Tom on my own.

I say, "I'll chance it. The worst he ever does is talk. One time he made a federal case out of me buying a Belafonte record he didn't like. Another time playing ball I cracked a window in a guy's Cadillac, and Pop acted like he was going to sue the guy for owning a Cadillac. You just never know."

Tom says, "With my dad, you *know*: I'm wrong."

Hilda comes back just then. She snaps, "If he's such a drug on the market, why don't you shut up and forget about him?"

"O.K., O.K.," says Tom.

The beach is getting filled up by now, so we pull on our clothes and head for the subway. Tom and Hilda get off in Brooklyn, and I go on to Union Square.

After dinner that night Mom is washing the dishes and Pop is reading the paper, and I figure I might as well dive in.

"Pop," I say, "there's this guy I met at the beach.

Well, really I mean I met him this spring when I was hunting for Cat, and this guy was in the cellar at Forty-six Gramercy, and he got caught and . . ."

"Wha-a-a-t?" Pop puts down his paper and takes off his glasses. "Begin again."

So I give it to him again, slow, and with explanations. I go through the whole business about the filling station and Hilda and NYU, and I'll say one thing for Pop, when he finally settles down to listen, he listens. I get through, and he puts on his reading glasses and goes to look out the window.

"Do you have this young man's name and address, or is he just Tom from The Cellar?"

I'd just got it from Tom when we were at the beach. He's at a Y in Brooklyn, so I tell Pop this.

Pop says, "Tell him to call my office and come in to see me on his next day off. Meanwhile, I'll bone up on City educational policies in regard to juvenile delinquents."

He says this perfectly straight, as if there'd be a book on the subject. Then he goes back to his newspaper, so I guess that closes the subject for now.

"Thanks, Pop," I say and start to go out.

"Entirely welcome," says Pop. As I get to the door, he adds, "If that cat of yours makes a practice of introducing you to the underworld in other people's cellars, we can do without him. We probably can anyway."

7
SURVIVAL

Cat hadn't got me into any more cellars, but I can't honestly say he'd been sitting home tending his knitting—not him.

One hot morning I went to pick up the milk outside our door, and Cat was sleeping there on the mat. He didn't even look up at me. After I scratched his ears and talked to him some, he got up and hobbled into the house.

I put him up on my bed, under the light, for inspection. One front claw was torn off, which is why he was limping, his left ear was ripped, and there was quite a bit of fur missing here and there. He curled up on my bed and didn't move all day.

I came and looked at him every few hours and wondered if I ought to take him to a vet. But he seemed to be breathing all right, so I went away and thought about it some more. Come night, I pushed him gently to one side, wondering what I better do in the morning.

Well, in the morning Cat wakes up, stretches, yawns, and drops easily down off the bed and walks away. He still limps a little, but otherwise he acts like nothing had happened. He just wants to know what's for breakfast.

"You better watch out. One day you'll run into a cat that's bigger and meaner than you," I tell him.

Cat continues to wait for breakfast. He is not impressed.

But I'm worried. Suppose some big old cat chews him up and he's hurt too bad to get home? After breakfast I take him out in the backyard for a bit, and then I shut him in my room and go over to consult Aunt Kate.

She sets me up with the usual iced tea and dish of cottage cheese.

"I had breakfast already. What do I need with cottage cheese?"

"Eat it. It's good for you."

So I eat it, and then I start telling her about Cat. "He came home all chewed up night before last. I'm afraid some night he's not going to make it."

"Right," says Kate. She's not very talky, but I'm sort of surprised. I expected she'd tell me to quit worrying, Cat can take care of himself. She starts pulling Susan's latest kittens out from under the sofa and sorting them out as if they were ribbons: one gray, two tiger, one yellow, one calico.

"So what you going to do?" she shoots at me, shoveling the kittens back to Susan.

"I—uh—I dunno. I thought maybe I ought to try to keep him in nights."

"Huh. Don't know much, do you?" she says. "Well, so I'll tell you. Your Cat has probably fathered a few dozen kittens by now, and once a cat's been out and mated, you can't keep him in. You got to get him altered. Then he won't want to go out so much."

"Altered?"

"Fixed. Castrated is the technical word. It's a two-minute operation. Cost you three dollars. Take him to Speyer Hospital—big new building up on First Avenue."

"You mean get him fixed so he's not a real

tomcat anymore? The heck with that! I don't want him turned into a fat old cushion cat!"

"He won't be," she says. "But if it makes you happier, let him get killed in a cat fight. He's tough. He'll last a year or two. Suit yourself."

"Ah, you're screwy! You and your cottage cheese!" Even as I say it I feel a little guilty. But I feel mad and mixed up, and I fling out the door. It's the first time I ever left Kate's mad. Usually I leave *our* house mad and go to Kate.

Now I got nowhere to go. I walk along, cussing and fuming and kicking pebbles. I come to an air-conditioned movie and go up to the window.

The phony blonde in the booth looks at me and sneers, "You're not sixteen. We don't have a children's section in this theater." She doesn't even ask. She just says it. It's a great world. I go home. There's no one there but Cat, so I turn the record player up full blast.

Pop comes home in one of his unexpected fits of generosity that night and takes us to the movies. Cat behaves himself and stays around home and our cellar for a while, so I stop worrying. But it doesn't last long.

As soon as his claw heals, he starts sashaying off again. One night I hear cats yowling out back and I go out with a bucket of water and douse them and bring Cat in. There's a pretty little tiger cat, hardly more than a kitten, sitting on the fence licking herself, dry and unconcerned. Cat doesn't speak to me for a couple of days.

One morning Butch, the janitor, comes up and knocks on our door. "You better come down and look at your cat. He got himself mighty chewed up. Most near dead."

I hurry down, and there is Cat sprawled in a corner on the cool cement floor. His mouth is half open, and his breath comes in wheezes, like he has asthma. I don't know whether to pick him up or not.

Butch says, "Best let him lie."

I sit down beside him. After a bit his breath comes easier and he puts his head down. Then I see he's got a long, deep claw gouge going from his shoulder down one leg. It's half an inch open, and anyone can see it won't heal by itself.

Butch shakes his head. "You gotta take him to the veteran, sure. That's the cat doctor."

"Yeah," I say, not correcting him. It's not just the gash that's worrying me. I remember what Aunt Kate said, and it gives me a cold feeling in the stomach: In the back-alley jungle he'd last a year, maybe two.

Looking at Cat, right now, I know she's right. But Cat's such a—well, such a *cat.* How can I take him to be whittled down?

I tell Butch I'll be back down in a few minutes, and I go upstairs. Mom's humming and cleaning in the kitchen. I wander around and stare out the window awhile. Finally I go in the kitchen and stare into the icebox, and then I tell Mom about the gash in Cat's leg.

She asks if I know a vet to take him to.

"Yeah, there's Speyer. It's a big, new hospital—good enough for people, even—with a view of the East River. The thing is, Mom, Cat keeps going off and fighting and getting hurt, and people tell me I ought to get him altered."

Mom wets the sponge and squeezes it out and polishes at the sink, and I wonder if she knows what I'm talking about because I don't really know how to explain it any better.

She wrings the sponge out, finally, and sits down at the kitchen table.

She says, "Cat's not a free wild animal now, and he wouldn't be even if you turned him loose. He belongs to *you,* so you have to do whatever is best for *him,* whether it's what you'd like or not. Ask the doctor and do what he says."

Mom puts it on the line, all right. It doesn't make me feel any better about Cat. She takes five dollars out of her pocketbook and gives it to me.

I get out the wicker hamper and go down to the cellar and load Cat in. He meows, a low resentful rumble, but he doesn't try to get away.

Cat in the hamper is no powder puff, and I get pretty hot walking to the bus, and then from the bus stop to the animal hospital. I get there and wait, and dogs sniff at me, and I fill in forms. The lady asks me if I can afford to pay, and with Mom's five bucks and four of my own, I say Yes.

The doctor is a youngish guy, but bald, in a white shirt like a dentist's. I put Cat on the table in front of him. He says, "So why don't you stay out of fights, like your mommy told you?"

I relax a bit and smile, and he says, "That's better. Don't worry. We'll take care of tomcat. I suppose he got this gash in a fight?"

"Yeah."

"He been altered?"

"No."

"How old is he?"

"I don't know. He was a stray. I've had him almost a year."

All the time he's talking, the doctor is soothing

Cat and looking him over. He goes on stroking him and looks up at me. "Well, son, one of these days he's going to get in one fight too many. Shall we alter him the same time we sew up his leg?"

So there it is. I can't seem to answer right away. If the doctor had argued with me, I might have said No. But he just goes on humming and stroking. Finally he says, "It's tough, I know. Maybe he's got a right to be a tiger. But you can't keep a tiger for a pet."

I say, "O.K."

An attendant takes Cat away, and I go sit in the waiting room, feeling sweaty and cold all over. They tell me it'll be a couple of hours, so I go out and wander around a lot of blocks I never saw before and drink some Cokes and sit and look up at the Fifty-ninth Street Bridge to Queens.

When I go back for him, Cat looks the same as ever, except for a bandage all up his right front leg. The doctor tells me to come back Friday and he'll take out the stitches.

Mom sees me come in the door, and I guess I look pretty grim, because she says, "Cat will be all right, won't he, dear?"

"Yes." I go past her and down into my room and let Cat out of the basket and then bury my head under the pillow. I'm not exactly ashamed of crying, but I don't want Mom to hear.

After a while I pull my head out. Cat is lying there beside me, his eyes half open, the tip end of his tail twitching very slowly. I rub my eyes on the back of his neck and whisper to him, "I'm sorry. Be tough, Cat, anyway, will you?"

Cat stretches and hops off the bed on his three good legs.

8

West Side Story

The regular park man got sunstroke or something, so I earned fourteen dollars raking and mowing in Gramercy Park in the middle of August. Gramercy Park is a private park. You have to own a key to get in, so the city doesn't take care of it.

Real paper money, at this time of year especially, is very cheering. I head up to Sam Goody's to see what records he's got on sale and what characters are buying them. Maybe I'll buy something, maybe not, but as long as I've got money in my pocket, I don't feel like the guy is glaring at me for taking up floor space.

Along the way I walk through the library, the big one at Forty-second Street. You go in by the lions on Fifth Avenue, and there's all kinds of pictures and books on exhibit in the halls, and you walk through to the back, where you can take out books. It's nice and cool, and nobody glares at you unless you either make a lot of noise or go to sleep. I can take books out of here and return them at the Twenty-third Street branch, which is handy.

Sam Goody's is air-conditioned, so it's cool too. There are always several things playing on different machines you can listen to. Almost the most fun is watching the people: little, fat, bald guys buying long-haired classical music, and thin, shaggy beatniks listening to the jazz.

I go to check if there are any bargains in the Kingston or Belafonte division. There's a girl standing there reading the backs of records, but I don't really catch a look at more than her shoes—little red flats they are. After a bit she reaches for a record over my head and says, "Excuse me."

"Sure." Then we catch each other's eye and both say, "Oh. Gee, hello."

Well, we're both pretty surprised, because this is the girl I met out at Coney Island that day with Nick when I had Cat with me, and now we're both a long way from Coney Island. This girl isn't one of the two giggly ones. It's the third, the one that liked Cat.

We've both forgotten each other's names, so we begin over with that. I ask her what she's been doing, and she's been at Girl Scout camp a few weeks, and then she earned some money baby-sitting. So she came to think about records, like me. I tell her I've been at Coney once this summer, and I looked around for her, which is true, because I did.

"It's a big place," she says, smiling.

"Say, you live out there, don't you? How come you get all the way in here by yourself? Doesn't your mom get in a flap? Mine would, if she knew I was going to Coney alone."

Mary says, "I came in with Mom. Some friend of hers has a small art exhibition opening. She said I could go home alone. After all, she knows I'm not going to get lost."

I say, "Gee, it'd be great to have a mother that didn't worry about you all the time."

"Oh, Mom worries." Mary giggles. "You should

have heard her when I said I liked *Gone With the Wind* and I didn't like *Anna Karenina.* I pretty nearly got disowned."

"What does she think about science fiction?" I ask, and Mary makes a face, and we both laugh.

I go on. "Well, my mom doesn't care what I read. She worries about what I eat and whether my feet are wet, and she always seems to think I'm about to kill myself. It's a nuisance, really."

Mary looks solemn all of a sudden. She says slowly, "I think maybe it'd be nice. I mean to have someone worrying about whether you're comfortable and all. Instead of just picking your brains all the time."

This seems to exhaust the subject of our respective mothers, and Mary picks up the record of *West Side Story* and says, "Gee, I'd like to see that. Did you?"

I say No, and to tell the truth I hadn't hardly heard of it.

"I read a book about him. It was wonderful," she says.

"Who?"

"Bernstein. The man who wrote it."

"What's *West Side Story* about, him?" I ask cautiously.

"No, no—he wrote the music. It's about some kids in two gangs, and there's a lot of dancing, and then there's a fight and this kid gets—well, it isn't a thing you can tell the story of very well. You have to see it."

This gives me a very simple idea.

"Why don't we?" I say.

"Huh?"

"Go see it. Why not? We got money."

"So we do," she says slowly. "You think they'll let us in, I mean being under sixteen?"

You know, this is the first girl I really ever talked to that talks like a person, not trying to be cute or something.

We walk around to the theater, and being it's Wednesday, there's a matinee about to start. The man doesn't seem to be one bit worried about taking our money. No wonder. It's two dollars and ninety cents each. So we're inside with our tickets before we've hardly stopped to think.

Suddenly Mary says, "Oops! I better call Mom! Let's find out what time the show is over."

We do, and Mary phones. She says to me, "I just told her I was walking past *West Side Story* and found I could get a ticket. I didn't say anything about you."

"Why, would she mind?"

Mary squints and looks puzzled. "I don't know. I just really don't know. It never happened before."

We go in to the show, and she is right, it's terrific. I hardly ever went to a live show before, except a couple of children's things and something by Shakespeare Pop took me to that was very confusing. But this *West Side Story* is clear as a bell.

We have an orangeade during intermission, and I make the big gesture and pay for both of them. Mary says, "Isn't it wonderful! I just happened to meet you at the beach, and then I meet you at Goody's, and we get to see this show that I've wanted to go to for ages. None of my friends at school want to spend this much money on a show."

"It's wonderful," I say. "After it's over, I'm going back to buy the record."

So after the show we buy it, and then we walk along together to the subway. I'll have to get off at the first stop, Fourteenth Street, and she'll go on to Coney, the end of the line.

It's hard to talk on the subway. There's so much noise you have to shout, which is hard if you don't know what to say. Anyway, you can't ask a girl for her phone number shouting on the subway. At least I can't.

I'm not so sure about the phone-number business either. I sort of can't imagine calling up and saying, "Oh, uh, Mary, this is Dave. You want to go to a movie or something, huh?" It sounds stupid, and I'd be embarrassed. What she said, it's true—it's sort of wonderful the way we just ran into each other twice and had so much fun.

So I'm wondering how I can happen to run into her again. Maybe the beach, in the fall. Let's see, a school holiday—Columbus Day.

The train is pulling into Fourteenth Street. I shout, "Hey, how about we go to the beach again this fall? Maybe Columbus Day?"

"O.K.!" she shouts. "Columbus Day in the morning."

"Columbus Day in the morning" sounds loud and clear because by then the subway has stopped. People snicker, and Mary blushes.

"So long," I say, and we both wave, and the train goes.

9
Fathers

That operation didn't make as much difference to Cat as you might think. I took him back to the clinic to get the stitches out of his leg and the bandages off. A few nights later I heard yowls coming up from the backyard. I went down and pulled him out of a fight. He wasn't hurt yet, but he sure was right back in there pitching. He seems to have a standing feud with the cat next door.

However, he's been coming home nights regularly, and sometimes in the cool part of the morning he'll sit out on the front stoop with me. He sits on a pillar about six feet above the sidewalk, and I sit on the steps and play my transistor and read.

Every time a dog gets walked down the street under Cat's perch, he gathers himself up in a ball, as if he were going to spring. Of course, the poor dog never knows it was about to be pounced on and wags on down the street. Cat lets his tail go to sleep then and sneers.

Between weathercasts I hear him purring, loud rumbly purrs, and I look up and see Tom there, stroking Cat's fur up backward toward his ears. Tom is looking out into the street and sort of whistling without making any sound.

"Gee, hi!" I say.

"Hi, too," he says. He strokes Cat back down the right way, gives him a pat, and sits down. "I just been down to see your dad. He's quite a guy."

"Huh-h-h? You got sunstroke or something? Didn't he read you about ten lectures on Healthy Living, Honest Effort, Baseball, and Long Walks with a Dog?"

"No-o-o." Tom grins, but then he sits and stares out at the street again, so I wait.

"You know," he says, "you give me an idea. *You* talk like *your* dad is a real pain, and that's the way *I* always have felt about *mine*. But your dad looks like a great guy to me, so—well, maybe mine could be too, if I gave him a chance. Your dad was saying I should."

"Should what? You should go home?"

"No. Your dad said I ought to write him a long letter and face up to all the things I've goofed on. Quitting NYU, the cellar trouble, all that. Then tell him I'm going to get a job and go to night school. Your dad figures probably he'd help me. He said he'd write him, too. No reason he should. I'm nothing in his life. It's pretty nice of him."

I try to digest all this, and it sure is puzzling. The time I ran down that crumb of a doorman on my bike, accidental on purpose, I didn't get any long understanding talks. I just got kept in for a month.

Tom slaps me in the middle of the back and stands up. "Hilda's gone back to work at the coffee shop. I guess I'll go down and see her before the lunch rush, and then go home and write my letter."

"Say 'Hi' for me."

"O.K. So long."

The weather cools off some, and Pop starts to talk about vacation. He's taking two weeks, last of August and first of September, so I start shopping around for various bits of fishing tackle and picnic gear we might need. We're going to this lake up in Connecticut, where we get a sort of motel cottage. It has a little hot plate for making coffee in the morning, but most of the rest of the time we eat out, which is neat.

We're sitting around the living room one evening, sorting stuff out, when the doorbell rings. I go answer it, and Tom walks in. He nods at me like he hardly sees me and comes into the living room. He shakes hands like a wooden Indian. His face looks shut up again, the way it did that day I left him in the filling station.

He reaches in his pocket and pulls out a letter. I can see a post-office stamp in red ink with a pointing hand by the address. He throws it down on Dad's table.

"I got my answer all right."

Pop looks at the letter and I see his foot start to twitch the way it does when he's about to blow. But he looks at Tom, and instead of blowing he just says, "Your father left town? No forwarding address?"

"I guess so. He just left. Him and that woman he married." Tom's voice trails off and he walks over to the window. We all sit quiet a minute.

Finally Pop says gently, "Well, don't waste too much breath on her. She's nothing to do with you."

Tom turns around angrily. "She's no good. She loafs around and drinks all the time. She talked him into going."

"And he went." There's another short silence, and Pop goes on. "Where was this you lived?"

"House. It was a pretty nice little house, too. Dark red with white trim, and enough of a yard to play a little ball, and I grew a few lettuces every spring. I even got one ear of corn once. We moved there when I was in second grade because my mom said it was near a good local school. I lived there till I went to college. I suppose he sold it, or got a loan, and they lit off to drink it up. Soon's they'd got *me* off their hands."

Tom bites off the last word. Suddenly I can see the picture pretty clear: the nice house, the father Tom always talked down and hoped would measure up. Now it's like somebody has taken his whole childhood and crumpled it up like a wad of tissue paper and thrown it away.

Mom gets up and goes into the kitchen. Pop's foot keeps on twitching. Finally he says, "Well, I steered you wrong. I'm sorry. But maybe it's just as well to have it settled."

"It's settled, all right," Tom says.

Mom brings out a tray of ginger-ale glasses. It seems sort of inadequate at a moment like this, but when Tom takes a glass from her he looks like he's going to bust out crying.

He drinks some and blows his nose, and Dad says, "When are you supposed to check in with the Youth Board again?"

"Tuesday. My day off. And I wind up the filling-station job the next week, right after Labor Day."

"Labor Day. Hm-m. We've got to get moving. If you like, I'll come down to the Youth Board with you, and we'll see what we can all cook up. Don't worry too much. I have a feeling you're just beginning to fight—really fight, not just throw a few stones."

"I don't know why you bother." Tom starts to stand up. But while we've been talking, Cat has been creeping up under the side table, playing the ambush game, and he launches himself at Tom just as he starts to stand. It throws him off balance and he sits back in the chair, holding Cat.

"You've got nothing to worry about," Pop says. "Cat's on your side."

10

Cat and the Parkway

Cat may be on Tom's side, but whether Pop is on Cat's side is something else again. I worry about this all the time we're planning the vacation. Suppose the motel won't take cats? Or suppose he runs away in the country? If he messes up the vacation in any way, I know Pop'll say to get rid of him.

I practice putting Cat back in the wicker hamper to see if I can keep him in that sometimes, but he meows like crazy. That'd drive Pop nuts in the car, and it certainly wouldn't hide him from any motel-keeper. So I just sit back and hope for the best, but I got a nasty feeling in the bottom of my stomach that some thing's going to go haywire.

Pop's pretty snappish anyway. He's working late nearly every night, getting stuff cleared up before vacation. He doesn't want any extra problems, especially not Cat problems. Mom's been having asthma a good deal lately, and we're all pretty jumpy. It's always like this at the end of the summer.

Tuesday night when he gets home, I ask Pop what's happened about Tom.

"We'll work something out," he says, which isn't what you'd call a big explanation.

"You think he can get back into college?"

"I don't know. The Youth Board is going to work on it. They're arranging for him to make up the midyear exams he missed, so he can get credit for that semester. Then he can probably start making up the second semester at night school if he has a job.

"Apparently the Youth Board knew his father had skipped—they've been trying to trace him. I don't think it'll do any good if they find him. Tom had better just cross him off and figure his own life for himself."

You know, I see "bad guys" in television and stuff, but with the people I really know I always lump the parents on one team and the kids on the other. Now here's my pop calmly figuring a kid better chalk off his father as a bad lot and go it alone. If your father died, I suppose you could face up to it eventually, but having him just fade out on you, not care what you did—that'd be worse.

While I'm doing all this hard thinking, Pop has gone back to reading the paper. I notice the column of want ads on the back, and all of a sudden my mind clicks on Tom and jobs.

"Hey, Pop! You know the florist on the corner, Palumbo, where you always get Mom the plant on Mother's Day? I went in there a couple of weeks ago, because he had a sign up, 'Helper Wanted.' I thought maybe it was deliveries and stuff that I could do after school. But he said he needed a full-time man. I'm pretty sure the sign's still up."

"Palumbo, huhn?" Pop takes off his glasses and scratches his head with them. He looks at his watch and sighs. "They still open?"

They are, and Pop goes right down to see the guy. He knows him fairly well anyway—there's

Mother's Day, and Easter, and also the shop is the polling place for our district, so Pop's in there every Election Day. He always buys some little bunch of flowers Election Day because he figures the guy ought to get some business having his shop all messed up for the day.

Dad comes back and goes over to the desk and scratches off a fast note. He says, "Here. Address it to Tom and go mail it right away. Palumbo says he'll try him out at least. Tom can come over Thursday night and I'll take him in."

Tom comes home with Pop Thursday about nine o'clock. They both look pretty good. Mom has cold supper waiting, finishing off the icebox before we go away, so we all sit down to eat.

"Tom's all set, at least for a start," Dad says. "He's going to start Tuesday, right after Labor Day. Palumbo can use him on odd jobs and deliveries, especially over the Jewish holidays, and then if he can learn the business, he'll keep him on."

"Never thought I'd go in for flower-arranging." Tom grins. "But it might be fun. I'm pretty fair at any kind of handiwork."

Remembering how quick he unlocked the padlock to get Cat out in the cellar, I agree.

He starts for his room after supper, and we all

say "good luck," "have a good time," and stuff. Things are really looking up.

I get up early the next morning and help Mom button up around the house and get the car loaded before Pop gets home in the afternoon. He hoped to get off early, and I've been pacing around snapping my fingers for a couple of hours when he finally arrives about six o'clock. It's a hot day again.

I don't say anything about Cat. I just dive in the back seat and put him behind a suitcase and hope he'll behave. Pop doesn't seem to notice him. Anyway he doesn't say anything.

It's mighty hot, and traffic is thick, with everyone pouring out of the city. But at least we're moving along, until we get out on the Hutchinson River Parkway, where some dope has to run out of gas.

All three lanes of traffic are stopped. We sit in the sun. Pop looks around, hunting for something to get sore about, and sees the back windows are closed. He roars, "Crying out loud, can't we get some air, at least? Open those windows!"

I open them and try to keep my hand over Cat, but if you try to hold him really, it makes him restless. For the moment he's sitting quiet, looking disgusted.

We sit for about ten minutes, and Pop turns off the motor. You can practically hear us sweating in the silence. Engines turn on ahead of us, and there seems to be some sign of hope. I stick my head out the window to see if things are moving. Something furry tickles my ear, and it takes me a second to register.

Then I grab, but too late. There is Cat, out on the parkway between the lanes of cars, trying to figure which way to run.

"Pop!" I yell. "Hold it! Cat's got out!"

You know what my pop does? He laughs.

"Hold it, my eyeball!" he says. "I've been holding it for half an hour. I'd get murdered if I tried to stop now. Besides, I don't want to chase that cat every day of my vacation."

I don't even stop to think. I just open the car door and jump. The car's only barely moving. I can see Cat on the grass at the edge of the parkway. The cars in the next lane blast their horns, but I slip through and grab Cat.

I hear Mom scream, "Davey!"

Our car is twenty feet ahead, now, in the center lane, and there's no way Pop can turn off. The cars are picking up speed. I holler to Mom as loud as I can, "I'll go back and stay with Kate! Don't worry!"

I hear Pop shout about something, but I can't hear what. Pretty soon the car is out of sight. I look down at Cat and say, "There goes our vacation." I wonder if I'll be able to catch a bus out to Connecticut later. Meanwhile, there's the little problem of getting back into the city. I'm standing alongside the parkway, with railroad tracks and the Pelham golf course on the other side of me, and a good long walk to the subway.

A cat isn't handy to walk with. He keeps trying to get down. If you squeeze him to hang on, he just tries harder. You have to keep juggling him, like, gently. I sweat along back, with the sun in my eyes, and people in cars on the parkway pointing me out to their children as a local curiosity.

One place the bulrushes and marsh grass beside the road grow up higher than your head. What a place for a kids' hideout, I think. Almost the next step, I hear kids' voices, whispering and shushing each other.

Their voices follow along beside me, but inside the curtain of rushes, where I can't see them. I hear one say, "Lookit the sissy with the kitty!" Another answers, "Let's dump 'em in the river!"

I try to walk faster, but I figure if I run they'll

chase me for sure. I walk along, juggling Cat, trying to pretend I don't notice them. I see a drawbridge up ahead, and I sure hope there's a cop or watchman on it.

The kids break out of the rushes behind me, and there's no use pretending anymore. I flash a look over my shoulder. They all yell, "Ya-n-h-h-h!" like a bunch of wild Indians, but they're about fifty feet back.

I grab Cat hard about the only place you can grab a cat, around one upper forearm, and I really run. The kids let out another war whoop. It's uphill to the bridge. Cat gets his free forepaw into action, raking my chest and arm, with his claws out. Then he hisses and bites, and I nearly drop him. I'm panting so hard I can't hardly breathe anyway.

A cop saunters out on my approach to the bridge, his billy dangling from his wrist. Whew—am I glad! I flop on the grass and ease up on Cat and start soothing him down. The kids fade off into the tall grass as soon as they see the cop. A stone arches up toward me, but it falls short. That's the last I see of them.

As I cross the bridge, the cop squints at me. "What you doing, kid? Not supposed to be walking here."

"I'll be right off. I'm going home," I tell him, and he saunters away, twirling his stick.

It's dark by the time I get to the subway, and most of another hour before I'm back in Manhattan and reach Kate's. I can hear the television going, which is unusual, and I walk in. No one is watching television. Mom and Pop are sitting at the table with Kate.

Mom lets loose the tears she has apparently been holding onto for two hours, and Pop starts bellowing: "You fool! You might have got killed jumping out on that parkway!"

Cat drops to the floor with a thud. I kiss Mom and go to the sink for a long glass of water and drink it all and wipe my mouth. Over my shoulder, I answer Pop: "Yeah, but if Cat gets killed on the parkway, that's just a big joke, isn't it? You laugh your head off!"

Pop takes off his glasses and scratches his head with them, like he always does when he's thinking. He looks me in the eye and says, "I'm sorry. I shouldn't have laughed."

Then, of all things, he picks up Cat himself. "Come on. You're one of the family. Let's get on this vacation."

At last we're off.

11
Rosh Hashanah at the Fulton Fish Market

We came back to the city Labor Day Monday—us and a couple million others—traffic crawling, a hot day, the windows practically closed up tight to keep Cat in. I sweated, and then cat hairs stuck to me and got up my nose. Considering everything, Pop acted quite mild.

I met a kid up at the lake in Connecticut who had skin-diving equipment. He let me use it one day when Mom and Pop were off sightseeing. Boy, this has fishing beat hollow! I found out there's a skin-diving course at the Y, and I'm going to begin saving up for the fins and mask and stuff. Pop won't mind forking out for the Y membership, because he'll figure it's character-building.

Meanwhile, I'm wondering if I can get back up to Connecticut again one weekend while the weather's still warm, and I see that Rosh Hashanah falls on a Monday and Tuesday this year, the week after school opens. Great. So I ask this kid—Kenny Wright—if I can maybe come visit him that weekend so I can do some more skin diving.

"Rosh Hashanah? What's that?" he says.

So I explain to him. Rosh Hashanah is the Jewish New Year. About half the kids in my school are Jewish, so they all stay out for it, and I always do too. Last year the school board gave up and made it an official school holiday for everyone, Jewish or not. Same with Yom Kippur, the week after.

Kenny whistles. "You sure are lucky. I don't think we got any holidays coming till Thanksgiving."

I always thought the kids in the country were lucky having outdoor yards for sports and recess, but I guess we have it over them on holidays—'specially in the fall: three Jewish holidays in September, Columbus Day in October, Election Day and Veterans' Day in November, and then

Thanksgiving. It drives the mothers wild.

I don't figure it'd be worth train fare to Connecticut for just two days, so I say good-bye to Kenny and see you next year and stuff.

Back home I'm pretty busy right away, on account of starting in a new school, Charles Evans Hughes High. It's different from the junior high, where I knew half the kids, and also my whole homeroom there went from one classroom to another together. At Hughes everyone has to get his own schedule and find the right classroom in this immense building, which is about the size of Penn Station. There are about a million kids in it—actually about two thousand—most of whom I never saw before. Hardly any of the Stuyvesant Town and Peter Cooper Village kids come here because it isn't their district. However, walking back across Fifth Avenue one day, I see one kid I know from Peter Cooper. His name is Ben Alstein. I ask him how come he is at Hughes.

"My dad wanted me to get into Peter Stuyvesant High School—you know, the genius factory, city-wide competitive exam to get in. Of course I didn't make it. Biggest Failure of the Year, that's me."

"Heck, I never even tried for that. But how come you're here?"

"There's a special science course you can qualify for by taking a math test. Then you don't have to live in the district. My dad figures as long as I'm in something special, there's hope. I'm not really very interested in science, but that doesn't bother him."

So after that Ben and I walk back and forth to school together, and it turns out we have three classes together, too—biology and algebra and English. We're both relieved to have at least one familiar face to look for in the crowd. My old friend Nick, aside from not really being my best friend anymore, has gone to a Catholic high school somewhere uptown.

On the way home from school one Friday in September, I ask Ben what he's doing Monday and Tuesday, the Jewish holidays.

"Tuesday I got to get into my bar mitzvah suit and go to synagogue and over to Brooklyn to my grandmother's. Monday I don't have to do anything special. Come on over with your roller skates and we'll get in the hockey game.'

"I skate on my tail," I say, because it's true, and it would be doubly true in a hockey game. I try quick to think up something else. We're walking down the block to my house, and there's Cat sitting out front, so I say, "Let's cruise around and get down to Fulton Fish Market and pick up some fish heads for my cat."

"You're a real nut, aren't you?" Ben says. He doesn't say it as if he minds—just mentioning the fact. He's an easygoing kind of guy, and I think most of the time he likes to let someone else make the plans. So he shrugs and says, "O.K."

I introduce him to Cat. Ben looks him in the eye, and Cat looks away and licks his back. Ben says, "So I got to get you fresh fish for Rosh Hashanah, huh?"

Cat jumps down and rubs from back to front against Ben's right leg and from front to back against his left leg and goes to lie down in the middle of the sidewalk.

"See? He likes you," I say. "He won't have anything to do with most guys, except Tom."

"Who's Tom?"

So I tell Ben all about Tom and the cellar and his father disappearing on him.

"Gee," says Ben, "I thought I had trouble, with my father practically telling me how to breathe better every minute, but at least he doesn't disappear. What does Tom do now?"

"Works at the flower shop, right down there at the corner."

Ben feels around in his pockets a minute. "Hey, I got two bucks I was supposed to spend on a textbook. Come on and I'll buy Mom a plant for the holidays, and you can introduce me to Tom."

We go down to the flower shop, and at first Tom frowns because he thinks we've just come to kid around. Ben tells him he wants a plant, so then he makes a big thing out of showing him all the plants, from the ten-dollar ones on down, so Mr. Palumbo will see he's doing a good job. Ben finally settles on a funny-looking cactus that Tom says is going to bloom pretty soon.

Ben goes along home and I arrange to pick him up on Monday. I wait around outside until I see Tom go out on a delivery and ask him how he likes the job. He says he doesn't really know yet, but at least the guy is decent to work for, not like the filling-station man.

I sleep late Monday and go over to Peter Cooper about eleven. A lot of kids are out in the playgrounds, and some fathers are there tossing footballs with them and shouting "Happy New Year" to each other. It sounds odd to hear people saying that on a warm day in September.

Ben and I wander out of the project and he says, "How do we get to this Fulton Street?"

I see a bus that says "Avenue C" on it stopping on Twenty-third Street. Avenue C is way east, and so is Fulton Street, so I figure it'll probably work out. We get on. The bus rockets along under the East Side Drive for a few blocks and then heads down Avenue C, which is narrow and crowded. It's a Spanish and Puerto Rican neighborhood to begin with, then farther downtown it's mostly Jewish. Lots of people are out on the street shaking hands and clapping each other on the back, and the stores are all closed.

Every time the bus stops, the driver shouts to some of the people on the sidewalk, and he seems to know a good many of the passengers who get on. He asks them about their jobs, or their babies, or their aunt who's sick in Bellevue. This is pretty unusual in New York, where bus drivers usually act like they hate people in general and their passengers in particular. Suddenly the bus turns off Avenue C and heads west.

Ben looks out the window and says, "Hey, this is Houston Street. I been down here to a big delicatessen. But we're not heading downtown anymore."

"Probably it'll turn again," I say.

It doesn't, though, not till clear over at Sixth Avenue. By then everyone else has got off and the bus driver turns around and says, "Where you two headed for?"

It's funny, a bus driver asking you that, so I ask him, "Where does this bus go?"

"It goes from Bellevue Hospital down to Hudson Street, down by the Holland Tunnel."

"Holy cow!" says Ben. "We're liable to wind up in New Jersey."

"Relax. I don't go that far. I just go back up to Bellevue," says the driver.

"You think we'd be far from Fulton Fish Market?" I say.

The driver gestures vaguely. "Just across the island."

So Ben and I decide we'll get off at the end of the line and walk from there. The bus driver says, "Have a nice hike."

"I think there's something fishy about this," says Ben.

"That's what we're going to get, fish," I say, and we walk. We walk quite a ways.

Ben sees a little Italian restaurant down a couple of steps, and we stop to look at the menu in the window. The special for the day is lasagna, and Ben says, "Boy, that's for me!"

We go inside, while I finger the dollar in my pocket and do some fast mental arithmetic. Lasagna is a dollar, so that's out, but I see spaghetti and meat balls is seventy-five cents, so that will still leave me bus fare home.

A waiter rushes up, wearing a white napkin over his arm like a banner, and takes our order. He returns in a moment with a shiny clean white linen tablecloth and a basket of fresh Italian bread and rolls. On a third trip he brings enough chilled butter for a family and asks if we want coffee with lunch or later. Later, we say.

"Man, this is living!" says Ben as he moves in on the bread.

"He treats us just like people."

Pretty soon the waiter is back with our lasagna and spaghetti, and he swirls around the table as if he were dancing. "Anything else now? Mind the hot plates, very hot! Have a good lunch now. I bring the coffee later."

He swirls away, the napkin over his arm making a little breeze, and circles another table. It's a small room, and there are only four tables eating, but he seems to enjoy acting like he was serving royalty at the Waldorf. When we're just finished eating, he comes back with a pot of steaming coffee and a pitcher of real cream.

I'm dolloping the cream in, and it floats, when a thought hits me: We got to leave a tip for this waiter.

I whisper to Ben, "Hey, how much money you got?"

He reaches in his pocket and fishes out a buck, a dime, and a quarter. We study them. Figure coffees for a dime each, and the total check ought to be $1.95. We've got $2.35 between us. We can still squeak through with bus fare if we only leave the waiter a dime, which is pretty cheap.

At that moment he comes back and refills our coffee cups and asks what we will have for dessert.

"Uh, nothing, nothing at all," I say.

"Couldn't eat another thing," says Ben.

So the waiter brings the check and along with it a plate of homemade cookies. He says, "My wife make. On the house."

We both thank him, and I look at Ben and he looks at me. I put down my dollar and he puts down a dollar and a quarter.

"Thank you, gentlemen, thank you. Come again," says the waiter.

We walk into the street, and Ben spins the lone

remaining dime in the sun. I say, "Heads or tails?"

"Huh? Heads."

It comes up heads, so Ben keeps his own dime. He says, "We could have hung onto enough for *one* bus fare, but that's no use."

"No use at all. 'Specially if it was yours."

"Are we still heading for Fulton Street?"

"Sure. We got to get fish for Cat."

"It better be for free."

We walk, threading across Manhattan and downtown. I guess it's thirty or forty blocks, but after a good lunch it doesn't seem too far.

You can smell the fish market when you're still quite a ways off. It runs for a half a dozen blocks alongside the East River, with long rows of sheds divided into stores for the different wholesalers. Around on the side streets there are bars and fish restaurants. It's too bad we don't have Cat with us because he'd love sniffing at all the fish heads and guts and stuff on the street. Fish market business is done mostly in the morning, I guess, and now men are hosing down the streets and sweeping fish garbage up into piles. I get a guy to give me a bag and select a couple of the choicer—and cleaner—looking bits. I get a nice red snapper head and a small whole fish, looks like a mackerel. Ben acts as if fish guts make him sick, and as soon as I've got a couple he starts saying "Come on, come on, let's go."

I realize when we're leaving that I don't even notice the fish smell anymore. You just get used to it. We walk uptown, quite a hike, along East Broadway and across Grand and Delancey. There's all kinds of intriguing smells wafting around here: hot breads and pickles and fish cooking. This is a real Jewish neighborhood, and you can sure tell it's a holiday from the smell of all the dinners cooking. And lots of people are out in their best clothes gabbing together. Some of the men wear black skullcaps, and some of them have big black felt hats and long white beards. We go past a crowd gathering outside a movie house.

"They're not going to the movies," Ben says. "On holidays sometimes they rent a movie theater for services. It must be getting near time. Come on, I got to hurry."

We trot along the next twenty blocks or so, up First Avenue and to Peter Cooper.

"So long," Ben says. "I'll come by Wednesday on the way to school."

He goes off spinning his dime, and too late I think to myself that we could have had a candy bar.

12
The Red Eft

Ben and I both take biology, and the first weekend assignment we get, right after Rosh Hashanah, is to find and identify an animal native to New York City and look up its family and species and life cycle.

"What's a species?" says Ben.

"I don't know. What's a life cycle?"

We both scratch our heads, and he says, "What animals do we know?"

I say, "Cat. And dogs and pigeons and squirrels."

"That's dull. I want to get some animal no one else knows about."

"Hey, how about a praying mantis? I saw one once in Gramercy Park."

Ben doesn't even know what it is, so I tell him about this one I saw. For an insect, it looks almost like a dragon, about four or five inches long and pale green. When it flies, it looks like a baby helicopter in the sky. We go into Gramercy Park to see if we can find another, but we can't.

Ben says, "Let's go up to the Bronx Zoo Saturday and see what we can find."

"Stupid, they don't mean you to do lions and tigers. They're not native."

"Stupid, yourself. They got other animals that are. Besides, there's lots of woods and ponds. I might find something."

Well, it's as good an idea for Saturday as any, so I say O.K. On account of both being pretty broke, we take lunch along in my old school lunchbox. Also six subway tokens—two extras for emergencies. Even I would be against walking home from the Bronx.

Of course there are plenty of native New York City animals in the zoo—raccoons and woodchucks and moles and lots of birds—and I figure we better start home not too late to get out the encyclopedias for species and life cycles. Ben still wants to catch something wild and wonderful. Like lots of city kids who haven't been in the country much, he's crazy about nature.

We head back to the subway, walking through the woods so he can hunt. We go down alongside the pond and kick up rocks and dead trees to see if anything is under them.

It pays off. All of a sudden we see a tiny red tail disappearing under a rotten log. I push the log again and Ben grabs. It's a tiny lizard, not more than two or three inches long and brick red all over. Ben cups it in both hands, and its throat pulses in and out, but it doesn't really try to get away.

"Hey, I love this one!" Ben cries. "I'm going to take him home and keep him for a pet, as well as do a report on him. You can't keep cats and dogs in Peter Cooper, but there's nothing in the rules about lizards."

"How are you going to get him home?"

"Dump the lunch. I mean—we'll eat it, but I can stab a hole in the top of the box and keep Redskin in it. Come on, hurry! He's getting tired in my hand I think!"

Ben is one of those guys who is very placid most of the time, but he gets excitable all of a sudden when he runs into something brand-new to him, and I guess he never caught an animal to keep before. Some people's parents are very stuffy about it.

I dump the lunch out, and he puts the lizard in and selects some particular leaves and bits of dead log to put in with him to make him feel at home. Without even asking me, he takes out his knife and makes holes in the top of my lunchbox. I sit down and open up a sandwich, but Ben is still dancing around.

"What do you suppose he is? He might be something very rare! How'm I going to find out? You think we ought to go back and ask one of the zoo men?"

"Umm, nah," I say, chewing. "Probably find him in the encyclopedia."

Ben squats on a log, and the log rolls. As he falls over backward I see two more lizards scuttle away. I grab one. "Hey, look! I got another. This one's bigger and browner."

Ben is up and dancing again. "Oh, boy, oh, boy! Now I got two! Now they'll be happy! Maybe they'll have babies, huh?"

He overlooks the fact that *I* caught this one. Oh, well, I don't want a lizard, anyway. Cat'd probably eat it.

Ben takes it from me and slips it in the lunchbox. "I'm going to call this one Big Brownie."

Finally he calms down enough to eat lunch, taking peeks at his catch between mouthfuls. As soon as he's finished eating, he starts hustling to get home so he can make a house for them. He really acts like a kid.

We get on the subway. It's aboveground—elevated—up here in the Bronx. After a while I see Yankee Stadium off to one side, which is funny because I don't remember seeing it when we were coming up. Pretty soon the train goes underground. I remember then. Coming up, we changed trains once. Ben has his eye glued to the edge of the lunchbox and he's talking to Redskin, so I figure there's no use consulting him. I'll just wait and see where this train seems to come out. It's got to go downtown. We go past something called Lenox Avenue, which I think is in Harlem, then Ninety-sixth Street, and then we're at Columbus Circle.

"Hey, Ben, we're on the West Side subway," I say.

"Yeah?" He takes a bored look out the window.

"We can just walk across town from Fourteenth Street."

"With you I always end up walking. Hey, what about those extra tokens?"

"Aw, it's only a few blocks. Let's walk."

Ben grunts, and he goes along with me. As we get near Union Square, there seem to be an awful lot of people around. In fact they're jamming the sidewalk and we can hardly move. Ben frowns at them and says, "Hey, what goes?"

I ask a man, and he says, "Where you been, sonny? Don'tcha know there's a parade for General Sparks?"

I remember reading about it now, so I poke Ben. "Hey, push along! We can see Sparks go by!"

"Quit pushing and don't try to be funny."

"Stupid, he's a general. Test pilot, war hero, and stuff. Come on, push."

"QUIT PUSHING! I got to watch out for these lizards!"

So I go first and edge us through the crowd to the middle of the block, where there aren't so many people and we can get up next to the police barrier. Cops on horseback are going back and forth, keeping the street clear. No sign of any parade coming yet, but people are throwing rolls of paper tape and handfuls of confetti out of upper-story windows. The wind catches the paper tape and carries it up and around in all kinds of fantastic snakes. Little kids keep scuttling under the barrier to grab handfuls of ticker tape that blow to the ground. Ben keeps one eye on the street and one on Redskin and Brownie.

"How soon you think they're coming?" he asks fretfully.

People have packed in behind us, and we couldn't leave now if we wanted to. Pretty soon we can see a helicopter flying low just a little ways downtown, and people all start yelling, "That's where they are! They're coming!"

Suddenly a bunch of motorcycle cops zoom past, and then a cop backing up a police car at about thirty miles an hour, which is a very surprising-looking thing. Before I've hardly got my eyes off that, the open cars come by. This guy Sparks is sitting up on the back of the car, waving with both hands. By the time I see him, he's almost past. Nice-looking, though. Everyone yells like crazy and throws any kind of paper they've got. Two little nuts beside us have a box of Wheaties, so they're busy throwing Breakfast of Champions. As soon as the motorcade is past, people push through the barriers and run in the street.

Ben hunches over to protect his precious animals and yells, "Come on! Let's get out of this!"

We go into my house first because I'm pretty sure we've got a wooden box. We find it and take it down to my room, and Ben gets extra leaves and grass and turns the lizards into it. He's sure they need lots of fresh air and exercise. Redskin scoots out of sight into a corner right away. Big Brownie sits by a leaf and looks around.

"Let's go look up what they are," I say.

The smallest lizard they show in the encyclopedia is about six inches long, and it says lizards are reptiles and have scales and claws and should not be confused with salamanders, which are amphibians and have thin moist skin and no claws. So we look up salamanders.

This is it, all right. The first picture on the page looks just like Redskin, and it says he's a Red Eft. The Latin name for his species is *Triturus viridescens,* or in English just a common newt.

"Hey, talk about life cycles, listen to this," says Ben, reading. " 'It hatches from an egg in the water and stays there during its first summer as a dull-green larva. Then its skin becomes a bright orange, it absorbs its gills, develops lungs and legs, and crawls out to live for about three years in the woods. When fully mature, its back turns dull again, and it returns to the water to breed.' "

Ben drops the book. "Brownie must be getting ready to breed! What'd I tell you? We got to put him near water!" He rushes down to my room.

We come to the door and stop short. There's Cat, poised on the edge of the box.

I grab, but no kid is as fast as a cat. Hearing me coming, he makes his grab for the salamander. Then he's out of the box and away, with Big Brownie's tail hanging out of his mouth. He goes under the bed.

Ben screams, "Get him! Kill him! He's got my Brownie!" He's in a frenzy, and I don't blame him. It does make you mad to see your pet get hurt. I run for a broom to try to poke Cat out, but it isn't any use. Meanwhile, Ben finds Redskin safe in the box, and he scoops him back into the lunchbox.

Finally, we move the bed, and there is Cat poking daintily with his paw at Brownie. The salamander is dead. Ben grabs the broom and bashes Cat. Cat hisses and skids down the hall. "That rotten cat! I wish I could kill him! What'd you ever have him for?"

I tell Ben I'm sorry, and I get him a little box so he can bury Brownie. You can't really blame Cat too much—that's just the way a cat is made, to chase anything that wiggles and runs. Ben calms down after a while, and we go back to the encyclopedia to finish looking up about the Red Eft.

"I don't think Brownie was really ready to lay eggs, or he would have been in the pond already," I say. "Tell you what. We could go back some day with a jar and try to catch one in the water."

That cheers Ben up some. He finishes taking notes for his report and tracing a picture, and then he goes home with Redskin in the lunchbox. I pull out the volume for C.

Cat. Family, *Felidae,* including lions and tigers. Species, *Felis domesticus.* I start taking notes: " 'The first civilized people to keep cats were the Egyptians, thirteen centuries before Christ. . . . Fifty million years earlier the ancestor of the cat family roamed the earth, and he is the ancestor of all present-day carnivores. The Oligocene cats, thirty million years ago, were already highly specialized, and the habits and physical characteristics of cats have been fixed since then. This may explain why house cats remain the most independent of pets, with many of the instincts of their wild ancestors.' "

I call Ben up to read him this, and he says, "You and your lousy carnivore! *My* salamander is an amphibian, and amphibians are the ancestors of *all* the animals on earth, even you and your Cat, you sons of toads!"

13

The Left Bank of Coney Island

Columbus Day comes up as cold as Christmas. I listen to the weather forecast the night before, to see how it'll be for the beach. "High winds, unseasonably low temperatures," the guy says. He would.

I get up at eight-thirty the next morning, though, figuring he'd be wrong and it would be a nice sunny day. I slip on my pants and shirt and go downstairs with Cat to have a look out. Cat slides out and is halfway down the stoop when a blast of cold wind hits him. His tail goes up and he spooks back in between my legs. I push the door shut against the icy wind.

Mom is sitting in the kitchen drinking her tea and she says, "My goodness, why are you up so early on a holiday? Do you feel sick?"

"Nah, I'm all right." I pour out a cup of coffee to warm my hands on and dump in three or four spoons of sugar.

"Davey, have you got a chill? You don't look to me as if you felt quite right."

"Mom, for Pete's sake, it's COLD out! I feel fine."

"Well, you don't have to go out. Why don't you just go back to bed and snooze and read a bit, and I'll bring you some breakfast."

I see it's got to be faced, so while I'm getting down the cereal and a bowl, I say, "Well, as a matter of fact, I'm going over to Coney Island today."

"Coney ISLAND!" Mom sounds like it was Siberia. "What in the world are you going to do there in the middle of winter?"

"Mom, it's only Columbus Day. We figured we'd go to the aquarium and then—uh—well, fool around. Some of the pitches are still open, and we'll get hot dogs and stuff."

"Who's going? Nick?"

"Nick wasn't sure—I'll stop by his house and

see." I'd just as soon steer clear of this "who's going" business, so I start into a long spiel about how we're studying marine life in biology, and we have to take some notes at the aquarium. Mom is swallowing this pretty well, but Pop comes into the kitchen just then and gives me the fishy eye.

"First time I ever heard of you spending a holiday on homework. I bet they got a new twist palace going out there."

I slam down my coffee cup. "Holy cats! Can't I walk out of here on a holiday without going through the third degree? What am I, some kind of a nut or a convict?"

"Just a growing boy," says Pop. "And don't talk so sassy to your mother."

"I'm talking to you!"

Pop draws in a breath to start bellowing, but Mom beats him to it by starting to wheeze, which she can do without drawing breath.

Pop pats her on the shoulder and gives me a dirty look. "Now, Agnes, that's all right. I'm not sore. I was just trying to kid him a little bit, and he flies off the handle."

I fly off the handle! How do you like that?

I give Mom a kiss. "Cheer up, Mom. I won't ride on the roller coaster. It's not even running."

I grab a sweater and gloves and money and get out before they can start anymore questions. On the subway I start wondering if Mary will show up. It's almost two months since we made this sort of crazy date, and the weather sure isn't helping any.

Coney Island is made to be crowded and noisy. All the billboards scream at you, as if they had to get your attention. So when the place is empty, it looks like the whole thing was a freak or an accident.

It's sure empty today. There's practically no one on the street in the five or six blocks from the subway station to the aquarium. But it's not quiet. There are a few places open—merry-go-rounds and hot-dog shops—and tinny little trickles of music come out of them, but the big noise is the wind. All the signs are swinging and screeching. Rubbish cans blow over and their tops clang and bang rolling down the street. The wind makes a whistling noise all by itself.

I lean into the wind and walk up the empty street. My sweater is about as warm as a sieve. I wonder if I'm crazy to have come. No girl would get out on a boardwalk on a day like this. It must be practically a hurricane.

She's there, though. As soon as I turn the corner to the beach, I can see one figure, with its back to the ocean, scarf and hair blowing inland toward me. I can't see her face, but it's Mary, all right. There isn't another soul in sight. I wave and she hunches her shoulders up and down to semaphore, not wishing to take her hands out of her pockets.

I come up beside her on the boardwalk and turn my back to the ocean, too. I'd like to go on looking at it—it's all black and white and thundery—but the wind blows your breath right back down into your stomach. I freeze.

"I was afraid you wouldn't come on a day like this," I say.

"Me too. I mean I was afraid *you* wouldn't."

"Mom and Pop thought I was crazy. I spent about an hour arguing with them. What'd your mother say?"

"Nothing. She thinks I'm walking alone with the wind in my hair, thinking poetic thoughts."

"Huh? What for?"

Mary shrugs. "Mom's like that. You'll see. Come on, let's go home and make cocoa or something to warm up, and then we'll think up something to do. We can't just stand here."

She's right about that, so I don't argue. Her house is a few blocks away, a two-family type with a sloped driveway going down into a cellar garage. Neat. My pop is always going nuts hunting for a place to park.

Mary goes in and shouts, "Hi, Nina! I brought a friend home. We're going to make some cocoa. We're freezing."

I wonder who Nina is. I don't hear her mother come into the kitchen. Then I turn around and there she is. Holy cow! We got some pretty beat-looking types at school, but this is the first time I've ever seen a beatnik mother,

She's got on a black T-shirt and blue jeans and old sneakers, and her hair is in a long braid, with uneven bangs in front.

Mary waves a saucepan vaguely at us both and says, "Nina—Davey—this is my mother."

So Nina is her mother. I stick out my hand. "Uh—how do you do?"

"Hel-looo." Her voice is low and musical. "I think there is coffee on the stove."

"I thought I'd make cocoa for a change," says Mary.

"All right." Nina puts a cigarette in her mouth and offers one to me.

I say, "No, thank you."

"Tell me . . ." She talks in this low, intense kind of voice. "Are you in school with Mary?"

So I tell her I live in Manhattan, and how I ran into Mary when I had Cat on the beach, because that makes it sound sort of respectable, not like a pickup. But she doesn't seem to be interested in Cat and the beach.

"What do you *read?* In your school?" she asks, launching each question like a torpedo.

I remember Mary saying something about her mother and poetry, so I say, "Well, uh—last week we read 'The Highwayman' and 'The Wreck of the Hesperus.' They're about—I mean, we were studying metaphors and similes. Looking at the ocean today, I sure can see what Longfellow meant about the icy . . ."

I thought I was doing pretty well, but she cut me off again.

"Don't you read any *real* poetry? Donne? Auden? Baudelaire?"

Three more torpedoes. "We didn't get to them yet."

Nina blows out a great angry cloud of smoke and explodes, "Schools!" Then she sails out of the kitchen.

I guess I look a little shook up. Mary laughs and shoves a mug of cocoa and a plate of cinnamon toast in front of me. "Don't mind Mother. She just can't get used to New York schools. Or Coney Island. Or hardly anything around here.

"She grew up on the Left Bank in Paris. Her father was an artist and her mother was a writer, and they taught her to read at home, starting with Chaucer, probably. She never read a kids' book in her life.

"Anything I ever tell her about school pretty much sounds either childish or stupid to her. What I really love is science—experiments and stuff—and she can't see that for beans."

"Our science teacher is a dope," I say, because she is, "so I really never got very interested in science. But I told Mom and Dad I was coming to the aquarium to take notes today, so they wouldn't kick up such a fuss."

Mary shakes her head. "We ought to get our mothers together. Mine thinks I'm wasting time if I even *go* to the aquarium. I do, though, all the time. I love the walrus."

"What does your pop do?"

"Father? He teaches philosophy at Brooklyn College. So I get it from both sides. Just think,

think, think. Father and Nina aren't hardly even interested in *food.* Once in a while Nina spends all day cooking some great fish soup or a chicken in wine, but the rest of the time I'm the only one who takes time off from thinking to cook a hamburger. They live on rolls and coffee and sardines."

Mary puts our cups in the sink and then opens a low cupboard. Instead of pots and pans it has stacks of records in it. She pulls out *West Side Story* and then I see there's a record player on a side table. What d'you know? A record player in the kitchen! This Left Bank style of living has its advantages.

"I sit down here and eat and play records while I do my homework," says Mary, which sounds pretty nice.

I ask her if she has any Belafonte, and she says, "Yes, a couple," but she puts on something else. It's slow, but sort of powerful, and it makes you feel kind of powerful yourself, as if you could do anything.

"What's that?" I ask.

"It's called 'The Moldau'—that's a river in Europe. It's by a Czech named Smetana."

I wander around the kitchen and look out the

window. The wind's still howling, but not so hard. I remember the ocean, all gray and powerful, spotted with whitecaps. I'd like to be out on it.

"You know what'd be fun?" I say out loud. "To be out in a boat on the harbor today. If you didn't sink."

"We could take the Staten Island ferry," Mary says.

"Huh?" I hadn't even thought there was really any boat we could get on. "Really? Where do you get it?"

"Down at Sixty-ninth Street and Fourth Avenue. It's quite a ways. I've always gone there in a car. But maybe we could do it on bikes, if we don't freeze."

"We won't freeze. But what about bikes?"

"You can use my brother's. He's away at college. Maybe I can find a windbreaker of his, too."

She finds the things and we get ready and go into the living room, where Nina is sitting reading and sipping a glass of wine.

"We're going on our bikes to the ferry and over to Staten Island," Mary says. She doesn't even ask.

"Oh-h-h." It's a long, low note, faintly questioning.

"We thought with the wind blowing and all, it'd be exciting," Mary explains, and I think, Uh-o, that's going to cook it. *My* mother would have kittens if I said I was going out on a ferry in a storm.

But Nina just says, "I see," and goes back to reading her book. I say good-bye and she looks up again and smiles, and that's all.

It's another funny thing—Nina doesn't seem to pay any attention to who Mary brings home, like most mothers are always snooping if their daughter brings home a guy. Without stopping to think, I say, "Do you bring home a lot of guys?"

Mary laughs. "Not a lot. Sometimes one of the boys at school comes home when we're studying for a science test."

I laugh, too, but what I'm thinking of is how Pop would look if I brought a girl home and said we were studying for a test!

14

Expedition by Ferry

As we ride through Brooklyn the wind belts us around from both sides and right in the teeth. But the sun's beginning to break through, and it's easy riding, no hills.

This part of Brooklyn is mostly rows of houses joined together, or low apartment buildings, with little patches of lawn in front of them. There's lots of trees along the streets. It doesn't look anything like Manhattan, but not anything like the country, either. It's just Brooklyn.

All of a sudden we're circling a golf course.

What d'you know? Right in New York City!

"Ever play golf?" The wind snatches the words out of my mouth and carries them back to Mary. I see her mouth shaping like a "No," but no sound comes my way. I drop back beside her and say, "I'll show you sometime. My pop's got a set of clubs I used a couple of times."

"Probably I better carry the clubs and you play. I can play tennis, though."

We pass the golf course and head down into a sort of main street. Anyway there's lots of banks and dime stores and traffic. Mary leads the way. We make a couple of turns and zigzags and then go under the parkway, and there's the ferry. It's taken us most of an hour to get from Mary's house.

I'm hoping the ferry isn't too expensive, so I'll have plenty of money left for a good lunch. But while I'm mooning, Mary has wheeled her bike right up and paid her own fare. Well, I guess that's one of the things I like about her. She's independent. Still, I'm going to buy lunch.

The ferry is terrific. I'm going to come ride ferries every day it's windy. The boat doesn't roll any, but we stand right up in front and the wind blows clouds of spray in our faces. You can pretend you're on a full-rigged schooner running before a hurricane. But you look down at that choppy gray water, and you know you'd be done if you got blown overboard, even if it is just an old ferryboat in New York harbor.

The ferry ride is fast, only about fifteen minutes. We ride off in Staten Island and start thinking where to go. I know what's first with me.

I ask Mary, "What do you like, hamburgers or sandwiches?"

"Both. I mean either," she says.

The first place we see is a delicatessen, which is about my favorite kind of place to eat anyway. I order a hot pastrami, and Mary says she never had one, but she'll try the same.

"Where could we go on Staten Island?" I say. "I never was here before."

"About the only place I've been is the zoo. I've been there lots of times. The vet let me watch her operate on a snake once."

This is a pretty surprising thing for a girl to tell you in the middle of a mouthful of hot pastrami. The pastrami is great, and they put it on a roll with a lot of olives and onions and relish. Mary likes it too.

"Is the vet a woman? Aren't you scared of snakes?"

"Uh-un, I never was really. But when you're watching an operation, you get so interested you don't think about it being icky or scary. The vet is a woman. She's been there quite a while."

I digest this along with the rest of my sandwich. Then we both have a piece of apple pie. You can tell from the way the crust looks—browned and a little uneven—that they make it right here.

"So shall we go to the zoo?" Mary asks.

"O.K." I get up to get her coat and mine. When I turn around, there she is up by the cashier, getting ready to pay her check.

"Hey, I'm buying lunch," I say, steaming up with the other check.

"Oh, that's all right." She smiles. "I've got it."

I don't care if she's *got* it. I want to *pay* it. I suppose it's a silly thing to get sore about, but it sort of annoys me. Anyway, how do you maneuver around to do something for a girl when she doesn't even know you want to?

The man in the deli gives us directions to get to the zoo, which isn't far. It's a low brick building in a nice park. In the lobby there are some fish tanks, then there's a wing for birds on one side, animals on the other, and snakes straight ahead.

We go for snakes. Mary really seems to like them.

She says, "The vet here likes them, and I guess she got me interested. You know, they don't really understand how a snake moves? Mechanically, I mean. She's trying to find out."

We look at them all, little ones and big ones, and then we go watch the birds. The keeper is just feeding them. The parrot shouts at him, and the pelican and the eagles gobble up their fish and raw meat, but the vulture just sits on his perch looking bored. Probably needs a desert and a dying Legionnaire to whet his appetite.

In the animal wing a strange-looking dame is down at the end, talking to a sleepy tiger.

"Come on, darling, just a little roar. Couldn't you give me just a soft one today?" she's cooing at him. The tiger blinks and looks away.

The lady notices us standing there and says, "He's my baby. I've been coming to see him for fourteen years. Some days he roars for me beautifully."

She has a short conversation with the lion, then moves along with us toward the small cats, a puma and a jaguar. She looks in the next cage, which is empty, and shakes her head mournfully.

"I had the sweetest little leopard. He died last week. Would you believe it? The zoo never let me know he was sick. I could have come and helped take care of him. I might have saved his life."

She goes on talking, sometimes to herself, sometimes to the puma, and we cross over to look at two otters chasing each other up an underwater tunnel.

"What is she, some kind of nut?" Mary says. "Does she think this is her private zoo?"

I shrug. "I suppose she's a little off. But so's my Aunt Kate, the one who gave me Cat. They just happen to like cats better than people. Kate thinks all the stray cats in the world are her children, and I guess this one feels the same way about the big cats here."

We mosey around a little bit more and then head back to the ferry. I make good and sure I'm ahead, and I get to the ticket office and buy two tickets.

"Would you care for a ride across the harbor in my yacht?" I say.

"Why, of course. I'd be delighted," says Mary.

A small thing, but it makes me feel good.

Over in Brooklyn I see a clock on a bank, and it says five o'clock. I do some fast calculating and say, "Uh-oh, I better phone. I'll never make it home by dinnertime."

I phone and get Pop. He's home early from work. Just my luck.

"I got to get this bike back to this kid in Coney," I tell him. "Then I'll be right home. About seven."

"What do you mean *this* bike and *this* kid? Who? Anyway, I thought you were already at Coney Island."

I suppose lawyers just get in the habit of asking questions. I start explaining. "Well, it was awfully cold over in Coney, and we thought we'd go over to Staten Island on the ferry and go to the zoo. So now we just got back to Brooklyn, and I'm downtown and I got to take the bike back."

"So who's 'we'? You got a rat in your pocket?"

I can distract Mom but not Pop. "Well, actually, it's a girl named Mary. It's her brother's bike. He's away in college."

All I can hear now is Pop at the other end of the line, laughing his head off.

"So what's so funny about that?"

"Nothing," he says. "Nothing. Only now I can see what all the shouting was about at breakfast."

"Oh."

"O.K. Now mind you get that girl, as *well* as the bicycle of the brother who goes to college, home safe. Hear? I'll tell your mother you narrowly escaped drowning, and she'll probably save you a bone for dinner. O.K.?"

"O.K. Bye."

Him and his jokes. Ha, ha, ha. Funny, though, him worrying about me getting Mary home safe, when her own mother doesn't worry any.

We start along toward her house slowly, as there's a good deal of traffic now. I'm wondering how to see Mary again without having to ask for her number and phoning and making a date. Something about telephoning I don't like. Besides, I'd probably go out to a pay phone so the family wouldn't listen, and that'd make me feel stupid to begin with.

Just then we start rounding the golf course, and I whack the handle bar of my bike and say, "Hey, that's it!"

"What's it?"

"Golf. Let's play golf. Not now, I don't mean. Next holiday. We've got Election Day coming up. I'll borrow Pop's clubs and take the subway and meet you here. How about ten o'clock?"

"Hunh?" Mary looks startled. "Well, I suppose I could try, or anyway I could walk around."

"It's easy. I'll show you." The two times I played,

I only hit the ball decently about four or five times. But the times I *did* hit it, it seemed easy.

We get to Mary's house and I put the bikes away and give her back her brother's jacket. "I guess I'll go right along. It's getting late. See you Election Day."

"O.K., bye. Say—thanks for the ferry ride!"

15

Dollars and Cats

Wednesday night before Thanksgiving I go down to the delicatessen to buy some Coke, so I can really enjoy myself watching TV. Tom is just finishing work at the flower shop, and I ask him if he wants to come along home.

"Nah. Thanks. I got to be at work early tomorrow." He doesn't sound too cheery.

"How's the job going?"

"O.K., I guess." We walk along a little ways. "The job's not bad, but I don't want to be a florist all my life, and I can't see this job will train me for anything else."

That seems pretty true. It must be tough not getting regular holidays off, too. "You have to work all day tomorrow?" I ask.

"I open the store up at seven and start working on orders we've already got. I'll get through around three or four."

"Hey, you want to come for dinner? We're not eating till evening."

Tom grins. "You cooking the dinner? Maybe you better ask your mother."

"It'll be all right with Mom. Look, I'll ask her and come let you know in the store tomorrow, O.K.?"

"Hmm. Well, sure. Thanks. I've got a date with Hilda later in the evening, but she's got to eat with her folks first."

"O.K. See you tomorrow."

"Right."

Mom says it's all right about Tom coming, so I go down and tell him in the morning. Turns out Mom has asked Kate to have dinner with us, too, which is quite a step. For Kate, I mean. I think she would have turned the invitation down, except no one can bear to hurt Mom's feelings. Kate's been in our house before, of course, but then she just came in to chat or have tea or something. It wasn't like an invitation.

She comes, and she looks like someone from another world. I've never seen her in anything but her old skirts and sneakers, so the "good clothes" she's wearing now must have been hanging in a closet twenty years. The dress and shoes are way out of style, and she's carrying a real old black patent-leather pocketbook. Usually she just lugs her old cloth shopping bag, mostly full of cat goodies. Come to think of it, that's it: Kate lives in a world that is just her own and the cats'. I never saw her trying to fit into the ordinary world before.

Cat knows her right away, though. Clothes don't fool him. He rubs her leg and curls up on the sofa beside her, still keeping a half-open eye on the oven door in the kitchen, where the turkey is roasting.

Tom comes in, also in city clothes—a white shirt and tie and jacket—the first time I ever saw him in them. He sits down on the other side of Cat, who stretches one paw out toward him negligently.

Looking at Kate and Tom sitting there on the sofa, both looking a little ill at ease, I get a funny idea. My family is starting to collect people the way Kate collects homeless cats. Of course, Kate and Tom aren't homeless. They're people-less—not part of any family. I think Mom always wanted more people to take care of, so she's glad to have them.

Kidding, I ask Kate, "How many cats at your home for Thanksgiving dinner?"

She stops stroking Cat a minute and thinks. "Hmm, Susan's got four new kittens, just got their eyes open. A beautiful little orange one and three tigers. Then there's two big kittens, strays, and one old stray tom. Makes eight, that's all. Sometimes I've had lots more than that."

"Doesn't the landlord ever object?" Pop asks.

Kate snorts. "Him! Huh! I pay my rent. And I have my own padlock on the door, so he can't come snooping around."

We all sit down to dinner. Pop gives Cat the turkey neck to crunch up in the kitchen. He finishes that and crouches and stares at us eating. Kate gives him tidbits, which I'm not supposed to do. I don't think she really wants to eat the turkey herself. She's pretty strictly a fruit and yogurt type.

After dinner Tom leaves to meet Hilda, and I walk home with Kate, carrying a bag of scraps and giblets for her cats. While she's fiddling with the two sets of keys to open her door, the man next door sticks his head out. "Messenger was here a little while ago with a telegram for you. Wouldn't give it to me."

"A telegram?" Kate gapes.

"Yeah. He'll be back." The man looks pleased, like he's been able to deliver some bad news, and pulls his head in and shuts his door.

We go into Kate's apartment, and cats come meowing and rubbing against her legs, and they jump up on the sink and rub and nudge the bag of scraps when she puts it down. Kate is muttering rapidly to herself and fidgeting with her coat and bag and not really paying much attention to the cats, which is odd.

"Lots of people send telegrams on holidays. It's probably just greetings," I say.

"Not to me, they don't!" Kate snaps, also sounding as if they better hadn't.

I go over to play with the little kittens. The marmalade-colored one is the strongest of the litter, and he's learned to climb out of the box. He chases my fingers. Kate finishes feeding the big cats, and she strides over and scoops him back into the box. "You stay in there. You'll get stepped on." She drops Susan back in with her babies to take care of them.

The doorbell rings, and Kate yanks open the door, practically bowling over an ancient little messenger leaning sleepily against the side of the door.

"Take it easy, lady, take it easy. Just sign here," he says.

She signs, hands him the pencil, and slams the door. The orange kitten has got out again, and Kate does come close to stepping on him as she walks across the room tearing open the telegram. He doesn't know enough to dodge feet yet. I scoop him back in this time.

Kate reads the telegram and sits down. She looks quite calm now. She says, "Well, he died."

"Huh? Who?"

"My brother. He's the only person in the world I know who would send me a telegram. So he's dead now."

She repeats it, and I can't figure whether to say I'm sorry or what. I always thought when someone heard of a death in the family, there'd be a lot of crying and commotion. Kate looks perfectly calm, but strange somehow.

"Has he been sick?"

Kate shakes her head. "I don't know. I haven't seen him in twenty years."

There is silence a moment, and then Kate goes on, talking half to herself and half to me. "Mean old coot. He never talked to anyone, except about his money. That's all he cared about. Once he tried to get me to give him money to invest. That's the last time I saw him. He has an old house way up in the Bronx. But we never did get along, even when we were kids."

"Did he have a wife or anything? Who sent the telegram?"

"He's had a housekeeper. Just as mean as him. She'd buy him day-old bread and dented cans of soup because they were cheaper. She suited him fine—saved him money and never talked to him. Well, she'll get his money now, if he left any. That's what she's been waiting for. She sent me the wire."

Twenty years, I think. That's a long time not to be speaking to your own brother, and him living just a ten-cent phone call away. I wonder. She couldn't just not give a hoot about him. They must have been real mad at each other. And mad at the whole world, too. Makes you wonder what kind of parents *they* had, with one of them growing up loving only cats and the other only money.

Kate is staring out the window and stroking an

old stray tomcat between the ears, and it hits me: there isn't a person in the world she loves or even hates. I like cats fine, too, but if I didn't have people that mattered, it wouldn't be so good. I say "So long" quietly and go out.

16
Fortune

"I always wondered if the poor soul had any relatives." That's what Mom says when I tell her about Kate's telegram. "And now she's lost her only brother. That's sad."

"I think it's sad she never talked to him for twenty years. All these years I've wished I had a brother," I say.

"If it's her only brother, she's going to have to do something about his estate," says Pop. That legal mind, it never rests. I guess he's got a point about this, though. How is Kate going to deal with lawyers, or undertakers, or anyone? She can't hardly stand to *talk* to people like that.

"What'll she have to do?"

"Maybe I better go see her tomorrow," says Pop. "There can be lots of things—see if he left a will, if he owes any taxes, if he has property that has to be taken care of or sold. You can't tell."

"Kate said he was a miser. Maybe he left her a million. Say, that'd be great!"

"Don't be a dope!" Pop snaps, and he really sounds angry, so I pipe down.

The next morning Pop tells me to go over and see how Kate is. "The way she feels about people, I don't like to just barge in. I'll come by in ten minutes, like I was picking you up to go to a movie or something."

I saunter round the corner onto Third Avenue and stop short. There are two newspaper cars pulled up in front of Kate's building, one red and one black, and a sizable knot of people gathered on the sidewalk. I move in among them.

"That crazy cat lady . . . he musta been a nut too . . . left her about a million . . . a lotta rich cats, how d'ya like that. . . ."

So I guess he did leave her money, and all of a sudden I see it isn't "great." It's going to be trouble. I push through the people and go upstairs without anyone stopping me. When I open Kate's door, old stray tomcat shoots out. He's leaving, and I can see why.

Kate's room is tiny, and it looks like it's filled with a mob. Maybe it's only half a dozen guys, but the photographers are pushing around trying to get shots and the reporters are jabbering.

Orange kitten sticks his head out of the box. Then out he comes, into the sea of feet. I drop him back in and try to get across to Kate. She's pretty well backed into a corner and looking ready to jump out the window. She has her arms folded in front of her, each hand clenching the other elbow, as if to hold herself together. A reporter with a bunch of scratch paper in his hand is crowding her.

"Miss Carmichael"—funny, I never even knew her last name before—"I just want to ask one or two questions. Could you tell us when you last saw your brother?"

"No, I couldn't," she snaps, drawing her head down between her shoulders and trying to melt into the wall.

"Watcha going to do with the money?" a photographer asks. He picks up a cat, one of the big stray kittens, and dumps it on Kate. The cat clings to her and the photographer says, "Hold it now. Just let me snap a picture."

He takes two steps back.

At the first step the room is silent. At the second step a shattering caterwaul goes up. He has stepped on the adventurous orange kitten.

The scream freezes us all, except Kate. She shoots out of her corner, knowing instantly what has happened. The kitten is jerking slightly now, and bright, bright blood is coming out of its mouth. With one violent, merciful stroke Kate finishes it. She picks the limp body up and wraps it neatly in a paper towel and places it in the wastebasket.

The room is still silent for one congealed instant. Kate seems almost to have forgotten the crowd of men. Then two of them make hastily for the door. The photographer shuffles his feet and says, "Gee, m'am, I didn't mean . . . I wouldn't for the world . . ."

Kate whirls and screams at him: "Get out! Get out, all of you! Leave me and my cats alone! I never asked you in here!"

At that moment my pop comes in the door. Of course he doesn't know anything about the kitten, but he takes in the general situation and herds the two remaining newspapermen to the door. He gives them his card and home address and tells them to look him up a little later.

My knees suddenly feel weak and I slump onto the sofa, and my eyes swivel round to the little package in the wastebasket. It would be the strongest one. I really never saw anything get killed right in front of me before. It hits you.

Pop is trying to calm Kate down. She's facing him, grabbing each sleeve of his coat. "What am I going to do? What can I do? I don't want his money. I don't want anything from anyone. I just want to be let alone!"

"Take it easy, Kate, take it easy. You don't have to let anyone into your apartment. About the inheritance, well, I'll have to look into that." Over his shoulder Pop signals to me to go home and get Mom.

I go home and explain the situation to Mom, and she comes back with me. One photographer and a couple of reporters are still hanging around, and the guy snaps a picture of me and Mom at the door. Mom scoots on up. Bad as I feel, I still get a charge out of getting my picture taken for a paper.

"Hey, kid," one of the reporters shoves in front of me, "about this Miss Carmichael. Does she act pretty strange, like talking to herself on the street and stuff?"

I see the story he's trying to build up. While it's true in a way, if you really know Kate it's not. Anyway, I'm against it. I say, "Nah. She's all right. She's just sort of scared of people, and she likes cats."

"How many cats she got?"

There have been up to a dozen on a busy day, but again I play it down. "She's got a mother cat with kittens. Sometimes a stray or two. Don't get sucked in by all that jazz these dumb kids around here'll give you."

"She gets all that money, you think she'll buy a big house, set up a home for stray cats?"

I shrug. "I don't know. She doesn't want the money anyway. She just wants to be let alone."

"Doesn't want the money!" the photographer chips in. "Boy, she must be *really* nuts! I'm going back to the office."

The reporter says he's going to wait and talk to my pop, and I go on upstairs to see what's doing.

Kate is sitting on the sofa, sniffling and wiping her eyes and muttering, but looking calmer. Mom is making tea. Pop is looking out the window, scratching his head.

Kate gulps and draws a big breath. "Tell them I don't want his old money. Tell them to give it to someone else. Tell them to leave me alone. I just want my own place and my cats. They can't make me move, can they? I've lived here thirty years. I couldn't go anyplace else."

She gulps and sniffs some more, and Mom brings her a cup of tea. The stray kittens jump up to see if it's anything good and nuzzle into her lap. Kate takes a sip of tea and asks Pop again, "They can't make me move, can they?" This seems to be what worries her most.

"No-o," says Pop, "it's only . . ."

He's interrupted by a knock on the door, and I go open it a crack. A guy says he's the landlord. As soon as Kate hears his voice, she yelps at him, "I paid my rent, first of the month like always. Don't you come bothering me!"

"It's about the cats," he says. "People outside saying you got a dozen cats in here. There's a law, you know."

He's a seedy-looking, whining kind of a man, and he looks real pleased with himself when he says there's a law about cats.

Kate jumps right at him. "I'm not breaking any laws. I know you. You just want to get me out of here and rent the place for more money. You leave me alone!"

The man whines, "There's a law, that's all. I don't want no violation slapped on my building."

Pop comes over and tells the man there's just a mother cat with kittens. "There's a couple of strays here, too, right now, but I'll take them home with me."

"There's a law, that's all. Also, I got a right to inspect the premises." Pop shows no signs of letting him in, and he shuffles and grumbles and goes away.

"Lock the door," Kate snaps. "I keep it locked all the time."

Pop says he's going home to make some phone calls and try to figure out what's going on. He takes down the name and address of Kate's brother and asks her if she's sure there are no other relatives. She says she never heard of any. Pop goes, and Kate insists that I lock the door after him.

She gets up and starts stirring around getting food out for the cats. She buys fish and chicken livers for them, even though she hardly eats any meat herself. She listens at the back door a moment to make sure no one's out there, then opens the door and puts out the garbage and wastebasket. There goes the adventurous kitten. You got to hand it to Kate. She has no sniffling sentimentality about her cats. Kitten's dead, it's dead, that's all. She doesn't mope over the limp mite of fur. In fact, anything to do with cats she's got sense and guts. They're her family. I don't know that I could have put that kitten out of its misery.

Just as long as the world doesn't throw any stray fortunes at her, Kate does fine. But when people get in her way, she needs someone like Pop.

Mom says she'll stick around a while and tells me to take the two stray kittens home, just in case the landlord comes back trying to make trouble.

"O.K., great—Cat'll have some company!"

Kate sniffs. "He'll hate it. Cats don't like other cats pushing into their house."

She's right, of course. I put the kittens down at home, and Cat hisses at them and then runs them under the radiator in the kitchen. Then he sits down in the doorway and glowers at them, on guard.

Things simmer down gradually. Mom and I and

sometimes Tom, who's right at the flower shop on the corner, take turns checking on Kate and doing shopping for her, or going with her so she doesn't get badgered by people. But pretty soon everyone in the neighborhood forgets all about her and her inheritance. They see her buying just the same old cat food and cottage cheese and fruit, and they probably figure the whole thing was a phony.

It wasn't though. Pop finds out her brother did leave a will. He lined up his funeral, left something to his housekeeper, something to a little restaurant owner way downtown—apparently that was his one big luxury, a decent meal twice a year when he went down to buy more stocks—and the rest to Kate.

Pop says it may take months or years to clear up the estate, but he says Kate can get her share all put in trust for her with some bank, and they'll take care of all the legalities and taxes and just pay her as much or little as she wants out of the income. And she can leave the whole kit and caboodle to a cat home in her will if she wants to, which will probably make her tightwad brother spin in his grave. I asked her once, and she said maybe she'd leave some to the Children's Aid, because there are a lot of stray children in New York City that need looking after, as well as cats. She's getting to think about people some.

17
Telephone Numbers

There are some disadvantages to not getting a girl's phone number. This sort of date I had with Mary for golf on Election Day fell through. In the first place, I was sick in bed with the flu, and Mom wouldn't have let me out for anything, and secondly, it was pouring rain. Without the phone number, there wasn't any way I could let her know, and I didn't even know a street address to write to later.

By the time I got finished with the flu, we were into Thanksgiving and then all the trouble with

Kate. Time passed and I felt rottener about standing her up without a word, and I couldn't get up my nerve to go out to Coney and just appear on her doorstep. I could have found the house all right, once I was out there.

The first week of Christmas vacation the phone rings late one afternoon and Pop answers it. He says, "Just one minute, please," and I know right away from his voice it isn't someone he knows.

"Young lady on the phone for you, Dave," he says, and he enjoys watching me gulp.

"Hullo?" a rather tight, flat little voice asks. "Is this Dave—uh, Mitchell—uh, I mean, with Cat?"

I recognize it's Mary, all right, even if she does sound strange and scared.

"Oh, hi!" I say. "Sure, it's me! I'm awfully sorry about that day we were going to play golf. I was in bed with the flu, and then I didn't know your phone number or . . ."

"Oh, that's all right," she says. "I wondered what happened."

There's a slight pause, and I see Pop grinning and pretending to read his paper. I turn around so I won't see him.

"Where are you now, out in Coney?" I ask Mary.

"No, as a matter of fact, I'm in Macy's." Her

voice trails off a little, but then she starts in again. "As a matter of fact, that's why I called. You see, I was supposed to meet Mom here at five, and she hasn't come, and I bought all these Christmas presents, and I forgot about the tax or something, and this is my last dime."

She stops. I see now why she sounds scared, and I get a curdled feeling in my stomach, too, because what if the dime runs out in the phone and she's cut off? I'll never find her in Macy's. It's too big.

"Pop!" I yelp. "There's this girl I know is in a phone booth in Macy's and her dime is going to run out and she hasn't anymore money. What'll I do?"

"Get the phone number of the booth and call her back. Here—" He gives me a pencil.

What a relief. Funny I never thought of that. You just somehow don't think of a phone booth having a number.

Mary sounds pretty relieved, too. I get the number and call her back, and with Pop making suggestions here and there we settle that I'll go over to Macy's and meet her on the ground floor near Thirty-fourth Street and Broadway at the counter where they're selling umbrellas for $2.89, which Mary says she can see from the phone booth.

"O.K." I say, and then I sort of don't want to hang up. It's fun talking. So I go on. "Look, just in case we miss each other at Macy's, what's your phone number at home, so I could call you sometime?"

"COney 7-1218."

"O.K. Well, good-bye. I'll be right over. To Macy's, I mean."

I grab my coat and check to see if I've got money. Pop asks if I'm going to bring her home for dinner.

"Gee, I don't know." I hadn't given a thought to what we'd do. "I guess so, maybe, if her mother hasn't come by then. I'll call you if we do anything else."

"O.K.," Pop says.

I go out and hustle through the evening rush-hour crowds to the subway. The stores are all open evenings now, for Christmas, so the crowds are going both ways.

I get to the right corner of Macy's, and I see Mary right away. Everyone else is rushing about and muttering to themselves, and she's standing there looking lost. In fact she looks so much like a waif that the first thing I say is, "Hi! Shall we go get something to eat?"

"Yes, I'm starved. I was just going to get a doughnut when I found I'd run out of money."

"Let's go home and you can have dinner with us then. But what about your mother? Won't she be looking for you?"

Mary shifts her feet and looks tired. "I don't know. Probably if she came and I wasn't here, she'd figure I'd gone home."

I try to think a minute, which is hard to do with all these people shoving around you. Mary starts to pick up her two enormous shopping bags, and I take them from her, still trying to think. At the subway entrance I see the phone booth.

"That's the thing," I say. "Why don't you call your house and see if your mother left a message or something?"

"Well . . ." Mary stands by the phone looking confused and in fact about ready to cry. I suddenly decide the best thing we can do is get home and sit down where it's quiet. Waiting fifteen minutes or so to phone can't make much difference.

We get home pretty fast and I introduce Mary to Mom and Pop. She sinks into the nearest chair and takes off her shoes.

"Excuse me," she says. "I just bought these heels, and it's awful wearing them!"

She wiggles her toes and begins to look better. Mom offers her a pair of slippers and Pop passes some potato chips.

Mom says, "Poor child, did you try to do all your Christmas shopping at once?"

"Well, actually, I was having fun just looking for a long while. I have two little cousins that I don't really have to get much for, but I love looking at all the toys. I spent quite a while there. Then I did the rest of my shopping in a rush, and everything is so crowded, and I got mixed up on my money or the sales tax and only had a dime left, and I missed my mother or she forgot."

She stretches out her toes to touch Cat, who is sitting in front of her. "I couldn't think what to do. It's so hard to think when your feet hurt."

"It certainly is," agrees Mom. She goes out to the kitchen to finish fixing dinner, and Pop suggests Mary better phone her home. She gets her father, and her mother has left a message that she was delayed and figured Mary would go home alone. Mary gives her father our address and tells him she'll be home by nine.

We must have hit a lucky day because we have a real good dinner: slices of good whole meat, not mushed up stuff, and potatoes cooked with cheese in them, and salad, and a lemon meringue pie from the bakery, even.

After dinner we sit around a little while, and Pop says I better take Mary home, and he gives me money for a cab at the end of the subway. When Mary gives the driver her home address, I say it over to myself a few times so I'll remember.

Suddenly I wonder about something. "Say, how'd you know *my* phone number?"

"I looked it up," she says simply. "There's about twenty-eleven Mitchells in the Manhattan phone book, but only one in the East Twenties, so I figured that must be you."

"Gee, that's true. You must have had an awful time, though, standing in the phone booth with your feet hurting, going through all those Mitchells."

Says Mary, "Oh, no. I did it one rainy afternoon at home, weeks ago."

Well, what do you know.

18

"Here's to Cat!"

The two stray kittens gradually make themselves at home. Somehow or other Cat has taught them that he's in charge here, and he just chases them for fun now and again, when he's not busy sleeping.

As for keeping cats in my room, that's pretty well forgotten. For one thing, Mom really likes them. She sneaks the kittens saucers of cream and bits of real hamburger when no one's looking, and she likes talking to them in the kitchen. She doesn't pick them up, but just having them in the room sure doesn't give her asthma.

The only time we have any trouble from the cats is one evening when Pop comes home and the two kittens skid down the hall between his legs, with Cat after them. He scales his hat at the lot of them and roars down the hall to me, "Hey, Davey! When are you getting rid of these cats? I'm not fixing to start an annex to Kate's cat home!"

"I'm sure Davey will find homes for them," Mom says soothingly, but getting a little short of breath, the way she does any time she's afraid one of us is losing his temper.

In fact, one thing this cat business seems to have established is that me and Pop fighting is the main cause of Mom's asthma. So we both try to do a little better, and a lot of things we used to argue and fight about, like my jazz records, we just kid each other about now. But now and then we still work up to a real hassle.

I've been taking a history course the first semester at school. It's a real lemon—just a lot of preaching about government and citizenship. The second semester I switch to a music course. This is O.K. with the school—but not with Pop. Right away when I bring home my new program, he says, "How come you're taking one less course this half?"

I explain that I'm taking music, and also biology, algebra, English, and French.

"Music!" he snorts. "That's recreation, not a course. Do it on your own time!"

"Pop, it's a course. You think the school signs me up for an hour of home record playing?"

"They might," he grunts. "You're not going to loaf your way through school if I have anything to say about it."

"Loaf!" I yelp. "Four major academic subjects is more than lots of the guys take."

Mom comes and suggests that Pop better go over to school with me and talk it over at the school office. He does, and for once I win a round—I keep music for this semester. But he makes sure that next year I'm signed up all year for five majors: English, French, math, chemistry, and European history. I'll be lucky if I have time to breathe.

I go down to the flower shop to grouse to Tom. It's after Valentine's Day, and business is slack and the boss is out.

"Why does Pop have to come butting into my business at school? Doesn't he even think the school knows what it's doing?"

"Aw, heck," says Tom, "your father's the one

has to see you get into college or get a job. Sometimes schools do let kids take a lot of soft courses, and then they're out on a limb later."

"Huh. He just likes to boss everything I do."

"So—he cares."

"Huh." I'm not very ready to buy this, but then I remember Tom's father, who *doesn't* care. It makes me think.

"Besides," says Tom, "half the reason you and your father are always bickering is that you're so much alike."

"Me? Like *him*?"

"Sure. You're both impatient and curious, got to poke into everything. As long as there's a bone on the floor, the two of you worry it."

Mr. Palumbo comes back to the shop then, and Tom gets busy with the plants. I go home, wondering if I really am at all like Pop. I never thought of it before.

It's funny about fights. Pop and I can go along real smooth and easy for a while, and I think: Well, he really isn't a bad guy, and I'm growing up, we can see eye to eye—all that stuff. Then, whoosh! I hardly know what starts it, but a fight boils up, and we're both breathing fire like dragons on the loose.

We get a holiday Washington's birthday, which is good because there's a TV program on Tuesday, the night before the holiday, that I hardly ever get to watch. It's called *Out Beyond,* and the people in it are very real, not just good guys and bad guys. There's always one character moving around, keeping you on the edge of your chair, and by the time it all winds up in a surprise ending, you find this character is not a real person, he's supernatural. The program goes on till eleven o'clock, and Mom won't let me watch it on school nights.

I get the pillows comfortably arranged on the floor, with a big bottle of soda and a bag of popcorn within easy reach. The story starts off with some nature shots of a farm and mountains in the background and this little kid playing with his grandfather. There's a lot of people in it, but gradually you get more and more suspicious of dear old grandpa. He's taking the kid for a walk when a thunderstorm blows up.

Right then, of course, we have to have the alternate sponsor. He signs off, finally, and up comes Pop.

"Here, Davey old boy, we can do better than that tonight. The Governor and the Mayor are on a TV debate about New York City school reorganization."

At first I figure he's kidding, so I just growl, "Who cares?" He switches the channel.

I jump up, tipping over the bottle of soda on the way. "Pop, that's not fair! I'm right in the middle of a program, and I been waiting weeks to watch it because Mom won't let me on school nights!"

Pop goes right on tuning his channel. "Do you good to listen to a real program for a change. There'll be another western on tomorrow night."

That's the last straw. I shout, "See? You don't even know what you're talking about! It's not a western."

Pop looks at me prissily. "You're getting altogether too upset about these programs. Stop it and behave yourself. Go get a sponge to mop up the soda."

"It's your fault! Mop it up yourself!" I'm too mad now to care what I say. I charge down the hall to my room and slam the door.

I hear the TV going for a few minutes, then Pop turns it off and goes in the kitchen to talk to Mom. In a little while he comes down and knocks on my door. Knocks—that's something. Usually he just barges in.

"Look here now, Dave, we've got to straighten a few things out quietly. Your mother says she told you you could watch that program, whatever it was. So O.K., go ahead, you can finish it."

"Yeah, it's about over by now." I'm still sore, and besides Pop's still standing in my door, so I figure there's a hitch in this somewhere.

"But anyway, you shouldn't get so sore about an old television program that you shout 'Mop it up yourself' at me."

"Hmm."

"Hmm, nothing."

"Well, I don't think you should turn a guy's TV program off in the middle without even finding out about it."

Pop says "Hmm" this time, and we both stand and simmer down.

I look at my watch. It's a quarter to eleven. I say, "Well, O.K. I might as well see the end. Sorry I got sore."

Pop moves out of the doorway. He says, "Hereafter I will only turn off your TV programs before they start, not in the middle."

Just as I get the TV on and settle down, the doorbell rings.

"Goodness, who could that be so late?" says Mom.

Pop goes to the door. It's Tom, and Hilda is with him. I turn off the television set—I've lost track of what's happening, and it doesn't seem to be the grandfather who's the spook after all. It's the first time Hilda has been to our house, and Tom introduces her around. Then there's one of those moments of complete silence, with everyone looking embarrassed, before we all start to speak at once.

"Hilda came to the beach with us," I say.

"I told Tom we shouldn't come so late," says Hilda.

Pop says, "Not late at all. Come in and sit down."

Hilda sits on the sofa, where Cat is curled up. He looks at her, puts his head back and goes on sleeping.

Mom brings coffee and cookies in from the kitchen, and I pour the rest of the popcorn into a bowl and pass it around. Tom stirs his coffee vigorously and takes one sip and puts the cup down.

"Reason we came so late," he says, "Hilda and I have been talking all evening. We want to get married."

Pop doesn't look as surprised as I do. "Congratulations!" he says.

Tom says, "Thanks" and looks at Hilda, and she blushes. Really. Tom drinks a little more coffee and then he goes on: "The trouble is, I can't get married on this flower-shop job."

"Doesn't pay enough?" Pop asks.

"Well, it's not just the pay. The job isn't getting me anywhere I want to go. So that's what we've been talking about all evening. Finally we went up to Times Square and talked to the guys in the Army and Navy and Air Force recruiting office. You know, I'd get drafted in a year or two, anyway. I've decided to enlist in the Army."

"Goodness, you may get sent way out West for years and years!" says Mom.

"No, not if I enlist in the Army. That's for three years. But I can choose what specialist school I want to go into, and there's this Air Defense Command—it's something to do with missiles. In that I can also choose what metropolitan area I want to be stationed in. I can choose New York, and we could get married, and I might even be able to go on taking college courses at night school, with the Army paying for most of it."

Pop says, "You sound like the recruiting officer himself. You sure of all this?"

"I'll have to check some more," says Tom. "The

recruiting officer, as a matter of fact, tried to persuade me to shoot for officers' training and go into the Army as a career. But then I would be sent all over, and anyway, I don't think Army life would be any good for Hilda."

"I can see you have put in a busy evening," says Pop. "Well, shove back the coffee cups, and I'll break out that bottle of champagne that's been sitting in the icebox since Christmas."

I go and retrieve my spilled bottle of soda. There's still enough left for one big glass. Pop brings out the champagne, and the cork blows and hits the ceiling. Cat jumps off the sofa and stands, half crouched and tail twitching, ready to take cover.

Pop fills little glasses for them and raises his to Tom and Hilda. "Here's to you—a long, happy life!"

We drink, and then I raise my glass of soda. "Here's to Cat! Tom wouldn't even be standing here if it wasn't for Cat."

That's true, and we all drink to Cat. He sits down and licks his right front paw.

The hairs on her neck rose and her eyes widened. Amaroq's ears went forward aggressively and she remembered that wide eyes meant fear to him. It was not good to show him she was afraid. Animals attacked the fearful. She tried to narrow them, but remembered that was not right either. Narrowed eyes were mean. In desperation she recalled that Kapu had moved forward when challenged. She pranced right up to Amaroq. Her heart beat furiously as she grunt-whined the sound of the puppy begging adoringly for attention. Then she got down on her belly and gazed at him with fondness.

The great wolf backed up and avoided her eyes. She had said something wrong! Perhaps even offended him. Some slight gesture that meant nothing to her had apparently meant something to the wolf. His ears shot forward angrily and it seemed all was lost.

JULIE OF THE WOLVES

by

Jean Craighead George

Pictures by John Schoenherr

HarperTrophy
A Division of HarperCollins*Publishers*

To Luke George who loves wolves
and the Eskimos of Alaska

JULIE OF THE WOLVES

Printed in the United States of America. For information address HarperCollins Children's Books, a division of HarperCollins Publishers, 10 East 53rd Street, New York, N.Y. 10022.

ISBN 0-06-021943-2
ISBN 0-06-021944-0 (lib. bdg.)
ISBN 0-06-440058-1 (pbk.)
First Harper Trophy edition, 1974.

CONTENTS

PART I
Amaroq, the wolf

PART II
Miyax, the girl

PART III
Kapugen, the hunter

PART I

Amaroq, the wolf

MIYAX PUSHED BACK THE HOOD OF HER SEALSKIN parka and looked at the Arctic sun. It was a yellow disc in a lime-green sky, the colors of six o'clock in the evening and the time when the wolves awoke. Quietly she put down her cooking pot and crept to the top of a dome-shaped frost heave, one of the many earth buckles that rise and fall in the crackling cold of the Arctic winter. Lying on her stomach, she looked across a vast lawn of grass and moss and focused her attention on the wolves she had come upon two sleeps ago. They were wagging their tails as they awoke and saw each other.

Her hands trembled and her heartbeat quickened, for she was frightened, not so much of the wolves, who were shy and many harpoon-shots away, but because of her desperate predicament. Miyax was lost. She had been lost without food for many sleeps on the North Slope of Alaska. The barren slope stretches for three hundred miles from the Brooks Range to the Arctic Ocean, and for more than eight hundred miles from the Chukchi to the Beaufort Sea. No roads cross it; ponds and lakes freckle its immensity. Winds scream across it, and the view in every direction is exactly the same. Somewhere in this cosmos was Miyax; and the very life in her body, its spark and warmth, depended upon these wolves for survival. And she was not so sure they would help.

Miyax stared hard at the regal black wolf, hoping to catch his eye. She must somehow tell him that she was starving and ask him for food. This could be done she knew, for her father, an Eskimo hunter, had done so. One year he had camped near a wolf den while on a hunt. When a month had passed and her father had seen no game, he told the leader of the wolves that he was hungry and needed food. The next night the wolf called him from far away and her father went to him and found a freshly killed caribou. Unfortunately, Miyax's father never explained to her how he had told the wolf of his needs. And not long afterward he paddled his kayak into the Bering Sea to hunt for seal, and he never returned.

She had been watching the wolves for two days, trying to discern which of their sounds and movements expressed goodwill and friendship. Most animals had such signals. The little Arctic ground squirrels flicked their tails sideways to notify others of their kind that they were friendly. By imitating this signal with her forefinger, Miyax had lured many a squirrel to her hand. If she could discover such a gesture for the wolves she would be able to make friends with them and share their food, like a bird or a fox.

Propped on her elbows with her chin in her fists, she stared at the black wolf, trying to catch his eye. She had chosen him because he was much larger than the others, and because he walked like her father, Kapugen, with his head high and his chest out. The black wolf also possessed wisdom, she had observed. The pack looked to him when the wind carried strange scents or the birds cried nervously. If he was alarmed, they were alarmed. If he was calm, they were calm.

Long minutes passed, and the black wolf did not look at her. He had ignored her since she first came upon them, two sleeps ago. True, she moved slowly and quietly, so as not to alarm him; yet she did wish he would see the kindness in her eyes. Many animals could tell the difference between hostile hunters and friendly people by merely looking at them. But the big black wolf would not even glance her way.

A bird stretched in the grass. The wolf looked at it.

A flower twisted in the wind. He glanced at that. Then the breeze rippled the wolverine ruff on Miyax's parka and it glistened in the light. He did not look at that. She waited. Patience with the ways of nature had been instilled in her by her father. And so she knew better than to move or shout. Yet she must get food or die. Her hands shook slightly and she swallowed hard to keep calm.

Miyax was a classic Eskimo beauty, small of bone and delicately wired with strong muscles. Her face was pearl-round and her nose was flat. Her black eyes, which slanted gracefully, were moist and sparkling. Like the beautifully formed polar bears and foxes of the north, she was slightly short-limbed. The frigid environment of the Arctic has sculptured life into compact shapes. Unlike the long-limbed, long-bodied animals of the south that are cooled by dispensing heat on extended surfaces, all live things in the Arctic tend toward compactness, to conserve heat.

The length of her limbs and the beauty of her face were of no use to Miyax as she lay on the lichen-speckled frost heave in the midst of the bleak tundra. Her stomach ached and the royal black wolf was carefully ignoring her.

"*Amaroq, ilaya,* wolf, my friend," she finally called. "Look at me. Look at me."

She spoke half in Eskimo and half in English, as if

the instincts of her father and the science of the *gussaks*, the white-faced, might evoke some magical combination that would help her get her message through to the wolf.

Amaroq glanced at his paw and slowly turned his head her way without lifting his eyes. He licked his shoulder. A few matted hairs sprang apart and twinkled individually. Then his eyes sped to each of the three adult wolves that made up his pack and finally to the five pups who were sleeping in a fuzzy mass near the den entrance. The great wolf's eyes softened at the sight of the little wolves, then quickly hardened into brittle yellow jewels as he scanned the flat tundra.

Not a tree grew anywhere to break the monotony of the gold-green plain, for the soils of the tundra are permanently frozen. Only moss, grass, lichens, and a few hardy flowers take root in the thin upper layer that thaws briefly in summer. Nor do many species of animals live in this rigorous land, but those creatures that do dwell here exist in bountiful numbers. Amaroq watched a large cloud of Lapland longspurs wheel up into the sky, then alight in the grasses. Swarms of crane flies, one of the few insects that can survive the cold, darkened the tips of the mosses. Birds wheeled, turned, and called. Thousands sprang up from the ground like leaves in a wind.

The wolf's ears cupped forward and tuned in on

some distant message from the tundra. Miyax tensed and listened, too. Did he hear some brewing storm, some approaching enemy? Apparently not. His ears relaxed and he rolled to his side. She sighed, glanced at the vaulting sky, and was painfully aware of her predicament.

Here she was, watching wolves–she, Miyax, daughter of Kapugen, adopted child of Martha, citizen of the United States, pupil at the Bureau of Indian Affairs School in Barrow, Alaska, and thirteen-year-old wife of the boy Daniel. She shivered at the thought of Daniel, for it was he who had driven her to this fate. She had run away from him exactly seven sleeps ago, and because of this she had one more title by gussak standards–the child divorcée.

The wolf rolled to his belly.

"Amaroq," she whispered. "I am lost and the sun will not set for a month. There is no North Star to guide me."

Amaroq did not stir.

"And there are no berry bushes here to bend under the polar wind and point to the south. Nor are there any birds I can follow." She looked up. "Here the birds are buntings and longspurs. They do not fly to the sea twice a day like the puffins and sandpipers that my father followed."

The wolf groomed his chest with his tongue.

"I never dreamed I could get lost, Amaroq," she went on, talking out loud to ease her fear. "At home on Nunivak Island where I was born, the plants and birds pointed the way for wanderers. I thought they did so everywhere . . . and so, great black Amaroq, I'm without a compass."

It had been a frightening moment when two days ago she realized that the tundra was an ocean of grass on which she was circling around and around. Now as that fear overcame her again she closed her eyes. When she opened them her heart skipped excitedly. Amaroq was looking at her!

"*Ee-lie,*" she called and scrambled to her feet. The wolf arched his neck and narrowed his eyes. He pressed his ears forward. She waved. He drew back his lips and showed his teeth. Frightened by what seemed a snarl, she lay down again. When she was flat on her stomach, Amaroq flattened his ears and wagged his tail once. Then he tossed his head and looked away.

Discouraged, she wriggled backward down the frost heave and arrived at her camp feet first. The heave was between herself and the wolf pack and so she relaxed, stood up, and took stock of her home. It was a simple affair, for she had not been able to carry much when she ran away; she took just those things she would need for the journey—a backpack, food for a week or so, needles to mend clothes, matches, her sleeping skin, and ground cloth to go under it, two knives, and a pot.

She had intended to walk to Point Hope. There

she would meet the *North Star*, the ship that brings supplies from the States to the towns on the Arctic Ocean in August when the ice pack breaks up. The ship could always use dishwashers or laundresses, she had heard, and so she would work her way to San Francisco where Amy, her pen pal, lived. At the end of every letter Amy always wrote: "When are you coming to San Francisco?" Seven days ago she had been on her way—on her way to the glittering, white, postcard city that sat on a hill among trees, those enormous plants she had never seen. She had been on her way to see the television and carpeting in Amy's school, the glass buildings, traffic lights, and stores full of fruits; on her way to the harbor that never froze and the Golden Gate Bridge. But primarily she was on her way to be rid of Daniel, her terrifying husband.

She kicked the sod at the thought of her marriage; then shaking her head to forget, she surveyed her camp. It was nice. Upon discovering the wolves, she had settled down to live near them in the hope of sharing their food, until the sun set and the stars came out to guide her. She had built a house of sod, like the summer homes of the old Eskimos. Each brick had been cut with her *ulo*, the half-moon shaped woman's knife, so versatile it can trim a baby's hair, slice a tough bear, or chip an iceberg.

Her house was not well built for she had never

made one before, but it was cozy inside. She had windproofed it by sealing the sod bricks with mud from the pond at her door, and she had made it beautiful by spreading her caribou ground cloth on the floor. On this she had placed her sleeping skin, a moosehide bag lined with soft white rabbit skins. Next to her bed she had built a low table of sod on which to put her clothes when she slept. To decorate the house she had made three flowers of bird feathers and stuck them in the top of the table. Then she had built a fireplace outdoors and placed her pot beside it. The pot was empty, for she had not found even a lemming to eat.

Last winter, when she had walked to school in Barrow, these mice-like rodents were so numerous they ran out from under her feet wherever she stepped. There were thousands and thousands of them until December, when they suddenly vanished. Her teacher said that the lemmings had a chemical similar to antifreeze in their blood, that kept them active all winter when other little mammals were hibernating. "They eat grass and multiply all winter," Mrs. Franklin had said in her singsong voice. "When there are too many, they grow nervous at the sight of each other. Somehow this shoots too much antifreeze into their bloodstreams and it begins to poison them. They become restless, then crazy. They run in a frenzy until they die."

Of this phenomenon Miyax's father had simply said, "The hour of the lemming is over for four years."

Unfortunately for Miyax, the hour of the animals that prey on the lemmings was also over. The white fox, the snowy owl, the weasel, the jaeger, and the siskin had virtually disappeared. They had no food to eat and bore few or no young. Those that lived preyed on each other. With the passing of the lemmings, however, the grasses had grown high again and the hour of the caribou was upon the land. Healthy fat caribou cows gave birth to many calves. The caribou population increased, and this in turn increased the number of wolves who prey on the caribou. The abundance of the big deer of the north did Miyax no good, for she had not brought a gun on her trip. It had never occurred to her that she would not reach Point Hope before her food ran out.

A dull pain seized her stomach. She pulled blades of grass from their sheaths and ate the sweet ends. They were not very satisfying, so she picked a handful of caribou moss, a lichen. If the deer could survive in winter on this food, why not she? She munched, decided the plant might taste better if cooked, and went to the pond for water.

As she dipped her pot in, she thought about Amaroq. Why had he bared his teeth at her? Because she was young and he knew she couldn't hurt him?

No, she said to herself, it was because he was speaking to her! He had told her to lie down. She had even understood and obeyed him. He had talked to her not with his voice, but with his ears, eyes, and lips; and he had even commended her with a wag of his tail.

She dropped her pot, scrambled up the frost heave and stretched out on her stomach.

"Amaroq," she called softly, "I understand what you said. Can you understand me? I'm hungry—very, very hungry. Please bring me some meat."

The great wolf did not look her way and she began to doubt her reasoning. After all, flattened ears and a tail-wag were scarcely a conversation. She dropped her forehead against the lichens and rethought what had gone between them.

"Then why did I lie down?" she asked, lifting her head and looking at Amaroq. "Why did I?" she called to the yawning wolves. Not one turned her way.

Amaroq got to his feet, and as he slowly arose he seemed to fill the sky and blot out the sun. He was enormous. He could swallow her without even chewing.

"But he won't," she reminded herself. "Wolves do not eat people. That's gussak talk. Kapugen said wolves are gentle brothers."

The black puppy was looking at her and wagging his tail. Hopefully, Miyax held out a pleading hand to him. His tail wagged harder. The mother rushed to him and stood above him sternly. When he licked her cheek apologetically, she pulled back her lips from her fine white teeth. They flashed as she smiled and forgave her cub.

"But don't let it happen again," said Miyax sarcastically, mimicking her own elders. The mother walked toward Amaroq.

"I should call you Martha after my stepmother,"

Miyax whispered. "But you're much too beautiful. I shall call you Silver instead."

Silver moved in a halo of light, for the sun sparkled on the guard hairs that grew out over the dense underfur and she seemed to glow.

The reprimanded pup snapped at a crane fly and shook himself. Bits of lichen and grass spun off his fur. He reeled unsteadily, took a wider stance, and looked down at his sleeping sister. With a yap he jumped on her and rolled her to her feet. She whined. He barked and picked up a bone. When he was sure she was watching, he ran down the slope with it. The sister tagged after him. He stopped and she grabbed the bone, too. She pulled; he pulled; then he pulled and she yanked.

Miyax could not help laughing. The puppies played with bones like Eskimo children played with leather ropes.

"I understand *that*," she said to the pups. "That's tug-o-war. Now how do you say, 'I'm hungry'?"

Amaroq was pacing restlessly along the crest of the frost heave as if something were about to happen. His eyes shot to Silver, then to the gray wolf Miyax had named Nails. These glances seemed to be a summons, for Silver and Nails glided to him, spanked the ground with their forepaws and bit him gently under the chin. He wagged his tail furiously and took Silver's slender nose in his mouth. She crouched before him, licked his cheek and lovingly bit his lower jaw. Amaroq's tail flashed high as her mouthing charged him with vitality. He nosed her affectionately. Unlike the fox who met his mate only in the breeding season, Amaroq lived with his mate all year.

Next, Nails took Amaroq's jaw in his mouth and the leader bit the top of his nose. A third adult, a small male, came slinking up. He got down on his belly before Amaroq, rolled trembling to his back, and wriggled.

"Hello, Jello," Miyax whispered, for he reminded her of the quivering gussak dessert her mother-in-law made.

She had seen the wolves mouth Amaroq's chin twice before and so she concluded that it was a ceremony, a sort of "Hail to the Chief." He must indeed be their leader for he was clearly the wealthy wolf; that is, wealthy as she had known the meaning of the word on Nunivak Island. There the old Eskimo hunters she had known in her childhood thought the riches of life were intelligence, fearlessness, and love. A man with these gifts was rich and was a great spirit who was admired in the same way that the gussaks admired a man with money and goods.

The three adults paid tribute to Amaroq until he was almost smothered with love; then he bayed a wild note that sounded like the wind on the frozen sea. With that the others sat around him, the puppies scattered between them. Jello hunched forward and Silver shot a fierce glance at him. Intimidated, Jello pulled his ears together and back. He drew himself down until he looked smaller than ever.

Amaroq wailed again, stretching his neck until

his head was high above the others. They gazed at him affectionately and it was plain to see that he was their great spirit, a royal leader who held his group together with love and wisdom.

Any fear Miyax had of the wolves was dispelled by their affection for each other. They were friendly animals and so devoted to Amaroq that she needed only to be accepted by him to be accepted by all. She even knew how to achieve this—bite him under the chin. But how was she going to do that?

She studied the pups hoping they had a simpler way of expressing their love for him. The black puppy approached the leader, sat, then lay down and wagged his tail vigorously. He gazed up at Amaroq in pure adoration, and the royal eyes softened.

Well, that's what I'm doing! Miyax thought. She called to Amaroq. "I'm lying down gazing at you, too, but you don't look at *me* that way!"

When all the puppies were wagging his praises, Amaroq yipped, hit a high note, and crooned. As his voice rose and fell, the other adults sang out and the puppies yipped and bounced.

The song ended abruptly. Amaroq arose and trotted swiftly down the slope. Nails followed, and behind him ran Silver, then Jello. But Jello did not run far. Silver turned and looked him straight in the eye. She pressed her ears forward aggressively and lifted her tail. With that, Jello went back to the puppies and the three sped away like dark birds.

Miyax hunched forward on her elbows, the better to see and learn. She now knew how to be a good puppy, pay tribute to the leader, and even to be a leader by biting others on the top of the nose. She also knew how to tell Jello to baby-sit. If only she had big ears and a tail, she could lecture and talk to them all.

Flapping her hands on her head for ears, she flattened her fingers to make friends, pulled them together and back to express fear, and shot them forward to display her aggression and dominance. Then she folded her arms and studied the puppies again.

The black one greeted Jello by tackling his feet. Another jumped on his tail, and before he could discipline either, all five were upon him. He rolled and tumbled with them for almost an hour; then he ran down the slope, turned, and stopped. The pursuing pups plowed into him, tumbled, fell, and lay still. During a minute of surprised recovery there was no action. Then the black pup flashed his tail like a semaphore signal and they all jumped on Jello again.

Miyax rolled over and laughed aloud. "That's funny. They're really like kids."

When she looked back, Jello's tongue was hanging from his mouth and his sides were heaving. Four of the puppies had collapsed at his feet and were asleep. Jello flopped down, too, but the black pup still looked around. He was not the least bit tired. Miyax watched him, for there was something special about him.

He ran to the top of the den and barked. The smallest pup, whom Miyax called Sister, lifted her head, saw her favorite brother in action and, struggling to her feet, followed him devotedly. While they romped, Jello took the opportunity to rest behind a clump of sedge, a moisture-loving plant of the tundra. But hardly was he settled before a pup tracked him to his hideout and pounced on him. Jello narrowed his eyes, pressed his ears forward, and showed his teeth.

"I know what you're saying," she called to him. "You're saying, 'lie down.' " The puppy lay down, and Miyax got on all fours and looked for the nearest pup to speak to. It was Sister.

"Ummmm," she whined, and when Sister turned around she narrowed her eyes and showed her white teeth. Obediently, Sister lay down.

"I'm talking wolf! I'm talking wolf!" Miyax clapped, and tossing her head like a pup, crawled in a happy circle. As she was coming back she saw all five puppies sitting in a row watching her, their heads cocked in curiosity. Boldly the black pup came toward her, his fat backside swinging as he trotted to the bottom of her frost heave, and barked.

"You are *very* fearless and *very* smart," she said. "Now I know why you are special. You are wealthy and the leader of the puppies. There is no doubt what you'll grow up to be. So I shall name you after my father Kapugen, and I shall call you Kapu for short."

Kapu wrinkled his brow and turned an ear to tune in more acutely on her voice.

"You don't understand, do you?"

Hardly had she spoken than his tail went up, his mouth opened slightly, and he fairly grinned.

"Ee-lie!" she gasped. "You do understand. And that scares me." She perched on her heels. Jello whined an undulating note and Kapu turned back to the den.

Miyax imitated the call to come home. Kapu looked back over his shoulder in surprise. She giggled. He wagged his tail and jumped on Jello.

She clapped her hands and settled down to watch this language of jumps and tumbles, elated that she was at last breaking the wolf code. After a long time she decided they were not talking but roughhousing, and so she started home. Later she changed her mind. Roughhousing was very important to wolves. It occupied almost the entire night for the pups.

"Ee-lie, okay," she said. "I'll learn to roughhouse. Maybe then you'll accept me and feed me." She pranced, jumped, and whimpered; she growled, snarled, and rolled. But nobody came to roughhouse.

Sliding back to her camp, she heard the grass swish

and looked up to see Amaroq and his hunters sweep around her frost heave and stop about five feet away. She could smell the sweet scent of their fur.

The hairs on her neck rose and her eyes widened. Amaroq's ears went forward aggressively and she remembered that wide eyes meant fear to him. It was not good to show him she was afraid. Animals attacked the fearful. She tried to narrow them, but remembered that was not right either. Narrowed eyes were mean. In desperation she recalled that Kapu had moved forward when challenged. She pranced right up to Amaroq. Her heart beat furiously as she grunt-whined the sound of the puppy begging adoringly for attention. Then she got down on her belly and gazed at him with fondness.

The great wolf backed up and avoided her eyes. She had said something wrong! Perhaps even offended him. Some slight gesture that meant nothing to her had apparently meant something to the wolf. His ears shot forward angrily and it seemed all was lost. She wanted to get up and run, but she gathered her courage and pranced closer to him. Swiftly she patted him under the chin.

The signal went off. It sped through his body and triggered emotions of love. Amaroq's ears flattened and his tail wagged in friendship. He could not react in any other way to the chin pat, for the roots of this signal lay deep in wolf history. It was inherited from generations and generations of leaders before him. As his eyes softened, the sweet odor of ambrosia arose from the gland on the top of his tail and she was drenched lightly in wolf scent. Miyax was one of the pack.

All through the sunny night she waited for Amaroq to come home with food for her and the pups. When at last she saw him on the horizon she got down on all fours and crawled to her lookout. He carried no food.

"*Ayi,*" she cried. "The pups must be nursing—that's why there's no meat." Slumping back on her heels, she thought about this. Then she thought again.

"You can't be nursing," she said to Kapu, and plunked her hands on her hips. "Silver growls when you suckle, and drives you away." Kapu twisted his ears at the sound of her voice.

"Okay," she called to him. "Where are you getting the food that makes you so fat?" He ignored her, concentrating on Silver and Nails, who were coming slowly home from the hunt.

Miyax went back to her pot and stuffed on the cold raw moss until her stomach felt full if not satisfied. Then she crawled into her cozy home in the hope that sleep would soothe her hunger.

She smoothed the silver hairs of her beautiful wedding parka, then carefully took it off and rolled it up. Placing it and her fur pants in a bag made of whale bladder, she tied it securely so that no moisture would dampen her clothes while she slept. This she had learned in childhood, and it was one of the old Eskimo ways that she liked, perhaps the only one. She had never violated it, even in the warm, gas-heated house in Barrow, for damp clothes could mean death in the Arctic.

When her outer garments were put away she took off the bright red tights her mother-in-law had bought for her at the American store in Barrow. Walking to the pond, she rinsed them and laid them in the sun. The cool air struck her naked body. She shivered and was glad that she had done one thing right—she had worn her winter clothes, not her light summer *kuspuck*, the woman's dress.

The wind gusted; Miyax scrambled through the low door and slid into her sleeping skin. The silken softness of the rabbit fur embraced her and she pulled the hood around her face so that only her nose was exposed. The fur captured her warm breath, held it against her face, and she became her own radiant stove. In this cozy micro-world she forgot her hunger and recalled what she already knew about wolves so that she could put it together with what she had observed.

Wolves are shy, Kapugen had said, and they desert their dens if discovered by man; yet this pack had not. Did Amaroq not know she was human? Perhaps not; she had never walked in his presence, the two-legged signal of "man" to wild animals. On the other hand he must know. Kapugen had said that with one sniff a wolf knew if you were male or female, adult or child, if you were hunting or not hunting—even if you were happy or sad. She concluded that Amaroq tolerated her because she was young, had no gun, and was sad— a lost child.

She next considered Nails. Who was he? Amaroq's dependable friend, that was true, yet she suspected he was even more than that—a spiritual father of the pups. Nails took orders from Amaroq, but stayed close to Silver and the little wolves. He was father when their real father was busy. He was Amaroq's serious partner. But Jello? Who was he? Where had he come from? Was he a pup of a previous year? Or had he joined the pack just as she had, by soliciting Amaroq for membership in his tribe? There was much to learn about her family.

Miyax did not know how long she slept, for midnight was almost as bright as noon and it was difficult to judge the passing of time. It did not matter, however; time in the Arctic was the rhythm of life. The wolf pups were barking their excited *yipoo* that rang out the hour of the end of the hunt. The pack was coming home. With visions of caribou stew in her head, she got out of her sleeping skin and reached for her clothes.

The puppies may not have been eating, but certainly Amaroq would have to bring Jello some food. He had been home all night. Stepping into the sunlight, she put on her tights, danced a moment, and then pulled on her furs. Leaning over the pond, she saw in the glassy water the hollows of her cheeks. She was pleased, for she looked almost like the gussak girls in the magazines and movies—thin and gaunt, not moon-faced like an Eskimo. Her hair! She leaned closer to the tundra looking glass. Her hair was a mess. Pressing it into place with her hands, she wished she had taken Daniel's wedding brush and comb with her. They lay unused in the corner of a table drawer in the house at Barrow.

Quickly she climbed the frost heave, lay down, and looked at the wolves. There was no meat to be seen. The three hunters were stretched out on their sides, their bellies extended with food. Jello was gone. Of course, she said to herself, he had been relieved of his duties and had backtracked the hunters to the kill. She winced, for she had been so certain that today she would eat. So I won't, she said to herself, and that's that.

Miyax knew when to stop dreaming and be practical. She slid down the heave, brushed off her parka, and faced the tundra. The plants around the pond had edible seeds, as did all of the many grasses. There were thousands of crane fly and mosquito larvae in the water, and the wildflowers were filling if not very nourishing. But they were all small and took time to gather. She looked around for something bigger.

Her black eyes were alert as several Lapland longspurs darted overhead. They might still have young in their nests. Staying on one side of the heave, so the wolves would not see her two-leggedness, she skipped into the grass. The birds vanished. Their dark pointed wings were erased from the sky as if they had sensed her deadly purpose. Miyax crouched down. Kapugen had taught her how to hunt birds by sitting still and being patient. She crossed her feet and blended into the plants, still as a stone.

Presently a grass blade trembled and Miyax saw a young bird fluttering its wings as it begged to be fed. A brown lark-like parent winged down and stuffed its open beak. Another youngster begged and the parent flew to it. Unfortunately, the second little bird was so far from the first that Miyax knew they were out of the nest and impossible to catch. She shifted her attention to the snow buntings.

A movement in the sky above the horizon caught her attention, and she recognized the pointed tail and black head of a jaeger. She knew this bird well, for it hunted the shore and tundra of Nunivak Island. A bold sea bird, it resembled its close relative the gull, but was not a fisher. The jaeger preyed upon lemmings, small birds, and occasionally carrion. Miyax wondered what prey it was hunting. Three more jaegers joined the first, circled close together as if over a target, then dropped out of sight below the horizon.

"The wolf kill!" she fairly shouted. "They're sharing the wolf kill."

Jumping to her feet, she lined up the spot where they had disappeared with a patch of brown lichens in the distance, and ran with joy along the invisible line. When she had gone a quarter of a mile, she stopped and looked back. The endless tundra rolled around her and she could not tell which frost heave was which.

"Oh, no!" she cried. She turned around and laboriously searched out the plants crushed by her feet. Near a pool she lost all sight of her steps and then with relief recognized an empty lemming nest, a round ball of grass that she had kicked open. She pounced on it, saw a flower she had trampled, and ran up the heave to it. From the top she looked across the distance to her own precious house.

She reminded herself not to be so careless again. "One can get lost out here," she said aloud.

Miyax flopped down in the grass to rest. Her hand touched a patch of Arctic peas. They were tiny but numerous; she took off her boot and then her sock, and filled its toe with the vegetables. When all were harvested, she swung the sock over her shoulder and, striding joyously, rounded her pond and plunked the peas in her pot. She rolled them around with her fingers and they rattled musically. She rolled them again and made up words to fit their rhythm:

> *Peas that go* tink, *peas that go* tot,
> *Peas that will never grow outside my pot.*

The puppies yapped and Silver ran out across the tundra. She leaped with grace, her fur gleaming like metal; then she swept into a dip in the landscape and vanished. Up from the horizon rose the jaegers, announcing that Silver had gone to the kill. Clutching the cooking pot to her breast, Miyax excitedly waited to see her bring back meat for the pups.

The jaegers circled, the longspurs tumbled on their wings, and at last Silver came home. Her mouth was empty.

"I just don't understand," she said to the pups. "What is keeping you alive?" Putting down her pot, she went to her lookout to try to solve the riddle.

Silver came up the long slope, gave the grunt-whine that summoned the pups, and Kapu ran to meet her. She pulled back her lips in a smile and nosed him affectionately. Then Kapu stuck his nose in the corner of her mouth. Silver arched her back, her neck rippled, and she choked up a big mound of meat. Kapu set upon it with a snarl.

"So that's it!" said Miyax. "The meat's in the belly-basket. Now what do I do?"

Kapu let Sister share the meal with him, but not Zing, Zat, and Zit—as Miyax had dubbed the three tawny pups who had little personality as yet. Zing rushed over to the resting Silver and cuddled up against her. He rammed his nose against her teats and taking one in his mouth, ravenously nursed. Silver tolerated this for a moment, then growled. He did not let go and she snapped at him. He pulled away, but when she stretched out he dove back into her belly fur again. With a loud bark she rolled onto her stomach and cut off her milk from him. Zing got up, walked over to Amaroq, and stuck his nose in the corner of his mouth. Amaroq regurgitated food.

The secret of the fat pups was out. They were being weaned from mother's milk to well-chewed and partially digested food.

They might eat food from the belly-basket for weeks before they were brought chunks of meat that Miyax could share, and so she went out into the grasses again to look for buntings. Soon Silver and Nails trotted off in the direction of the kill. Having fed the puppies, they were now feeding themselves. Miyax cautiously peered around the heave. Jello had not gone with them. Yet he had been to the kill. He would have food in his belly-basket.

When the jaegers arose into the air she picked up the pot and climbed once again to the top of her frost heave. Getting to her hands and knees, she gave the grunt-whine call. "Look at me. I'm nice," it said.

Jello strode toward her. So pushed around was he by Silver, so respectful of Amaroq and even Nails, that he was excited by a voice more humble than his own. He even lifted his tail and head higher than Miyax had ever seen him do, and, acting like the boss wolf, loped up her frost heave. Curious Kapu trotted behind.

As Miyax scurried to meet Jello, he hesitated, growled softly, and urinated. "Don't be scared," she said and whimpered. He circled closer. Quickly rising to her knees, grunting the note of friendship, she slipped her hand over his head and clasped the top of his nose firmly in her fingers.

"I'm boss," she said as his tail and head went down in deference to the symbol of leadership. She started to slip her hand into the corner of his mouth, but he jerked away. Then Kapu, as if he understood what Miyax wanted, swept up to Jello and nuzzled his mouth. Jello heaved, opened his jaws, and deposited food on the ground.

"I'll live! I'll live!" Miyax cried jubilantly as Jello turned, put his tail between his legs, and raced back to the other pups. Kapu sat down and watched with wrinkled forehead as she scooped the meat into the pot. When she had retrieved every morsel, she gently closed her lips on the bridge of his nose. His tail wagged respectfully and he gazed softly into her eyes.

"Kapu," she whispered. "We Eskimos have joking partners—people to have fun with—and serious partners—people to work and think with. You and I are both. We are joking-serious partners." He wagged his tail excitedly and blinked. "And that's the best of all." She reached out to hug him, for his eyes were mellow and his fuzz irresistible. But he was like water and slipped through her hands.

On two knees and one hand, holding the pot with the other, Miyax hobbled toward her camp. Kapu bit her heel softly and she glanced over her shoulder. His head was cocked and his tail swished slowly.

"What are you saying now?" she asked. He gave the grunt-whine for attention.

Of course, she was his big sister and he wanted to play. Reaching into her pocket she pulled out a mitten and before she could flash it in front of his nose, he had leaped, caught it, and was pulling and shaking her whole arm and torso with incredible strength.

Miyax let go lest she spill her meat, and Kapu rolled head over heels into the lichens. Taking a firm grip on the mitten, he flattened his ears in spirited fellowship, dashed down the slope and up to his den. There he turned to see if she was following.

"Bring back my mitten," she called. "I need it." He flashed the wolf smile of apology, shook the mitten, and romped into the midst of his other brothers.

Kapu scratched a wide swath on the ground with his hind feet. The three tawny pups sniffed the mark and Zit sat down before it. Bold Kapu had written his signature and it was deep and impressive. Miyax wondered if the mitten victory was responsible. It was quite a trophy to win.

Placing her pot by her fireplace, she walked out on the tundra and gathered dry grass and lichens in her sock, for there was, of course, no wood to burn. Although caribou droppings were a better fuel, she was too fearful of getting lost to hunt them. Piling the grass and lichens in the center of the stones, she went into her house, took a small cookie tin from her pack, and removed one precious match. Then she lit the tinder.

The grass burst into flame and the lichens smoldered slowly, giving her time to dig the peat that the dead grasses had laid down for thousands and thousands of years. Gradually the peat glowed, the water boiled, and an hour later Miyax had a pot of caribou stew.

"At last!" she said. On it floated great chunks of golden grease, more delicious than the butter from the gussak store. She put a savory bite in her mouth, sucked the juices, then chewed a long time before she swallowed. She must not eat too fast or too much. Kapugen had said that an old lady, rescued from the snow after weeks of starvation, so stuffed herself that she died the next day.

Munching another bite, she went out to the grass clump to check on buntings, and a long time later returned to eat two more chunks of caribou. The rest, though she longed for it, she stored inside her house. Then she patted her stomach and told it to wait.

For the first time in days she could think of something other than food. Her mind turned to the problem of which direction was north and in which direction lay the town of Point Hope. The dips and heaves of the tundra spread out all around her and still looked the same in every direction.

"Oh, ho!" she said aloud. "More lichens grow on one side of the frost heaves than on the other." She pondered this, as well as the oblong shape of her pond, which was caused by the flow of the ice as it moved with the wind. But did the wind come down from the north or out of the west on the North Slope of Alaska? She did not know. Next, she noted that the grasses grew in different spots than the mosses, and the more she studied, the more the face of the tundra emerged; a face that could tell her which way was north, if she had listened more carefully to Kapugen.

Her legs began to buckle and her body swayed. She crumpled to her knees, for the food was making her both dizzy and sleepy. She staggered into her fur-carpeted house and lay down.

MIYAX'S EYELIDS FLUTTERED; THE BLACK LASHES parted, then framed her wide eyes like ferns around a pool. She had eaten, slept for many hours; and the dull, tired feeling of starvation was gone. She felt bright and very much alive.

Rolling to her stomach, she propped herself on her elbows, and reached into her pot to eat. She ate a lot. The food in the pot lowered drastically. When but two meals remained, she made up her mind to tell Amaroq she wanted a whole shank of caribou. Wolves did bring food to their dens. Kapugen had seen them walk long miles in spring, with legs and ribs for the mothers who stayed in the ground with their pups for almost ten days after birth.

Well, she had no puppies to induce Amaroq to feed her, so she pondered again. Kapugen had once told her of a wolf who was wounded by the hoofs of a caribou. He limped to a rock cave and lay down to recover. Every night his leader trotted over the snow, bringing him meat until he was well and could rejoin the pack.

Miyax did not want to suffer a wound, but it

seemed to her that in order to be fed by wolves one had to be helpless.

"If that's the case," she said to herself, "I should be buried in food. I'm helpless enough. I cannot fell a caribou or catch a bird. And I'm lost, besides." She thrust her head out the door.

"Amaroq, I'm helpless," she cried. The chilly air tingled her nose and she noticed that the cotton grasses by the pond were seeding out into white puffs. This was worrisome, for they marked the coming of autumn, the snows, and the white-outs. White-outs could be dangerous. When the cotton grass heads were gone, the winds would lift the snow from the ground to the air and she would not be able to see her feet. She would be imprisoned wherever she stood . . . maybe for days . . . maybe till death.

Amaroq howled the long note to assemble. Silver and Nails barked a brief "Coming," and it was the beginning of a new day for Miyax and the wolves. Although the clocks in Barrow would say it was time to get ready for bed, she was getting up, for she was on wolf time. Since there was no darkness to hamper her vision, night was as good a time to work as day, and much better if you were a wolf girl. Rehearsing whimpers and groveling positions as she climbed to her lookout, she got ready to tell Amaroq how helpless she was in his own language.

He was awake, lying on his side, watching Sister's

paw twitch as she slept. He got up and licked the restless sleeper as if to say "All's well." The paw relaxed.

Miyax whimpered and twisted her head appealingly. Amaroq shot her a glance and wagged his tail as if she had said "Hello," not "I'm helpless."

Suddenly his head lifted, his ears went up, and Amaroq sniffed the wind. Miyax sniffed the wind and smelled nothing, although Amaroq was on his feet now, electric with the airborne message. He snapped his hunters to attention and led them down the slope and off across the tundra. Jello stayed home with the pups.

The pack moved in single file almost to the horizon, then swerved and came back. Shading her eyes, Miyax finally saw what the wind had told Amaroq. A herd of caribou was passing through. She held her breath as the hunters sped toward a large buck. The animal opened his stride and gracefully gained ground. He could so easily outrun the wolves that Amaroq let him go and trotted toward another. This one, too, outdistanced the pack and Amaroq swerved and tested another. Just as Miyax was wondering how the wolves ever caught anything, Amaroq put on full speed and bore down on a third.

This animal could not outrun him, and when Amaroq attacked he turned and struck with his powerful hoofs. Like a bouncing ball the leader sprang away. Nails and Silver fanned out to either side of the beast, then veered and closed in. The caribou bellowed, pressed back his ears, zigzagged over a frost heave, and disappeared from sight.

"They're chasing the weakest," Miyax said in astonishment. "It's just like Kapugen said—wolves take the old and sick."

She looked from the empty tundra to the busy den site. Kapu was staring at her, his eyes narrowed, his ears thrown forward aggressively.

"Now why are you so hostile?" she asked, then looked at her feet and legs. "Ee-lie, Ee-lie." She dropped to all fours and smiled apologetically.

"*Ayi,* Kapu. You've never seen a man in all your life. What is it that tells you to beware? Some spirit of your ancestors that still dwells in your body?"

She gave the grunt-whine and Kapu pressed down his ears, snatched up a bone and brought it over to her. She grabbed it, he tugged, she pulled, he growled, she giggled, and Jello called Kapu home. He cocked an ear, rolled his eyes, and ignored the baby-sitter.

"You're naughty," she said and covered a grin with her hand. "Martha would scold me for that."

Kapu dropped the bone. She leaned down, picked it up in her teeth, and tried to run on all fours. She had barely begun to move away when Kapu leaped on her back and took her bare neck in his teeth. She started to scream, checked herself and, closing her eyes, waited for the teeth to pierce her skin. They did not even bruise, so controlled was this grip that said "Drop the bone." She let it go, and in one swish Kapu leaped to the ground and snatched it.

As she started after him something struck her boot and she looked around to see Zit, Zat, and Sister at her heels. Zing charged up the knoll, hit her arm with great force, and knocked her to the ground. She growled, flashed her teeth, and narrowed her eyes. Kapu dropped the bone and lay down. Zing backed up, and for a moment not a puppy moved.

"Phew." She smiled. "That did it."

Too late she remembered that such a smile was an apology, a sort of "I didn't mean it," and before she could growl all five little wolves jumped on her again.

"Stop!" She was angry. They sensed it and backed away. "Shoo! Go!" She waved her arm above her head and the threatening pose spoke louder than all her words. Drooping their tails, glancing warily at her, they trotted away—all but Kapu. He licked her cheek.

"Dear Kapu." She was about to stroke his head, when he picked up the bone and carried it back to the den. But he was not done with play. He never was. Kapu was tireless. Diving into a tunnel, he came out on the other side and landed on Jello's tail.

When Miyax saw this she sat back on her heels.

Open-ended tunnels reminded her of something. In the spring, wolf packs stay at a nursery den where the pups are born deep in the earth at the end of long tunnels. When the pups are about six weeks old and big enough to walk and run, the leaders move the entire group to a summer den. These are mere shelters for the pups and are open at two ends. For a few weeks the packs stay at this den; then they leave and take up the nomadic winter life of the wolf.

The cold chill of fear ran up Miyax's spine—the wolves would soon depart! Then what would she do? She could not follow them; they often ran fifty miles in a night and slept in different spots each day.

Her hands trembled and she pressed them together to make them stop, for Kapugen had taught her that fear can so cripple a person that he cannot think or act. Already she was too scared to crawl.

"Change your ways when fear seizes," he had said, "for it usually means you are doing something wrong."

She knew what it was—she should not depend upon the wolves for survival. She must go on her own. Instantly she felt relieved, her legs moved, her hands stopped shaking, and she remembered that when Kapugen was a boy, he had told her, he made snares of rawhide and caught little birds.

"Buntings, beware!" she shouted and slid down to her camp. Stepping out of her pants, she slipped off her tights and cut a swath of cloth from the hip with her ulo. She tore the cloth into small strips, then ate some stew, and started off to hunt birds. Every so often she tied a bit of red cloth to a clump of grass or around a conspicuous stone. If she was going to hunt in this confusing land, she must leave a trail to lead her home. She could not smell her way back as the wolves did.

As she tied the first piece of cloth to a bent sedge, she looked down on a small pile of droppings. "Ee-lie," she said. "A bird roost. Someone sleeps here every night." Quickly she took the thongs from her boots, made a noose, and placed it under the sedge. Holding the pull-rope, she moved back as far as she could and lay down to await the return of the bird.

The sun slid slowly down the sky, hung still for a moment, then started up again. It was midnight. A flock of swift-flying Arctic terns darted overhead, and one by one dropped into the grasses. Ruddy turnstones called sleepily from their scattered roosts, and sandpipers whistled. The creatures of the tundra were going to sleep, as they did also at noon in the constant daylight. Each called from his roost—all but the little bird of the sedge. It had not come back.

A bird chirped three feet from her face, and Miyax rolled her eyes to the left. A bunting on a grass blade tucked its bill into the feathers on its back, fluffed, and went to sleep. Where, she asked, was the bird of the sedge? Had it been killed by a fox or a weasel?

She was about to get to her feet and hunt elsewhere, but she remembered that Kapugen never gave up. Sometimes he would stand motionless for five hours at a seal breathing hole in the ice waiting for a seal to come up for a breath. She must wait, too.

The sun moved on around the sky and, when it was directly behind her, the sleeping bunting lifted its head and chirped. It hopped to a higher blade of grass, preened, and sang its morning song. The sleep was over. Her bird had not come back.

Suddenly a shadow passed. A snowy owl, white wings folded in a plummeting dive, threw out his feathered feet and struck the little gray bunting. The owl bounced up, and came down almost on Miyax's outstretched hand, the bird caught in his foot. Her first instinct was to pounce on the owl, but she instantly thought better of that. Even if she could catch him, she would have his powerful claws and beak to contend with, and she knew what damage they could do. Besides, she had a better idea—to lie still and watch where he flew. Perhaps he had owlets in the nest, for these little birds took almost six weeks to get on their wings. If there were owlets, there would also be food, lots of it, for the male owls are constantly bringing food to the young. Once, she had counted eighty lemmings piled at the nest of a snowy owl.

So close was the *ookpick*, the white owl of the north, that she could see the clove markings on his wings and the dense white feathers that covered his legs and feet. His large yellow eyes were pixieish, and he looked like a funny little Eskimo in white parka and mukluks. The wind stirred the wolverine trim on Miyax's hood and the owl turned his gleaming eyes upon her. She tried not to blink and belie the life in her stone-still body, but he was suspicious. He turned his head almost upside down to get a more acute focus on her; then unwinding swiftly, he lifted his body and sped off. His wings arched deeply as he steered into a wind and shot like a bullet toward the sun. As Miyax rolled to a sitting position, the owl scooped his wings up, braked, and dropped onto an exceptionally large frost heave. He left the bird and flew out over the tundra, screaming the demonic call of the hunting ookpick.

Miyax tied another red patch on the sedge, rounded a boggy pond, and climbed the heave where the owl lived. There lay an almost dead owlet, its big beak resting on the edge of the stone-lined nest. It lifted its head, laboriously hissed, and collapsed. The owlet was starving, for there was only the bunting, when there should have been dozens of lemmings. It would not live, in this time of no lemmings.

She picked up the bunting and owlet, regretting that she had found a provider only to lose him again.

The male owl would not bring food to an empty nest.

Collecting her red markers as she walked home, she kicked open old lemming nests in the hope of finding baby weasels. These small relatives of the mink, with their valuable fur that turns white in winter, enter lemming nests and kill and eat the young. Then they move into the round grassy structures to give birth to their own young. Although Miyax kicked seven nests, there were no weasels—for there were no lemmings to eat.

When in sight of her house she took a shortcut and came upon a pile of old caribou droppings—fuel for her fire! Gleefully, she stuffed her pockets, tied a marker at the site for later use, and skipped home dreaming of owlet stew.

She plucked the birds, laid them on the ground, and skillfully cut them open with her ulo. Lifting out the warm viscera, she tipped back her head and popped them into her mouth. They were delicious—the nuts and candy of the Arctic. She had forgotten how good they tasted. They were rich in vitamins and minerals and her starving body welcomed them.

Treats over, she sliced her birds into delicate strips and simmered them slowly and not too long.

"Chicken of the North," Miyax gave a toast to the birds. Then she drank the rich juices and popped the tender meat in her mouth. Had she been a boy this day would be one to celebrate. When a boy caught his first bird in Nunivak, he was supposed to fast for a day, then celebrate the Feast of the Bird. When he killed his first seal his mother took off her rings, for he was a man, and this was her way of bragging without saying a word.

Silly, she said to herself, but nevertheless she sang Kapugen's song of the Bird Feast.

Tornait, tornait,
Spirit of the bird,
Fly into my body
And bring me
The power of the sun.

Kapu yapped to say that the hunters were coming home, and Miyax washed out her pot and went to her lookout to tell them goodnight. Amaroq and Jello were facing each other, ruffs up, ready to fight. Before Jello could attack, Amaroq lifted his head and Jello bowed before him. The dispute was over. No blood was shed. The difference had been settled with the pose of leadership.

Miyax wondered what had happened to put them at odds with each other. Whatever the problem, Jello had surrendered. He was on his back flashing the white fur on his belly that signaled "I give up!"—and no one, not even the pups, could strike him.

"The white flag of surrender," she murmured. "Jello lost." Amaroq walked gracefully away.

He was not done with what he had to say, however. With a dash, he picked up her mitten and tore it to shreds, then rolled in its many pieces and stood up. Nails, Silver, and the pups sniffed him and wagged their tails in great excitement. Then Amaroq narrowed his eyes and glanced her way. With a chill she realized he was going to attack. She flattened herself like an obedient pup as he glided down his slope and up hers. Her breathing quickened, her heart raced.

When Amaroq was but five feet away and she could see each hair on his long fine nose, he gave the grunt-whine. He was calling her! Cautiously she crawled toward him. He wagged his tail and led her down the hill, through the sedges, and up the long slope to the wolf den. Patiently adjusting his stride to her clumsy crawl he brought her home to the pack, perhaps against Jello's will—she would never know.

At the den site he promptly ignored her and went to his bed, a dish-like scoop in the soil on the highest point. Circling three or four times, scratching the earth to prepare it for sleep, he lay down.

Miyax glanced out of the corner of her eyes to see Nails preparing his bed also with scratches and turns. Silver was already in her scoop, snapping at the nursing Zing. Jello was off by himself.

Now it was Miyax's turn to say she was home. Patting the ground, circling first to the left and then to the right, she lay down and pulled her knees up to her chin. She closed her eyes, but not completely.

Through her lashes she peeked at Amaroq for reassurance, just as she had seen the other wolves do. The wind played across his black ruff and his ears twitched from time to time as he listened to the birds and winds in his sleep. All was well with the world, and apparently with her, for Amaroq rested in peace.

But Miyax could not sleep. The sun reached its apogee and started down the blue sky of early afternoon. The elegant Arctic terns cut swirls in the sky, a spider crept under a stone, and the snow buntings flitted and called. From some distant spot a loon cried. Then the pale green of evening was upon the land and Miyax closed her eyes.

She awoke with a start a short time later and looked about in puzzlement. The sky vaulted above her. A grass blade tickled her face, and she remembered where she was—up on the frost heave with the wolf pack! Breathing deeply to quell a sense of uneasiness, she finally relaxed, unrolled, and sat up. Kapu was curled against her leg. His feet were flipping and he yipped as if challenging some wolf badman in his dreams. Softly she stroked his fur.

"All's well," she whispered and his paws stopped moving. He sighed and dreamed on peacefully.

She glanced around. All of the wolves were asleep, although they usually went hunting when the sky was lime-green. Perhaps they knew something she didn't know. Sniffing and turning her head, she saw nothing different from any other evening. Then in the distance a thick wall of fog arose. It blotted out the horizon, the far dips and heaves, the grasses, the pond, and finally her own frost heave. The fog streamed up the wolf slope and enveloped the members of the pack one by one until only Kapu was visible. Fogs were part of the Arctic summer, rolling in from the sea for only an hour or for many days, but Miyax had never given them much thought. Now she remembered that when the fog rolled over Barrow, airplanes were grounded, ships and boats had to be anchored, and even the two jeeps in town sat where they had stopped in the fog. She also remembered that people were prisoners of the fog, too. They could not see to hunt.

Now, if the wolves did not bring her some meat, she might not eat for days. She could resort to the belly-basket again, but Jello was jumpy and she doubted if she had enough courage to put her hands in the mouths of the others. Perhaps Kapu would share his meals with her.

"Kapu?" He sighed and pushed tighter against her. The whiskers that protected his sensitive nose and warned him of objects nearby, twitched as her breath touched them. His lips curled up. Whatever he was dreaming about now must be funny, she thought.

She hoped so, for her wide-awake dream was hardly amusing—it was desperate.

She was looking at Silver stretched not far away in a thin spot of fog. Zing, the incorrigible Zing, was nursing again. Silver growled. The pup rolled to his back, paws outstretched like an upside-down chair. Then Sister moved out of the fog. She snuggled up to her mother, suckled two or three times, more for comfort than food, and fell back to sleep.

This brief sucking of the pups had started Silver's milk flowing. Miyax stared at this unexpected source of food.

She inched forward on her stomach and elbows until she was close to the mother. Miyax had drunk the milk of other wild mammals on Nunivak and each time had found it sweet and good. True, the walrus and musk oxen had been milked by her father, but if he had done it, why couldn't she? Slipping her hand beneath a nipple she caught several drops, keeping her eyes on Silver to discern her mood. Slowly Miyax brought the milk to her mouth, lapped, and found it as rich as butter. She reached out again, but as she did so, Silver closed her jaws on Miyax's shoulder and held her immobile. She stifled a scream.

Suddenly Amaroq appeared and lifted his head. Silver let go. Miyax rubbed her shoulder and crept back to Kapu. He was awake, peering up at her, his head on his paws. When their eyes met, he flipped one ear humorously and Miyax sensed he had been through this, too.

"Guess I'm weaned," she said. He wagged his tail.

The fog thickened and, like an eraser on a blackboard, wiped out Amaroq and Silver and the tip of Kapu's tail. She cuddled closer to Kapu, wondering if Amaroq would hunt tonight. After a long time she decided he would not—his family was content and well fed. Not she, however; two drops of milk were scarcely life-sustaining. She patted Kapu, crawled off in the fog, and stood up when she thought she was safely out of sight. Amaroq snarled. She dropped to her knees. His tail beat the ground and she gasped.

"I know you can't see me," she called, "so how do you know what I'm doing? Can you hear me stand up?" His tail beat again and she scrambled to her house, awed by the sensitivity of Amaroq. He knew about fogs and the sneaky ways of human beings.

The sedges around her pond were visible if she crawled, and so on hands and knees she rounded the bank, picking seeds, digging up the nutlike roots of the sedges, and snatching crane fly larvae from the water. As she crept she ate. After what seemed like hours of constant foraging she was still hungry—but not starving.

She came back to her house in a fog so thick she could almost hold it in her hands. For long hours she was suspended between sleep and wakefulness. She listened to the birds call to keep in touch with each other in the fog. Like herself they could not smell their food; they needed to see. As time dragged on, she sang to pass the hours. At first she invented rhymes about the tundra and sang them to tunes she had learned at school. When she tired of these melodies she improvised on the songs of her childhood. They were better suited to improvisation, for they had been invented for just this purpose—to pass the hours in creative fun when the weather closed in.

She sang about the wolves, her house, and the little feather flower on her table; and when she had no more to say, she crawled to her door and looked out. The fog was somewhat lighter. She could see the empty pot by her fireplace and, low overhead, a few birds in the sky.

Then an airplane droned in the distance, grew louder, then fainter, then louder again. The pilot was circling, waiting to see if the weather might suddenly clear so he could land. The same thing had happened to her when she was flown from Nunivak to Barrow. As their plane came over the town, a dense fog rolled in and the pilot had circled for almost an hour.

"If we cannot land on this turn," he had finally announced over the intercom, "we will head straight back to Fairbanks." But suddenly the fog had cleared, and they had landed in Barrow.

The sound of the plane grew louder. Through the thinning fog, she saw the commercial plane that flew from Fairbanks to Barrow and back. Her heart pounded. If the pilot could see her he might send help. She ran out to wave, but the fog had swirled in again and she could barely see her hand. The engines accelerated, and the plane sped off in what must be the direction of Fairbanks. She listened to its sound and, bending down, drew a line in the soil in the direction it had gone.

"That way should be Fairbanks," she said. "At least I know that much."

Picking up pebbles, she pounded them into the line to make it more permanent, and stood up. "That way," she said, pointing in the opposite direction, "is the coast and Point Hope."

Amaroq howled. Nails barked. Then Amaroq slid into a musical crescendo that Silver joined in. Their voices undulated as each harmonized with the other. Jello's windy voice barked out and, like the beat of drums, the five pups whooped and yipped. Miyax rubbed her chin; something was different about this hunt song. It was eerie and restless. It spoke of things she did not understand and she was frightened.

The fog cleared again and she saw Amaroq, his hunters, and the pups running across the tundra. Even Jello was with them. Were they leaving her? Was this their day to take up the wandering life of the wolves? Was she now on her own? Picking up her red markers, she crawled around her frost heave and frantically gathered the leafy plants that the caribou eat. She stuffed mushroom-like fungi in her pockets, and bits of reindeer moss. She could no longer afford to pass up anything that might be edible.

As she worked on her hands and knees, she felt a rhythmical beat, like the rumble of Eskimo drums. Pressing her ear to the ground she heard the vibration of many feet—a herd of caribou was not far away.

The fog thinned more and Kapu came into view. As alert as an eagle, he was sniffing the wind and wagging his tail as if reading some amusing wolf story. She sniffed too, but for her the pages were blank.

The vibrations in the earth grew stronger; Miyax drew back, as out of the fog came a huge caribou, running her way. His head was out straight and his eyes rolled wildly. At his neck, leaping with the power of an ocean wave, was Amaroq. Nails was diving in and out under his legs, and at his flank dashed Silver. Miyax held her breath, wondering whether to run or dodge.

Then Amaroq jumped, floated in the air for an instant, and sank his teeth into the shoulder of the beast. He hung on while Silver attacked from the side. Then he dropped to the ground as the bull bellowed. The fog closed in briefly, and when it thinned the caribou was poised above Amaroq, his cleaver-like hoofs aimed at his head. There was a low grunt, a flash of hoofs, and the huge feet cut uselessly into the sod; for Amaroq had vaulted into the air again and had sunk his teeth in the animal's back. Snarling, using the weight of his body as a tool, he rode the circling and stumbling beast. Silver leaped in front of the bull trying to trip him or slow him down. Nails had a grip on one hind leg. The caribou

bucked, writhed, then dropped to his knees. His antlers pierced the ground; he bellowed and fell.

He was dying, his eyes glazed with the pain-killing

drug of shock; yet his muscles still flexed. His hoofs flailed at the three who were ending the hunt with slashes and blood-letting bites.

After what seemed to Miyax an eternity, the bull lay still. Amaroq tore open his side as if it were a loaf of bread and, without ceremony, fell to the feast.

Kapu and the little wolves came cautiously up to the huge animal and sniffed. They did not know what to do with this beast. It was the first one they had seen and so they wandered curiously around the kill, watching their elders. Amaroq snarled with pleasure as he ate, then licked his lips and looked at Kapu. Kapu pounced on a piece of meat and snarled, too; then he looked at Amaroq again. The leader growled and ate. Kapu growled and ate.

Miyax could not believe her good fortune—an entire caribou felled practically at her door. This was enough food to last her for months, perhaps a year. She would smoke it to make it lighter to carry, pack it, and walk on to the coast. She would make it to Point Hope.

Plans racing in her head, she squatted to watch the wolves eat, measuring, as time passed, the enormous amounts they were consuming—pounds at each bite. As she saw her life-food vanishing, she decided she had better get her share while she could, and went into her house for her knife.

As she crept up toward the bull she wondered if she should come so close to wolves that were eating.

Dogs would bite people under similar conditions. But dogs would refuse to share their food with others of their kind, as the wolves were doing now, growling pleasantly and feasting in friendship.

She was inching forward, when Kapu splintered a bone with his mere baby teeth. She thought better of taking her share; instead she waited patiently for the wolves to finish.

Amaroq left the kill first, glanced her way, and disappeared in the fog. Silver and Nails departed soon after and the pups followed at their mother's heels.

"Ee-lie!" Miyax shouted and ran to the food. Suddenly Jello came out of the fog and leaped upon a leg of the kill. She drew back. Why had he not eaten with the others? she asked herself. He had not been baby-sitting. He must be in some kind of wolf disgrace, for he walked with his tail between his legs and he was not allowed to eat with the pack.

When he too had feasted and left, she walked over to the caribou and admired the mountain of food. Impulsively, she paid tribute to the spirit of the caribou by lifting her arms to the sun. Then, scoffing at herself for being such an old-fashioned Eskimo, she sharpened her man's knife on a stone and set to work.

The skin was tough and she marveled that the wolves tore it so easily. Even as she peeled it away from the flesh with her knife, she was surprised how difficult it was to cut and handle, but she worked diligently, for the pelt was almost as valuable as the meat. Hours and hours later, the last bit of hide came free and she flopped on her back to rest.

"Such hard work!" she gasped aloud. "No wonder this job is given to Eskimo men and boys." With a sigh she got to her feet, dragged the skin to her house, and laid it out to dry. Scraping and cleaning the skin was something she knew more about, for that was a woman's job, but she was too busy to do that now. It was time to carve and eat! She cut open the belly and lifted out the warm liver, the "candy" of her people. With a deft twist of the ulo, she cut off a slice and savored each bite of this, the most nourishing part of the animal. So rich is the liver that most of it is presented to the women and girls, an ancient custom with wisdom at its core—since women give birth to babies, they need the iron and blood of the liver.

All during the wolf sleep Miyax stayed up, cutting off strips of caribou and hanging them over the fire. As she worked, a song came to mind.

Amaroq, wolf, my friend,
You are my adopted father.
My feet shall run because of you.
My heart shall beat because of you.
And I shall love because of you.

She stood up, peeked around the heave, and added,

"But not Daniel. I'm a wolf now, and wolves love leaders."

The umbrella of fog had lifted and Miyax ran up the side of her frost heave to see how her family was. They were sleeping peacefully—all but Amaroq. He shot her a glance, lifted his lips, and spoke with his teeth.

"Oh, all right. Ee-lie, Ee-lie." Miyax got down on all fours. "But how am I going to follow you if you won't let me walk? I am me, your two-legged pup." She stood up. Amaroq lifted his eyebrows, but did not reprimand her. He seemed to understand she could not change. His tail banged once and he went back to sleep.

HUNTS CAME AND WENT. THE SMOKE CURLED UP from Miyax's fire, and caribou strips shrank and dried. One night she watched the dipping sun, trying to guess the date. It must be the second week of August, for the sun sat almost on the rim of the earth.

The wolves had no doubt about the date; they were using a calendar set by the pups, and today was the second day of exploration. Yesterday, Silver had taken them out on the tundra to chase caribou and now they were bouncing around her, ready to go again. Kapu dashed off a few steps, came back, and spun in a circle. Silver finally gave the signal to go, and led him and the others down the hill and out behind the pond.

Miyax watched them trot off to learn about the scent of caribou and the joy of chasing foxes. She wished she could learn such things, too. Shouldering her pack, she wandered through the grasses in search of fuel, a much less exciting assignment. About an hour later she saw Silver and the pups and paused to watch them chase a lively young buck. Kapu ran with a skill that almost matched his mother's. Miyax waved to them and started home.

As she rounded the pond she squinted at the sun again, for it had not climbed up the sky but was still sitting on the horizon. This worried her; it was later than she thought. Autumn was almost here. A glance across the barrens reaffirmed this. The flowers were gone; the birds flocked in great clouds, and among them were eider and old squaw ducks that kept to the rivers and beaches except when they migrated south. Finally, she saw, like hundreds of huge black fingers, the antlers of the caribou beyond the turn of the horizon. They were moving to their wintering ground ahead of the deep freeze and the snow.

She wondered why they passed so close to their enemies the wolves, then recalled how swiftly they could run. The young and the healthy ones did not fear the wolves, and the sick and the old were doomed in winter. Her caribou had been so infested with the larvae of nose flies it had not been able to eat. A weakling, it had become food to give strength both to her and to the wolves.

After storing her fuel she returned to the kill to cut off more strips to smoke. As she approached she saw Jello there and she felt uneasy, for the wolves had not touched the caribou since the night they had felled it. She liked to think they had given it to her.

Jello snarled. "That's not nice," she said. "Go away!" He growled fiercely and she realized she had not seen him with the rest of the pack for several sleeps. He was not even baby-sitting now, for the pups went out with their mother at night. She shouted again, for she needed every bite of that meat. Hearing anger in her voice he stood up, the hairs on his back rising menacingly. She backed away.

Hurrying to camp, she got out her man's knife and began to dig. Every Eskimo family had a deep cellar in the permafrost into which they put game. So cold is the ground that huge whales and caribou freeze overnight, preserved for the months to come. Miyax dug to the frost line, then whacked at the ice until, many hours later, she had chopped three feet into it. This was not the eighteen-foot-deep cellar of her mother-in-law, but perhaps it would keep the rest of her food from Jello. Cautiously she went back to the kill. Jello was gone. Working swiftly, she chopped off the best pieces and dragged them to her refrigerator.

Then she covered the hole with a large slab of sod.

She was heating a pot of stew when Kapu came around the hill with a bone in his mouth. Miyax laughed at the sight, for although he ran like an adult on the tundra, he was still a puppy with games on his mind. She lifted a chunk of cooked meat from the pot and held it out to her brother.

"It's good," she said. "Try some Eskimo food." Kapu sniffed the meat, gulped, licked his jaws, and whined for more. She gave him a second bite; then Silver called and he trotted obediently home. A few minutes later he was back for another bite.

"Maybe you'll learn to like it so much, you'll travel with me," she said, and threw him another chunk of meat. "That would be nice, for I will be lonely without you." Kapu suddenly looked at her and pressed back his ears. She understood his problem instantly and danced lightly from one foot to the other.

"It's all right, Kapu," she said. "Amaroq has agreed that I can go on two feet. I am, after all, a person."

Unnumbered evenings later, when most of the meat was smoked, Miyax decided she had time to make herself a new mitten. She cut off a piece of the new caribou hide and was scraping it clean of fur when a snowstorm of cotton-grass seeds blew past her face. "Autumn," she whispered and scraped faster. She saw several birds on the sedges. They were twisting and turning and pointing their beaks toward the sun as they took their readings and plotted their courses south.

With a start, Miyax noticed the sun. It was half-way below the horizon. Shading her eyes, she watched it disappear completely. The sky turned navy blue, the clouds turned bright yellow, and twilight was upon the land. The sun had set. In a few weeks the land would be white with snow and in three months the long Arctic night that lasted for sixty-six days would darken the top of the world. She tore a fiber from the skin, threaded her needle, and began to stitch the mitten.

About an hour later, the sun arose and marked the date for Miyax. It was August twenty-fourth, the day the *North Star* reached Barrow. Of this she was sure, for on that day the sun lingered below the horizon for about one hour. After that, the nights lengthened rapidly until November twenty-first, when the sun disappeared for the winter.

In bed that evening, Miyax's spirit was stirred by the seeding grass and the restless birds and she could not sleep. She got up, stored some of the smoked meat in her pack, spread the rest in the sun to pack later, and hurried out to the caribou hide. She scraped all the fat from it and stuffed it in the bladder she had saved. The fat was excellent fuel, and gave light when burned. Finally she crept to her cellar for the rest of the meat and found Jello digging through the lid of sod.

"No!" she screamed. He snarled and came toward her. There was nothing to do but assert her authority. She rose to her feet and tapped the top of his nose with her man's knife. With that, he stuck his tail between his legs and slunk swiftly away, while Miyax stood still, surprised by the power she felt. The knife made her a predator, and a dangerous one.

Clutching her food, she ran home, banked the fire, and put the last of the meat on the coals. She was about to go to bed when Kapu bounced down her heave, leaped over her house, and landed silently by her side.

"Oh, wow!" she said. "I'm so glad to see you. Jello scares me to death these days." She reached into her pot for a piece of cooked meat for him and this time he ate from her fingers. Then he spanked the ground to play. Picking up a scrap from the mitten, she swung it around her head. Kapu leaped and snatched it so easily that she was startled. He was quick and powerful, an adult not a pup. She hesitated to chase him, and he bounded up the heave and dashed away.

The next morning when she went out to soften the hide by pounding and chewing it, she saw two bright eyes peering at her from behind the antlers, about all that was left of her caribou. The eyes belonged to an Arctic fox and she walked toward him upright to scare him away. He continued to gnaw the bones.

"Things are tough, eh, little fox?" she whispered. "I cannot drive you away from the food." At the sound of her voice, however, his ears twisted, his tail drooped, and he departed like a leaf on the wind. The fox's brown fur of summer was splotched with white patches, reminding Miyax again that winter was coming, for the fur of the fox changes each season to match the color of the land. He would soon be white, like the snow.

Before sundown the temperature dropped and Miyax crawled into her sleeping skin early. Hardly had she snuggled down in her furs than a wolf howled to the south.

"I am here!" Amaroq answered with a bark, and the distant wolf said something else–she did not know what. Then each pack counted off and when the totals were in, Miyax's wolves yipped among themselves as if discussing the tundra news–a pack of twelve wolves to the north. So wild had their voices been that Miyax crept to her door to call Kapu to come and ease her fears. She started with surprise. There by her pond was Amaroq. The wind was blowing his fur and his tribe was gathered around him, biting his chin, kissing his cheeks. With a sudden sprint he sped into the green shadows of sunrise and one by one his family fell in behind, according to their status in the pack. Nails ran second, then Silver, Kapu, Sister, Zit, Zat, Zing, and finally, far behind came Jello.

Miyax at last was sure of what had happened to Jello. He was low man on the totem pole, the bottom of the ladder. She recalled the day Amaroq had put him down and forced him to surrender, the many times Silver had made him go back and sit with the pups, and the times that Kapu had ignored his calls to come home to the den. He was indeed a lowly wolf—a poor spirit, with fears and without friends.

Scrambling to her feet she watched the pack run along the horizon, a flowing line of magnificent beasts, all cooperating for the sake of each other, all wholly content—except Jello. He ran head down, low to the ground—in the manner of the lone wolf.

"That is not good," she said aloud.

An Arctic tern skimmed low and she jumped to her feet, for it was flying with a determination that she had not seen in the birds all summer. Its white wings cut a flashing V against the indigo sky as it moved due south across the tundra. There was no doubt in her mind what that steady flight meant—the migration was on.

"Good-bye!" she called sadly. "Good-bye."

Another tern passed overhead, then another, and another. Miyax walked to the fireplace and threw on more fuel.

Amaroq howled in the distance, his royal voice ringing out in a firm command. Somehow, she felt, he was calling her. But she could not go on this hunt. She must finish smoking every morsel of meat. Hurriedly she picked up her markers and started off for more fuel.

Several hours later, her tights bulging with caribou chips, she saw the wolves again. Amaroq, Nails, and Silver were testing the herd and Kapu was pouncing and bouncing. She knew what that meant; the hour of the lemmings was returning. Of this she was sure; she had often seen the dogs, foxes, and children hop and jump after lemmings in this same laughable way.

"I'm glad to know that," she called to her friend, and hurried back to the fire.

As the chips glowed red, Miyax saw another Arctic tern flying the same route as the others. Quickly she drew its course across the mark on the ground to Fairbanks; then, peeling off a strip of sinew, she stood in the center of the X and held the ends of the thread in both hands. When one arm was pointing to the coast and the other was pointing in the direction the bird was taking, she cut off the remainder of the strip.

"There," she said, "I have a compass. I can't take the stones with me, but every time a tern flies over, I can line up one arm with him, stretch the sinew out, and my other hand will point to the coast and Point Barrow."

That night she unzipped a small pocket in her

pack and took out a battered letter from Amy.

. . . And when you get to San Francisco, we will buy you summer dresses, and because you like curls, we'll curl your hair. Then we'll ride the trolley to the theater and sit on velvet seats.

Mom says you can have the pink bedroom that looks over the garden and down on the bay and the Golden Gate Bridge.

When are you coming to San Francisco?

Your pen pal,
Amy

"The theater," she whispered, "and the Golden Gate Bridge." That night she slept with the letter under her cheek.

In the evening of the following day Miyax hastily put on her clothes and crawled up the frost heave. Like a good puppy she got down on her stomach.

"Amaroq," she called. "I'm ready to go when you are!"

The wind blew across the wolf den, shattering the heads of the cotton grass and shooting their seedlets south with the birds. No one answered. The wolves were gone.

PART II

Miyax, the girl

THE WIND, THE EMPTY SKY, THE DESERTED EARTH— Miyax had felt the bleakness of being left behind once before.

She could not remember her mother very well, for Miyax was scarcely four when she died, but she did remember the day of her death. The wind was screaming wild high notes and hurling ice-filled waves against the beach. Kapugen was holding her hand and they were walking. When she stumbled he put her on his shoulders, and high above the beach she saw thousands of birds diving toward the sea. The jaegers screamed and the sandpipers cried. The feathered horns of the comical puffins drooped low, and Kapugen told her they seemed to be grieving with him.

She saw this, but she was not sad. She was divinely happy going somewhere alone with Kapugen. Occasionally he climbed the cliffs and brought her eggs to eat; occasionally he took her in his arms and leaned against a rock. She slept at times in the warmth of his big sealskin parka. Then they walked on. She did not know how far.

Later, Kapugen's Aunt Martha told her that he had lost his mind the day her mother died. He had grabbed Miyax up and walked out of his fine house in Mekoryuk. He had left his important job as manager of the reindeer herd, and he had left all his possessions.

"He walked you all the way to seal camp," Martha told her. "And he never did anything good after that."

To Miyax the years at seal camp were infinitely good. The scenes and events were beautiful color spots in her memory. There was Kapugen's little house of driftwood, not far from the beach. It was rosy-gray on the outside. Inside, it was gold-brown. Walrus tusks gleamed and drums, harpoons, and man's knives decorated the walls. The sealskin kayak beside the door glowed as if the moon had been stretched across it and its graceful ribs shone black. Dark gold and soft brown were the old men who sat around Kapugen's camp stove and talked to him by day and night.

The ocean was green and white, and was rimmed

by fur, for she saw it through Kapugen's hood as she rode to sea with him on his back inside the parka. Through this frame she saw the soft eyes of the seals on the ice. Kapugen's back would grow taut as he lifted his arms and fired his gun. Then the ice would turn red.

The celebration of the Bladder Feast was many colors—black, blue, purple, fire-red; but Kapugen's hand around hers was rose-colored and that was the color of her memory of the Feast. A shaman, an old priestess whom everyone called "the bent woman," danced. Her face was streaked with black soot. When she finally bowed, a fiery spirit came out of the dark wearing a huge mask that jingled and terrified Miyax. Once, in sheer bravery, she peeked up under a mask and saw that the dancer was not a spirit at all but Naka, Kapugen's serious partner. She whispered his name and he laughed, took off his mask, and sat down beside Kapugen. They talked and the old men joined them. Later that day Kapugen blew up seal bladders and he and the old men carried them out on the ice. There they dropped them into the sea, while Miyax watched and listened to their songs. When she came back to camp the bent woman told her that the men had returned the bladders to the seals.

"Bladders hold the spirits of the animals," she said. "Now the spirits can enter the bodies of the newborn seals and keep them safe until we harvest them again." That night the bent woman seemed all violet-colored as she tied a piece of seal fur and blubber to Miyax's belt. "It's an *i'noGo tied*," she said. "It's a nice little spirit for you."

Another memory was flickering-yellow—it was of the old men beating their drums around Kapugen's stove. She saw them through a scarf of tiny crystals that was her breath on the cold night air inside the house.

Naka and Kapugen were on their hands and knees, prancing lightly, moving swiftly. When Naka tapped Kapugen's chin with his head, Kapugen rose to his knees. He threw back his head, then rocked back on his heels. Naka sat up and together they sang the song of the wolves. When the dance was over the old men cheered and beat their paddle-like drums.

"You are wolves, you are real wolves," they had cried.

After that Kapugen told her about the wolves he had known on the mainland when he went to high school in Nome. He and his joking partner would hunt the wilderness for months, calling to the wolves, speaking their language to ask where the game was. When they were successful, they returned to Nome with sled-loads of caribou.

"Wolves are brotherly," he said. "They love each other, and if you learn to speak to them, they will love you too."

He told her that the birds and animals all had languages and if you listened and watched them you could learn about their enemies, where their food lay and when big storms were coming.

A silver memory was the day when the sun came over the horizon for the first time in winter. She was at the beach, close to Kapugen, helping him haul in a huge gleaming net. In it was a beautiful white whale. Out of sight on the other side of the whale, she could hear the old men as they cheered this gift from the sea.

The whale was a mountain so high she could not see the cliffs beyond, only the sunlit clouds. Kapugen's huge, black, frostbitten hand seemed small as it touched the great body of the whale.

Not far away the bent woman was dancing and gathering invisible things from the air. Miyax was frightened but Kapugen explained that she was putting the spirit of the whale in her i'noGo tied.

"She will return it to the sea and the whales," he said.

Walking the tundra with Kapugen was all laughter and fun. He would hail the blue sky and shout out his praise for the grasses and bushes. On these trips they ate salmon berries, then lay in the sun watching the birds. Sometimes Kapugen would whistle sandpiper songs and the birds would dip down to see which of their members had gotten lost in the grass. When they saw him and darted away, Kapugen would laugh.

Fishing with Kapugen was murky-tan in her memory, for they would wade out into the river mouth where the stone weirs were built and drive the fish into nets between the walls. Kapugen would spear them or grab them in his hand and throw them to the men in the wooden boats. Occasionally he skimmed after the biggest cod and halibut in his kayak and he would whoop with joy when he caught one and would hold it above his head. It gleamed as it twisted in the sun.

Summers at seal camp were not as beautiful to Miyax as the autumns and winters, for during this season many families from Mekoryuk came to Nash Harbor to hunt and fish and Kapugen was busy. Sometimes he helped people set nets; sometimes he scouted the ocean in his kayak as he searched for seal colonies.

During these hours Miyax was left with the other children on the beach. She played tag and grass ball with them and she pried prickly sea urchins off the rocks, to eat the sweet meat inside. Often she dug for clams and when Kapugen returned he would crack them open and smack his lips as he swallowed them whole.

The Eskimos from Mekoryuk spoke English almost all the time. They called her father Charlie Edwards and Miyax was Julie, for they all had two names, Eskimo and English. Her mother had also called her Julie, so she did not mind her summer name until one day when Kapugen called her that. She stomped her foot and told him her name was Miyax. "I am Eskimo, not a gussak!" she had said, and he had tossed her into the air and hugged her to him.

"Yes, you are Eskimo," he had said. "And never forget it. We live as no other people can, for we truly understand the earth."

But winters always returned. Blizzards came and the temperatures dropped to thirty and forty below zero, and those who stayed at hunting camp spoke only in Eskimo and did only Eskimo things. They scraped hides, mended boots, made boats, and carved walrus tusks. In the evenings Kapugen sang and danced with the old men, and all of their songs and dances were about the sea and the land and the creatures that dwelled there.

One year, probably in September, for the canvas tents were down and the campground almost empty, Kapugen came into the house with a sealskin. It was a harbor seal, but had so few spots that it was a rare prize.

"We must make you a new coat," he had said. "You are getting big. Since your mother is not here to help us, I will do her work. Now watch and learn."

The skin was metallic silver-gold and so beautiful that even the velveteen parkas of the children from Mekoryuk paled by comparison. Miyax stroked it lovingly as Kapugen lay her old coat upon it and began to cut a larger one. As he worked he hummed, and she made up words about the seal who wanted to be a coat. Presently they became aware of the distant throb of a motorboat. The sound grew louder, then shut off at the beach. Footsteps crunched, the cold air rushed in the door, and there was Martha, Kapugen's aunt. She was thin and her face was pinched. Miyax disliked her immediately, but was spared the necessity of speaking nicely to her, for Martha had words only for Kapugen.

She talked swiftly in English, which Miyax barely understood, and she was angry and upset. Martha shook her finger at Kapugen and glanced at Miyax from time to time. The two were arguing very loudly when Martha pulled a sheet of paper from her pocket and showed it to Kapugen.

"No!" he shouted.

"We'll see!" Martha screamed, turned around, and went toward the boat where a white man waited. Kapugen followed her and stood by the boat, talking to the man for a long time.

The next morning Miyax was awakened as Kapugen lifted her up in his arms and held her close. Gently he pushed the hair out of her eyes and, speaking softly in Eskimo, told her she was going to live with Aunt Martha.

"There's a law that says you must go to school

. . . and I guess you should. You are nine years old. And I must go to war. The government is fighting somewhere."

Miyax grabbed him around the neck, but did not protest. It never occurred to her that anything that Kapugen decided was not absolutely perfect. She whimpered however.

"Listen closely," he said. "If anything happens to me, and if you are unhappy, when you are thirteen you can leave Aunt Martha by marrying Daniel, Naka's son. Naka is going to Barrow on the Arctic Ocean. I shall make arrangements with him. He is like me, an old-time Eskimo who likes our traditions. He will agree."

Miyax listened carefully, then he put her down and hastily packed her bladder-bag, wrapped her in an oilskin against the wild spray of the sea, and carried her to the boat. She sat down beside Martha and stared bravely at Kapugen. The motor started and Kapugen looked at her until the boat moved, then he turned his back and walked quickly away. The launch sped up a huge wave, slammed down into a foaming trough, and Kapugen was no longer visible.

With that Miyax became Julie. She was given a cot near the door in Martha's little house and was soon walking to school in the darkness. She liked to learn the printed English words in books, and so a month passed rather happily.

One morning when the air was cold and the puddles around the house were solid ice, an old man from seal camp arrived at the door. He spoke softly to Martha, then pulled his hood tightly around his face and went away. Martha came to Miyax's bed.

"Your father," she said, "went seal hunting in that ridiculous kayak. He has been gone a month this day. He will not be back. Bits of his kayak washed up on the shore." Martha stumped to the fire and turned her back.

Julie ran out of the house into the dark morning. She darted past the store, the reindeer-packing house, the church. She did not stop until she came to the beach. There she crouched among the oil drums and looked out on the sea.

The wind blew across the water, shattering the tips of the waves and shooting ice-sparklets north with the storm. "Kapugen!" she called. No one answered. Kapugen was gone. The earth was empty and bleak.

GRADUALLY JULIE PUSHED KAPUGEN OUT OF HER heart and accepted the people of Mekoryuk. The many years in seal camp alone with Kapugen had been dear and wonderful, but she realized now that she had lived a strange life. The girls her age could speak and write English and they knew the names of presidents, astronauts, and radio and movie personalities, who lived below the top of the world. Maybe the Europeans once thought the earth was flat, but the Eskimos always knew it was round. One only needed to look at the earth's relatives, the sun and the moon, to know that.

One day as she walked home across the snowy town she caught up with her schoolmates, Judith and Rose. Their boots squeaked in the cold and their voices sounded far away, for the temperature was far below zero. Judith invited her into her house and the three of them huddled close to the oil stove. Judith and Rose chatted, but Julie's eyes wandered around the room and she saw for the first time a gas cooking stove, a couch, framed pictures on the wall, and curtains of cotton print. Then Judith took her into her own room and she beheld a bed with a headboard, a table, and a reading lamp. On the table lay a little chain on which hung a dog, a hat, and a boat. This she was glad to see—something familiar.

"What a lovely i'noGo tied!" Julie said politely.

"A what?" asked Judith. Julie repeated the Eskimo word for the house of the spirits.

Judith snickered. "That's a charm bracelet," she said. Rose giggled and both laughed derisively. Julie felt the blood rush to her face as she met, for the first but not the last time, the new attitudes of the Americanized Eskimos. She had much to learn besides reading. That night she threw her i'noGo tied away.

English and math came easily to her, and by the end of the year Julie was reading and writing. That summer she worked at the mission beside the church sweeping the floor and greeting the visitors from the lower states who came to see real Eskimos. She read the encyclopedia when there was nothing else to do.

The next year Julie worked at the hospital on weekends. After school she cut out dresses in the domestic science room and sewed them on the electric machines. She bobbed her hair and put it in rollers to make the ends curl.

One Sunday, as she was coming home from the hospital, a jeep pulled up beside her and a gussak hailed her. He leaned on the steering wheel, a warm smile on his face.

"I'm Mr. Pollock. I own stock in the Reindeer Corporation here on the island," he said. "And I have a daughter your age. The last thing she asked me before I left San Francisco was to find a girl in the town of Mekoryuk on Nunivak Island and ask if she would like to exchange letters. How about being her pen pal?"

Julie needed no explanation for that term. Many letters came into the mission from children in the States who wanted to write letters. She had never done so before, but now she was ready.

"I would like that," she answered.

"My daughter's name is Amy," he said, taking a

letter from his inside pocket. "She told me to give this to the nicest girl I could find—and that's you, with your twinkling eyes and rosy cheeks."

Julie smiled and slowly took the extended letter, then skipped off to open it in the privacy of the mission library. She was enchanted by what she read:

Hello, my new friend,

I am Amy Pollock and I have blue eyes and brown hair. Next month I will be twelve years old, and I hope I'll be five feet tall by then. I have a quarter of an inch to go. I wear a size nine dress and a size six shoe, which my mother finds embarrassingly big. Frankly, I like my big feet. They get me up and down the steep hills of San Francisco and shoot me through the water like a frog when I swim. I am in the eighth grade and am studying French. I hate it, but would like to learn Eskimo. My father goes to Alaska often and he has taught me a few words. They are pretty words that sound like bells, but I can't spell them. Can you? How do you spell the word for "daylight"? Quaq?

I take dancing lessons, which I love, and I also like to play baseball with the kids that live on our hill. When I grow up I think I'll be a dancer, but it is an awful lot of work. One of the dancers at the San Francisco Opera House said so, so maybe I'll be a schoolteacher like my aunt and have the whole summer off.

Last month at school we saw your island on a television show. It was so beautiful, with the birds flying over it and the flowers blooming on its hills, that I wanted to write to someone who lives there, a girl like me.

Here is a picture of my house. That is me standing on one foot on the patio wall. Please write soon.

Your new friend,

Amy

P.S. When are you coming to live with us in San Francisco?

Julie folded the letter and whispered to herself: "Daylight is spelled A-M-Y."

The wonders of Mekoryuk dimmed as weekly letters from Amy arrived. Julie learned about television, sports cars, blue jeans, bikinis, hero sandwiches, and wall-to-wall carpeting in the high school Amy would soon be attending. Mekoryuk had no high school. The Eskimo children of the more prosperous families were sent to the mainland for further schooling, something which Aunt Martha could not afford. But, she thought, if she married Daniel, perhaps Naka could send her to school.

As the winter passed, Martha became irritated with her. She nagged Julie for wearing her hair short, and complained about Judith. "She's disrespectful of her parents," she snapped. "And she's bad." That's all she would say except, "The old ways are best."

After that Martha gave her chores to do on weekends and refused to let her attend the movies with her friends. The winter nights in the dark little house became nightmares. Julie waited for letters from Amy and the call from Naka.

The call came suddenly. One morning in June as Julie was dressing to go to the store, the head of the Indian Affairs in Mekoryuk appeared at the door. He explained that Naka had written, requesting Julie to come to Barrow and marry his son.

"You are now thirteen," the man said, "and I have in my files an agreement for this arrangement signed by Kapugen and Naka." Martha sputtered and whispered in her ear that she could say no if she wanted to.

"The old ways are best," Julie said, and Martha could not protest.

The next day transportation was arranged for her by the Bureau of Indian Affairs and Julie packed her few possessions in a moosehide bag and walked to the airport with Martha. The old lady dragged behind, taking slow steps, and by the time they reached the airport she was limping.

"What shall I do when I'm too crippled to get out of bed?" she said angrily. Julie was about to remind her how strong her legs had been a few hours ago, but had time to say no more than good-bye. The pilot himself escorted her up the steps into the gleaming cabin and showed her how to fasten her seat belt.

Cautiously she looked at the upholstery, the overhead lights, the open door to the pilot's cabin—then she closed her eyes. She was afraid the plane could not really fly. The engines roared, the ship moved, and minutes later she opened her eyes to see the houses of Nunivak shrink to specks and the island grow smaller and smaller. When it was but a jewel in the sea, she touched her seat and her armrest and stared down at herself.

"I'm sitting in the sky!" she said to the man beside her. He winked and she pressed her head against the window. She was an eagle seeking out new pinnacles. After a long time she relaxed and her wonder at the miraculous airship changed to curiosity.

"What makes us stay up here?" she asked the man.

"That's not a good question," he said, and she lapsed into silence. The plane landed in Anchorage, then Fairbanks. Here she was put on another plane, a smaller one—the only one that flew to remote Barrow.

Rugged mountain passes and valleys passed below her; the trees became smaller and more scarce, then disappeared entirely as the craft shot out over the North Slope and the pilot announced that they were crossing the Arctic Circle. The gussaks cheered and opened bottles to toast the mythical line, but hardly had they taken sips than the windows became white and the plane was bumping along through a summer fog.

They made wide circles over Barrow for an hour and a half before the pilot announced they would try once more to find an opening in the fog, then head back to Fairbanks. Julie had her nose pressed tightly to the window, for she could see the long threads that spoke of a clearing. Suddenly Barrow appeared below, its houses huddled against the ice-piled shore like a cluster of lonely birds.

As the plane began its descent into Barrow, Julie could see in the distance the towers of the Distant Early Warning System that marked the presence of the military in Barrow, and a narrow road along the coast that led to a group of buildings. The pilot announced that they belonged to the Navy and the University of Alaska. "The Arctic Research Laboratory," he said, "where scientists study the Arctic. People from all over the world come here to investigate the top of the world. We now know a lot about living in the cold."

The wheels struck the runway and the plane pulled up by a small wooden house on the tundra, the terminal building. For a moment Julie had misgivings about her fate; then the stewardess brought her coat and escorted her to the door. She looked down at two people she knew must be Naka and his wife, Nusan. Daniel was hiding behind them. Slowly Julie walked down the steps, crossed the stretch of macadam and took Naka's hand. He was dressed in a Navy Arctic field jacket and his eyes were dark and smiling. She remembered those eyes from her color wheel of memories and she felt better.

Nusan was dressed in a kuspuck trimmed with Japanese lace flowers and she was smiling at Julie. They had not met before. Nusan had never gone to seal camp.

Then Julie saw Daniel. She knew from his grin and dull eyes that something was wrong with him. Nusan must have seen the disappointment that flashed over her face, for she put her arm around Julie.

"Daniel has a few problems," she said quickly. "But he's a very good boy, and he's a good worker. He cleans the animal cages at the research lab. He will be like a brother to you."

With those words Julie relaxed, and pushed him out of her mind. He would just be a brother. That was fine. She looked at the little houses surrounded by boats, oil drums, tires, buckets, broken cars, and rags and bags, and happily followed her new parents home.

The very next day, however, to Julie's surprise, there was a wedding. The minister came to Naka's house with two strangers and Nusan took Julie into the kitchen and gave her a beautiful sealskin suit. She helped her to dress. Daniel put on a dark blue shirt and gussak pants. They were told to stand in the doorway between the living room and kitchen, and the minister began to read. Daniel grasped her hand. His was as clammy with anxiety as hers. She stared at the floor wondering if Kapugen had known that Daniel was dull. She would not believe he did.

When the reading was over Daniel escaped to the kitchen and sat on his bed. He began to tinker with a radio and mumble to himself. Naka walked outside with the minister and the two strangers, and Nusan sat down at her sewing machine.

"I've got to finish these boots for a tourist," she said. "Make yourself at home." The sewing machine hummed and the radio droned on. Julie stepped outside and sat down on an oil drum. The streets were hushed for it was the rest hour. She did not know how long she sat in quiet terror, but it was a long time. Presently a little girl came around a rusted ship's engine, pulling a smaller girl by the hand.

"Come on," she ordered the reluctant child. "It's time for the blanket toss." As they hurried along, other children gathered from all directions and clustered in front of the community house. Several men unfolded a huge skin. Eskimos and tourists took hold of it. A child got in the center, bounced, and then was flipped twenty feet up in the air, like a toy rocket. Giggling, the child kicked her feet as if she were running, and came gracefully down.

Julie looked away. Snow buntings whirled around

the house, an Arctic tern darted over the ocean, and the waves lapped the ice that was piled high on the shore. She was desperately homesick for Mekoryuk. She dropped her head on her knees.

"Julie?" a tall girl tapped her arm. "I'm Pearl Norton, Pani NalaGan." She began speaking in Innuit. Julie shook her head.

"We'd better use English," she said. Pearl nodded and laughed.

"I said, 'Let's go to the quonset.' " Julie jumped to her feet and followed Pearl around a broken box, over a battered auto door, and into an alley. In silence they passed the wooden hotel, where a tourist was huddled on the porch out of the wind; then they stepped onto the main street, where the stores stood. Crossing the street they entered an enormous quonset hut. When Julie's eyes had adjusted to the dim light she could see a dozen or more young men and girls, some in blue jeans and field jackets, some in kuspucks and parkas. They were seated at tables or leaning against pinball machines as they listened to rock and roll music. Pearl bought a Coke, got two straws, and they sat down at a table near the door.

"I know how you feel, Julie. I was married last year," Pearl began. "Don't pay any attention to it. No one does. All you have to do is leave the house or run away and everything's forgotten. Most of these arrangements are for convenience. I'm sure you are here to help Nusan make parkas and mittens for the tourists." Pearl leaned back. "Even in the old days they didn't make kids stick with these marriages if they didn't like each other. They just drifted apart."

Julie listened, her head swimming in confusion . . . Daniel, marriage, parkas, tourists, jukeboxes, pinball machines . . . divorce.

"I must go," Julie said. "Can I talk to you again?"

"I'll meet you here tomorrow. All the kids come here to have fun."

Daniel was gone when Julie stepped into the kitchen and nervously glanced around.

"Do you know how to sew?" Nusan yelled from the floor where she was cutting a short length of rabbit fur.

"A little," Julie answered as she unzipped her coat and folded it carefully.

"You shall know a lot when I'm through with you," Nusan replied and pointed to a large box in the corner. "Yard goods and rickrack. We have to make thirty parkas for the airlines by the end of the month. They lend them to the tourists who come here. None of them know how to dress. They'd freeze without parkas." Nusan threaded a needle and whipped the rabbit fur onto the top of a mukluk. She glanced up at Julie.

"You'll do nicely," she said. "You're smart and you're pretty."

Julie saw little of Daniel that summer and even less of him after school started. And so, by October she was beginning to enjoy her new home. She cooked and sewed for Nusan, studied at night, and had a few

hours in the afternoon when she met Pearl at the quonset.

As the months passed, the letters from Amy became the most important thing in Julie's life and the house in San Francisco grew more real than the house in Barrow. She knew each flower on the hill where Amy's house stood, each brick in the wall

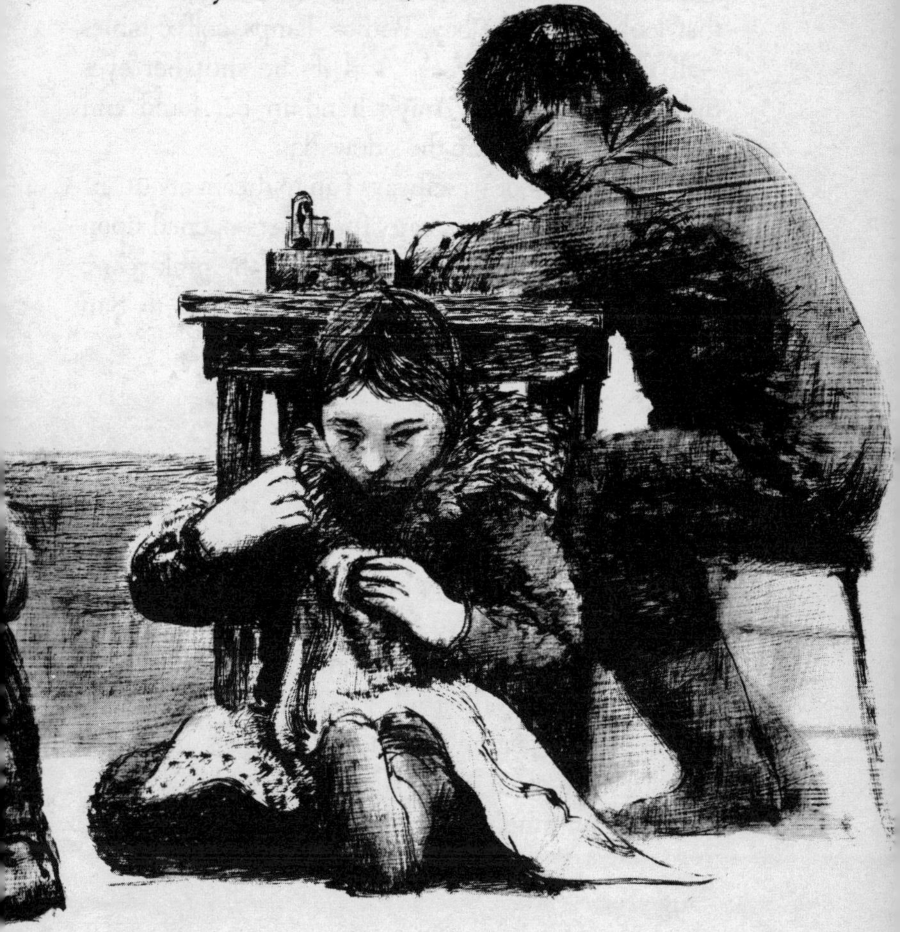

around the garden, and each tall blowing tree. She also knew the curls in the wrought-iron gate, and how many steps led up to the big front door; she could almost see the black-and-white tile on the floor of the foyer. If she closed her eyes she could imagine the arched doorway, the Persian rug on the living-room floor, the yellow chairs and the huge window that looked over the bay. Radios, lamps, coffee tables —all these she could see. And if she shut her eyes tight, she could feel Amy's hand in her hand and hear Amy's big feet tap the sidewalk.

The second floor was always fun to dream about. At the top of the winding stairs four doors opened upon rooms lit with sunshine. And one was the pink room, the one that would be hers when she got to San Francisco.

DURING THE WINTER JULIE CAME TO UNDERSTAND Naka. At first she thought he had a very important job, for he would be gone for days, often weeks, and be very tired and angry when he came home. He slept sometimes for two days. But when the subzero weather set in, Naka stayed home, and Julie realized that he did not work at all. He drank. The more he drank the angrier he became. Sometimes he struck Nusan; more often he picked a fight with his neighbor. Finally, numbness would overcome him and he would drop on the bed like a huge limp seal and sleep for days.

When he awoke he would be pleasant again, sitting in the fur- and scrap-filled room, making moose-hide masks for the summer tourist trade. He would sing the old songs of seal camp, and tell Julie about the animals that he and Kapugen had known. On those occasions, she would understand why Kapugen had loved him.

One night he struck Nusan over and over again. When she screamed and hit back, Julie ran to the quonset to look for Pearl. She was not there, but in a corner sat Russell, the young man who had been campaigning around the village, begging the Eskimos to vote "No" on requests for liquor licenses by the local restaurants.

Julie sat down. "Naka is evil again," she said. "His spirit has fled."

Russell nodded. "He, like many others, cannot tolerate alcohol. There's a man from San Francisco who does lots of business in Alaska. He has been able to help people like Naka. He helped my father. And me," Russell added. "Now we all join together and help each other not to drink. But Naka must agree to see him. If he does I'll try to get in touch with—"

Julie leaned forward, knowing exactly what Russell was going to say. "Mr. Pollock," she whispered.

"Ee-lie. How did you know?"

The pink room in San Francisco had a new dimension.

January twenty-fourth was a day of celebration. Beginning about the twenty-first, the top of the world began to glow like an eclipse as the sun circled just below the horizon. The Americans began to smile and the Eskimos put away their winter games of yo-yo and darts. Excitement mounted higher and higher each day.

The morning of the twenty-fourth Julie and Pearl ran all the way to school, for this was the most beautiful day of the year, the day of the sunrise.

Just before noon Julie and her classmates put on their parkas and mittens and skipped out the school door in awesome silence. The gussak principal was already outside watching the southeastern sky anxiously. His face seemed to say he really did not believe the miracle would happen.

"There it is!" a little boy shouted, as a brilliant light, first green then red, exploded on the horizon. Slowly the life-giving star arose until it was round and burning red in the sky. The Eskimos lifted their arms and turned their palms to the source of all life. Slowly, without any self-consciousness, every gussak raised his arms, too. Not one person snickered at the old Eskimo tradition.

For an hour and a half the sun moved above the

horizon, reminding the Eskimos that the birds and mammals would come back, that the snow would melt, and that the great ice pack that pressed against the shore would begin to retreat and set them free to hunt and fish.

Even on Nunivak there was no such wonderful day, for the sun appeared for a little while every day of the year.

"Bright sun, I missed you so," Julie whispered, and her palms felt vibrant with life.

The little house in Barrow became home as Julie fitted into Nusan's routine, and summer was upon the land before she knew it. Tourists arrived at the hotel every day; the research lab buzzed with activity. Julie stitched, sewed, and occasionally visited Pearl and her family.

Late one evening Nusan came back from the store. "Naka's in jail," she said angrily. "I've got to go get him. Finish these mukluks." She pointed. "A man wants them tomorrow." She hurried out the door and Julie picked up the boots. She was cutting a tiny black square to sew into the intricate band at the top when the door opened and Daniel came in.

She did not look up, for she knew his routine. He would fix himself a TV dinner, open a Coke, and sit on his cot listening to the radio.

"You!" he shouted. She looked up in surprise.

"You. You're my wife."

"Daniel, what's wrong?"

"They're laughing at me. That's what's wrong. They say, 'Ha, ha. Dumb Daniel. He's got a wife and he can't mate her. Ha.' "

He pulled her to her feet and pressed his lips against her mouth. She pulled away.

"We don't have to," she cried.

"They're laughin'," he repeated, and tore her dress from her shoulder. She clutched it and pulled away. Daniel grew angry. He tripped her and followed her to the floor. His lips curled back and his tongue touched her mouth. Crushing her with his body, he twisted her down onto the floor. He was as frightened as she.

The room spun, and grew blurry. Daniel cursed, kicked violently, and lay still. Suddenly he got to his feet and ran out of the house. "Tomorrow, tomorrow I can, I can, can, can, ha ha," he bleated piteously.

Julie rolled to her stomach and vomited. Slowly she got to her feet. "When fear seizes," she whispered, "change what you are doing. You are doing something wrong."

She got her red tights from a box on the shelf, slipped into a warm shirt, and put on her wedding parka and pants. Next she opened a box under the bed and picked out a pair of warm woolen socks. Shoving her feet into her boots she laced and knotted them. Daniel's old pack was under his cot. She got that, then opened a cardboard box by the stove and took out her man's knife and ulo which she had brought from Nunivak. Then she grabbed handfuls of wooden matches and dropped them into a moisture-proof cookie can.

She opened the door and walked calmly through the midnight light to Pearl's house. Stealing quietly past her sleeping brothers and parents, she crept into Pearl's room.

"Pearl, I'm leaving," Julie whispered.

Almost instantly Pearl was awake. "Daniel?"

Julie nodded. "He is dumb. Everyone's teasing him."

Pearl slipped out of bed and together they crept to the kitchen. When the door was closed Pearl sat down.

"Where are you going?"

"I won't tell you. Then they won't bother you. I need food."

Pearl glanced at the shelves above the stove and pushed a box under them; she took down bread, cheeses, dried fruits, meats, and a bag of oats and sugar.

"That's fine," Julie said. "I only need enough for a week or so. But I need to borrow a sleeping skin and ground cloth. I'll mail them back when I get where I'm going."

Pearl slipped out to the shed and came back with the sleeping skin and hide.

"They're a wedding present." She smiled. "You can keep them. No one uses these old-timers."

"Some needles, please," Julie said, "and that'll be all." Stuffing the sleeping skin into her pack, she tied the caribou hide to the bottom and shouldered her load.

"Are you sure you'll be all right?" Pearl asked.

"My father was a great hunter. He taught me much. If Nusan asks where I am, tell her you saw me walking out on the ice. She won't look for me long after that."

With a sob Julie threw her arms around Pearl, then stepped out the door and closed it quietly behind her. She walked to the beach, climbed onto the ice, and looked back. No one was on the street but a single tourist who was photographing the sun in the sky. His back was to her. Julie ducked below the ice rim and made her way along it on hands and feet until she was beyond the village and out of sight of the rooftops of Barrow. Then she stood up and looked at the ocean.

"Julie is gone," she said. "I am Miyax now."

She leaped lightly up the bank and onto the tundra. Her stride opened wider and wider, for she was on her way to San Francisco.

PART III

Kapugen, the hunter

THE MEMORIES VANISHED. THE WIND SCREAMED *oooooooooeeeeeeeeeee*. Miyax touched the lichens on the top of her frost heave.

"Amaroq," she called again, then ran down the slope and climbed to the wolf den. The site was silent and eerie and the puppies' playground was speckled with bleached bones like tombstones in a graveyard.

She picked one up and saw that it was jagged with the marks of little teeth. With some carving, it could be made into the comb she had been wanting. Glancing around, she saw the club-like base of an antler. "A weapon," she said. "I may need it."

A snowy owl floated past, turning his head as he peered down at her curiously.

"I'll see you in San Francisco," she called. He set

his eyes on some distant goal, bowed his wings, and flew southward as silently as the shadow he cast.

The wind twisted a strand of her hair, and as she stood on the wolf hill she felt the presence of the great animals she had lived with: Amaroq, Nails, Silver, Kapu. She wondered if she would ever see them again. The wind gusted; she turned and walked slowly back home, trailing her fingers on the tips of the sedges and thinking about her departure. At the top of her frost heave, she froze in her tracks. Her house was crushed in and her sleeping skins were torn and strewn over the grass. The meat she had laid out on the grass was gone. Her icebox was opened and empty.

"Ayi!" she cried. "My food! My life! I'm dead!"

Running from broken house to dumped cooking pot to icebox, she felt needles of fear move up her spine, spread into her arms, and pierce her whole body. Who had done this? What bestial creature had taken her food? She looked desperately around and saw, crouched in the reeds almost beside her, the angry Jello. His tail was swishing slowly, his ears were forward. She understood his message and stepped back. Then she knew that was wrong; she must not give in. Hand tightening on the antler club, brandishing it, growling, she flung herself upon him and bit the top of his nose. His eyes widened, his ears and body drooped, and his tail went between his legs.

He groveled on his belly and came up to her smiling, head lowered humbly.

Desperate, furious, she lunged at him. Jello rolled to his back and flashed the white hair of surrender. She did not strike; she could not strike a coward.

"Jello!" she cried. "Why? Why did you do it?"

Holding him in abeyance with the antler, she glanced around the ruins of her home and took stock of the damage. All the food in the cellar and on the ground was gone, and her pack was not in sight. Brandishing her weapon, growling at Jello, she backed toward the sod house, kicked back the ruins, and saw the pack under the crushed roof. It was intact. Jello had not found the meat in it. Her mind raced. She had a little food and Kapu had told her that the lemmings were coming back. She could yet make it.

"*Gnarlllllllllll,*" she snapped at Jello and lowered her club. He rolled over, stood up and, tail between his legs, fled into the twilight.

When he was gone she stood for a long time. Finally she picked up her sleeping skin and tore a fiber from the new hide. She got out her needle and, sitting with her legs out straight in the manner of Eskimo women, began to sew.

A lemming ran across a lichen patch. She stopped working and watched the little animal add a mouthful of grass to its round nest. A movement caught her eye and she glanced up to see a least weasel washing his belly on the other side of the knoll. New white fur was splotched across his gold back. He finished his toilet, and when he sat down he disappeared under the reindeer moss. "You are tiny," she said and smiled. Another cycle was beginning. The animals who preyed on the lemmings were also coming back.

Miyax put her needle away, rolled her ground skin into a tight bundle, and tied it to the bottom of the

pack. Then she got her pot and sleeping skin, her ulo and man's knife, the bones and her flowers. She packed them, tied a thong to the new caribou skin so she could drag it behind her, and lined up her pointer stones with a distant frost heave.

"It's time to go," she said and walked away, not looking back.

Many hours later she opened her pack, spread her skins, and took out a strand of smoked meat. A snowshoe hare screamed and, recognizing the cry of death, Miyax picked up her club and ran off to take the rabbit from its killer. Rounding a clump of grass she came upon an enormous wolverine, the king of the Arctic weasel family. Slowly he lifted his head.

The wolverine was built low to the ground, and his powerful front feet were almost as big as a man's hand. Utterly fearless, he looked her in the face.

"Shoooo," she said and jumped at him. He left the rabbit and came toward her. She jumped back and raised her club. He leapt lightly to the side, snarled, and sauntered away. Gingerly she snatched the hare, turned, and fled back to camp. The wolverine's fearlessness sent goose bumps up her spine. Hastily throwing the hare on the caribou skin she was dragging for just such a purpose, she walked on.

A tern floated past. She took out her sinew, held her arm under the bird, and singing aloud strode toward Point Hope.

At sunset the clouds were dark and soft-edged, like bears. They could dump a foot of snow or a sprinkle of snow. She dug a niche in the side of a heave with her man's knife, folded her ground skin into an envelope, and pushed it into the cave. With deft hands she pressed her sleeping skin into the envelope, then undressed. The fur nestled her, and when each toe and finger was warm she peered solemnly out of her den. The sky darkened, the clouds lowered, and the wind blew like a charging buck. In less than a minute she could see no more than the fur around her face. The snow had come.

Buried in her skins like an animal in its lair, Miyax wondered about Amaroq and Kapu. Would they be curled in furry balls, or would they be running joyously through the first storm of the winter, following their noses to game?

When she awoke the sun was out, the sky was clear, and only a feathering of snow covered the tundra—just enough to make it winter. Before she had dressed, however, the crystals had melted—all but a few on the north sides of the slopes, that spoke of things to come.

Miyax pulled a snarl out of her hair with her fingers, then looked around. Someone was watching her. Running to the top of a low hill, she scanned the flatness. A dozen stout caribou, their white necks gleaming in the sunlight, browsed in the distance; but there was nothing else. She laughed at herself, went back to her camp, and ate a piece of smoked meat. Rolling her skins and shouldering her pack, she walked to her caribou skin to pick up the leads. It was empty. Someone had taken her rabbit in the night. A wolverine, she thought; but there was not a footstep to tell which way the thief had gone.

She spun around. Again she felt as if someone were watching her. Again there was no one; there was only a large flock of terns in the sky. Taking a bearing on them with her sinew and adjusting her pack, she gave the skin-drag a yank and walked on.

All day the birds moved overhead. She walked a straight line to the ocean, for the pools had frozen and she could follow her compass without deviating.

When the eerie feeling of being watched persisted, Miyax began to wonder if the vast nothingness was driving her mad, as it did many gussaks. To occupy her mind she sang as she gathered caribou droppings and put them on her drag:

Amaroq, wolf, my friend,
You are my adopted father.
My feet shall run because of you.
My heart shall beat because of you.
And I shall love because of you.

That evening she stopped early, built a bright fire and cooked a stew, adding to it a sweet-leather lichen from the tundra. While the pot simmered and the steam hung above it like a gray spirit, she took out a needle and thread and mended a hole in her old mitten.

The earth trembled. She glanced up to see two of the largest caribou she had ever beheld. She could tell by the massiveness of their antlers that they were males, for those of the females are more slender and shorter. As the two ran side by side, the gleam of their headpieces told her it was the breeding season of the caribou. When the last fuzzy antler-coating of summer is rubbed off and the horns glow and shimmer, the mating season begins—a season of bellowing and short tempers.

Suddenly the lead bull circled and came toward the other. Both lowered their heads and clashed antlers with a clanging crack that sounded like a shot. Neither was hurt. They shook their heads and stepped back, tossed their antlers, and bellowed. Colliding again, they pawed the ground and then peacefully trotted away. Miyax wondered who they were fighting over, for not a female was to be seen. All the bravado and glamour seemed lost on the grass and the sky.

Nevertheless, when she had eaten she picked up her pack, tugged on her cumbersome drag, and moved on; for the thundering animals told her she was along the migration path and she did not want to camp in the middle of a caribou love nest.

Far from the herd, she stopped by a pond and made her bed. She was not sleepy, so she took out the wolf-puppy bone and, holding the ulo between her knees, carved a tooth in the comb.

Orange and purple shadows crept over the land as

the sun went down that night, and Miyax crawled into her sleeping skin noting that the days were growing shorter. She felt restless like the birds and mammals, and in the middle of the night she awakened and peered out at the sky. A star twinkled in the half-lit dome—the first of the year! She smiled, sat up, and hugged her knees.

The guidepost of her ancestors, the North Star, would soon be visible and would point her way when the birds had all gone South.

Softly across the distance a wolf barked, then another. The first bark was one of inquiry, a sort of "Where are you and what are you doing?" The answer was a casual "I am here." The next call, however, was disquieting. The wolf seemed to be saying there was danger in the air. Miyax looked around to see what it might be. Then the wolf changed the subject and shifted to a joyous howl. As the others joined in she recognized the hunt song of her pack. Amaroq's rich tones rose and fell like a violin; then came the flute-like voice of Silver. Nails's voice arose, less strong than Amaroq's, bringing variation to the theme. Cupping her hands behind her ears, she listened intently. Yes, the pups were singing too, sounding very mature and grown up—until Kapu added his laugh-bark.

She listened for Jello to sound forth. He did not. The concert ended abruptly and she heard other sounds in the dimness. A lemming screamed in death, and a flock of migrating eider ducks called out their positions to each other.

Suddenly something moved. She bolted out of bed and grabbed her club. The grass crackled behind her and she spun around. Sedges bobbed to say it was only the wind.

"Ayi!" She was disgusted by her fears. She kicked a stone to change something, since she could not change what she was doing, as Kapugen advised. Feeling better, she slid back in her sleeping skin. "I guess," she said to herself, "that the sun's been up so long I've forgotten the sounds of the night." As she waited for sleep she listened to the polar wind whistle, and the dry grasses whined like the voice of the old bent lady.

"Jello!" she screamed, sitting bolt upright. He was almost beside her, his teeth bared as he growled. Then he picked up her pack and ran. She jumped out of bed and started after him, for her very life was in that pack—food, needles, knives, even her boots. The wind chilled her naked body and she stopped to collect her wits. She must act with wisdom. She must think! Her clothes, where were her clothes? They, too, were gone. No, she remembered they were safe in the bladder bag under the caribou skin.

Quickly she pulled them out and clutched them to her chest, but they were of little comfort. She could go nowhere without boots; nor could she make new ones. Her needles and ulo, the tools of survival, were all in the pack. Shivering, she slid into bed and cried. A tear fell on the grass and froze solid.

"My tombstone."

She lay very still wondering how long it would take for life to leave her.

When she opened her eyes it was daylight and the warm yellow of the land gave her hope. She could eat her caribou skin if she had to. Rolling to her stomach, she smelled something sweet and recognized the scent of wolf urine. It had been dropped at the edge of her bag and was frozen but fresh. Someone had greeted her during the night. It could not have been Jello for the scent did not have the bitter odor of an angry and desolate wolf. Furthermore, it was sparsely given, not the dousing given to hostile objects. It must have been Amaroq. She sniffed again but her nose was not sensitive enough to read the other messages in the urine that meant "all is well." Yet its light and loving scent gave her a sense of security and she smiled at the sun, dressed, and put her mind to inventing boots.

Wrapping the drag around one foot and her sleeping skin around the other, she clomped awkwardly through the grass in a wider and wider circle hoping that Jello, having eaten her meat, would have abandoned the pack. She did not care about the food anymore. Her ulo and needles and matches were more important to find. With them she could make shoes, hunt, and cook. She marveled at how valuable these simple things were, how beautiful and precious. With them she could make a home, a larder, a sled, and clothes. And the cold air was equally precious. With it she could, like her father, freeze leather and sinew into sleds, spears, and harpoons. She would not die here if she could find her ulo and needles.

As she carefully searched the ground she began to think about seal camp. The old Eskimos were scientists too. By using the plants, animals, and temperature, they had changed the harsh Arctic into a home, a feat as incredible as sending rockets to the moon. She smiled. The people at seal camp had not been as outdated and old-fashioned as she had been led to believe. No, on the contrary, they had been wise. They had adjusted to nature instead of to man-made gadgets.

"Ayi!" she gasped. On the side of a ground swell lay Jello, his body torn in bloody shreds, his face contorted. Beside him lay her backpack!

Instantly she knew what had happened; Amaroq had turned on him. Once Kapugen had told her that some wolves had tolerated a lone wolf until the day he stole meat from the pups. With that, the leader gave a signal and his pack turned, struck, and tore the lone wolf to pieces. "There is no room in the wolf society for an animal who cannot contribute," he had said.

Jello had been so cowed he was useless. And now he was dead.

Slowly she opened her pack. The food was gone but her needles, ulo, and boots were tucked in the pockets where she had put them. They were now more wonderful to Miyax than airplanes, ocean liners, and great wide bridges. As she put on her shoes she checked for her man's knife and matches. They were there, too. Life was hers again! Slinging her pack to her shoulders, she placed a stone at Jello's head and turned away.

"You've got to be a super-wolf to live," she said. "Poor Jello was not." She left him to the jaegers and foxes.

"Amaroq, wolf, my friend," she sang as she walked along. "Amaroq, my adopted father."

Reaching Point Hope seemed less important, now that she had come to truly understand the value of her ulo and needles. If she missed the boat she could live well until another year. Her voice rang out happily as she sang and followed the birds and her compass.

ONE EVENING AS SHE LOOKED FOR A CAMPSITE, she felt lonely. To amuse herself she thought of the hill where the white house stood in San Francisco.

When it seemed almost real enough to touch, and very beautiful, it vanished abruptly; for the tundra was even more beautiful—a glistening gold, and its shadows were purple and blue. Lemon-yellow clouds sailed a green sky and every wind-tossed sedge was a silver thread.

"Oh," she whispered in awe, and stopped where she was to view the painted earth. As she dropped her pack it clanged out a frozen note, reminding her again that autumn was over. The season had been brief; the flash of bird wings, the thunder of migrating herds. That was all. Now it was winter, and the top of the soil was solid. No blue sea would be lapping the shores of Barrow; instead the Arctic Ocean would be a roaring white cauldron forming ice that would join the land with the polar cap.

She was not afraid. Singing her Amaroq song, she gathered grass and rolled it into cylinders. With deft strokes she chopped a hole in the icebound lake, soaked the grass sticks, and laid them out in the air to freeze. Hours later they had snapped and crackled into ice poles. She cut the drag in two pieces and, pushing the poles under one piece, she erected a tent.

Inside her shelter she cut a long thread of hide and twisted it into a snare. A snowshoe rabbit trail ran along the lake and she set off to find the resting place of the one who had made it. The air was cold and she blew her breath into the wolverine trim of her parka hood. There it hung and warmed her face.

Amaroq called and she called back, not to tell him she needed food as she had once done, but to tell him where she was.

A lemming burst out of the grass near her foot and she spun around to look for its nest and young. Not finding them, she turned back in time to see a fox ripple like a ribbon as he pounced and sped off with the lemming. She grinned, made a mental note to be quicker, and walked carefully along the rabbit trail. Finally she came upon a concave dish in the ground —the roost. In it the rabbit would hide from enemies or rest when not eating. She spread her snare, elevated it with an ice stick, and paid out enough hide-line to be out of the sight of the hare.

Flat on her stomach she watched the roost. Minutes turned into hours and the pinks and greens of sunset colored the frozen prairie. Suddenly down the trail, ears back, feet flying, came the rabbit. It made a sharp turn and plopped to a halt in its roost. Miyax yanked and caught its left hind foot. She killed it quickly, and ran back to camp.

The grass rustled and she turned around. "Kapu!"

He was trotting down the rabbit trail with a leg of caribou in his mouth. His head bucked as he fought the awkward weight of the meat.

"Kapu!" she repeated. He wagged his tail, took a

better grip on his burden, and trotted up to her. He dropped it at her feet. With a skip and a leap she told him in wolf language how glad she was to see him. He replied by dashing around in a small circle, then in three big circles. Finally he stopped and wagged his tail.

"Is this for me?" she asked pointing to the leg. He spanked the ground with his front paw, leaped to the side, and spanked the ground again. With a grin she reached in her pocket, found a strip of caribou hide, and thrust it at him. Kapu snatched it, and with one pull not only wrested it from her, but sent her sprawling on her back. Tail held straight out, he streaked like a rocket across the lichens, turned, and came back with the hide. He shook it in front of her, daring her to take it away.

"You're much much too strong for me now, Kapu," she said and slowly got to her feet. "I can't play with you anymore." Shaking the hide, he danced, barked, and then ran over the tundra until he was but a speck in the distance.

Miyax laughed, and dragged the caribou leg back to her tent. She cut it up and built a small fire. She skinned the rabbit, saving the fur to line her new mitten.

As the stew cooked, the crackling cold inspired her to dance. She stepped forward on the vast stage at the top of the world and bowed to her immense audience.

Curving her arms out, bending her knees, she hopped on one foot and beat time with the other. Then she glided and shifted her weight, gracefully executing a combination of steps which the bent woman had danced long ago at seal camp. When she came to the refrain, however, she did not do the dance about evil spirits, but improvised—as Eskimos do at this point. She told the story of a young wolf who had brought the lost girl a shank of meat, and ended the performance with a Kapu-like caper. She spun laughing to a stop. She was warm. Her blood tingled.

"Ee-lie," she thought. "The old Eskimo customs are not so foolish—they have purpose. I'm as warm as the center of a lemming's nest."

As the sky darkened, Kapu came back. He barked softly.

"I know what you want," she called, holding out a large piece of cooked meat. Kapu took it so gently from her fingers that she could not even feel his teeth. As she watched him run off into the night, her eyes lifted to the sky. There, twinkling in the distance, was the North Star, the permanent light that had guided the Eskimos for thousands of years. She sang:

Bright star, still star,
Lead me to the sea . . .

Hastily, she cut the remaining half of her caribou skin into four strips and a circle. Cracking open the ice on the lake, she weighted the pieces with stones and sent them to the bottom.

Around midnight she awoke to hear her wolves in the distance talking softly among themselves—probably paying tribute to Amaroq as they moved along the trail, she thought. Peering out of her tent she saw that the star was gone. A cold flake struck her nose, melted, fell into her fur, and froze. The wind blared, the wolves called joyously, and Miyax snuggled deep in her furs. Let it snow. Kapu had known it was coming and had brought food for her.

She slept until daybreak, saw that it was still snowing, and dozed, off and on, through the white, wild day as the weasels and foxes did. That night the sky cleared, and at dawn she crawled out of her skins. The tundra was white with the snow that would lock up the Arctic till June. The cold had deepened.

After breakfast she cracked open the lake ice again, pulled out the water-soaked circle and laid it out on the ground. Using her man's knife, she turned up the edges, tied them in place, and let the cup freeze in the air. As it hardened she stepped into the bottom, tramped it into a bowl, and then cut two holes in one side. Through these she ran leather thongs and tied them together.

Next she took two strips of skin from the water

and held them in place while they froze to the bottom of the bowl, in the shape of flat rockers. Then she stood up. Her sled was done.

Working quickly, for she had only a few hours of daylight, she formed tear-shaped hoops out of the last two strips. These she laid out to freeze. When they were solid she webbed them with hide, made loops for her toes, and put on her snowshoes. They crackled and snapped, but kept her up on the drifts. Now she could travel the top of the snow.

She cut the rest of the caribou leg into bite-size chunks and stored them in her sled. Then, adjusting her mittens in the darkness, she took a bearing on the North Star and started off.

Her icy sled jingled over the wind-swept lakes and she sang as she traveled. The stars grew brighter as the hours passed and the tundra began to glow, for the snow reflected each twinkle a billion times over, turning the night to silver. By this light she could see the footsteps of the wolves. She followed them, for they were going her way.

Just before sunrise the wolf prints grew closer together. They were slowing down for the sleep. She felt their presence everywhere, but could not see them. Running out on a lake, she called. Shadows flickered on the top of a frost heave. There they were! She quickened her stride. She would camp with them and do the dance of the-wolf-pup-feeding-the-lost-girl for Kapu. He would surely run in circles when he saw it.

The shadows flattened as she walked, and by the time she reached the other shore they had turned into sky and vanished. There were no footsteps in the snow to say her pack had been there and she knew the Arctic dawn had tricked her eyes. "Frost spirits," she said, as she pitched her tent by the lake and crawled into bed.

By the yellow-green light of the low noon sun Miyax could see that she had camped on the edge of the wintering grounds of the caribou. Their many gleaming antlers formed a forest on the horizon. Such a herd would certainly attract her pack. She crawled out of bed and saw that she had pitched her tent in a tiny forest about three inches high. Her heart pounded excitedly, for she had not seen one of these willow groves since Nunivak. She was making progress, for they grew, not near Barrow, but in slightly warmer and wetter lands near the coast. She smelled the air in the hopes that it bore the salty odor of the ocean, but it smelled only of the cold.

The dawn cracked and hummed and the snow was so fine that it floated above the ground when a breeze stirred. Not a bird passed overhead. The buntings, longspurs, and terns were gone from the top of the world.

A willow ptarmigan, the chicken of the tundra, clucked behind her and whistled softly as it hunted seeds. The Arctic Circle had been returned to its permanent bird resident, the hardy ptarmigan. The millions of voices of summer had died down to one plaintive note.

Aha, ahahahahahaha! Miyax sat up, wondering what that was. Creeping halfway out of her bag, she peered into the sky to see a great brown bird maneuver its wings and speed west.

"A skua!" She was closer to the ocean than she thought, for the skua is a bird of the coastal waters of the Arctic. As her eyes followed it, they came to rest on an oil drum, the signpost of American civilization in the North. How excited she would have been to see this a month ago; now she was not so sure. She had her ulo and needles, her sled and her tent, and the world of her ancestors. And she liked the simplicity of that world. It was easy to understand. Out here she understood how she fitted into the scheme of the moon and stars and the constant rise and fall of life on the earth. Even the snow was part of her, she melted it and drank it.

Amaroq barked. He sounded as if he was no more than a quarter of a mile away.

"*Ow, ooo,*" she called. Nails answered, and then the whole pack howled briefly.

"I'm over here!" she shouted joyously, jumping up

and down. "Here by the lake." She paused. "You know that. You know everything about me all the time."

The wind began to rise as the sun started back to the horizon. The lake responded with a boom that sounded like a pistol shot. The freeze was deepening. Miyax lit a fire and put on her pot. A warm stew would taste good and the smoke and flames would make the tundra home.

Presently Amaroq barked forcefully, and the pack answered. Then the royal voice sounded from another position, and Silver checked in from across the lake. Nails gave a warning snarl and the pups whispered in "woofs." Miyax shaded her eyes; her wolves were barking from points around a huge circle and she was in the middle. This was strange—they almost always stayed together. Suddenly Amaroq barked ferociously, his voice angry and authoritative. Silver yelped, then Nails and Kapu. They had something at bay.

She stepped onto the lake and skipped toward them. Halfway across she saw a dark head rise above the hill, and a beast with a head as large as the moon rose to its hind feet, massive paws swinging.

"Grizzly!" she gasped and stopped stone-still, as the huge animal rushed onto the ice. Amaroq and Nails leapt at its face and sprang away before the bear could strike. They were heading it off, trying to prevent it from crossing. The bear snarled, lunged forward, and galloped toward Miyax.

She ran toward her tent. The wind was in her face and she realized she was upwind of the bear, her scent blowing right to him. She darted off in another direction, for bears have poor eyesight and cannot track if they cannot smell. Slipping and sliding, she reached the south bank as the grizzly staggered forward, then crumpled to its knees and sat down. She wondered why he was not in hibernation. The wolves had been sleeping all day—they could not have wakened the bear. She sniffed the air to try to smell the cause, but only odorless ice crystals stung her nose.

The pack kept harassing the sleepy beast, barking and snarling, but with no intention of killing it. They were simply trying to drive it away—away from her, she realized.

Slowly the bear got to its feet and permitted itself to be herded up the lake bank and back to where it had come from. Reluctantly, blindly, it staggered before the wolves. Occasionally it stood up like a giant, but mostly it roared in the agony of sleepiness.

Yapping, barking, darting, the wolves drove the grizzly far out on the tundra. Finally, they veered away and, breaking into a joyous gallop, dashed over the snow and out of sight. Their duty done, they were running—not to hunt, not to kill—but simply for fun.

Miyax was trembling. She had not realized the size and ferocity of the dark bear of the North, who is called "grizzly" inland, and "brown bear" along the coasts—*Ursus arctos*. Large ones, like the grizzly her wolves had driven away, weighed over a thousand pounds and stood nine feet tall when they reared. Miyax wiped a bead of perspiration from her forehead. Had he come upon her tent, with one curious sweep of his paw he would have snuffed out her life while she slept.

"Amaroq, Nails, Kapu," she called. "I thank you. I thank you."

As she packed to travel on, she thought about her escorts. Wolves did not like civilization. Where they had once dwelled all over North America they now lived in remote parts of Canada, in only two of the lower forty-eight states, and in the wilderness of Alaska. Even the roadless North Slope had fewer wolves than it did before the gussaks erected their military bases and brought airplanes, snowmobiles, electricity, and jeeps to the Arctic.

As she thought about the gussaks she suddenly knew why the brown bear was awake. The Americans' hunting season had begun! Her wolves were in danger! The gussaks were paid to shoot them. A man who brought in the left ear of a wolf to the warden was rewarded with a bounty of fifty dollars. The bounty was evil to the old men at seal camp, for it encouraged killing for money, rather than need.

Kapugen considered the bounty the gussaks' way of deciding that the amaroqs could not live on this earth anymore. "And no men have that right," he would say. "When the wolves are gonc there will be too many caribou grazing the grass and the lemmings will starve. Without the lemmings the foxes and birds and weasels will die. Their passing will end smaller lives upon which even man depends, whether he knows it or not, and the top of the world will pass into silence."

Miyax was worried. The oil drum she had seen when the skua flew over marked the beginning of civilization and the end of the wilderness. She must warn her pack of the danger ahead. She had learned to say many things to them; but now, the most important of all, the ear-twist or bark that would turn them back, she did not know.

How, she thought, do I shout "Go away! Go far, far away!" She sang:

Go away, royal wolf,
Go away, do not follow.
I'm a gun at your head,
When I pass the oil drum.

Threads of clouds spun up from the earth and trailed across the tundra. They marked the beginning of a white-out. Miyax changed her plans to travel that night, crept into her shelter, and watched the air turn white as the snow arose from the ground and hung all around her. She closed her tent flap and took out her pot. In it she put a piece of fat from the bladder-bag and a scrap of sinew. She lit the sinew and a flame illuminated her tiny home. She took out the comb.

As she carved she saw that it was not a comb at all, but Amaroq. The teeth were his legs, the handle his head. He was waiting to be released from the bone. Surprised to see him, she carved carefully for hours and finally she let him out. His neck was arched, his head and tail were lifted. Even his ears had a message. "I love you," they said.

A bird called faintly in the darkness. Miyax wondered what kind it was and what it was doing so far north at this date. Too sleepy to think, she unlaced her boots, undressed, and folded her clothes. The bird called from the edge of her sleeping skin. Holding her candle above her head, she crept toward the door and peered into the bright eyes of a golden plover. He was young, for he wore the splotched plumage of the juvenile and still had a trace of baby-yellow around his beak. He slumped against her skins.

Gently she slipped her hand under his feet, picked him up, and brought him close to her. His black and gold feathers gleamed in the sputtering light. She had never beheld a plover so closely and now understood why Kapugen had called them "the spirit of the birds." The plover's golden eye and red noseband made it look like one of the dancers in the Bladder Feast.

"You are lost," she said. "You should be far from here. Perhaps in Labrador. Perhaps even in your winter home on the plains of Argentina. And so you are dying. You need insects and meat. But I'm so glad you're here." Then she added, "I shall call you Tornait, the bird spirit."

She eased the bird inside her warm sleeping skin, cut off a small piece of caribou meat, and held it out. Tornait ate ravenously, then rested. She fed him once more, and then he tucked his head in his back feathers and went to sleep.

The following night the white-out was still so dense she could not see the ground when she crept out for snow to melt and drink.

"I won't go on tonight," she said to Tornait when she came inside. "But I do not care. I have food, light, furs, fire, and a pretty companion." That evening she polished her carving of Amaroq and talked to Tornait. The plover was incredibly tame, perhaps because he lived in the most barren parts of the world where there were no people, perhaps because he was lonely. Tornait ran over her skins, flitted to her head and shoulders, and sang when she sang.

On the next afternoon the white-out was but a frosty mist. Miyax was cooking dinner when Tornait drew his feathers to his body and stood up in alarm. She listened for a long time before she heard the snow scream as footsteps pressed it. Scrambling to the door, she saw Kapu in the mist, frost on his whiskers.

"Hi!" she called. He did not turn around for he was looking at something in the distance. Presently Amaroq swept into view and stopped beside him.

"Amaroq!" she shouted. "Amaroq, how are you?" Tossing her head in wolf happiness, she crawled out of her tent on all fours and nudged him under the chin. He arched his neck grandly. Then, with a glance at Kapu, he ran out on the lake. The young wolf followed, and, laughing joyously, Miyax crawled after them both. She had not gone far before Amaroq stopped and glared at her. She stayed where she was. The regal pair leaped away, snow billowing up from their strides like smoke.

Getting to her knees she looked for Silver, Nails, and the other pups, but they did not follow the pair. Miyax rocked back on her heels. Could it be that the leader of the pack was teaching the leader of the pups? She nodded slowly as she comprehended. Of course. To be a leader required not only fearlessness and intelligence, but experience and schooling. The head of a wolf pack needed to be trained, and who better to do this than Amaroq?

"And I know what you'll teach," she called out. "You'll teach him which animal to harvest. You'll teach him to make all decisions. You'll teach him how to close in on a caribou, and where to bed the wolf pack down; and you'll teach him to love and protect."

The white-out vanished, the stars blazed out, and San Francisco called to Miyax. It was time to move on. Kapu was now in school.

"But how shall I tell them not to follow me anymore?" she asked Tornait as she crawled back into her tent.

"Of course!" she gasped. She had been told by Amaroq himself how to say "stay back" when he had wanted Kapu alone. He had walked forward, turned around, and glared into her eyes. She had stopped in her tracks and gone home. Eagerly she practiced. She ran forward, looked over her shoulder, and glared.

"Stay, Amaroq. Stay where you are!"

Humming to herself she took down her tent, rolled it into a bundle, and threw it on the new sled. Then she stuffed her pack and tucked Tornait in the hood of her parka. Sticking her toes in her snowshoes, she took a bearing on the constant star. The snow squeaked under her feet, and for the first time she felt the dry bite of the cold right through her parka and boots. To her this meant the temperature was zero, the point every year when she began to feel chilly. Dancing and swinging her arms to get warm, she picked up the thongs of her sled and walked toward the sea. The sled glided lightly behind her.

She did not hear the airplane; she saw it. The low sun of noon struck its aluminum body and it sparkled like a star in the sky. It was a small plane, the type bush pilots use to carry people over the roadless tundra and across the rugged mountains of Alaska where cars cannot go. Presently its sound reached her ears and the throb of the engines reminded her that this was the beginning of the season when bush pilots took the gussaks out to hunt. The craft tipped its wings and zigzagged across the sky. When it continued to zag she realized the pilot was following a meandering river where game wintered. A river, she thought; rivers led to the sea. I am nearing the end of my journey; Point Hope might be but one sleep away. She quickened her pace.

The airplane banked, turned, and came toward her. It seemed as big as an eagle as it skimmed low over the ground. Bright flashes of fire burst from its side.

"They *are* hunting," she said to Tornait. "Let's get in the oil drum. I look like a bear in these clothes."

Just before she reached the drum she crossed the footsteps of Amaroq and Kapu. They had passed this way only moments ago, for the snow crystals their warm feet had melted were not yet frozen again. The plane continued to come toward her. Apparently she had been seen. She kicked snow over her sled and pack and crawled to the front of the barrel. It was sealed. She could not get inside. Scurrying to the other end she found that it, too, was closed. Desperately she threw herself under the curve of the drum and lay still. Much of her was still exposed. Flailing her hands and feet, she stirred up the light snow. It arose like a cloud and settled upon her as the plane soared above.

Shots rang out. The plane roared away and Miyax opened her eyes. She was still alive and the air hunters were over the river. The plane banked and flew back, this time very low. Tornait struggled.

"Be still," she said. The gunfire snapped again and, eyes wide open, she saw that it was not aimed at her.

"Amaroq!" Horrified, she watched him leap into the air as a splatter of shots burst beside him. Digging in his claws, he veered to the right and left as Kapu ran to join him. Teeth bared, angrily growling, Amaroq told him to go. Kapu sped off. The plane hesitated, then pursued Amaroq.

Shots hit the snow in front of him. He reared and turned.

"Amaroq!" she screamed. "Here! Come here!"

The plane swerved, dove, and skimmed about thirty feet above the ground. Its guns blasted. Amaroq stumbled, pressed back his ears, and galloped across the tundra like a shooting star. Then he reared, and dropped on the snow.

He was dead.

"For a bounty," she screamed. "For money, the magnificent Amaroq is dead!" Her throat constricted with grief, and sobs choked her.

The plane banked and came back. Kapu was running to Amaroq. His ears were pressed to his head and his legs moved so swiftly they were a blur. Bullets showered the snow around him. He leaped, dodged, and headed for the oil drum. His wide eyes and open mouth told Miyax he was afraid for the first time in his life. Blindly he ran, and as he came by she reached out and tripped him. He sprawled across the snow and lay still. While the plane coasted off to make another turn, she covered Kapu with flakes.

The snow turned red with blood from his shoulder. Miyax rolled under the barrel.

The air exploded and she stared up into the belly of the plane. Bolts, doors, wheels, red, white, silver, and black, the plane flashed before her eyes. In that instant she saw great cities, bridges, radios, school books. She saw the pink room, long highways, TV sets, telephones, and electric lights. Black exhaust enveloped her, and civilization became this monster that snarled across the sky.

The plane shrank before her eyes, then turned and grew big again. Tornait flew to the top of the barrel, screaming his alarm cry and beating his wings.

Kapu tried to get up.

"Don't move," Miyax whispered. "They're coming for Amaroq." Knowing Kapu did not understand, she reached out and softly stroked him, singing: "Lie still. Lie still." She watched him slump back in the snow without a sound.

The plane returned at so low a level she could see the men in the cockpit, their coat collars pulled up around their necks, their crash helmets and goggles gleaming. They were laughing and watching the ground. Desperately Miyax thought about Silver, Nails, and the pups. Where were they? They must be clear targets on the white snow. Maybe not—they were light in color, not black.

Suddenly the engine accelerated, the wing flaps pressed down, and the craft climbed, banked, and sailed down the river like a migrating bird. It did not turn around.

Miyax buried her fingers in Kapu's fur. "They did not even stop to get him!" she cried. "They did not even kill him for money. I don't understand. I don't understand. *Ta vun ga vun ga,*" she cried. *"Pisupa gasu punga."* She spoke of her sadness in Eskimo, for she could not recall any English.

Kapu's blood spread like fish ripples on the snow. She wriggled to him and clamped her thumb on the vein that was gushing. She held the pressure—a minute, an hour—she did not know how long. Then Tornait called hungrily. Cautiously she lifted her hand. The bleeding had stopped.

"Ta gasu," she said to Kapu. She brushed the snow off her sled and took out her poles. She set up her tent beside the barrel, banked the snow around the bottom to seal out the wind, and spread her ground cloth

under it. When she tried to push Kapu into the shelter she found him too heavy. He lifted his head, then dropped it wearily. Miyax decided to build the tent around him. She took everything down and started all over again.

This time she eased the ground skin under him inch by inch until he lay on the fur. Then she kicked the oil drum to free it from the ice, rolled it close to him, and erected her tent against it. She sealed the gaps with snow.

The drum was old, for it had different markings than those around Barrow, but like them, it was barely rusted. The frigid winters and the dry desert-like conditions of the tundra prevent metals, papers, garbage, and refuse from deteriorating as it does in warmer zones. In the Arctic, all artifacts are preserved for ages. Even throwing them into the oceans does not work a change, for the water freezes around them, and in the ice floes they come back on the shores. The summer sun unveils them again.

Miyax melted snow, cut off meat for Tornait, and fed him. He flew down from the barrel and ran into the tent. Hopping onto her furry sleeping skin, he puffed his feathers, stood on one foot, and went to sleep.

With the stew bubbling, Kapu resting, and Tornait asleep, Miyax dared to think of Amaroq. She would go and bid him good-bye. She tried to get up, but she could not move. Grief held her in a vise-like clamp.

About an hour later Kapu lifted his head, rolled his eyes around the cozy interior of the tent, and accepted chunks of stew. Miyax petted his head and told him in Eskimo to lie still while she looked at his wound. It was long and deep and she knew it must be sewn together.

Taking a piece of sinew from the ground skin, she threaded it into her needle and pierced the soft flesh. Kapu growled.

"*Xo lur pajau, sexo,*" she sang soothingly. "*Lupir*

pajau se suri vanga pangmane majo riva pangmane." Monotonously repeating over and over the healing song of the old bent lady, she hypnotized Kapu as she closed the wound. The perspiration was running down her cheeks when she was done, but she was

able to tell him that he would get well and return to lead their pack.

The sun set in a navy blue sky, and the stars sparkled on and off as they spoke of their vast distances from the earth. About midnight the inside of the tent began to glow green and Kapu's eyes shone like emeralds. Miyax peered out the flap door. Fountains of green fire rose from the earth and shot to the top of the black velvet sky. Red and white lights sprayed out of the green. The northern lights were dancing. The lakes boomed, and Nails howled mournfully beyond the tent.

Miyax howled back to tell him where she was. Then Silver barked and the pups called, too. Each voice sounded closer than the last; the pack was coming toward the oil drum as they searched for Amaroq and Kapu.

Miyax stepped into the light of the aurora. It was time to bid Amaroq farewell. She tried to go forward but her feet would not move. Grief still held them useless. Clutching her left knee in both hands, she lifted her foot and put it down; then she lifted the other and put it down, slowly making her way across the turquoise snow.

Amaroq lay where he had fallen, his fur shining in the strange magnetic light.

"Amaroq . . ." She took her carving from her pocket, and got down on her knees. Singing softly in

Eskimo, she told him she had no bladder for his spirit to dwell in, but that she had his totem. She asked him to enter the totem and be with her forever.

For a long time she held the carving over his body. Presently, the pain in her breast grew lighter and she knew the wolf was with her.

The stars had slipped down the sky when at last she stood up and walked swiftly back to Kapu.

All night Miyax sat beside him and listened to Silver, Nails, and the pups.

"*Ow ow ow ow owwwwwww*," they cried in a tone she had never heard before, and she knew they were crying for Amaroq.

THE SUN WENT DOWN ON NOVEMBER TENTH NOT TO arise again for sixty-six days. In the darkness Kapu got up to exercise by walking out on the tundra and back. Tornait was not so comfortable in the continuous night. He slept in Miyax's furs most of the time, waiting for the dawn. When it did not come, hunger awoke him; he ran from his roost to Miyax, pecked on her boot, and fluttered his wings for food. Then the darkness would say to him "sleep," and he would run back to his roost, pull his foot into his breast feathers, and close his eyes.

For her part, Miyax found the clear nights quite

manageable. She could hunt caribou chips by star and moonlight, cook outside, and even sew. When the sky was overcast, however, the tundra was black and she would stay inside, light her candle, and talk to Kapu and Tornait.

At these times she began to shape the antler-weapon into a more elaborate design. As she worked she saw five puppies in it. Carefully she carved out their ears and toes until they were running in single file, Kapu in the lead. She grew tired, took out Amaroq's totem, and thought about his life and brave spirit.

"The pink room is red with your blood," she said. "I cannot go there. But where can I go? Not back to Barrow and Daniel. Not back to Nunivak and Martha . . . and you cannot take care of me anymore."

Snowstorms came and went; the wind blew constantly. One starry night Miyax heard a whimper and opened the tent flap to see Silver at the door. She had a large hare in her mouth, and although Miyax was glad for food, she was distressed to realize that her pack was not eating well. Disorganized without Amaroq, they were forced to hunt rabbits and small game. These would not sustain them. Miyax reached out, petted Silver on the shoulder, and felt her bony back. Without a leader the pack would not live through the winter.

Silver nudged her hand, Miyax opened the flap wider, and the beautiful wolf came in. She dropped the rabbit and walked over to Kapu. He got to his feet, and arching his neck, lifted his head above hers. She greeted him, wagging her tail excitedly. Then she tried to bite the top of his nose to tell him she was the leader, but Kapu drew up tall. Gently he took her nose in his mouth. She bit him under the chin, hailing the new chief.

Kapu pushed past her and slipped out of the tent. Silver followed the prince of the wolves.

In the darkness he sang of his leadership, but, too weak to run, turned wearily back to the tent.

A new grandeur attended his movements as he came through the door and Miyax squeezed his chin. He lay down and watched her skin the rabbit.

She gave him the flesh and went out to hunt lemmings for herself. Since the end of summer the little rodents had doubled, tripled, even quadrupled their numbers. By following their runways she found seven nests and caught eighty furred young. She skinned and cooked them, and found them delicious. The next night Silver brought her a part of a moose. She had not killed it, for it was old and frozen. Miyax knew she had been down to the river. No moose wandered the tundra.

Several sleeps later Kapu ran over the snow without stumbling and Miyax decided it was time to move to the river. Game would be more abundant in the dwarf willows that bordered the waterways. There rabbits and ptarmigan gathered to eat seeds out of the wind, and moose wintered on the twigs of the willows. Perhaps Silver and Nails would find a sick yearling and with help from the pups be able to kill it. Life would be kinder there.

She packed, put Tornait in her parka hood and, picking up her sled ropes, set off once more. Kapu limped as he walked beside her, but less and less as they plodded along. The exercise seemed to help him and by the end of the night he was running fifty steps to her one. Often he took her hand and mouthed it affectionately.

The river would not be hard to find, for she had marked its position by the faithful North Star and so, hours later, as the constellation of the hunter moved to the other side of her, she reached the brushy bank. In the distance loomed the massive wall of the Brooks Range, the massive mountains that rimmed the North Slope on the south. Her journey was coming to an end. The rivers that flow out of the Brooks Range are close to the sea.

After making camp Miyax and Kapu went out to snare ptarmigan and rabbits. Silver called from a short distance away and they answered her.

Hours later when Miyax crawled into her sleeping skin the wolves were so near that she could hear the pups scratching the snow as they made their beds.

As she had anticipated, the hunting was excellent, and upon checking her snares the next day she found three rabbits and two ptarmigan. For several days she was busy skinning and cooking.

One night while Miyax sewed a new boot, Kapu licked her ear and trotted off. When he did not come back by the time the moon had swung all the way around her tent and was back again, a whole day, she went out to look for him. The snow glowed blue and green and the constellations glittered, not only in the sky, but on the ice in the river and on the snow on the bushes and trees. There was, however, no sign of Kapu. She was about to go to bed when the horizon quivered and she saw her pack running the bank. Kapu was in the lead. She crawled into her tent and awakened Tornait.

"Kapu's leading the hunt. All's well," she said. "And now we must leave them."

At dawn she hastily took down her tent, hoisted her pack to her back, and stepped onto the frozen river where walking was easier. Many miles along her way she came upon wolverine tracks and followed them up to a den. There, as she suspected, lay several rabbits and ptarmigan. She loaded them on her sled and returned to the river, listening to Tornait peep soft plover songs in the warmth of her parka hood.

She kissed his beak gently. They were helping each other. She kept him warm and fed him and he radiated heat in her hood. But more important, his whisperings kept her from being totally and hopelessly lonely without Kapu and her wolf pack.

With every mile she traveled now, the oil drums became more and more numerous and the tracks of the wolverine more and more scarce. Like the wolf, the wolverine is an animal of the wilderness, and when Miyax saw no more tracks she knew she was approaching man. One night she counted fifty drums on a spit in the river, and there she made camp. She must stop and think about what she wanted to do.

When she thought of San Francisco, she thought about the airplane and the fire and blood and the flashes and death. When she took out her needle and sewed, she thought about peace and Amaroq.

She knew what she had to do. Live like an Eskimo —hunt and carve and be with Tornait.

The next day she took out her man's knife and cut blocks of snow. These she stacked and shaped into a house that was generously large. If she was going to live as the Eskimos once lived, she needed a home, not just a camp.

When her ice house was completed and her skins were spread over the floor, she sat down and took out the totem of Amaroq. Her fingers had rubbed him to a soft glow in her pocket and he looked rich and regal. Placing him over her door, she blew him a kiss, and as she did so, happiness welled up in her. She knew he was taking care of her spirit.

Time passed, fountains of the magnetic northern lights came and went, and the moon waxed and waned many times. Miyax found her life very satisfying. She became an expert at catching small game and she took great pleasure in carving. When she had finished the carving of the puppies, she found a stone by the river and began chipping it into an owl. Always she listened for her pack, but they did not call. She was both glad and miserable.

Miyax was not without things to do. When she was not hunting, or carving, she danced, sewed, chopped wood or made candles. Sometimes she tried to spell Eskimo words with the English alphabet. Such beautiful words must be preserved forever.

One night she began a tiny coat of ptarmigan feathers for Tornait. He had been shivering lately, even in her parka hood, and she was concerned about him. She stitched the plumes to a paper-thin rabbit hide and fashioned a bird-like coat.

On the moonrise when the coat was finished and she was trying to slip it on Tornait, she heard in the distance the crackle of feet on the ice. The sound grew louder and she poked her head into the night to see a man on the river running beside his sled and team of dogs. Her heart leaped—an Eskimo hunter, one of her own pack, truly. Rushing onto the river ice she waited until the sled drew close.

"Ayi!" she called.

"Ayi!" a voice answered, and within minutes the hunter pulled the sled up beside her and greeted her warmly. Nestled in the furs was the man's woman and child. Their eyes glistened softly in the moonlight.

Miyax's voice was hoarse from disuse, but she managed to greet them happily in Eskimo and invite them into her house for a sleep. The woman was glad to stop, she told Miyax in the Upick dialect, as she climbed from the sled. They had not rested since they had left Kangik, a town on Kuk Bay at the mouth of the Avalik River, the river they were on.

At last Miyax knew where she was. Kangik was inland from Wainwright and still many sleeps from Point Barrow. But she no longer cared.

"I'm Roland," the man said in English as he unloaded his sleeping skins on the floor of the igloo and spread them out. "Are you alone?"

Miyax smiled at him as if she did not understand and put a twisted spruce log on the fire. When it blazed and man and woman were warming their backs, Roland asked her again, but this time in Upick, her own beautiful tongue. She answered that she was.

"I'm Alice," the pretty mother said. Miyax gestured hopelessly. "Uma," the woman said, pointing to herself. "Atik," she said, pointing to the man and, lifting the baby above her head, called him Sorqaq. Miyax found the names so nice that, as she took her cooking pot from the fire to offer her guests hot ptarmigan, she hummed and sang. Then she went to her sleeping skin, picked up Tornait, and held him before Sorqaq, who was now on his mother's back in her kuspuck. He peeked over her shoulder, laughed at the bird, kicked, and disappeared. In his excitement he had lost his knee grip and had dropped to his mother's belt. Miyax laughed aloud. Uma giggled and gave him a boost; his round face reappeared and he reached for the bird.

Miyax suddenly wanted to talk. Speaking rapidly in Eskimo, she told her guests about the river, the game, the fuel, and the stars—but not about the wolves or her past. They listened and smiled.

When dinner was over Atik talked slowly and softly, and Miyax learned that Kangik was an Eskimo village with an airport and a mission school. A generator had been built, and electricity lighted the houses in winter. A few men even owned snowmobiles there. Atik was proud of his town.

Before going to bed he went out to feed the dogs. Then Uma talked. She said they were headed for the mountains to hunt caribou. When Atik returned, Miyax told him he did not need to go to the mountains—that a large herd was yarded not far up the river. She drew a map on the floor and showed him where the wintering grounds of the caribou lay. He was happy to learn this, he said, for the Brooks Range was treacherous in winter; whole mountainsides avalanched, and storms brewed up in mere minutes.

Uma nursed the baby, tucked him into their furs, and softly sang him to sleep as the fire began to die down. Presently her head nodded, and she slipped into bed, where Atik joined her.

Miyax alone was awake, visions of Kangik filling her head. She would go there and be useful. Perhaps she would teach children how to snare rabbits, make parkas, and carve; or she might live with some family that needed her help. She might even work in the store. In Kangik she would live as her ancestors had, in rhythm with the animals and the climate. She would stay far away from San Francisco where men were taught to kill without reason. She did not fall asleep for hours.

Tornait awoke first and called softly. Miyax dressed, cut off a piece of meat, and held it out to him. He snatched the food and swallowed it noisily. That awoke the baby and the baby awoke Uma, who reached out, took him to her breast, and rocked him as she lay in the furry warmth of her skins. It was almost zero in the house and she did not hurry to get up.

Atik awoke, yawned, and roared, "I'm hungry." Uma laughed and Miyax put the pot on the fire. Atik dressed, went out to his sled, and brought back bacon, bread, beans, and butter. Miyax had forgotten there were such good things and her mouth fairly watered as she smelled them cooking. At first she refused the food when Uma offered it, but seeing how disappointed she was she accepted the bacon and sucked on it quietly, remembering with pain the tastes of Barrow.

After breakfast Atik went out to harness the dogs, Miyax cleaned up, and Uma played with her baby. As she tossed him she chatted happily about her love for Atik and how excited she had been when he decided to take her on the hunt. Most Eskimo wives were left home these days; with the advent of gussak frozen foods, cooks were no longer needed for the hunt. And the women never tanned hides anymore; all skins for the tourist trade must go to Seattle to be tanned correctly for the temperate climates where most were shipped.

Uma rambled on. Atik had been raised in Anchorage and knew very little about hunting, for his father had been a mechanic. But he had died, and Atik was sent to live with his grandfather in Kangik. He had become enamored of hunting and fishing and became so skilled that when his grandfather died he was adopted by the greatest of all living Eskimo hunters.

"Kapugen taught Atik where the seals live and how to smell a caribou trail."

Miyax stopped cleaning her pot. Her blood raced hot, then cold. Turning slowly around she stared at Uma.

"Where was this Kapugen born?" she asked in Eskimo.

"He has never said. He paddled up the river one day, beached his kayak, and built a house where he landed. All I know is that he came out of the Bering Sea. But he was wealthy in the Eskimo sense—intelligent, fearless, full of love—and he soon became a leader of Kangik."

Miyax did not take her eyes off Uma's lips as they formed soft words of Kapugen. *"U i ya* Kangik?" she asked.

"Yes, but not in the center of town where the rich men live. Although Kapugen is also rich, he lives in a simple green house on the river bank. It is upstream, beside the wilderness, where the people he loves feel free to visit."

Trembling with eagerness, Miyax asked Uma to tell her more about Kapugen, and Uma, spilling over with enthusiasm, told how the town and its people had grown poor and hungry several years ago. The walrus had all but vanished from the coast; the gray whales were rare, and the seals were few and far between. The Bureau of Indian Affairs put most everyone on pensions, and so they drank and forgot all they knew. Then Kapugen arrived. He was full of pride and held his head high. He went out into the wilderness and came back with musk-oxen. These he bred and raised. The men helped him; the women made the fur into thread and then into mittens and beautiful sweaters and scarves. These were sold to the gussaks who paid high prices for them, and within a few years the people of Kangik became independent and prosperous.

"But there is still a need for caribou and wolverine furs for clothing and trim," she said, "so Kapugen and Atik go hunting every winter to supply the town."

"Kapugen did not come this year," she went on. "He let me come instead." She smiled, slipped her baby into her kuspuck, tightened her belt, and stood up. "Kapugen is wise and strong."

Miyax turned her back to Uma. She must not see the quivering of her body at every mention of her father's name. He had been dead to her, for so long that she was almost frightened by the knowledge that he lived. Yet she loved each cold chill that told her it was true.

Outside the dogs began fighting over their rations, and Atik's whip cracked like a gunshot. Miyax shivered at the sound. She thought of Amaroq and tears welled in her eyes but did not fall, for she was also thinking about Kapugen. She must find him. He would save the wolves just as he had saved the people of Kangik.

"Amaroq, Amaroq," she sang as she fluffed up her furs. Uma turned to her in surprise.

"You are happy after all," she said in Eskimo. "I thought perhaps this was the beginning of your periods and that your family had sent you to a hut to be alone. The old grandmother who raised me did that, and I was miserable and so unhappy, because no one does that anymore."

Miyax shook her head. "I am not yet a woman."

Uma did not inquire further, but hugged her. Then she put her baby in her kuspuck and crept out the door to join Atik in the starlit darkness. It was day and the constellations of the Southern Hemisphere were shining overhead. The dogs were biting their harnesses and fighting each other, and Atik was trying to make them hold still. Suddenly they lunged in all directions and the sled was moving. Atik picked up Uma and the baby, put them on the sled and, calling his grateful thanks to Miyax, took off.

She waved until they were lost in the darkness, then rushed into her house, rolled up her sleeping skins, and loaded her sled. She hoisted her pack to her back and picked up Tornait. Carefully she slipped the feather coat around his breast and, leaving his wings free, tied the little coat on his back. He looked silly. She laughed, rubbed her nose against his beak, and tucked him into the hood of her parka.

"*Amna a-ya, a-ya-amna,*" she sang as she slid to the river, put on her snowshoes, and strode down the snapping ice bed.

She had gone about a mile when she heard Kapu bark. She knew it was he. His voice was unmistakable. Terrified, she turned around.

"Stay! Stay!" she screamed. The wind picked up her words and blew them down the river. Kapu ran up to her, followed by Nails and the pups. All were yipping authoritatively as they told her to join them.

"I cannot," she cried. "My own Amaroq lives. I must go to him!"

She walked forward a few steps, and turned and glared as the wolf leader had done. For a moment they hesitated, as if not believing her message. Then they dashed away and ran up the river. They called from the bank, and then they were gone.

Miyax had spoken her last words to her wolves.

She thought of Kapugen and hurried on. What would she say to him? Would they rub noses when they met? Surely he would hug his favorite child and let her enter his house, tan his hides, sew his clothes, cook his food. There was so much she could do for this great hunter now; prepare caribou, catch rabbits, pluck birds, and even make tools with water and the freezing air. She would be very useful to him and they would live as they were meant to live—with the cold and the birds and the beasts.

She tried to recall Kapugen's face—his dark eyes and the brows that drooped kindly. Would his cheeks still be strong and creased by laughter? Would he still have long hair and stand tall?

A green fountain of magnetic light shot up into the sky, its edges rimmed with sparks. The air crackled, the river groaned, and Miyax pointed her boots toward Kapugen.

SHE COULD SEE THE VILLAGE OF KANGIK LONG BEfore she got to it. Its lights twinkled in the winter night on the first bench of the river near the sea. When she could make out windows and the dark outlines of houses, she pulled her sled to the second bench above the river and stopped. She needed to think before meeting Kapugen.

She pitched her tent and spread out her sleeping skins. Lying on her stomach, she peered down on the town. It consisted of about fifty wooden houses. A few were large, but all had the same rectangular design

with peaked roof. Kangik was so snowy she could not see if there was trash in the streets, but even if there had been she would not have cared. Kapugen's home had to be beautiful.

The village had one crossroad, where the church and mission stood. On either side of them were the stores, which Miyax recognized by the many people who wandered in and out. She listened. Dog teams barked from both ends of town, and although she knew there were snowmobiles, the village was essentially a sled-dog town—an old-fashioned Eskimo settlement. That pleased her.

Her eyes roamed the street. A few children were out romping in the snow and she guessed that it was about ten o'clock in the morning—the time Eskimo children were sent out to play. By that hour their mothers had completed their morning chores, and had time to dress the little ones and send them outside, cold as it was.

Below the town, she could see the musk-oxen Uma had spoken about. They were circled together near the gate of their enclosure, heads facing out to protect themselves from wolves and bears. Her heart thrilled to see these wondrous oxen of the north. She could help Kapugen take care of the herd.

Two children burst out of a house, put a board across a barrel like a seesaw, and took their positions standing on either end of the board. They began jumping, sending each other higher and higher, and coming down on the board with incredible accuracy. Miyax had seen this game in Barrow, and she watched the flying figures with fascination. Then she slowly lifted her eyes and concentrated on the houses.

There were two green houses near the wilderness. She was debating which one was Kapugen's when the door opened in the smaller one and three children tumbled out. She decided he must live in the other one—with the windows, the annex, and two wooden boats in the yard.

A woman came out of Kapugen's house and hurried across the snow.

"Of course," Miyax thought. "He has married. He has someone to sew and cook for him. But I can still help him with the oxen."

The woman passed the church and stopped at the mission door. She was engulfed in light for an instant, then the door closed behind her. Miyax arose. It was time to seek out her father. He would be alone.

Her feet skimmed the snow as she ran down the hill and across the road, where the children were hitching a dog to a sled. They giggled, and Tornait answered their high birdlike voices from inside her hood.

As Miyax neared the green house she took Tornait in her hand and ran right up to the door. She knocked.

Footsteps sounded from a far corner of the house. The door opened and there stood Kapugen. He was just as she remembered him—rugged, but with dark gentle eyes. Not a word came to her mind. Not even his name or a greeting. She was too moved by the sight of him to speak. Then Tornait peeped. She held him out.

"I have a present for you," she said at last in Eskimo. The feather coat rustled and Tornait's amber head pulled into the covering like a turtle.

"What is it?" Kapugen's voice was resonant and warm and seemed to come from the seashore at Nunivak where the birds sang and the sea was framed with the fur of his parka. "Come in. I've never seen such a bird." He spoke English and she smiled and shook her head. He repeated his invitation in Upick. Miyax stepped across the threshold and into his home.

The big room was warm and smelled of skins and fat. Harpoons hung on the wall, and under the window was a long couch of furs. The kayak hung from the ceiling, and a little stove glowed in the center of the room. Kapugen's house in Kangik looked just like Kapugen's house in seal camp. She was home!

Tornait hopped to the floor, his feather coat blooming behind him like a courting ptarmigan. He ran under a fur.

"He wears a coat!" Kapugen laughed and got down on his knees to peer at the bird.

"Yes," Miyax said. "He is the spirit of the birds. He is a golden plover."

"A golden plover, the spirit of the birds? Where did you hear that?" Kapugen arose and pushed back her parka hood.

"Who are you?"

"Julie Edwards Miyax Kapugen."

The great frost-blackened hands ran softly over her face.

"Ee-lie," he whispered. "Yes, you are she. You are beautiful like your mother." He opened his arms. She ran into them and for a long time he held her tightly.

"When they sent you to school," he said softly, "Nunivak was too much to bear. I left and began a new life. Last year when at last I was rich I went back to get you. You were gone." His fingers touched her hair and he hugged her once more.

The door opened and the woman came in. "Who have we here?" she asked in English.

Miyax saw that her face was pale and her hair was reddish gold. A chill spread over her. What had Kapugen done? What had happened to him that he would marry a gussak? What was his new life?

Kapugen and his woman talked—she loudly, Kapugen quietly. Miyax's eyes went around the room again. This time she saw not just the furs and the kayak, but electric lamps, a radio-phonograph, cotton curtains and, through the door to the annex, the edge of an electric stove, a coffee pot, and china dishes.

There were bookshelves and a framed picture on the wall of some American country garden. Then she saw a helmet and goggles on a chair. Miyax stared at them until Kapugen noticed her.

"Aw, that," he said. "I now own an airplane, Miyax. It's the only way to hunt today. The seals are scarce and the whales are almost gone; but sportsmen can still hunt from planes."

Miyax heard no more. It could not be, it could not be. She would not let it be. She instantly buried what she was thinking in the shadows of her mind.

"Miyax," the wife said in bad Upick, "I teach in the school here. We shall enroll you tomorrow. You can learn to read and write English. It's very difficult to live even in this Eskimo town without knowing English."

Miyax looked at Kapugen. "I am on my way to San Francisco," she said softly in Upick. "The gussaks in Wainwright have arranged transportation for me. I shall go tomorrow."

A telephone rang. Kapugen answered it and jotted down a note.

"I'll be right back," he said to Miyax. "I'll be right back. Then we'll talk." He hugged her. Miyax stiffened and looked at the helmet.

"Ellen, fix her some food," he called as he put on his coat, a long American-made Arctic field jacket. He zipped it with a flourish and went out the door.

Ellen went into the kitchen and Miyax was alone.

Slowly she picked up Tornait, put on her sealskin parka, and placed the little bird in her hood. Then she snapped on the radio, and as it crackled, whined, and picked up music, she opened the door and softly closed it behind her. Kapugen, after all, was dead to her.

On the second bench of the river above town she found her tent and pack, threw them onto her sled and, bending forward, hauled on it. She walked on up the river toward her house. She was an Eskimo, and as an Eskimo she must live. The hour of the lemming was upon the land, cycling slowly toward the hour of Miyax. She would build snowhouses in winter, a sod house in summer. She would carve and sew and trap. And someday there would be a boy like herself. They would raise children, who would live with the rhythm of the beasts and the land.

"The seals are scarce and the whales are almost gone," she heard Kapugen say. "When are you coming to live with us in San Francisco?" called Amy.

Miyax walked backward, watching the river valley. When the last light of Kangik disappeared, the stars lit the snow and the cold deepened far below zero. The ice thundered and boomed, roaring like drumbeats across the Arctic.

Tornait peeped. Miyax turned her head, touched

him with her chin, and felt his limpness. She stopped walking and lifted him into the cold.

"Tornait. What is wrong with you? Are you sick?" Swiftly opening her pack, she took out some meat, chewed it to thaw it, and gave it to the bird. He refused to eat. She put him inside her parka and pitched her tent out of the wind. When she had banked it with snow, she lit a small fire. The tent glowed, then warmed. Tornait lay in her hands, his head on her fingers; he peeped softly and closed his eyes.

Many hours later she buried him in the snow. The totem of Amaroq was in her pocket. Her fingers ran over it but she did not take it out. She sang to the spirit of Amaroq in her best English:

The seals are scarce and the whales are almost gone.
The spirits of the animals are passing away.
Amaroq, Amaroq, you are my adopted father.
My feet dance because of you.
My eyes see because of you.
My mind thinks because of you. And it thinks, on
this thundering night,
That the hour of the wolf and the Eskimo is over.

Julie pointed her boots toward Kapugen.

Onion John

Onion John

JOSEPH KRUMGOLD

Illustrated by Symeon Shimin

HarperTrophy
A Division of HarperCollins*Publishers*

ONION JOHN

 For information address HarperCollins Children's Books, a division of HarperCollins Publishers, 10 East 53rd Street, New York, NY 10022.
Manufactured in the United Kingdom by HarperCollins Publishers Ltd.

Library of Congress Catalog Card Number: 59-11395
ISBN 0-690-59957-9
ISBN 0-690-04698-7 (lib. bdg.)
ISBN 0-06-440144-8 (pbk.)

First Harper Trophy edition, 1984.

For

my wife

HELEN

Chapter 1

Up until I turned twelve years old the kind of friends I had were what you'd expect. They were my own age more or less. Most of them were born here in Serenity along with me. And all of us went to the same school together.

As long as those were the friends I had, nothing too serious ever happened to any of us, except a broken arm now and then or six stitches in somebody's scalp or scarlet fever. The worst was when we were six years old and Eechee Ries had to be pulled out of the pond behind the closed down piano factory. Eech had to get worked over with a Pulmotor. They had him breathing again in about ten minutes and he came out fine. That was the worst. Until I got to know Onion John and we two came to be the best of friends.

Onion John was a lot different from anyone I ever hung out with before. Like his age. No one actually knew how old he'd be. But considering he was six feet and three inches tall with a mustache, it was a good guess that Onion

John was well along in years. Anyway, he was a lot older than I am.

He used to live up on Hessian Hill, Onion John did, in a house he built out of piled up stone and four bathtubs and no running water. Once a month he'd get up in the middle of the night, according to the way the moon was, to cook up a stew with chunks of lead in it and maybe some chipped stone he collected and half a rabbit sometimes and always a little wood alcohol to make a blue flame. It wasn't a stew for eating. It was to get gold out of the moon, to make his fortune.

I never saw any fortune come out of what Onion John was cooking. And now I guess I never will. Because everything's changed for Onion John, on account of us getting to be friends the way we did.

It happened the day we played Rockton Township for the Little League Pennant. Onion John didn't come out to watch the ball game, actually. He came to go shopping in the garbage dump behind center field which is the position that I play. The Serenity dump for John was the same as the supermarket is for most people. He went there for whatever he needed. And if he didn't find what he was looking for he usually came across something he could use just as well. So the sight of Onion John out there on the garbage dump, that day, there was nothing too different in that.

Except everything else about the afternoon was so different I took special notice, more than ever before, of

Onion John. It was the biggest ball game I ever played in. And the most important ball player on the Serenity team was me. Not that I'm the best one. There's George Connors who bats fourth, he's the best slugger our age with this trick, he has, of twisting his wrists when he steps into a ball. Ries, who almost drowned that time, he's our best pitcher. And in the field, Bo Hemmendinger is the handiest.

I'm lucky. The only way I ever managed to stay on the team was because of all the luck I had. The part I liked about the Little League was the bus rides we took when we played away from home, the singing, and what happened every afternoon just batting it around at practice. The most I ever looked for out of a ball game was not to get noticed, particularly.

Yet I was the one the whole championship depended on. According to Mr. Miller who was the editor of the only newspaper we have in town, the *Lamp*.

I'd just come into the hardware store to bring my father his cooked lunch, the way I'd been doing all that summer, and while the bell on top was still jingling, I heard, "Congratulations, Andy. You're in the news."

It was dark inside the store with all the shades pulled down, especially after the glitter the sun made outside. When I made him out, I saw my father over in kitchenware waiting on Mrs. Kinnoy. "It's on the desk! Take a look at yourself."

Across the front page of the *Lamp* was this headline

about us. LITTLE LEAGUERS MEET ROCKTON LIONS IN PENNANT TILT. When I saw the picture of the ball team underneath the headline, I asked my father, "Who am I? Which one?"

The sort of picture it was you could make out Mr. Donahue on one side. He runs the barber shop down at the bridge and he coaches us. And on the other side you could make out my father. He's the president of the Rotary Club and they collected to buy us our bats and gloves and things. They were tall.

But in between, all you could see was twelve uniforms all in a row with hardly any faces to them because of the way things were smudged. We all looked the same, Burke, Hemmendinger, Ries, Schwarz, Connors, Maibee and Berry, like a bunch of dark shadows standing in the fog with the word SERENITY across our chest.

This is the special way that the *Lamp* prints a lot of its pictures and I never minded it before. Most of the time I know what the picture is supposed to look like anyway, whether it's the Episcopal Church, or the firehouse, or construction starts on the new $125,000 school. Except this time I'd just as soon not have to suppose, seeing it was my first picture in the paper.

"Who are you?" my father turned around to answer me. "Why don't you look underneath." Below the picture were all our names from left to right and the fifth was *Andrew J. Rusch, Jr.* I counted out to the fifth blur and it didn't look familiar. I folded the paper under my arm and went over to where my father was shaking his head at the two fingers Mrs. Kinnoy held up. "No laundry faucet ever took a washer that size," he told her.

In a hardware store you go crazy with sizes. You take washers, they go from an eensy quarter inch right up to two and a half, even three inches for a valve in a water main. If someone comes in without a worn washer or without the faucet itself to get fitted, you're licked. Unless you use the kind of a system my father has.

He led the way to the back wall where we keep pipe samples and fittings and he told Mrs. Kinnoy to pick out the faucet back there that looked like the one she had at home. He left her with one finger to her lips and he turned to me.

"How'd you like it?" He took the paper for another look.

"There don't seem much use to a picture, if all you can recognize is your name."

"This is it." Mrs. Kinnoy turned from the shelf with a faucet in her hand. "Rimco. That's even the trademark. What's wrong?" she asked when she looked at me.

She examined the paper with my father and it reminded Mrs. Kinnoy of her high school graduation picture when all that came out was her sash. "What a shame!" she said. "Why don't you call Ernie Miller and let him hear how you feel, Andy. Just tell him."

"I feel all right."

"That's no way to talk." My father had his arms crossed and he held on to his elbows. "Not for some one who's going to the moon." We joked about me going to the moon sometimes, me and my father, because of the good marks I brought home in arithmetic. "Out in space you've got to stand on your own two feet."

He led the way across the store. "I'd like Ernie Miller to learn he can't do this! The time's come when he ought to stop mutilating the good people of this town."

He brought us to where we have an office partitioned off behind three show cases, on one side cutlery and in the front fishing items and on the third side, guns. He dialed. I was ready to hear my father let Mr. Miller have it, when he handed the phone across the counter.

"Me?"

"Go ahead. You're the one's disappointed."

I wasn't so disappointed. But my father was right. It wasn't his picture in the paper. And I couldn't stand there with the phone in my hand, all the yelling came out of it. I said, "Hello."

It wasn't a good time to talk to Mr. Miller. He told me Judge Brandstetter had just called to complain about some T's that were missing out of his name. And the whole Connors family was taking oxygen because their girl got engaged and the *Lamp* never even mentioned it. "And now you're telling me you're mutilated!" Whatever it was he pounded, it sounded like a drum. "All right, let me see you get out there and win that championship tomorrow. If you think you rate special attention from the *Lamp,* Andy, then you're the one I'm going to watch. But if you lose, well then my boy, maybe then, I'll have something to complain about."

"Me lose? How can I? There's eight others on the team."

"You're the only one who called. Now show me why you're so important!" Mr. Miller hung up.

That's how I became the most important ball player all of a sudden on the Serenity team. And not only that. Everything else about the game was what you'd never expect. The ball park was jammed with the biggest crowd we ever had, better than forty people. And when the Rockton rooters showed up, there were twenty more of those. The Lions, every one on their team had grown six inches in the two weeks since we beat them by one run. They looked bigger than I ever expected. And I never expected everyone to start talking how we should lose.

But Coach Donahue told us, "I don't care if you lose. Just let me see a lot of pepper out there."

And my father. "Losing's just a number on a scoreboard, Andy. Don't think about it. Let yourself go and have fun."

And my mother. "Baseball's a sport. It makes you healthy." Her idea was that you got just as healthy losing as you did when you won.

Maybe it was all strategy. To keep us from getting nervous. I didn't see the good of it, as strategy. It didn't keep me from getting nervous. I was afraid some of the others would follow the strategy and then we really would lose. And with Mr. Miller sitting behind first base in his white droopy straw hat, it could mean this was the last game I'd ever play for the Little League after he finished writing me up in the *Lamp.*

The only thing wasn't a surprise that afternoon was the sight of Onion John out back in the garbage dump putting together a pile of old brick. Wherever you happened to be in Serenity, Onion John was what you'd expect. He was like the street lights turning up after supper when it got dark. Or the afternoon shadows moving under the locust trees in the park across from the courthouse. He was there when you were on your way to school, or fishing for blue gill in the creek and when you ran down to the A&P for your mother. He was always around.

He was even the kind of noise you didn't pay any attention to. The whirr of a lawn mower in back of Miss Rorty's house. Or shears clicking behind Judge Brandstetter's high hedge. And he'd be one of the first things you saw in the morning when you happened to look out the window, this long overcoat moving down the street with a pair of heavy sneakers below and a knitted hat that came to a point above, and over his shoulder a burlap bag always bulging and in his other hand, a spade. Mostly I never gave John a second look.

But that day I could've been a million miles away from Serenity, if it weren't for Onion John. He was the only thing around that looked familiar. And when I headed for center field I'd just as soon kept right on going out to the garbage dump to spend the afternoon there. Where it was like every other day. Onion John didn't turn around at all the rooting and horn blowing for the game to get started. He didn't care whether we lost or won or whether we played, even, for the championship at all.

I yelled hello at him.

He looked up and yelled back. I couldn't understand because Onion John doesn't talk English.

Ben Wolf, the umpire behind home plate, yelled, "Play ball!"

Chapter 2

I looked around for an old buttercup that sticks out of the ground where I usually stand. In the first game of the season I made a blind reach with my bare hand and came down with the ball, sliding on my shoulder, to find it waving underneath the peak of my hat, all yellow. Ever since it's been a lucky piece, like a four leaf clover. I hardly had time to find it before Eechee Ries let go with his first pitch. But I did and I was all set, as set as I'd ever be, when the game started.

Their first time at bat, the Rockton Lions didn't get anywhere. The lead off man struck out. The next dribbled to short. And then an easy pop up made it one, two, three. Not a ball came out of the infield. So it couldn't have been very interesting for Mr. Miller if all he was watching was me.

All he could see was the way I kept my hat tight and my belt up and my pants legs pulled down. It was inside, where everything went on. My back went into every pitch, to get a little extra into Eechee's delivery. And the muscles in my legs began to ache, helping everybody to run a little faster. I don't know what my stomach was doing but every ball that hit the catcher's mitt echoed down there. If Mr. Miller thought everything depended on me, that's the way it worked out, inside. I played every position on the team to keep those first three Lions from getting a hit.

Maybe that's why I got such a clout myself, at the first ball pitched to me, just to be able to do something on the outside. I ended up on third base with Maibee and Connors going over the plate and Serenity two whole runs ahead. We were out in front. And it was one hundred per cent pure homogenized luck. It came in way over my head, the ball did. I couldn't hold back. The bat went boom. And there I was on third.

I stood on top of the base and listened to the roar. It looked as if everybody in the stands had hiccups the way they kept pounding each other on the back. It looked like there was a change in strategy. Mr. Donahue and my father and my mother, too, they jumped and got hoarse along with everyone else, holding two fingers in the air. The big idea seemed to be we ought to go ahead and win now instead of not caring if we lose.

Bill Berry took a last strike and left me stranded on third base. I headed for my buttercup out in center field. Onion John was still going on the way you'd expect, if no one else was. He was still picking up old brick, chipping away with a hammer to loosen the cement. He had a pretty good pile built up. I thought maybe I could get him interested in baseball, now we were ahead. I shouted at him, "Two big ones for Serenity." I held up both arms. "And a big goose egg for Rockton."

Onion John let out a bellow like the game was over and we had the pennant sewed up. Only it wasn't the score. It was the brick he was working on, had him excited. He came out of the dump holding two of them up and laughing as if they were rubies. One thing about Onion John, whatever he was doing, if someone came along he was always ready to stop and talk things over.

I had to wave him back. There was a Rockton batter up at the plate. Besides I wouldn't know what he was talking about even if there was time to listen. The way John spoke was his own secret. Most of the words he used were full of *x*'s and *z*'s and noises like *ptchky* and *grvtch*. It was a high speed language full of jokes, from the way he carried on. Every so often, talking away, he'd get too much for himself and bust out. There was no way of telling whether the jokes were that good or not. The only part of his conversation I ever understood was the end of it. He said, "Well, good day," each word separate and clear and then you knew he was finished with whatever he was telling you.

That's what he said now when he saw that I was busy. He pulled at the point on the top of his hat and he said,

"Well, good day." I watched him go back into the dump.

With the first pitch I got my insides into the ball game, again, and my muscles. Up to now the only things Mr. Miller could write about me had to be at least good. But there were five more innings to go where anything could happen.

It was right then, on top of the second inning, when the game just about came to an end for me. There was a Lion on third. Then a walk from Ries put a Lion on first. Two on. And two out. I kicked up a chunk of dirt around the buttercup. It held up great the buttercup did, in the first inning when I got my hit. I tried to keep it working for that last out.

The Lion at bat swung. At the sound of the hit I started running. That's the way a good outfielder's supposed to work. All he has to hear is the crack of the bat and he knows where the ball's going. I swung around and I headed for a black spot right in front of the garbage dump, where it was burnt. I had a full breath and I went, straight for the deep end of center field.

"Go, man. Go, go, go." It was Eechee on the mound.

I looked over my shoulder. The ball was coming down behind me.

"Go, go, go!"

Where'd he want me to go? The ball was dropping right on the spot I started from.

"No!"

That was my father. I turned. The whole place went dead quiet, everything stopped. Even the ball seemed to hang up high where it was. The ball park was a picture in the paper. My father stood on the top of the bench, still, his finger pointed into the sky. My mother's face was hid in her hands, her elbows sticking straight at me. Mr. Miller had his white hat stretched out like he was waiting for the ball to drop into it.

The only sound was the clink of Onion John's hammer. It kept time and he started to sing a little tune. There were three deep notes and everything snapped back to life. The ball dropped as I ran and I dove for it. There was a scream. The ball went past me. A grunt from the stands came rolling out over the infield.

Everybody wanted me to do something different.

"Go, go, go!" Eechee wouldn't let up.

"Third, Andy. Get it to third."

"Here—me. Give me the toss. Me!"

"Watch it."

"Get it home."

There was no use getting it home, or doing anything much. The Rockton man was home. It was a home run with two men on base coming in ahead. Three to two. The picture was three for them, two for us, with me stretched out flat in center field.

The ball was in the dump. I don't see how anyone could know so little about baseball but Onion John figured the game was over. Maybe it was because he saw me taking it easy, just lying on the grass. Anyway he picked up the ball and brought it out to where I was with the idea, now I wasn't so busy, we could have that talk. When he saw my uniform all streaked and dirty he thought to make me feel better. Instead of giving me the ball, he reached underneath his overcoat, and then underneath a second overcoat. He wore them summer and winter. He finally got down to his pants pockets and he brought out a nickel.

I reached for the ball. John rubbed it clean in his hands and gave it to me. I gave him a smile to thank him. He settled down for a visit. He pointed to the clouds over the Munkachunk Mountains and came out with a lot of noises that, at least, cheered him up. And to tell the truth they were pretty good looking clouds at that, big thunderheads crowding up high over the hills.

"Let me have it, Andy." It was Bo Hemmendinger yelling from second base.

"I got to go now," I told Onion John.

"Well, good day," he stretched his hat off his head.

I tossed the ball to Bo and he relayed it to Ries. I went back to where I was standing and there wasn't any buttercup. The header I took scooped it out of the ground neat as a bulldozer. I kept looking for it the rest of the inning and right after Rockton was tagged for their last out, I saw it. It was laying underneath a hunk of dirt and it was starting to dry up.

"It's the breaks," said my father at the bench. "You can't get all the breaks, Andy. To come right down to it, that's part of the fun of the game."

I didn't know we were playing for fun again. It was confusing the way the strategy shifted back and forth. I turned around to see how Mr. Miller looked. He sat there in his white hat looking like nothing in particular. I guess he was making up his mind what to write in next Thursday's *Lamp.*

"Plenty of time left," said my father. "Three to two and there's four and a half innings to go. We're only one run behind."

"What happens," I didn't go into the buttercup part, "if you don't feel so lucky anymore?"

"You make your luck." My father pulled up my belt in back. "If you need any. It's nothing you have to count on, Andy. Not you, if you just let yourself go loose and natural. You're a natural ball player. You've got it."

My father was right.

I won the ball game. I hit a homer in the last half of the sixth with two on. And there it was, Serenity 5, Rockton 3. What's more there wasn't anything lucky about it. I knew I was going to get the home run even before it happened. I knew just the groove the ball was coming in on. I knew how I got my left foot out, and my hip, was just the right way. It was the longest ball anyone hit all afternoon. And from the way the place went to pieces, the bomb that went off, even Onion John turned around to watch. All that was left for me to do was run around the bases. And to be happy along with everybody else.

And I certainly was. Now that I was rounding first, and second and third, Mr. Miller didn't have anything to write except Serenity was champ of the Little League. He didn't have anything to print about me, unless it was how I helped to get the pennant. I didn't have to say goodbye to anybody. Not to Eech or Hemmendinger or Bitsy or George Connors. They were the ones I was going to be with for the rest of the summer, same as always.

"You see!" My father tackled me high as I came in from home plate. "That's the kind of a guy you are!" He lifted me up on the bench where I was harder to reach and got less of a pounding. "You're a winner!"

The auto horns blew with everyone getting back into their cars, five honks and then three. Five and three, all keeping time together.

"Ries's drug store!" My father stuffed us back into our windbreakers. "Flips and splits, everybody. They're all on me." He took my cap off. "What'll you have, slugger?"

"A plate of chocolate ice cream."

"That's what you always have. Go ahead, spread yourself. You've had a big day."

"Except for those four and a half innings." Hauling our bats and buckets and the rest, the mob of us walked back to where the cars were. The yelling and the horns kept up. "The only place I wanted to be most of the game was out in back there, on the garbage dump with Onion John. Especially, those innings."

"What's a couple of innings? I was sure you'd come through."

"Were you?"

"Positive." He shook the back of my neck.

"I wasn't. Not about winning. And not about pepper. Or having fun. Or getting healthy, what went on inside I wasn't even sure about that."

"There wasn't any question in my mind. I knew."

He sorted us out for the ride back to town. "Quit crowding! No more than six kids to a car."

"I think I'll hoof it," I told him.

"Get in, there's plenty of room."

"Through the dump, I'll get down to the drug store as fast as you."

"Sure, but why walk?"

"I want to see what goes on out there, with Onion John."

"John?" My father shoved Hemmendinger's backside into the car and slammed the door. "Up to you." He took the bat I was carrying out of my hand. "John won't be interested in how the game turned out."

"Even so. Now it's all over, I thought I'd walk through the dump."

It was quiet out there, with the horns finished and the crowd gone. John was glad I'd come because he was so proud to show me the pile of brick he had. It was a fine looking collection of brick. A lot of them were almost whole, with only corners broken off.

He had a lot to tell me. So I sat down on the brick and listened. None of it came across. But even so, it was nice to get out there at last. And once you took notice of Onion John, you couldn't help but be interested to watch him talk, no matter what it was he said. With his hands chopping and slicing, and his eyes so busy, and his cheeks and shoulders working, I never saw anybody get such a workout from just a conversation.

When he laughed, I got to doing it too, he was having such a good time. Then I thought I caught a couple of words.

"Cows in the sky?" I asked him. "Is that what you said?"

He stopped and his eyes went wide, looking at me. He nodded. They were right, the words I'd heard. No one else ever understood anything he said except, of course, "Well, good day."

He let me have the same mouthful over again. This time it was just noise again, none of it hung together. But the thing is, I'd done it once! That was important enough to Onion John. He stared at me like I was a magician.

He came over and we shook hands again. "Mayaglub-pany!" he said. Later I found out what that meant. "Friends." And that's what we got to be, after the Rockton game, that afternoon.

Chapter 3

We put in a lot of time together the next few days, experimenting. There had to be something I did those couple of seconds out on the garbage dump that brought him in so clear. I didn't know what it was and Onion John didn't know either. But there had to be something about me that was worth looking into.

We investigated me all over town, wherever it was we happened to meet. Most of the time we put in was on the bridge on High Street. This is the coolest sight we have in Serenity, where the water comes spilling out of the mill pond back into Musconetty Creek. We don't have a mill any longer, only McSwain's Feed Store where the mill used to be. But the dam's still in great shape and you can spend hours watching the green water curl over and come up white and bubbling as it goes under the bridge. The two of us hung on a rail, thinking of different tests to make and then trying them.

Onion John would try talking slow or fast, or in little

chunks with big spaces between, or even in single words. He'd speak in a high voice or very deep, or he'd whisper. Then he'd stop and watch me, to see what'd happen. For all the smooth shining water I watched go barreling over that dam, we didn't get anywhere.

The thing is Onion John understood English, a lot of it anyway. And I could get him to repeat words, like a second grader. But that wasn't what we were after. It was the slam bang, mile a minute clatter he made, if I could get that tuned in again then Onion John would be free to say whatever he had in mind. Our problem was the same as in spying, when you're up against trying to decipher a code.

We were on Water Street one noon time. It was dead hot and I'd just come back from swimming. I met up with Onion John on the way down to the hardware store. I felt lazy. There wasn't anything moved in all the heat on Water Street except the one stop light we have in town, at the corner of High, going from red to green to red again. All there was to listen to was humming that came from the bushes and flowers in front of the houses and every so often the croak of a frog from the pond behind the piano factory. And Onion John, who never let up. We could've been the only ones in Serenity with all the quiet and the burnt up smell there was that August. Onion John went on about the smell and the terrible weather we were having, without rain, and the scandal it was.

"What kind of scandal?" I asked him.

John stopped. He almost tripped. He grabbed me by the shoulders. I looked up and got blinded with the sun. Then it hit me. I'd been listening to him for the last two minutes. I'd understood most everything he said.

We held on to each other. We tried to keep everything the way it was, quiet. We took a couple of steps and got back to walking. John didn't let out a word. Then walking together, him as tall as he was with me looking up at him every so often, he took a chance. He let go.

John told me this was the worst summer he'd ever seen in Serenity. The kind of dry spell we were having the whole world could get burnt if rain didn't come. It was a scandal the way people went around not caring, not trying to do anything about it.

I've talked about the weather all my life. But I never heard anything so amazing as that. It all came across. What John had to say about the weather was absolutely clear. We had it. I knew how to listen to Onion John. There was a way to it and I could see just the way it was. And there couldn't be any fluke to what happened. John went on about the weather and I understood him! I couldn't hold back any longer.

"Mayaglub!" I yelled, trying for that word back on the dump.

"Mayaglubpany!" he shouted to show me how it went.

We stood on the corner of High and Water Street and we let go at each other. "Mayaglubpany!"

The window over Ries's drug store opened and Eechee looked out, with a piece of bread in his hand from the lunch he was having.

"What's up?" he shouted.

"Wait'll you hear!"

"What?"

"Onion John."

I took Eech up to Hessian Hill that afternoon to listen to him. We found Onion John tying rocks in a tree. The tree grew sheepnose apples. They're a yellow kind that comes down to three rounded points like the muzzle of a sheep, if you want to think about it that way. You wouldn't want a better apple to eat, more juicy. And they're early. The first apple you have every year, usually, was out of the sack Onion John brought to town when you happened to meet him and he'd give you one.

We climbed up to help, even though neither of us had ever heard of anybody tying rocks in a tree. John had nine of them, big as softballs. His idea was that the rocks would make the apples ashamed, hanging so close by and heavy. And the apples would try hard to catch up and become big and heavy too.

It didn't seem like much of an idea to me. But then, I never did let on about the buttercup I had in center field. That was only an idea too, and how could you tell about it, whether it worked or not? Without saying what I thought, I passed on to Eech how John explained about the rocks.

"How do you know what he said?" Eech asked me. "I mean why can't I hear him."

"Getting the hang of it takes time. Listen some more."

All the time we worked in the tree, Onion John never stopped talking so Eech had plenty to listen to. When he got the last rock hung, Eech sat down in the leaves above me. "Not a word! I'd just as soon listen to a broken crank shaft, all I get out of him."

"You're not doing it right, come on down."

John dusted off a couple of places for us, with his hat, down in the crotch of the tree. When we sat down he took a couple of onions out of his overcoat pocket for us. And even though they were beauties, because he grew the best onions around, neither Eech nor I felt like one.

John ate onions the way other people ate apples or pears. And always he used his big jackknife, slicing each mouthful. Holding the slice between the blade and his thumb, he ate very slowly.

Talking away, John waved his hand along the river. From up there in the tree on Hessian Hill you could see where the river came out of the water gap and turned and flashed around into the rapids, south of town, near a new plant down there called General Magneto. John shook his fist at the clouds. They were the same kind of thunderheads as on the day of the ball game, white and piled up over the hills like a sky full of fresh dried laundry. John mooed. He ate a piece of onion and looked as if he were going to cry.

He put two fingers alongside his ears and he growled. He leaned over to me and he whispered. He laughed. And he slapped the tree.

"Is that so?" I asked John. "Why do they eat shadows?"

"Who eats shadows?" Eech lay hold of my T-shirt and pulled me around. "Where do you get shadows? I have an earache from listening so hard."

"That's the trouble. You can't listen to him that way, not too hard."

I explained to Eechee how trying to follow John so close was the mistake I made first off. It was only when I didn't pay any particular attention to him, when I didn't care so much, that I started to get the drift. I described to Eech how you had to watch Onion John and keep hearing what he said all together, without trying. "You know what it's like? Like listening to the band concert on Sunday night."

"The American Legion Band? I hear that fine."

"Well, you don't try to listen to the flute separate, do you, or the big horn or each note one after the other? You kind of take it all in together. They play 'Stars and Stripes' and you get to know what it's about just by listening to everything at once. Not each little toot. And it's the same with him, the way you have to listen to Onion John."

"Except 'Stars and Stripes' is a tune. It don't mean anything. If there was anything you had to say, like pass the butter, you could bang out 'Stars and Stripes' from here to next January. And it won't get you any butter."

"As far as that goes." I turned to Onion John who watched us, very interested, as we talked. "Would you please pass the butter?"

John lifted his shoulders to apologize he didn't have any butter. He brought out another onion to see if that would do instead.

"No thanks."

"What does that prove?" asked Eech. "Except he understands English. I know that."

"And he speaks it too. Only it's mixed up with a lot of other odds and ends, his own kind of sounds. That's why you have to listen to him in a new kind of way. Lazy, and not too close. And pretty soon all the words he's got hidden start to come out. They surprise you."

"Okay." Eech leaned back where he was sitting and stretched out and closed his eyes. "Is this lazy enough?"

"You got to watch him too. That's as important a part as all the rest."

Eech opened his eyes. "Start him up."

"The shadows?" I turned to Onion John. "Why do they eat shadows?"

John went back into high. He sailed his hands past us. He whistled. Talking fast, he gathered the air around him into big piles. He put a big bunch of air on my lap. And another big bunch on Eechee. Then he whispered again to both of us, winking. He finished with the same kind of laugh as before.

"Ever hear anything like that?" I asked Eech.

"It's just no use." Eech sat up. "It all goes by me like a fast freight. What's he talking about?"

I explained to Eech how bad John was worried about the weather. And how sore he was at the thunderheads, the way they'd been hanging over the Munkachunks day after day without doing anything. It was their fault, John said, we didn't get rain.

According to John, the thunderheads were scouts for the rest of the clouds, scattered like a herd of cows over the sky, grazing through the blue up there further than you could see. The thunderheads came on first and they'd mutter and mumble at each other to decide whether this was a good place for the others to collect. The way you see a couple of cows pick out one end of a field, sometimes. And then the others would gather along when they're quiet from eating and are full and ready to be milked.

If the thunderheads decide they like a place, they start up a wind to whistle the rest in. And from all over the sky, the clouds bunch up and flock together eating the shadows on the ground as they come. Because that's what they live on, Onion John explained. A cloud sops up shadows the way a cow eats alfalfa until the herd grows so big and full the sky is packed tight and there aren't any more shadows. All that's left is a gray day.

And once they are full up, pretty soon the rain that's in

the clouds comes spreading out, blowing across the fields, driving through the trees and running off the roof. They let out a storm. And to keep the rain coming harder and harder, the big thunderheads rumble and bellow and go charging through the herd, their horns sharp as lightning.

"You're right," Eech sat forward from his branch. "I never heard anything like that before."

"The only trouble is those thunderheads have been looking over this valley the last four or five days without doing anything. John argues we have to make up their minds for them."

"Whose minds? The clouds?"

I nodded. That was one of the reasons John was so happy I could understand him. Now I could tell everybody how to manage. The whole town had to stop eating for a day and drink only water. And then there had to be a procession. With the most important up front, the mayor, and the president of the bank, Mr. Weems, and all the ministers and school teachers leading the rest of us down to the creek. We had to carry torches and sing a special hymn. And at the end we had to toss the mayor in the creek with all his clothes on.

Eechee shook his head when I told him. "Old Man Weltershot. In the creek? Never happen in a million years."

"Everyone would certainly enjoy it, him and his big hat."

"That part, maybe. But who'd go for not eating all day?"

"I guess not." Eech and I didn't see where anyone in Serenity would go parading around with torches on the off chance it might rain. And that's what I told John. He was very disappointed. He threw away the little piece of onion he had left and snapped his jackknife shut and the next thing he said, I didn't understand at all. He went on talking to himself and it must've been in his own language. Not a word came through.

"What's he saying?"

"I don't know." I was afraid I'd lost the knack I had.

"He looks real sad."

"He's bound, that's why, on having a procession. Look Eech!" I explained the part where Onion John whispered. "He said it didn't have to be everybody in town. He says the more the better, but even a few people would do. Maybe even us, we three might work. Should I ask him?"

"For a procession that'd be sparse, only us two and John."

"We could spread out."

"I guess we could." Eech picked a leaf and twirled it. "But why? Do you think it'll do any good?"

"It'll make him happy. And it can't do any harm. And what if it works. We'll be the first ones in Serenity who ever made it rain!"

"I guess it can't do any harm." Eech let his leaf float away. "Okay. If you want to."

"Onion John," I said. He turned from looking at the

river. "Would three do it? Eech and I will help, if you want."

I waited while he thought it over. It would be terrible if after only a couple of hours I couldn't hear him right anymore. I remembered the trick was not to be so tight. I relaxed. John finally nodded and started off. I didn't have anything to worry about. I heard him. He made sense.

He described to us that even one person could manage, as far as that went. Except the fewer there were, the harder it was for each one. Those there were had to believe that much harder the procession would work. He asked us how we felt about it. Eech and I didn't see any harm in believing hard. When I promised we'd do everything we could, Onion John bounced right back.

"He wants us to fast all day tomorrow," I told Eech. "Not even breakfast. And to drink twice as much water as ever. And we have to meet him up here three hours before sundown."

"I can't get over you," said Eech. "The way you understand him."

It was wonderful, just to be able to sit around in a tree with Onion John and hear everything he had to say. He told us about his life. He was born in a high valley in some mountains there were way on the other side of Europe and everything they did in his home town was different, the way they danced and ate and spoke. John liked it there. Except that he wanted an acre of land where he could be by himself. And around his home, there wasn't any left.

An uncle of his was going to New York City and John went along, but there wasn't any land left there either. The way he came out to around Serenity was with the railroad, building the branch line that goes through the county. It was only a temporary job. He quit when he came to Long Meadows, about twenty miles below town, to grow vegetables in the muck fields, almost pure mud that they have down there. He enjoyed that, raising fine celery and onions. But it wasn't the same as having his own place.

So it was like coming home, for Onion John, when he found the two acres on Hessian Hill where nobody minded if he settled down. It was because of all the rocks, John figured, the place was empty. John used the rocks to build his house and before long the garden he grew had everyone startled. Especially the onions he turned out which was the way he got his name.

Along with the vegetables they bought, John found enough people around town who wanted him to keep up their lawns and shrubs at thirty-five cents an hour. He refused to take any more. He figured the price he set twenty-five years ago was about right and any extra they gave him would be charity. He thought everyone around Serenity was nice enough, letting him stay up on Hessian Hill all by himself, and he didn't want anything extra. It was impossible for Onion John to imagine a nicer place than Serenity, friendly as all the people were.

That's why he was so glad, and he shook his fist at the thunderheads, we were getting together to make it rain. It would help everyone in town.

"Anyway," said Eech, as we climbed down out of Onion John's sheepnose tree, "I don't see where it can do any harm."

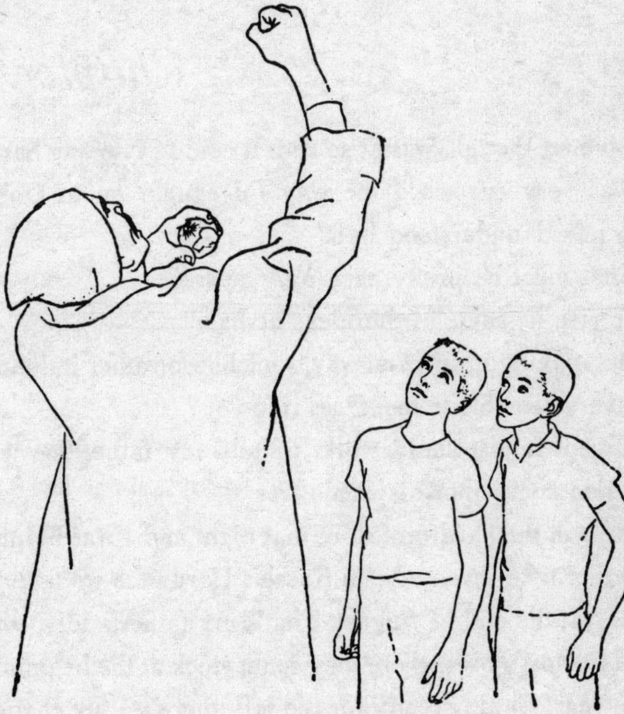

Chapter 4

My father, though, wasn't so sure it couldn't do any harm. He was very surprised the way I'd caught on to Onion John, how I understood him.

"That must be pretty exciting," he said.

"It sure is, some of the ideas he has."

"But making it rain that way, somehow or other it doesn't seem very sensible to me. Does it to you?"

"Except it just could work." I told my father the way John tied rocks into his apple tree.

It was in the hardware store that night and I was helping my father take inventory. In Rusch's Hardware we take inventory at the end of August. That's my father's idea compared to most stores where they count stock at the beginning of the year. Getting ready for the fall, there's a big change-over in the store anyway, moving out the summer merchandise, garden tools and fishing equipment and picnic stuff. What you start to feature is guns, axes and saws, animal traps and such. So in addition to rearranging for the new season, and finding out what's on hand, and what there is to reorder, we take inventory. When we take a rest from counting, my father and I talk things over, all sorts of things. It was one of those times I told him about Onion John, and how he shames his apples into growing.

"And you've got to admit, Onion John brings down some of the best early apples we get in town."

"He certainly does. But don't you think that might be a coincidence, Andy? Onion John's a great gardener. He'd grow good apples even without rocks."

"Maybe the same coincidence will work if we try for rain. As long as we get wet weather, what's the difference how it's done. You can't go anywhere without hearing about the dry spell, how serious it is."

"It's bad, there's no doubt about that. We stand to lose twelve to fifteen hundred dollars. In this store alone. If the farmers don't make it, we don't."

"Then what's the harm of trying?"

"There's no particular harm," my father smiled, "except for someone who might be going to the moon."

I laughed. Every time my father mentioned about going to the moon I saw myself in a space suit with my head in a bubble.

"What's the joke? Actually, there's any number of people who will be going to the moon, Andy, during your life time. Think of it. Why shouldn't one of them be you?"

"But a chance like that. You can't take it too serious."

"Why not? You're good in math. And if you keep going there's no reason why you can't make it up to M. I. T., the college we've talked about in Massachusetts."

"The Institute of Technology?"

"And once you're out of there," he nodded, "with a good scientific background, you can go anywhere. Even to the moon. There's no reason why you shouldn't take that seriously. As serious, anyway, as you do Onion John."

"Except Onion John's now. He's here in Serenity. And it's tomorrow afternoon, the procession. The moon's way ahead, it's years from now. Even if you want to think about it."

"You have to start sometime, Andy. Taking a sensible attitude toward what goes on. And the sooner you begin, getting your mind trained to see the logical reason for things, the better chance you'll have. That is, if you're at all interested in going to the moon."

"Who wouldn't be? Except it's so far away."

"Even if it is, I don't think cooking up a storm with Onion John is any way to train yourself. The harm is that you may get confused."

"I'll watch out," I promised my father. "And if I do, would you mind if we tried with Onion John? We've just gotten to be friends. And it would make him happy. And everyone else too, if his idea worked."

"Well, no, I don't think I mind." My father picked up

the clipboard that had the list of all the different items. "If it's nothing you really believe in. And you just go out there for the fun of it."

He started to check through his sheets to find out where we left off. I figured I had to tell him how it worked.

"You can't go out there for the fun of it. It's not like a ball game. John says you have to believe in it, hard."

"He did?" My father looked over the top of his clipboard. "Well even so, I guess this once won't be so bad. Besides, we'd better get back to work."

Mostly inventory gets done at night when there's no customers. It's all counting. If you try to take care of trade and at the same time keep a lot of numbers in your head, chances are it'll take twice as long.

As it is, we put in a week to ten nights to go through the place. There's over five thousand different items in our hardware store, not counting all the sizes in each item. Mostly it's me and my father working together, except for two nights when Walt, who clerks for us, stays on.

The nights we put in seem a good way, to me, for the summer to come to an end. The store's always dark, with only one light on because we don't want people to think we're open. And it's a little like we were in a big barn counting over our own kind of harvest, all the different things we have. Some of them are old, the wooden spigots for instance we keep for cider barrels and wine. And some are new, just out. like electric eye door openers. Going down the shelves, with all the shadows climbing around and the night dead quiet except for us counting, inventory is the most serious time we have together, my father and I.

He might say, "Lag bolts? Six inch?"

Then I answer, "Two dozen, plus one, two, three, four, five. Twenty-nine in all."

He says, "Check. Lag bolts, four inch?"

I'm up on the rolling ladder we have that goes down the length of wall behind the counter. I go over them and I look down. "Four and a half dozen of the four inch."

"Four and a half dozen." He writes it on his list that's held to his clipboard. "Right. Now about lead screw anchors?"

We go on for about a half hour that way, him asking and me giving him all the answers, between each break. But that night he stopped five minutes after we got started again.

"Talking about rain," he looked up to me on the ladder, "you know, don't you, there's a perfectly sound scientific way of making rain. Did you ever hear of seeding clouds?"

"Somewhere I did." Any idea that came from my father would certainly satisfy John. Long as it brought damp weather. "But I forget how it works?"

"What they do is, they scatter dry ice."

"Makes you think of snow, doesn't it?"

"So it does. But the purpose of seeding a cloud with dry ice is to chill it. Some of the tiny particles freeze and start

falling, picking up other droplets as they come. Until each one collects a full sized raindrop, like a snowball rolling down a hill. That's the process. And multiplied a couple of billion times for every cloud, you get rain. That's the way they do it."

"Sounds like a pretty clever way."

"It's certainly logical. And a lot of times it works."

"Not all the time? Why not?"

"No, not every time. There must be too many different

factors to hit. Wind, temperature, different seasons, dust in the air. There's a lot goes into getting it right."

"But tell me," I came down a couple of rungs on the ladder. "How do they know when they do get it right? I mean, suppose it does rain. How do they know the difference, whether it's because they seeded or it just rained anyway?"

"Well, I don't know if they can ever be absolutely sure."

"I see." It seemed to me like there could be as much coincidence to it as with Onion John, hanging rocks up for his apples.

"But at least, Andy, it's a reasonable approach. You can see the sense to it."

"I can see that, sure. No matter how much rain John would get, tossing the mayor around instead of dry ice, there'd be no sense to that. So why don't I explain it to John, how to do it your way? We could get dry ice from Eechee Ries, out of the soda fountain down at the drug store. Maybe enough for a pretty good shower."

"It's not that simple," my father shook his head. "The spraying's handled out of an airplane. A special crew, and special equipment, there's a whole outfit you have to call in to do the job."

"Of course, there'd have to be." I must've sounded pretty silly to my father, as if the three of us could ever toss dry ice high enough to hit any clouds. I climbed back up the ladder. "I guess we'll just call off the procession and leave it up to that outfit. Whenever it gets here." At least I could tell John something was being done. I found the place on the shelf where I was working. "I think we're up to pliers, aren't we?"

"Pliers," said my father. "But we're not hiring any such outfit, Andy." I turned to listen. "A job like seeding clouds costs thousands of dollars. Serenity can't afford to take that kind of a gamble. It's too big a deal for this town."

"But then, if not that, what are you going to do?"

"Nothing. We're going to let the weather take care of itself and get back into the hardware business. Back to inventory and pliers."

"Right." At least with pliers there wasn't anything you had to decide about them. My father asked me, "Long reach duck bill pliers?" I said, "Nine." And he said, "Check!" We went through regular slip joint pliers, ignition pliers, long chain nose pliers, cutting nippers and diagonals. As long as we stuck to the hardware business, my father and I, it was pretty easy knowing what to do. And working there together with the night getting late, we finished up the shelves behind the long front counter.

My father asked, "Knuckle joint planes?"

I said, "Three."

"Ries's," said my father. That's the way we knocked off every night, to go down to the drug store. My father'd have a cup of coffee and I'd have a plate of chocolate ice cream. We turned off the light and our steps sounded louder leaving the store, the way they always do in the dark. Outside, the full moon traveled through the big thunderheads that still hung up there in the sky.

"I've been thinking about tomorrow afternoon," I told my father. "I think we ought to go ahead with Onion John. As long as you don't mind."

"You still think so?"

"Well, there's a lot of sense to dry ice but there's nothing you can do about it. That's one thing. And even if we could, dry ice doesn't work any better than Onion John when you look at the coincidence. And with Onion John it's cheaper. There's not so much of a gamble. And it would certainly help the hardware store, if it did work somehow. And everyone."

"I wouldn't worry about that." My father looked up at the sky and he spoke quietly. "We probably will get rain. The seven o'clock news said we were going to get a break in the next thirty-six hours. A storm's moving in from the northeast."

The moon was gone for a second. It came back to turn the night white, and our faces like chalk, and the shadows along the street went sharp and black.

"Then I certainly think we ought to go ahead."

"In heaven's name, why, Andy?"

"Well if conditions are so favorable. I'd just as soon try when we got the odds on our side. That makes it better."

"Andy!" My father kicked a piece of rock off the pavement, into the road. He put his hands in his pockets and he walked away from me, down Water Street.

I caught up with him. "What's wrong?"

"Only me." He laughed down at the sidewalk going past. "I ought to be able to get this over to you. Why you can't go back to playing with the moon up there and the clouds, as if you had them on the living room carpet. Seems easy enough until I try."

Usually this is the best part of inventory. When we go down to Ries's after working on a job together. I didn't want anything to come up between us.

"You got it over clear enough. If you don't want me to go ahead with Onion John, I won't."

"That's not the point, Andy. Of course you can go ahead. If you're not persuaded, then I'm certainly not going to forbid you spending the afternoon with Onion John. It's not that important."

"Unless we get rain."

"Well, we can wait and see how that works out."

Mrs. Ries was behind the counter. I asked her to please be sure not to serve Eechee any breakfast. She couldn't see the reason why Eechee should miss all his nourishment. And rather than go into any more explanations, I told her never mind. It was simpler to take care of it myself.

Chapter 5

I was down to High Street by seven o'clock the next morning. And I got hold of Eech before he swallowed anything except, he told me, a little toothpaste. That couldn't hurt. I held on to him all day long, hardly passing up a faucet without taking a drink. We were hungry and waterlogged, getting up to Hessian Hill.

The procession couldn't start until sundown, and in the three hours we had there was plenty to do. First thing when I met Onion John, was to say, "Hello." He said hello, and I asked him, "How are you?" He had no complaints except for a small crick in the back, and I asked him, "What's new otherwise?" There was nothing new otherwise. And I was certainly glad to hear it all. Testing him out, everything he said still made sense.

Most of our time went into finding the right kind of torches to carry. These had to be young cedar trees just four years old. They had to be cedar because the wood smokes a lot and the smell has a lot of carry to it. And the reason for four years old was the last wet summer we had, when the river flooded, was four years back. So it stood to reason, any tree started that year would be best for getting more wet weather.

Walking across fields with Onion John and into woods was as good as going for a hike through a mail order catalog. Almost everything he came across had some use to him. John pointed out rocks, trees, bushes and even a black snake that were good for all sorts of things, for lumbago and making soup and improving your eye sight. That's the reason the sack of his was always bulging. He was forever picking up samples.

We found the cedars we wanted in a swamp in back of Tracy's farm, right below Hessian Hill. From the rings they had and the smell, and even the taste after he chewed on a couple of leaves, John gave us his word they were the best four-year-old cedars he ever saw.

The next we had to do was meditate. This was to get us into the mood of believing hard and there's nothing to it. You sit down and keep still and you think over anything you did that was wrong or bad. It took me a little while to decide. Finally I thought about missing the fly ball in the Rockton game. How much wronger can you get? And then I thought about taking a peek at Bo Hemmendinger's arithmetic paper, the last test we had at school. Which was bad enough. I had both points covered and I was ready to quit.

Except John and Ries kept going. I thought Eech was

carrying it a little too far. He never did anything all that wrong or bad to take the time he did. Waiting for those two, I meditated a little extra. About my father. And about Technology. And going to the moon. I always had in mind to stay on in Serenity and run the hardware store the way my father did. And leaving was a new idea to get used to. That's as far as I went meditating, when Onion John came out of his trance. He sang us a hymn.

It was the hymn we had to use in the procession. We had to learn it. And we couldn't, neither Eech nor I. The voice John used, way down deep like he was singing in a barrel, we couldn't match that. And the words were impossible. I couldn't get through the first three without fetching up lockjawed.

"Can't he do the singing?" Eech gave up. "And us come in for the drums. Boom. Boom. We could do that."

"We can't go," I gave him Onion John's opinion, "unless we sing. Otherwise he's going to have to hold a one man procession." Moving his hands like he was playing six games of checkers, John explained how one man held a procession. "It takes a lot of running around he says, but at least everyone in it is singing. That's important."

"Pete's sake." Eech scratched his head with both hands. "After all the fasting and the water we've drunk! Tell him we have to go along, Andy."

I thought of a song we knew that might do just as well as the hymn. We sang it for John, Eechee carrying the melody and me doing the slides. John thought the tune was all right. And when we promised him there wasn't a wetter song in the English language, that fixed it. We arranged that he'd sing his special hymn and we'd sing my idea which was, "Anchors Aweigh, My Lads, Anchors Aweigh."

The problem was settled just in time. We heard the closing whistle of the new factory down the river, General Magneto. The afternoon was still and clear enough for the blast to carry all that way. We hurried to get started because the procession had to reach the creek just as the sun went out of sight.

John led us to the very top of Hessian Hill, on to a clean grazed over pasture, and we spread apart in a line with about fifty steps between us. We lighted up our torches and John was right, I never saw cedar burn so gummy black and strong. The idea of the smoke was to attract the attention of the thunderheads. Heavy and curling, the smoke had the look of young clouds starting out and that was something they'd notice. And the dry peppery smell the cedar sent up, that was to give the clouds some idea of how burnt it was down here, how brittle and dry.

The sun was headed straight down, when we lit our torches, burning a big ragged hole in the thunderheads. And the torches seemed to work. The whole valley turned roaring red. There wasn't a sound on the top of the hill, except some yakking crows, but the piled up flame spread out in the sky and the gold and the purple made you want to cover your ears. It looked as if the clouds were raging to see what we wanted.

There was a yell from John, "Advance!" and we took out. John's hymn started and he turned to wave his torch for us to get going. I heard Eech sound off with "Anchors Aweigh" and I joined in. I was extra light, with more float to every step, coming off Hessian Hill. That could come from not eating all day. Or it's what happens when you take to singing to a lot of clouds.

All the way down to the creek, we walked only along the crests of the hills so that we threw the longest possible shadows. Because that's what they eat, clouds are interested in shadows. Some we cast down the slopes below were better than a block long. And on top of them, the shadow of the lifting smoke off our torches built us up even bigger. It was a surprise how good a procession we were, just the three of us, once we took on all that size.

The sight of us almost wrecked a truck. We were going through a field on the Bemeth place, where the corn was still low on account of the drought, when a big two ton job came around a bend in the road below us. The driver must've went rigid. He jammed into a ditch and stayed there while we went singing out of sight. He had plenty to listen to. John's heavy voice went rolling over the country like there was a church leading us, with its windows open. I never heard an organ go any deeper.

Straight down it wouldn't be more than half a mile to

the creek. The way we went though, keeping to the crests, it was three times that distance. The lower we dropped, the more the slopes evened out and the less stretch we got to our shadows. But then we started to hit more hollows, where it was darker and the lights of our torches showed up better through the trees. That gave the procession as good a look as before.

We reached the bridge at Conroy's Bend right on time, just as the sun touched down on the Munkachunks. We tossed our torches into the Musconetty, to show the clouds that's all they had to do to put out the burning and the dried up smell. All it took was a little water. And then came the sacrifice, which was a way of saying please when you ask a favor.

At least years ago, hundreds, this part used to be a real sacrifice. Back then, they'd take the prettiest young girl around, a sort of Miss America who didn't know too much and hadn't dated around a lot yet, and they'd throw her into the water with a stone around her neck. The up-to-date modern way is to throw in the most important man in the procession without a stone so he has a chance to get out.

Onion John elected himself to be the sacrifice because he was a man, at least, without considering who was the most important. Eechee and I agreed. It would be a lot easier for Onion John to come home dripping than either of us.

We fixed up a launching platform with an old plank

we found and a branch we used for a pole. We balanced the two on the rail and John climbed aboard, crosswise, with his hands in his pockets for the smooth roll that'd give him. Eech and I started "Anchors Aweigh" and we lifted. John went barreling down the incline, picking up speed, and he was out beyond the rail hanging over the water, when he howled.

I almost dropped the pole, not knowing what happened. John tried to wriggle back. He got a finger hold on a beam of the bridge and he yelled for us to lean down on our end.

"Why?" yelled Eech.

"He wants to come up on the bridge again."

"He can't walk out on us now." Eech didn't move his plank. "This is the best part."

"He says it's all off," I told Eech. "The whole procession."

John was sorry and he apologized. He forgot his water stone. This was a clear piece of quartz you could almost see through. By rights it should be in his pocket when he got sacrificed. John left it back in his place and there was no time to get it because the sun was half gone. The whole procession was spoiled, he was afraid. It would never work. There was no reason to drop him in the water.

"There sure is," said Eech. "I want to see him splash. I've been waiting for this all day long."

"That's no good reason to dump him. The reason we got to dump him," I explained, "is the radio. After what the forecast says, that ought to balance out the water stone."

"Did it say rain?"

"By tomorrow morning. And he'll feel terrible, when it comes down. If we dump him, now, he can take the credit."

"He sure can. You're right, that's a much better reason."

"Then let's," I said. "Let go."

The plank swung out of Eechee's hand and the pole out of mine. John roared as our launching platform flipped over the rail. The roar ended in a gurgle and in the splash that came up, Eech and I got almost as wet as Onion John. The point of his knitted hat came out of the water and went straight up until John stood with the creek to his middle, staring at us.

"Don't get mad," I asked him. "It really is going to rain."

John shook his head and let out a circle of spray. No it wasn't, he said, the procession was spoiled.

"But look, John!" I had to get him to finish the ceremony some way. "Long as you're in there, can't we see the end. So we'll know what to do the next time."

Next time, John told me, he was going to handle the procession all by himself.

"Then we'll never get a chance to see it all. Can't you show us now?"

With the drip coming off his nose and chin, John shrugged his shoulders as if to say, why not?

This is the way he finished off the procession. He stood

in the creek and he sang his hymn very slow. He took off his outside overcoat and filled it with water. He carried it like a bag over his shoulder and he came back up on the bridge. Eech and I took corners of the coat and we helped him toss the water out to make a big wet splotch across the dusty planks. Then he dropped the coat over the bridge and let it float downstream. The coat going down the river was supposed to be the body, the way it happened in the old days, of the sacrifice. Finally he said a short prayer and with tight fingers he touched his forehead, both shoulders and the exact center of his stomach.

"Amen," he said.

"You're not sore?" I asked him.

He didn't answer. But from the look on his face and the droop of his mustache, he wasn't happy. I hated to think we mightn't be friends anymore. But I was sure he'd see I was right to dump him, next morning when it rained.

He lifted the point of his hat. "Well, good day," he said, each word perfect.

"See you tomorrow," I said.

We watched him start up the hill through the dark that was gathering along the creek bottom. He dripped as he went and sloshed. He swung his sleeves at the bushes along the road, giving them the benefit of how wet he was. He stopped to take off his hat and he wrung it over a small flower.

That was as much water as came out of our procession.

Chapter 6

The next morning turned out dry.

"Eighty-two in the shade," my mother looked around from the sink when I came into the kitchen. "You boys must've slipped up someplace. The sun's a furnace."

"But how can that happen?"

"We used to believe in ants," she said. "Stepping on them. It never worked."

"That's not what I'm talking about!"

"Great day!" My father came through the door. "Where's the umbrellas, Andy? I thought we'd need them this morning."

"So did I."

"Too bad." My father shook his head at all the beautiful sunshine in the backyard. "This is going to be a shock to Onion John."

"You don't know the half of it," I told him. "He's liable not to want to talk to me anymore. The way today turned out."

"Just because it didn't rain?" My father sat down at the table. "Well Andy, anyone who thinks he can turn on a cloud the way you do a faucet, he ought to expect a little disappointment."

"But he didn't think so. That's just it. He forgot his water stone. John was positive it wasn't going to rain. It was the radio. That's what I was counting on. The radio was wrong."

"Was it?" asked my mother.

"Now that I think of it!" My father put down his orange juice. "It was."

"How can that happen?"

"Well, they're only human on the radio." My mother sat down with us.

"Don't they have barometers?"

My father finished his orange juice. "Yes, they have barometers, and hydrographs and isotherms, a lot of those things."

"How come none of them seem to work as well as John's water stone?"

"It's the way you look at it," said my father. "There's a big difference between Onion John and the radio. John thinks he can make it rain. The radio doesn't pretend any such thing. It only predicts when it's going to rain."

"Except it doesn't."

"That's right. They have their instruments and yet, sometimes, they do make a mistake. And they allow for it, for a reasonable margin of error. But with all his water stones and torches," said my father, "Onion John will never get it to rain. It's not an error. It's impossible. The point is, he can't." My father shoved his glass away. "Now finish your orange juice."

In the twelve years I've known my father up until then, and for three days later as well, he was always right. Three days later it rained. It started about five o'clock in the morning, before daybreak, the second day of school. The whole sky turned over like a tipped bucket and down it came in a steady wash until you couldn't see any raindrops through the window or any drip from the trees. Just water, streaming. The house shook with the roar.

Eechee Ries stopped by to pick me up for school. And my father came our way. We went downtown together in our slickers and raincaps and stopped at the bridge on High Street to look at the Niagara foaming over the spillway. The force of the water was frightening, the way it came at you over the falls.

"Look!" said Eech. Out of the foam twisted a cedar tree. It was small and burnt exactly like the torches we carried in the procession. Standing in the rain we watched the burnt stick of cedar go under the bridge.

"Onion John." Eech reached for me and I almost dropped the books I was carrying under my slicker. "He was going to hold a one man procession. Maybe he did It was John, he started this."

I looked at my father, who only smiled. "After all," I told Eech, "it's only a burnt piece of cedar. It could've come from anywhere."

Then, there wasn't any doubt about it. Over the dam it floated, getting lost in the foam and coming clear again to go under the bridge. It was Onion John's coat, the second overcoat he had. Eechee and I stared at each other. We wiped the driving rain off our face. We heard a far off hymn.

It was Onion John coming down Water Street. He didn't have any overcoat on, just an old piece of tarp wrapped around him and dragging on the sidewalk behind. He kept time with one hand, singing away happy as a bull frog.

"Onion John!" yelled Eech. "You did it."

Onion John lost hold of his tarp, waving back at us. He hurried up to where we were and Eech grabbed his hand. "Congratulations!" said Eech.

They shook hands and Onion John turned to me. He had this big smile on his face and I could see he wasn't sore about getting ducked. I didn't know whether to congratulate him for making it rain, my father was so sure he couldn't.

My father was wrong. And he knew it. He showed us he was wrong. He took John's hand and he held his arm. "Congratulations." My father didn't need any more proof. "This is just what we've been waiting for!" He patted the wet tarp on John's shoulder. "You did great."

No one could have appreciated Onion John more than my father. I heard him tell Mr. McSwain that the storm was better for Serenity than money in the bank. It was a shot in the arm, all up and down the valley, for the corn that was so stunted. It brought on a third cutting of hay. It came just in time. And there was just enough, without any floods or washed out roads. Even at the hardware store, my father guessed we'd catch up on the fifteen hundred dollars we were going to lose.

And the total cost of the whole thing was no more than John's two overcoats.

That wasn't any problem, even though right after the storm no funerals came along. John got most of the things he wore out of funerals. He attended them all because he didn't have any family of his own and he liked to take whatever happened, to anybody in Serenity, personally. He was the one who cried the loudest in a cemetery, to make up for not being able to say how he felt. And usually the family gave Onion John any men's clothes that were left over. But that was never the reason he came. John would come to anyone's funeral, no matter what size he was.

When no one died right then, I took care of the overcoats. Through the kids at school. They all knew it was Onion John started the storm, after Ries finished talking. Onion John was the greatest thing ever happened to Serenity, to listen to Ries. And the next greatest, because I understood him, was me. I began to get as much a reputation as George Connors, the star athlete we have, or Bill Berry who's double jointed or Bo Hemmendinger who gets the biggest allowance. So all I had to mention was that my friend Onion John needed overcoats. And they brought half a dozen down to the hardware store, the kids in our class, extra ones they found at home.

John picked an army officer's coat to wear on the outside and a long one with velvet lapels for underneath. They looked awful. But when John saw himself in a strip of sheet aluminum back there in the storeroom, he twirled on his heel. He called himself, a fine prince.

My father came through while he was at it, to pick up

three gallons of white paint. I couldn't understand my father. "Suits you perfect!" he said to Onion John.

"You don't really mean that?" I followed my father back into the store. "He looks all out of shape."

"I know." My father piled the cans on the counter. "But why spoil it for him? He's pleased."

"The way he looks, though!"

"You've got to humor him. He's a lot younger than you are, in many ways, or Dick Ries. And if he gets a kick out of those overcoats, well, it's the same as the pride he took when he thought he made it rain. He really believed it."

"Didn't you?" I watched my father as he went over to the desk to check on the order he was filling. I'd gone along as if my father and I thought the same way, now, about Onion John.

"Didn't I what?" he looked up.

"Is that what you were doing down at the bridge? You were only humoring him?"

"Of course." He straightened up. "Now, Andy! You're not going to tell me that you believed Onion John was the cause of that storm, are you?"

I did not answer my father's question. I said, "Well, it is hard to believe." Which was true enough. But I saw then that the best way to handle any question about Onion John, with my father, was not to talk about it. And it worked out all right, handling it that way, for a while.

Chapter 7

In Serenity, there's a lot goes on for Halloween. Some of it the kids think up for themselves, like almost wrecking things but never so bad that later they can't be fixed. Scribbling an automobile with a wax candle is part of that, and hauling off someone's gate to another part of town, and draping up a tree with a couple of rolls of toilet paper. Then there's prizes the Chamber of Commerce thinks up, for being artistic. You draw pictures with crayon on store windows, barns and witches and cats, and the best one gets five dollars.

The idea of the Chamber of Commerce is to keep everybody so busy coloring windows they won't have the time for any wrecking. But by working hard, the kids around Serenity manage to do both.

In addition to those things, there's four of us who give ourselves a party. We've done it for three years, Ries, Hemmendinger, Bitsy Schwarz and me. Soon as school starts we begin saving two and a half dollars each to chip into the party. It's a good deal for everyone but Hemmendinger, with his allowance. Eech gets it by working down at the drug store, and me with my father, and Bits by running deliveries for the A&P. It's not that we're hogs and we need all that money for food. There's a lot you have to spend for decorations.

That's because where we hold the party is in Hemmendinger's barn, or Schwarz's woodshed, or this year the plan was for our cellar. These are all places we know. And to make them look different takes more money than you'd expect in crepe paper and serpentines, and cardboard pumpkins, ghosts and skeletons. A lot of work goes into it too. We need about a week, getting together after school, to fix a place so it's hard to recognize.

The day before Halloween, the four of us do our shopping for the banquet. It's always the same every year. The main course is Mocha Cake which we have made to order down at Struhlmeyer's. It has to be a pretty big cake to hold all the writing on it, *Good Wishes, Rusch, Schwarz, Hemmendinger, Ries.* Then there's eclairs which are chocolate and vanilla cream puffs. For other courses we have Napoleons and two kinds of ice cream and rice pudding. The rice pudding's mostly for Bo, so we have that first the way you'd start off with soup. On the side, we have two little paper cups at each place, one filled with salted nuts and the other with chocolate creams. To drink we have Kiowa Club Ginger Ale which stings your throat if it goes down fast and makes your nose itch. It gives you the feeling it could be hard liquor you were drinking and that's an excuse for acting drunk if you feel like it.

It's pretty wild once we get going. All of us try to hold off long as we can, admiring the decorations and how nice the table is set. But that never takes too much time, seeing that everyone there worked at getting things ready. And soon as we start eating, that's about all there's left to do. The kind of meal it is, it slides down pretty fast. And we never can eat as much as we thought we could, which is always a surprise year after year. Once we're full, the party's about over except for drinking Kiowa Club and getting drunk and taking swipes at each other and yelling while we pull down the serpentines and crepe paper and the rest of the decorations we put up. The whole affair never lasts more than fifteen or twenty minutes.

It wouldn't be worth it, except for all the talk goes on beforehand during the weeks we save up the money. And afterwards, when we get out to spend the night around town and we tell the others what a swell party we had. Before and after, the party sounds like such a good idea that's why we decide every year to go ahead with it.

This particular Halloween though wasn't going to be the same exactly as the years before. One thing different, I had a date with my father for after the banquet and so did the other three. The Rotarys were putting on a program, which was a father-and-son evening where a magician was going to saw the executive secretary, Mr. Kinnoy, in half.

"I wouldn't want to miss a thing like that," I told my father. "Even if we have to call off the banquet."

"You don't have to. The program doesn't get going until eight-thirty. If you fellows start at seven, the way you plan, you ought to be finished long before then. You can have your party and come over to the club, both."

Along with that difference, the date I had with my father, was the invitation we gave to Onion John. It was Bo's idea.

"He's an expert, isn't he," Bo asked Eech and me, "on spooks and spirits? So if on the Fourth of July you have the mayor to make a speech, and on Armistice Day you have the American Legion and on Christmas you have Santa Claus, how about us having Onion John for Halloween?"

It was great with me, seeing Onion John was my best friend. And it was okay with the others, too, for John to be a guest even though that meant he didn't have to chip in or help decorate. There was always more than enough.

From the moment he walked into the cellar, Onion John changed the whole way we went at our party. Like with the decorations, this was the first time anyone besides ourselves had ever seen how nice we were fixed up. One step through the door, Onion John stopped and put down his burlap bag. He moaned as if he had a cramp. It was only because everything was so elegant. We followed him around

while he examined every pumpkin, witch and skeleton in front and in back. I never saw anyone get so bowled over by three dollars and eighty-seven cents worth of decorations.

We were ready to eat. But first John had to thank us for asking him. We stood at the table and I told the others how John appreciated our invitation with all his heart and soul.

"Especially his soul," I explained. "Because back at the start that's what Halloween was, the Feast of All Souls."

"They had a feast? I never knew they even ate anything, souls?" asked Bo. "How come?"

"Back there at the start," I passed along everything John told me, "there was only two big days in the year. No Washington's Birthday or Labor Day or anything like that. One day was in the spring, around May Day, when they'd let the cows out to pasture to go up into the hills and graze. They'd celebrate that. And then when it got cold and they brought their cows down again, they had Halloween."

"Where do the souls come in?" asked Bo.

"If you bring cows in for the winter to be snug and warm, you'd certainly do the same for your relatives, wouldn't you? And back then, it didn't make any difference whether they were live ones or dead ones. So if you had an uncle who passed away, or an aunt, you didn't leave them out in the wind and the dark where they'd get chilled to the bone. You invited them in to gather around the fire with the rest of the family. That's why, this particular night, they called it the Feast of All Souls."

"And what Bo asked," said Eech. "What do they eat, the souls at the feast?"

"John doesn't know."

Eech couldn't believe there was something John didn't know.

"I do," said Bits. "What they eat is filets."

Eech saw the joke before the rest of us. "Filet of sole." He roared and we joined in. I explained to John how filet of sole was a type of fish and he laughed too. But not for long. There was a danger, he had to warn us about, that came on Halloween.

"Can't we eat now?" asked Bo. "We can hear about that along with our rice pudding."

John held up his hands to keep us from sitting down. With all the traffic there was on Halloween, he told us, everyone holding open house for whatever souls they knew, there were others who tried to sneak in. These would be mean spirits who weren't friendly to anyone, such as hobgoblins, demons, witches and vampires as well as the ghosts of hung murderers. Halloween was the one big chance for such as these to come out of hiding and sidle in where they didn't belong, into the homes of decent people.

Eech figured that's how kids got started wrecking on

Halloween, when it could be blamed on these mean spirits.

"You're probably right." Bo reached for the rice pudding.

"Hold on!" I told Hemmendinger. "Before we eat, John says we ought to ward off any witches and the rest who are around. It's not only they can spoil the feast. They give you boils, distemper and dropsy."

"How long does it take to ward them off?" asked Bo.

It took about fifteen minutes. What we did was to fumigate the cellar. John pulled a load of laurel leaves out of his burlap bag and filled up an old ash barrel we had next to the furnace. Then he sprinkled this with a can of triple blessed oil.

"What's so triple blessed about it?" asked Bo. It was nothing but a rusty quart can of oil, the kind you'd get in a gas station. There were two wads of paper stuck into where the holes were punched. Bo pulled out one of the papers and stuck his finger in. We watched the oil drip back into the can. "Looks to me like plain crankcase oil, and plenty dirty too."

We gathered around while John explained. He whispered how he'd hidden the can of oil for almost a month underneath the pulpit of the Presbyterian Church. That made three Sunday's worth of psalms, prayers and sermons that flowed into it.

"You couldn't get much more blessing packed into one quart of oil," said Eech.

"I guess not." Bo brought a kitchen match out of his pocket. "Can I be the one to light the barrel?"

"With a match?" I stopped Bo because of what Onion John told me. "That's no way. You have to set it off with a piece of living fire."

The way you make living fire, John showed us, is with oak wood. Oak is worse than rat poison for demons. John brought two small slabs of it out of his bag. Also a thin round stick and a small bow, the kind you'd have for a bow and arrow. The thin stick gets looped into the bow and it gets held between the two slabs. And to bring out the living fire, you work the bow back and forth like you were playing a bull fiddle.

Onion John picked Bits and me for this job. Because Bitsy was the first born in his family, being the oldest, and I was the first born in mine, being the only one there was. John turned out the electric bulb we had in the cellar. In the pitch black, he said, "Advance!"

Bits and I held the stick between the two slabs of wood and pulled against each other on the bow. All we got for a while was a wheeze out of the stick as it twirled. Soon a glow began, in the dark, a tiny circle barely red. John started to recite, a bunch of jawbreakers like the words in that hymn he sang. John recited louder and louder as the circle got redder and louder still, when some of the wood shavings scattered around the bottom of the stick sparked up.

He dumped the living fire that sprouted into the leaves in the barrel. On account of the oil, most of what came out was smoke.

It was the smoke we wanted, John explained. Any fiends around were knocked senseless by the smoke. And to make it rougher on them when they dropped, John had us turn all the chairs upside down with their feet sticking in the air. I found a lot of other stuff to mangle them with. We bumped around in the dark and stuck up a rake, an axe, a bag of old golf clubs and a crow bar. For witches, the cellar was worse than a booby trap. By then it was pretty bad on us too, considering the smoke.

"Where's the door?" Bitsy started coughing. "Let me out of here!"

"For heaven's sakes!" It was my mother at the top of the stairs. "What goes on down there? Andy!"

The others headed for the basement door to the outside. I ran upstairs.

"Look at this kitchen," said my mother. It took me a little while, coming out of the dark, before I was able to look. Then I could see the big refrigerator and the stove all white and shining. And of course, a lot of smoke. And my father standing in the dining room door holding on to a magazine.

"Everything under control?" he asked.

"It's only a little fire in a barrel. It's almost out by now. We were fumigating for witches. With Onion John."

"John? Is he with you?"

It wasn't that I tried to keep it any secret from my father, the invitation. It never came up, any reason to mention it.

"I didn't know you ever had any older people," my mother said, "at your banquet."

"It's only Onion John's special," I explained, "when it comes to Halloween. There's a lot of history in what he knows. How Halloween started with souls eating. And why demons go flying around tonight. It's educational."

"And you're sure it's safe down there?" my mother flapped her apron at the smoke.

"For everyone but witches."

"Well look, Andy," my father folded his magazine. "Suppose you hop down there and empty the fire into the furnace. And we'll get going. It's late."

"But we can't. We haven't started to eat yet."

"Why not? It's practically eight o'clock. Don't you want to go to the Rotarys?"

"Sure. Who'd want to miss seeing the executive secretary get sawed in half? Of course I want to go."

"Of course he does!" My mother stopped waving her apron.

"All we got left to do, is eat. It won't take more than a couple of minutes."

"Besides there's the others," my mother told my father. "Herm Ries and Mr. Hemmendinger, they're waiting for their boys too."

"There's a half hour," my father looked at his watch. "That ought to give you enough time. Get going, Andy. I'll wait for you."

"And don't gulp," said my mother. "There's plenty of time to eat properly."

We had the cellar to air out, and the stuff to put away that we stuck up, and the fire to dump into the furnace before we started eating. And when we did sit down at the table, John took out of his second overcoat some big thick plumbers' candles, the kind sell at six for a quarter. Everyone had a lighted candle in front of his plate. As far as making the place hard to recognize the candles turned out better than the decorations. They changed even us. We looked more serious, each of us sitting in the dark behind a little flame.

At last, we started. Bo poured out the ginger ale. Then John stood up and held his glass and rattled away for a couple of minutes.

"He hopes we won't get distemper," I told the others. "And we get through the winter. It's a toast. Everyone has to give a toast."

Bitsy thought a bit and got up. "Melba," he said. "That's a toast." Eech got up and said, "French." I said, "Dry." And Bo said, "Buttered." We drank our ginger ale.

No one got drunk. We went to work on our rice pudding, talking about broomsticks, the kind witches ride.

I always wondered why a witch would ever pick anything so uncomfortable to travel on and John knew why. It wasn't a broom at all, back at the beginning. Only a sheaf of corn stalks, or wheat, or hay. This was the last bunch the farmers cut in the fields and they brought it home to save over the winter. It was called the Corn Mother. And the idea was to keep it through the time when the ground was hard with frost and couldn't grow anything until the spring came and the earth warmed up. Then the farmer would spread the Corn Mother out in the fields to remind the dirt how it grew crops the year before. It was a reminder. And if you didn't have the Corn Mother, if it got lost or stolen, there was a chance the dirt around a farm would forget what it was supposed to do and it would just sit there, flat as a super highway, not growing.

"So the witches would steal the Corn Mother," Bo finished up his rice pudding, "to cross up the farmers?"

John said that was the case. And the farmers would disguise the Corn Mother by putting a stick in it to make it look like a broom, as a way of crossing up the witches. They caught on though, as anyone can see by walking through a five and dime store and looking at all the stuff with witches on it. Everyone of them is riding a broom.

"Seems logical," said Ries. "If they were out to get something only to clean with, you'd see witches riding vacuums."

By then we'd worked our way past Napoleons, cream puffs and eclairs and reached our main course, the Mocha

Cake with the writing on it. John stopped to get his fiddle out of the burlap bag when Bo looked at the wrist watch he wears. "Holy Hannah. It's eight-thirty. My old man's waiting to go to the Rotarys."

"Mine too," said Eech.

"We'd better get out of here," said Bits.

"Without any cake?" Eech put down the eclair he was eating.

"Maybe we can get a couple of more minutes, if it's okay to be a little late." I stood up from the table. "I'll be right back."

The kitchen was dark when I got upstairs. My mother was in the living room having coffee with Eechee's Ma and Mrs. Hemmendinger and Mrs. Kinnoy.

"Your father's at the club," she told me before I had a chance to ask. "He went on ahead with Herman Ries and Mr. Hemmendinger. They're waiting for you there."

"If it's only a couple of more minutes, do you think they'd mind?"

"Pa asked me to give you a message. He says he's leaving this up to your judgment. You can come over whenever you're finished."

"Whenever?" That sounded like a good arrangement.

"Your father says you're welcome any time at all."

"Any time at all," I told the others when I got downstairs. They were relieved to hear there wasn't any rush. Especially when Onion John got started with his fiddle.

He was down at the end of the cellar where it was black except for a square red glow, like a stage, lighted up by the open furnace door. The violin John had was a wreck, patched all over with friction tape. But the sounds that came out were as good as new.

The number John played reminded you a little of "Old McDonald Had a Farm" except it was lowered a couple of notches and came out ten times slower. No one applauded when John finished and he looked at us again.

"What's it mean," Bitsy asked, "a song like that?"

Onion John told us the story of the song. It was about a man floating down a river in a boat who sees someone on shore that looks just like himself. It's as if he were seeing himself in a mirror. He tries to get into shore. But there's no way to manage the boat and it floats downstream. At the end, the one on shore waves and calls out. The man on the boat can't hear. And then he does. What the man on shore yells, in the last line of the song, is "Farewell."

"The story isn't much," said Bits. "But at least, you have to admit that the tune is beautiful."

Onion John had a couple of faster numbers, with more snap to them. There was a dance went with the last one. It was called a Clock Dance and John did it by going around in a circle, stomping heel and toe on the straightaways and scissoring his feet on the curves. He did it twice around, playing the fiddle all the while. None of us could even do it once without tripping.

By then we'd finished eating and the Mocha Cake that was left over spelled out a word. There was 'Hem' from Hemmendinger. 'Arz' from Schwarz. 'Ri' from Ries. And 'Ch' from Rusch. Hemarzrich. It sounded like Onion John's kind of word. But it didn't mean anything in his language either. We decided we'd make it a secret word. To mean—*trouble*. We arranged when anyone of us was in trouble, all he'd have to say was *Hemarzrich.* and the others would have to help.

In my judgment, it was time we got over to the Rotarys. The candles were burning out, anyway, and the brightest part of the cellar was in front where the moonlight came in through the windows.

It was when Onion John saw the moon that the big delay came. It was a perfect moon for making gold, full and near in a wide clean sky. But the miracle was, it came on Halloween! Never in Onion John's life had the two come together, on the same night, before. It meant, with his eyes wide John whispered, that our fortunes were made.

What decided us we had the time to make our fortunes was the sight of Mr. Kinnoy, the executive secretary, walking down the empty street.

"He's whole," said Bits. "They must've called off the program."

We went ahead with Onion John. He had everything he needed for stewing gold in his burlap bag, fern seeds and some sticks of lead, wood alcohol and some special stones,

the kind that philosophers used. By rights, we had to be in clean clothes but I found some sheets on the back line to wrap ourselves in. What with prayers and washing up and hymns and a little meditating, again, there was a lot of preparation before we had a pot filled with the proper ingredients.

John put it into the furnace. He poured wood alcohol in

the pot and a blue flame came out. He began a deep hum and he started to sway. Standing there in front of the furnace door, watching the flame, the four of us picked up his sway.

I heard a whisper. "Andy." It was my mother, far off. I listened and it came again, "Andy."

I swayed backwards a couple of steps and sneaked off without bothering the others. Before I got through the dark to the top of the kitchen stairs, my mother said, "It's after one."

When I came into sight she asked, "Is that my sheet?" She didn't wait for an answer. "This is no time to be playing ghosts!"

"We're not." I came into the kitchen and when I could see again, there was my father standing. "We're making gold."

My father interrupted my mother. "Okay, Andy. Ask him to leave."

"Who? Onion John? We wouldn't know how to go on without him."

"Get that man out of this house!"

"He's run into a miracle. It's the first time it ever happened in all his life."

"I don't care about that, Andy."

"Can't you humor him, just a bit more?"

"Not any more."

By now my eyes were accustomed to the kitchen and I

looked around at everything. The refrigerator broke out with a high hum.

"You just want me to get him out of here?"

"That's all."

"It's my fault we didn't get over to the Rotarys. We went by my judgment."

That didn't make any difference to my father and mother. They stood there looking at me in the sheet. I took it off and I folded it carefully.

"If you'd tell me what you want me to do," I asked my mother, "with the sheet?"

She took it out of my hands.

I went back down into the dark again. "*Hemarzrich,*" I said to the others at the furnace. I never thought I'd get to use the word so soon.

It worked, for a secret word, the way we'd arranged. They put on the light. I told Onion John what he had to do. I figured he'd cry because he never cares who's around. Instead, he rubbed his mustache into shape.

They gave me their sheets, until I had an armful. Onion John picked up his burlap bag and the four of them left. I didn't know where to put the sheets down, not in a dirty cellar. I was lucky to find a laundry basket near the door. I took out the pot that was stewing in the furnace and I dumped it into the ash barrel. Everything, except for Onion John's stones. I picked those out so that I could give them back to Onion John next time I saw him, whenever that'd be.

Chapter 8

Next morning, my father was gone by the time I came down. I brought my lunch over to the hardware store, from school, and I found him with his two fingers pointed at a letter in the typewriter. It was pretty clear my father didn't want me to be friends with Onion John. But how bad, didn't he want me to be friends? Enough, so I shouldn't see Onion John any more? Or enough, I shouldn't even say hello to Onion John if I passed him on the street?

I started to ask but my father shook his head. "Not now, Andy. I'm in the mood to write the Biltgud Electric Company." That's an outfit sold us half a dozen popup toasters that poppedup slow. My father punched Biltgud across his typewriter, then the bell sounded and he swung around in his chair.

"It isn't Onion John worries me. It's us, the way we're behaving. You. We fix up a date and you just let it slide. And me. I go higher than a kite. That's not like us, is it?"

"No," I said. "Usually we get along pretty well."

"That's because any problems we have, somehow or other we settle them. That's what we ought to do here."

"How?"

"I don't know." My father looked at the typewriter and hammered with a finger at one key. "As a start, I'd say we ought to forget last night."

"I'm ready." It was little enough to get us settled, me and my father. "And I guess I ought to use better judgment."

"That's a good idea. If you're not so sure about it, suppose you talk it over with me. Beforehand. And not wait until one o'clock in the morning."

"All right," I promised. "And about Onion John?"

My father swung back to his typewriter. "I want to get this off to Biltgud."

So I didn't know where I stood with Onion John when I saw him heading straight for the hardware store late that afternoon. He came down Water Street right up to the front steps that led to the door. My father was busy with Walt, the clerk, setting up a display for shotgun ammunition. By taking a five-foot slide down the aisle, I managed to reach the door in time. I waved to Onion John and pointed, to get him to go back to the alley we have behind the store. Whatever my father had in mind, I was sure he wouldn't want Onion John in the store anymore than in the house.

I wandered past my father and Walt. Onion John was

going a blue streak by the time I reached him in the alley. For him, Halloween had turned out to be a disaster. It wasn't only the gold had him wrought up. When he got back to Hessian Hill the night before, he found his front door sitting on the roof. It was no more than what you had to expect on Halloween. And John wouldn't have minded, except both hinges were twisted off the door and one hinge was broke in half. He'd actually come to buy a pair of hinges, our biggest and strongest.

"Couldn't you find any out on the garbage dump?" I asked him.

John flopped his hands against his overcoat. He'd put in hours on the dump and the nearest he found to hinges, he said, was an old washing machine. I couldn't see where that even came close to what he needed.

"You wait right here," I told him. Luckily, the hinges were behind the front counter on the other side from where my father was with Walt. I meandered in and picked up a pair of six-inch, barn door strap hinges. I didn't hide the hinges, especially, except I held them against my side with my arm.

They were just what John had in mind.

"They'll last you a lifetime. Zinc plated steel. The best we have. Only eighty-four cents a pair."

John took another look at the hinges and judged they were worth twenty-seven cents. I said okay. I thought I'd chip in the rest out of my wages to make up, something anyway, for the fortune he'd lost the night before. John looked up from the hinges but the smile he had went over my head. "Well, good day," he pulled up the point of his hat as if he were leaving.

"Good day," came from behind me. My father stood with his arms crossed, holding on to his elbows, looking at us.

"John didn't come here for a friend," I showed him the hinges. "He's a customer."

"Then why didn't he come into the store?"

"I just didn't think that was any way to solve our problem, the way you feel about Onion John."

"But this way, Andy? This is no way! Hiding out in an alley."

Onion John had his purse unsnapped and was ladling out nickels and dimes. I acted business like, counting the change he put in my hand. "Twenty, twenty-five, twenty-six, twenty-seven." I gave my father the money. "That's on account. The rest is what I owe. On account of the gold we spoiled last night. I figured he ought to get a bargain."

I gave John the hinges. "I hope you find these satisfactory. If you don't, you can return them to Rusch's Hardware Store anytime at all and get a refund."

John thanked me, bobbing his head at my father, and he turned to hurry down the alley.

"Onion John!" my father yelled. John stopped and my father went after him. "Look here a second, will you. About last night, about the gold, about me stopping you. Don't get that wrong. It's not that I don't like you, John. It's only this whole business of making gold, well, I'm against it. It's wrong." My father looked around the alley to think how to explain it. "It could lead to inflation."

John turned to me to tell him what inflation was. I couldn't. My father showed us how if everybody started making gold, then it wouldn't be worth so much. And you'd have to pay more and more for the things you wanted.

"Those twenty-seven cent hinges," my father pointed at them in John's hand, "could go up to forty or fifty dollars with inflation."

John was amazed. He confessed to me he had never thought there was any danger in making gold. And for that matter, neither had I.

"He sees what you mean," I told my father. "Next when it comes time to make gold, he won't try to make so much."

"I'm glad we understand each other," said my father. "There's nothing personal to it, John. It's just a question of economics. Personally, I like you. I think you're a fine man."

John smiled because he was always proud to hear when anyone liked him. "He likes you too," I translated to my father. "He thinks you're a fine man."

My father nodded to thank John. The two of them had fine smiles.

"It certainly seems you two like each other," I said.

"Of course. Why shouldn't we?"

"Then why is it you can't get to be friends?"

"I guess you and I don't have too much in common, do we, John?" My father laughed. Until he looked at me. It turned into a surprised look, as if I'd just come into the alley. "Except one thing, of course. Andy. He seems to understand us both pretty well."

"If you were," I pointed out to my father, "friends that is, it would certainly help solve our problem."

My father nodded to me and then to John. "There's no reason why you shouldn't think of me as your friend, John. I wish you would. If there's anything I can do, I'd be glad to help. I'm not much at making it rain but if there's anything else, let me know."

John said there wasn't any help he needed. "But he's glad you want to be friends with him. And the next time you're up on Hessian Hill he asks you to drop by his place for a visit." I never imagined they'd get along this well. "Once he gets his door fixed, in a day or two."

"What's wrong with his door?"

I told my father the trouble John had for Halloween. "But these hinges, they're not meant for any house door." My father shook his head. "You'd use this kind of hardware on a barn, a whopping big barn door. Come on, John. I'll show you what you need." He started down the alley and then he slowed to turn around. "Or better yet. It's practically closing time. What say we let Walt close up? And us three, we take a run out to Hessian Hill right now. How about that, John? Let's go see what you really need up there."

I'd have called anyone crazy if they tried to tell me that morning I'd end up riding out to Hessian Hill with Onion John and my father in the same car. All the weeks I'd put in trying to keep the two of them apart, I could see that was wrong. What was more natural, if there's trouble between your best friend and your father, than to get them together?

John dusted off his best chair, a rocker with its runners off. But my father didn't sit down, he was so interested in seeing the inside of John's house. He stood in the middle of the room and he didn't move. Except for his head. This went around as far as it could go, then the rest of my father turned to see what was left.

John had built over an old foundation where somebody's house, long ago, burned down. He built of rock cemented together with clay and straw mixed. He kept it whitewashed outside so it looked nice.

Inside he had a complete wooden floor except for one corner where there was a hole. This was so he could throw cans down into the basement and anything else he couldn't burn that might turn out to be useful later.

"I think this is the first house I've ever seen," said my father, "without wall to wall flooring."

For furniture, John had a strong iron bed on which he

kept all his clothes. Sometimes, this piled up according to the number of funerals going on and made a good thick blanket to sleep under. He also had a beautiful table made of shiny mahogany with three legs and a barrel to hold up the fourth corner. There were four chairs, all whole. And a stove that didn't look very good but the way it burnt kept the place as warm as the Fourth of July.

But most of the room in his house, and there was only one room, was taken up by bathtubs. There were four white bathtubs side by side. John got them from the dump and it seemed a mystery to him why anyone would ever want to throw away a bathtub. First because they were beautiful and second because they were useful. For storing things. For bathing, John used a bucket. In one bathtub, John kept beets and cabbages. The other was mostly for onions and some potatoes. The third he filled with the dust he got from sweeping out churches.

"He actually brings dust in?" asked my father. "In here?"

I had to explain the dust wasn't for use inside. John spread it over his vegetable garden. The church dust was blessed, same as the oil he had, and it was as fine for his vegetables as any fertilizer.

The fourth bathtub was for newspapers. John used a lot of newspapers, not to read of course but to start fires with and to eat off. For these purposes, he collected the Serenity *Lamp* and the daily paper from down the river, *The Easton*

Globe. But for papering the walls, which he did every year, John used only *The New York Times.* Judge Brandstetter who subscribed to the *Times* told John it was the best newspaper. And John liked to use the best there was when he could get it. It made a nice quiet wallpaper without any murders, so far as you could read, or robberies.

There were only two decorations on the wall. One was John's patched up violin. And the other was a picture, painted red and gold on wood, so faded you had to come close to make out it was an old gentleman wearing a beard and a crown. This was *Saint Stepan.* He hailed from the same place as where John was born. The upkeep on *Stepan* was the biggest household expense John had. There was a candle lighted in front of him, night and day. And even though John burnt the candle in a glass and shoved a wick through the drippings, so they'd burn over again, the light bill on *Stepan* ran high.

"Who'd ever think there was any place like this in Serenity?" said my father. "But how about that door? I guess that's the only thing concerns us. Let's have a look at it."

John brought out his new hinges. And he waited while my father squatted to look over the door jamb.

"No sir. Those hinges won't do." My father stood up. "No hinges will do. This jamb here is split and it's rotted. There's nothing to screw on to. And even a new jamb," he examined the stone work around the door, "won't work. There's no studding here to fasten against. And if there

were, the wall's shot. The cement work, or the clay whatever it is, the whole wall's crumbling."

John said he had a lot of good red clay around, and straw, to fix it up.

"It's not worth it. Not with this kind of field stone. You'd have to start from the ground up, collecting stone." He turned to us shaking his head. "What you need, John, isn't just a pair of hinges. What you need is a whole new house."

Everyone needs a new house, John shrugged. "But as long as that's impossible," I told my father, "he wants you to explain what kind of hinges will work."

My father wasn't listening to me. He stepped backwards, to the outside of the house, and he looked the place over. "What Onion John needs," he said it all over again to himself, "is a new house."

"Yes," I repeated. "But as long as that's impossible—."

"It's not impossible." My father had a very quiet smile as he left me and Onion John. "Not at all impossible."

He walked slowly around the house. When he showed up at the corner again he stopped long enough to pick, with his forefinger, at the mortar between the stones. Then he came back to where we stood.

"Onion John," my father looked very happy. "I think you're about due for a complete change."

"How do you mean?"

"I think we ought to rebuild Onion John from the ground up."

Onion John and I stared at each other. My father talked like a magician.

"The first thing we're going to do is build Onion John a new house."

"Us three?"

My father laughed. "The Rotary Club. Ever since last summer we've been looking for a project. Since we put the raft off the beach down in the river. This is it! We'll build John a new house. The Rotary Club will."

"Would they ever do it?"

"There's a good chance they will. Onion John's been around an awful long time. Everybody likes him, the way he's taken care of himself all these years. And I think the time's come when the town ought to do something to help him. This is the project we've been looking for. I think they'll go for it. I really think every one of them will go for it."

John took me by the arm to ask if I wouldn't please explain.

"My father thinks you'd make a great project. For the people in the town. So you could have a new house up here."

Onion John said he didn't want anyone to go out of their way to fix his house.

"Not fix," said my father. "Brand new. You'll live like the rest of us. With heating and electricity, a refrigerator and running water and a new bathtub."

John raised his hands for my father to stop. A new house, he asked me, with another bathtub?

"And this one's going to be brand new," I told him. "Nothing off the dump."

John's eyes went wide. The new bathtub was what got him! My father and I stood there, in the growing dark, watching to see whether he'd laugh or cry. There's no telling, when he's happy, what he'll do. He started out with laughing. But then his eyes watered up and he cried too. He switched back and forth between one and the other and at the end his face was full of tears and teeth, both. He took my father by the shoulders and then threw a bear hug around him.

"He certainly thanks you."

"It's not me," my father laughed. "It's the club. They're going to have to vote on it first."

"But you're pretty sure, aren't you, they'll do it?"

"I'm almost positive!"

I couldn't hold back any longer. I knew the word now and I let it go. "Mayaglubpany!" John let go of my father and joined in. "Mayaglubpany!"

"What's that?"

"Friend."

My father tried the word a couple of times until he got it straight. And the three of us yelled together, like it was a high school cheer, "Mayaglubpany!" We finished out of breath. Then my father fixed up John's door, for the time being, and we left John standing out in front of his house, a shadow in the open door that was lighted by *Saint Stepan's* candle, waving at us.

"This might even be as much fun as making it rain," said my father. "What do you think, Andy?"

"I never imagined this." I watched the headlights stretching down the hill. "A thing like this! How'd you ever get the idea of building John a new house?"

"Well, for one thing, he needs it. That's sure." My father shifted into second to take care of the steep grade down Hessian Hill. "And another thing, Andy, to be honest about it, was you."

"Me?"

My father nodded. "If we're going to be friends with Onion John, there's only two ways to go about it. Either you go back with him into the fourteenth century some place. And you learn how to fight dragons."

"Who does any of that?"

"Or fumigate for witches, the same thing. On the other hand, we can bring John up, to where we live today. I just thought that would be more practical for John. And you too. And everyone concerned. It doesn't seem likely we'll ever run into a dragon."

"I guess not." I laughed. "And better than practical it's wonderful. The way it works out, you and John and the new house, all together. If it works out that way."

"It will," said my father. "I think it will."

Chapter 9

And my father was right. He passed along the suggestion about Onion John at the next lunch meeting there was of the Rotary Club. There's one every Friday. Before the Rotarys got through their main plate, which was creamed tuna on toast that Friday, a good many were talking about Onion John. Most of the talk was comparing Onion John with the raft they put out on the river. Most thought the house was just as good an idea, except it would cost a lot more.

Then they got around to how everybody would chip into the project from their different businesses, lumber and wiring and piping, and charge it off as an advertisement. That was one way to bring the cost down.

And another was the notion of everybody working on the house instead of hiring labor. For the whole club, all the members, to do the carpentering and the bricklaying and to build the place themselves. Not only would that help with the cost, it was early American. Back in history that was the way they had of putting up houses and barns. Every one pitched in for all of one day, back then, and they called it a building bee.

By the time the Rotarys got to dessert, which was slices of vanilla ice cream and strawberry sauce, there were a lot who thought this old-fashioned way was a good scheme even though the house itself would be up-to-date. At least it made the budget small enough so you could talk about it.

After lunch there's a business meeting where they smoke cigars. Before they got very far into it there was already a majority in favor of building Onion John a new house. And after my father and a couple of others got through reminding the rest how much John was liked around Serenity, and how well John took care of himself for so many years, everyone agreed it would be a fine project to build him a proper place to live.

Except for a while, Ernie Miller, the editor of the *Lamp*. Ernie thought that Onion John, so far as anyone could see, was pretty happy as he was. And besides Ernie wanted to know how would Onion John support a new house on thirty-five cents an hour to pay for electric bills and oil for heating and general upkeep. The new house would mean a different way of going at things, for Onion John, and Ernie didn't know how good that was.

There was a discussion to straighten Ernie out, and a resolution. All those Onion John worked for promised to pay him a dollar an hour, whether John wanted it or not, because no one can take any less except if he breaks the law.

After that, Ernie joined in and there was a unanimous vote to build John his new house. There were cheers when the meeting broke up. This was not for Onion John. Every week when there's a motion to adjourn the Rotarys cheer.

I knew all about the meeting even though, of course, I wasn't there. I heard a good deal from my father. And then I heard it all over again, with a lot more added, just by sitting back. Everyone knew I was Onion John's best friend. And the whole school wanted to talk to me about the things they'd heard at home. I listened to the same things again and again. I didn't want anyone to get the impression I was snooting him, just because I happened to be such a close friend of John's. Or because my father happened to be Andrew J. Rusch. So I let them go ahead.

"I heard your father was great," said Ries. "He said Onion John's a permanent part of Serenity. As much a part of the town as the bridge on High Street or the paving. We take care of one, your Pop said. Let's take care of the other."

"Is that what he said?" I'd ask.

Even Connors. Ordinarily with George Connors, if it's something you can't throw like a football, or you can't jump like an ashcan, or you can't race against, he acts like it's not very important.

"But when your father talked of the Umbangis," said

George, "how we send billions of dollars all over the world trying to civilize the Umbangis and natives like that! I thought it was pretty good when he said we ought to do the same for Onion John right here in our own backyard."

"Well!" I'd say.

But the real reason they were all excited was not so much what anyone said. It was how the idea opened up and spread. The Rotarys gave the project a name, Onion John Day. And as the news got around, a lot more than the Rotarys joined in. The ladies auxiliary and different women's clubs figured on putting up a canopy for breakfast and lunch and digging a barbecue pit for supper to keep the crowd fed. And then the High School band came in on Onion John Day to furnish music for everyone's morale while they were working. And then the ambulance corps in case of accidents, and then the other men's clubs, until practically everyone in Serenity was lending a hand.

It looked like Onion John Day was going to be as big as anything we'd had in town since the Seventh National Guard came back from Korea, when most of us were too young to get any fun out of it. The best part of way back then, so far as anyone recalled, was the free eats out in the courthouse square. On Onion John Day we were all piling in to do something, not just eat hot dogs. The seventh and eighth grades, for instance, it was us they were leaving Onion John's old house up to. We were going to tear it down. We were organized into the Demolition Committee and a lot of comparing went on, between us, about the best ways of wrecking a house.

The whole of Serenity was organized. Ordinarily what you belonged to in town was your own family, or the class you were in, or the farm you ran or the store. During those weeks what you belonged to, if anyone asked, was a committee. Even the third grade, they belonged to the Debris Committee. That meant, during Onion John Day, they'd go around picking up nails and bits of lumber and strips of shingle that fell off the roof and they'd keep it all sorted out and in piles.

There was a committee for Trucking, for Tool Repair and Supply, and a Coffee Break Committee and Solicitation, which was where if something was needed, an extra tractor or chairs for the band to sit on, you went out and asked. Eechee was on Solicitation. There was a Press and Publicity Committee that Ed Maibee asked to get on because of the liking he had for envelopes, the taste of them. Press and Publicity sent out a lot of envelopes. There were always meetings to be announced and there were items had to be sent to the newspapers. There were even a couple of writeups came from Press and Publicity that were printed in the daily paper down in Easton, *The Globe*, how Serenity was getting together to put up a house in one day.

My father was on the Executive Committee. He was the Chairman. Onion John wasn't on any committee. It was a little lonely for him.

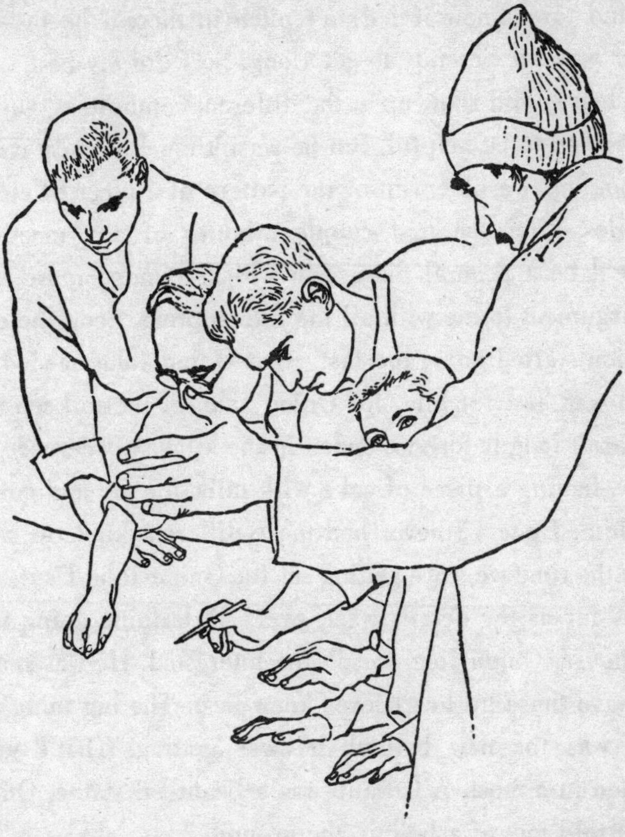

I saw a lot of Onion John, myself, on business. If the Architectural Committee wanted him to look at a blueprint, or Curtains and Slipcovers wanted him to look at yard goods, naturally I had to go along. There was no other decent way of talking to Onion John, except through me. It took up a lot of my time. Not that I minded, handling a job that important. The truth is, everyone at school and most around town knew if I didn't pitch in there'd be just no other way for Serenity to get along. So I did my best.

When he did show up at the different committees, Onion John tried to be helpful. But he wasn't much when it came to looking at a blueprint or the pattern of a piece of cloth. Besides, after the first couple minutes of any meeting, there'd be a general discussion which sounded more like an argument to me with all the interrupting. Soon the discussion started going too fast, what Onion John needed or what was best for him, for Onion John or me to keep up. It wasn't long before we ended in the kitchen, wherever we were, having a piece of cake with milk for me and coffee for him. I guess I never had more different kinds of cake than the time we were getting set for Onion John Day.

As far as the details went, every little thing going into the house, Onion John wasn't too interested. He was ready to leave those up to whoever knew best. The big thing for him was the new bathtub he was getting. That's what tickled him most. A bathtub was a beautiful statue, Onion John told me, of a hole in the ground.

It almost ruined Onion John Day, the bathtub did, and even the friendship there was between Onion John and my father. We went up to Hessian Hill two days before the Sunday when the big day was going to be to check the plans for wiring the new stove. My father went to measure and I went along.

When we got up to John's place, there was an axe working in the woods behind his garden and that was John. We yelled and let him have the auto horn a couple of times and went into his house. It was warm inside, and dark and dry with a comfortable smell because of all the vegetables John had stored. With the day so wet, rain until mid-afternoon and now so overcast and cold, it was a good place to come into. We waited for John, in the shadows. The only light came from *Saint Stepan* and from a couple of cracks in the stove where the fire popped. We stood with our back to the stove, rubbing, to get rid of the chill we'd collected.

John came in with an armful of wood, laughing as if he'd just heard a good joke from somebody outside. But it was just because we were there. He dropped the wood and lit up a kerosene lamp and put a pot of water on to boil. He told us how nice it was we came to visit because he knew we were so busy with Onion John Day.

My father rolled out a set of blueprints and went down to his knees to go to work with a tape measure. I told John what was up, how my father had to check the electric wiring for the stove. John laughed as if this were even a bigger joke than the one he might've heard outside.

"Frolka?" That's what John called his wood stove. The name it had, lettered on the oven, was Frolic. John thought it was crazy putting wires into Frolic. All it needed was wood.

My father looked up at him with a smile. "You're not going to have to live with Frolic anymore. All that's over with, John. Schwarz is getting you a GL 124, the latest there is."

John was confused. He looked at me. I described how he could get rid of the old stove now that he was getting a brand new white shiny model, all electric.

"Frolka!" John hurried over and helped my father, practically lifting him to his feet. He set my father down in one chair and me in another. He hardly finished a word he spoke, fast as he went. It was hard to follow.

But one thing was clear. John wasn't going to get rid of any Frolic. He'd had the stove for eighteen years. It was more an old friend than just an appliance. It had a special way of cooking food, especially *pradzhnik*. And besides it heated the place. And besides he knew how to work it.

My father talked very patiently. How much cleaner a new stove was and how much easier, with no wood to chop. How the place would be heated with oil. About electricity, and how easy it was to work with nothing but a switch.

John shook his head, on and on, until my father said, "Think of Mr. Schwarz. It'll be a blow to him. He's proud of giving you that stove. How do you think he'll feel if you let everyone else in on this. And Mr. Schwarz, you take his stove and hand it back to him. He'll feel you have something against him."

He'll be sad? John asked me.

"Very sad," said my father.

John went over and looked at Frolic. He warmed his

hands over the top of it. Finally his shoulders lifted. All right, he turned back to us, he didn't want to make Mr. Schwarz sad. We could tell him he could bring his new stove and put it where the old one was.

"It can't go exactly there." My father rolled out the blueprints again. "Not without shifting the whole electrical circuit. The stove'll have to go closer to the wall." He pointed to how things were going to be. "That'll change the bathroom slightly. But even so, relocating the bathroom is a lot less trouble."

John wanted to know about the bathroom. My father explained how this was a small separate room with white plastic tile on the walls. John listened very carefully. Then he asked my father a favor, not to make any separate room for the new bathtub. The couple of times a month he'd be alone in the tub, it was a shame to hide it away in a little room by itself.

"He wants it out here." I hadn't realized, myself, what Onion John had in mind. "With the other four bathtubs."

"The other four what?"

"He thinks it'd be nice to have the five bathtubs right out here, all in a row."

"No, Andy. I don't think you or Onion John understands." My father worked the blueprints back into a tube. He slapped them against his hand. "Please tell Onion John that the whole idea is to build him a regular, respectable house. There can't be any four bathtubs in the living room.

Or five! Just one, tucked away in its own small room where maybe he'll enjoy using it more than once or twice a month." My father raised a finger. "Explain there's only going to be one bathtub in this house."

"The way his heart seems to be set on five," I said, "I don't think he's going to like it."

"Andy! Onion John, please take a look." My father spread the blueprints out on the table and pointed where there was going to be a sofa and a coffee table and an overstuffed chair and a floor lamp. Together with a table for eating off and a kitchen arrangement at one end of the room, the place was pretty well taken up.

I had Onion John right, though. He didn't like it.

"He says he don't need a special table for drinking coffee, or those other things. He'd just as soon have the bathtubs."

"John!" My father spoke word by word and loud. "It's not proper, or right, or civilized."

I listened to Onion John and got back to my father. "All he wants to know is, who'll it make unhappy. Anybody?"

"That's not the point. We're trying to get him to live normal and comfortable. Can't you get him to see that?"

I gave my father the last of what John said. "Long as it doesn't make anybody unhappy, he'd just as soon go and have the five of them out here in a row. And be happy himself."

"Great heavens." My father turned to look through the

window at the gray outside. "Who ever thought of this!"

John's back was turned to me, too. He warmed his hands at the stove.

I stood in the middle. It couldn't end here, my father and Onion John being friends. I sided with my father. After all, Onion John couldn't have a better friend, all my father was doing. And I sided with John. After all, long as no one else was sad why couldn't he be happy? There had to be some way to handle this.

"How about it?" I asked my father.

"Never mind." He watched the mist that was coming up outside. "Let me think."

"Onion John?"

He let out a word that turned six corners and doubled back on itself to end, the way it sounded, as if he spit. He didn't turn around.

I waited. I looked at what was in front of me. It was a story in *The New York Times* that started WAR CLOUDS GATHER IN INDONESIA. I looked to see what the war was about. A gobble came up outside, not so far away, like the call of a turkey.

"That!" I said. "You know what? I think that's an English bird."

Pheasant, John turned.

"Cock pheasant." My father looked at both of us. "Close by!"

We heard another gobble. Without a word, my father

dashed out the door. By the time John had his gun from behind the stove my father was back with the twelve gauge over-and-under shotgun he carries in the trunk of his car all season. In his other hand he had a pair of rubber-footed hunting boots.

No one said anything about the argument. My father changed into his boots. John rummaged underneath his bed. He came out with a long beautiful feather, green, red and white, the tail feather off a cock bird. He ran it into both barrels of my father's shotgun.

"What're you doing?" asked my father.

"Makes your gun shoot straighter, John says, the tail off a bird from the year before."

John opened the fire door of the stove and tossed the feather in.

"Isn't he going to use it on his own gun?"

John explained you could use only one feather for one gun. He didn't have any others. "Well, thank you," said my father, "for giving me the break, whatever good it is."

Outside it had turned sharper, the cold, and a real fog had climbed over Hessian Hill. John led us beyond the rise of the hill and we dropped toward the swamp below. We spread out. My father and Onion John kept pace with each other, about fifteen yards of brush between them. I went on a little ahead, with the idea if I kicked up anything they'd have plenty of time for a shot, bird-dogging it.

We worked our way very slowly down the side of the

hill, the three of us in a triangle. Every few steps we pulled up to listen for the cock again. The cover was very low and in the fog rolling past all you could see was my father and John and me. We were the only things black and solid. Besides us, there was only gray winding into white here and there and then fading out.

We started quietly into the swamp. No one spoke. There wasn't anything to talk about, here. The gobble sounded again, off to our left. My father waved for me to go in, the two of them holding their elbows out, loose. I changed direction, feeling out each step in the boggy ground. There was a whirring blast stopped me, startled, even though every second I'd been expecting a bird to break cover.

"Yours, John!" my father yelled. "Take it!"

The bird rose, past the sound of the shot that came from Onion John. It glided into the lighter gray above. There was another shot, my father. The bird pulled up as if it just remembered something it left behind, in the brush below. It came down scrambling, the way you start downstairs two steps at a time and then you go out of control.

"Gosh!" yelled my father. "Wasn't that beautiful?" he asked me as they came up. We were on our way to where the bird dropped. I was just about to answer when it came, another exploding whirr. The bird rose out of nowhere and headed straight for us.

"John!" yelled my father.

There was hardly time to swing a gun. John was wide.

And low, with the bird practically overhead. My father cracked me with his elbow as he turned. He shot. I didn't mind the quick hurt in my cheek. I watched the bird. It started to fight for a hold up above, reaching with its wings for fog to hang on to, and missing. The pheasant fought its way down and disappeared.

"Andy!" My father was on his knees in front of me. "Did I hurt you?"

"No. It's okay."

He watched for a couple of seconds waiting to see if I was going to let go. I never felt less like crying. Not with the three of us, after how it was up at the house, having such a good time.

On his knees still, my father looked up into the sky. "That was it!" he said. "That was absolutely it. I never thought I'd ever get a shot like that."

John kept saying, again and again, like a prayer, a long slow word full of *s*'s.

The two of them went on repeating themselves. We collected the birds and started back for John's. "I practically took that shot off my hip. Right off here." He showed us. "I didn't think it could be done. You don't suppose—" Whatever his thought was, it ended in a laugh. "You don't suppose," he started over again, to John, "your tail feather had anything to do with it."

John was absolutely positive. It was exactly how the tail feather was supposed to work.

"Well," said my father, "I don't know."

When we got back to the house, with the two pheasants turned bright as rainbows under the light at the table, my father said it again. "I don't know. It sounds weird to me but if that's what you think, we'll leave it up to you."

It turned out he was talking about the bathtubs. "We won't close in your new bathroom, John. We'll put it over in the corner, behind a screen. Whenever you want to have it out in the living room, you can take the screen away."

That sounded fine to John. And the other four bathtubs?

"Well, we're going to redo the cellar downstairs. It's almost going to be another room. Suppose we put the other four bathtubs down in the basement where you can go and admire them, whenever you feel like it."

John thought for a second and then he agreed. It sounded like a fair arrangement. He and my father each took a pheasant and they shook hands. John came with us to the car and he watched us take off.

After a while, my father stopped thinking. "No," he hit the steering wheel, "there's just no sense to it!" I didn't know whether he was talking about the tail off the pheasant or the bathtubs. But by then, it didn't make too much difference. We weren't broken up, the three of us, and Onion John Day was still coming up, only two days away.

Chapter 10

You gotta get up.

You gotta get up.

You gotta get up, this morning."

It was still dark at five-thirty of Onion John Day when the massed bugles blew from the courthouse tower. This was the opening event, Reveille. Anyone who could play a trumpet or a bugle, from the High School Band or the Veterans', collected at the courthouse to wake the town up.

I lay in bed and listened, to the end. There wasn't one wrong note. It sounded real professional, the opening event.

Except halfway through pulling my pajama top over my head, they started up again. I hadn't seen on the program where there were going to be any encores. I figured this one was a blast for the extra heavy sleepers.

But when they blew again for the third time, there didn't seem any sense to it. It came just as I got the cap off the toothpaste. By then, for sure, everybody in town was on their feet.

That was the end of Reveille. But a single trumpet, sweet and slow, came through when I was brushing my hair. It was "Home On The Range." It was Ben Wolf, from the sound of it, the number he always played at band concerts.

What happened was thirteen horn players showed up. No more than four could crowd into the tower. They played in shifts. Three times four is twelve and the one left over was Ben Wolf. So they let him play any solo he wanted. It was useless to keep grinding out Reveille over and over.

I had to make the first car out. It left High and Water Street, according to the time table in the printed program, at 5:52 AM.

Everything on the time table was for odd minutes like that, 1:03 or 10:28. It was Mr. Donahue, his notion. The good of it was no one'd keep track of the odd minutes, he thought. And they'd get where they were supposed to be ahead of time. At 1:00 instead of 1:03. Or at 10:25 instead of 10:28. That way the schedule wouldn't get all fouled up with people straggling around. Besides it sounded better organized, like we were running a railroad.

I left the house at 5:43. The dark was slacking off now. The sun was scheduled to rise in just an hour, at 6:44. A lot of the houses along the street had lights on. Past the bright windows, through the quiet, I half ran the four blocks downtown. You could feel the hurry there was, in the still morning, everybody tearing toast and gulping coffee and wading into cornflakes.

John's place was a lighted square, from the road, his window. When we opened the door the only thing on was the candle for *Saint Stepan.* He was in front of the candle, kneeling with his head down. We waited at the door and watched the shape of Onion John as he said his prayers. He crossed himself. He came to his feet and he blew out the candle. It was the first time I ever saw Onion John's house black, with no flame where *Stepan* was.

A match struck and the lamp over the table lit up the house. And the man who stood there turning down the wick so it wouldn't smoke, he was a surprise.

Onion John was wearing only one overcoat, the underneath one with the velvet lapels. And instead of heavy sneakers he had on a pair of patent leather shoes, a little pointed, that used to belong to Grandpa McSwain who died at the age of eighty-four. And the hat he put on, now his prayers were over, was a fedora practically brand new. The fedora was creased exactly right, the way you'd expect.

But when he talked, Onion John sounded the same as always. He told us how good we all looked. He got out chairs for us to sit down and visit.

"Visit?" Mr. Kinnoy looked at his watch. "It's 6:03. We're the Committee on Personal Arrangements, John, and we're two minutes late as it is."

Late, John wanted to know, for what?

"For the schedule," said Mr. Kinnoy.

John apologized he kept us waiting. He took longer than

usual with *Saint Stepan* for all the things he had to be thankful about. John used another minute, explaining, before Mr. Kinnoy interrupted.

"We're due out of here at 6:22." The Committee on Personal Arrangements, he explained, had to empty the place of all John's things. "But your valuables, John, I wish you'd take care of them yourself. You can stow them in my station wagon."

John nodded. He looked around and picked up an old iron skillet off the table and tried to make up his mind whether it was valuable.

"Please!" said Mr. Kinnoy. "Just what's important."

John nodded. From the wall, he took his old fiddle. And his shotgun from behind the stove. From under the bed he came up with an old shiny spade that had its fifth handle, he once told me, fitted into it. He put this stuff on the table and on top, the picture of *Saint Stepan.* Then a prayer book. It was the only book he had. But today he had another one, the printed program of Onion John Day. It was the size of a small magazine with a green cover that had a drawing, without too much resemblance to it, of Onion John. Inside, there was mostly advertisements. But John couldn't read anyway, neither the program nor the prayer book. So the inside wasn't very important. That finished the pile of what was valuable. I helped John carry it all out to Mr. Kinnoy's wagon. In the little light spreading outside he asked me what a schedule was.

"Look," I pointed.

There was a far off rumble. And over the hill came a glare that spread through the sky until suddenly it narrowed down to a long beam of headlights. Right after, came another pair of headlights shooting high in the air. They leveled off as the top of the hill was reached. They were the first trucks from Burke's Lumber Yard, a couple of big two-ton trailers. Behind them came a smaller panel truck, from Struhlmeyer's bakery. Then a sedan, smaller still. This would be Mrs. Ries and a car full of ladies, including my Ma. They and the bakery truck were in Food and Refreshments, breakfast division. In the still morning, all you could hear was the roar of the convoy.

"That's a schedule," I told John. "They're right on time. It's the most important thing happens today. Everyone keeping up to schedule."

Now we had a moment to visit, I started to ask him why he was wearing such a new kind of outfit. John left me. He hurried into the house. Before I even reached the door, he was out again with the rocker in his arms, the one without any runners. He went out of sight around a corner.

Inside, Personal Arrangements was in full swing, taking the bed apart, emptying the bathtubs, moving out the table. I gave a hand with the table, tipped over on its side so it could be jockeyed through the door, when John came back. He put his shoulder to the corner George Connors was holding, and shoved.

"That does it!" said George. "We're wedged."

Mr. Kinnoy looked around from the bed where he was working. Mostly to get John out of the way, I imagine, he said, "How about those things on the stove, John. Will you handle them?"

John was done with the stove by the time we got the table unstuck. He swept the pots off the top into a burlap bag and pulled pans out of the oven until the clatter filled the house. Because we blocked the door, he threw the bag out the window. He was back with us at the table just as we were starting to move. He leaned into it and we were wedged tighter than before.

"You know what I think?" Mr. Kinnoy held on to the headboard of the bed and glanced out the window. "With all those cars starting to come in, John, you ought to go out there and show them where to park."

There was a good deal of traffic, from the noise. John agreed. He had to crawl underneath the table to get out of the house. And we had the place just about empty, the chairs and a cupboard, his clothes and the bathtubs, we had the stovepipe down and we were just starting to move Frolic when we heard a crash. It was someone's fender, sure, got collapsed.

In a second, John stood at the door again. Mr. Hemmendinger who was in charge of Parking and Traffic thought it best if he came back to check if the house was cleaned out right. John wanted to help with the stove. But

Mr. Kinnoy shook his head to show that we had it under control. John looked around the room, bare now with only some sticks of firewood left in the corner. He watched us carry Frolic out the door.

"6:29," said my father. You could hear him a quarter of a mile around. He'd come up in the loud-speaker truck of Berry's Television and Radio Repair. That was going to be my father's job all day, keeping the schedule going over the loud-speaker. "The house is clear for salvage," he said. Anything useful, like doors and windows, had to be collected by Salvage, before the house was torn down. "And breakfast! Chow's up for anyone hasn't eaten."

John wanted me to go with him to find my father. It was getting light now. There were a couple of dozen cars parked. And just coming in off the road were three school buses. One would have the Band. And another, my crowd, Demolition. I couldn't remember from the program who was in the third. My father was easy to spot, in the one truck that had a horn on top. Ben Wolf was with him. Besides playing a trumpet, Ben Wolf's a bookkeeper who works down in the new factory, General Magneto. He was helping my father to keep the bills straight and the receipts, as well as the schedule. The two of them had a lot of papers in the truck.

"John!" My father saw us. "Well, that looks better."

John straightened the brim of his fedora so it stood out flat all around.

"It's yours!" Now I knew why it was familiar. "It's your best hat," I said to my father. "Next to the one you bought last Easter."

"John and I thought he might dress a little special today, considering how special a day it is. More like everyone else."

John nodded to show how much he agreed with that idea. He asked me to put a question to my father.

"Because he's not on any committee, he wants you to tell him what to do. He's ready to try anything."

"The first thing's breakfast." My father pointed over to where they'd set up a tent with wide awnings for the ladies to cook under. "You hungry, John?"

John nodded as if the most important thing to be, according to the schedule, was starved. It was my mother who waited on us, at a counter made out of planks laid over sawhorses. We'd eaten, my father and I. He had a cup of coffee and I had a glass of milk. But John had the whole works laid out for him, juice and Crusted Toasties and doughnuts and a platter of coffee cake. "Or for the guest of honor," my mother stood with her hands on the counter, "we could manage eggs. With ham or bacon?"

"John's only breakfast I ever saw," I told my mother, "is salted fish or sardines and black bread and a powerful piece of cheese. And onions of course. He always has an onion."

"I don't know about the rest," my mother looked into the cartons behind her, "but we can certainly fix him up with these." They were as big as baseballs, the onions she put on the counter, and they were beauties.

"Not for breakfast!" My father pointed with his spoon. "Not onions."

John glanced around at the three of us. He told me that my mother didn't have to go to any extra trouble. He shoved the onions away, slowly because they were such good lookers. Then he said he didn't want any onions. And he started with the orange juice and Crusted Toasties.

I left my milk and I went around Onion John, to sit on the other side of my father. "Why don't we tell him he can go ahead and eat the onions?"

"But he doesn't want them."

"That's only what he said."

"Why would he do that?"

"I think he's trying to act like everyone else. The way we want him to. Just to please us."

"But maybe he doesn't actually want any onions."

"He's a friend of mine, Pop. The thing is, I know about him."

"He's a friend of mine, too." And of course, that was so It was the best thing could happen. "And do you know what I think," my father took a swallow of coffee. "I think he's changing."

"All of a sudden, overnight."

"It's a start. Those onions, he may be losing his taste for those. Once he starts living differently, you never can tell. He might end up a completely different kind of human being, Onion John."

"Actually?"

"I think he might."

At 6:44 there was a growl that rolled up as the band started its first number, right on schedule. "The World Is Waiting For The Sunrise." The timing couldn't be any more perfect because the sun rose too, on schedule. The bright yellow rim of it climbed the road to Hessian Hill.

Onion John put down his spoon to listen to the band. It looked to be out of politeness. My mother told him the music was only for morale. And Onion John went back to his Toasties.

I watched the light of the gasoline lamps under the canopy thin out. With Onion John Day only starting, there were already a lot of changes in Onion John. If he kept on trying so hard, it could be that he might change into a completely different human being. My father's guess was as good as mine. Or maybe better, now that he was a friend of Onion John's. That problem at least was solved. The way the two of them got along, and how fine they understood each other.

Listening to the music and watching the sun come up on Onion John Day, both at once, I figured the way they got along was enough to be happy about.

Chapter 11

Tearing down John's house turned out to be as good as anyone ever expected. It started with fifteen of us, all from my class, battering away from the inside.

The battering ram we had was a long four-by-eight-inch beam they were going to use for the ridge pole of the roof. Our job was to get the walls of the house to fall outward, out on the ground where the rock could be cleaned up easy. No bulldozer could get inside the house to do the job. The seventh and eighth grades could demolish a house fast as any bulldozer, if it came to that, once we got going.

We all hung on to the long piece of timber and waited for the next one to make the first move.

John started it. He was with Mr. Ries and Donahue and a couple of others who were standing by inside to see we were careful. John looked up from Mr. Ries' wrist watch. "Advance!" He picked up a sledge hammer. "Advance!" He took a swing and put a crack into *The New*

York Times. John let loose with another thud and daylight showed.

"One and a two," said Eech. "Three!"

The line of us let heave. And the timber rammed through, clean past the stones of the wall to push out a small jagged triangle. We tried again, and a whole chunk of wall came splintering down. From then on, no one held back.

Except it's by mistake, how many chances do you get to wreck anything? And when you do put out a window with a football, or get shoved through a picket fence, the next thing you have to do is run. Up at Onion John's we had a chance to concentrate, to work out different ideas how to demolish. When we finished with the battering ram, everyone had their own special approach to wrecking.

George Connors used an old baseball bat that only lasted a couple of swings and split. Some tried with a sledge hammer but Eech and I figured those were too heavy. And some with an axe or a regular hammer, which we thought were too light. Eechee and I used a crowbar. He supplied most of the muscle, behind me, at the end of the bar. And me up front, I did the guiding. We had power and accuracy both.

We didn't try so much for speed, like the others walloping away. We found the way to score was to pick out the right rock to hit. So we studied our way along and twice with a single swing, we started landslides that left gaps in the wall a yard wide. But the touchdown we made, the real home run for us, was the wall behind where the stove used to be, the west wall. The key rock had the shape of a horse's head and all the other rocks branched away from it.

"Wait!" Eech waved everybody to the other end of the room. "Hold them back, Mr. Donahue," said Eech. "You ready, Andy?"

The place was quiet and all I said was "Check!" We took the sideways step we'd developed and got our backs into the swing of the bar as we let it out.

Crunch. There was the dry grinding sound of a crack that started slow. Then another crack opened and built into a roar. Everything was hid. The inside of the house went yellow and white with the dust rolling back. The roar kept up. It got louder. Until I could see it was the people outside, through where the wall used to be, cheering.

The entire wall was gone. The roof would've come down if it weren't propped with beams. Eechee and I walked out through the rubble and shook hands with anyone who wanted, including Onion John.

He said we did fine.

"It's the way you built it." We couldn't take all the credit. "I never saw a house any better built for tearing down."

"8:11," said my father through the loud-speaker. "Cleaning and Grading. Get a dozer over to the building site. Demolition's complete. Move that rock out of there."

"8:24. Ditching. The water line's marked to the spring. Start your back hoe at the house."

Every time my father made an announcement there was a lot of rushing around. From the cars where they were parked in the corn field next to John's, or from the job that was finished to the one that was getting started. And with the band going every twelve minutes, "The Washington Post March," or "Poet and Peasant," or "Oh, What A Beautiful Morning," or "The Thunderer," Onion John Day got to be as busy and happy as a fair. Everybody was dressed in their roughest clothes, loud shirts and heavy boots and aprons and overalls, until you hardly recognized them. A locomotive engineer dressed in stripes and a high peaked hat turned out to be Judge Brandstetter, of all people. You had to look close at who came along.

Mostly when I saw Onion John he had somebody stopped to ask what time it was. I was sorry I told him about the schedule. He was forever on the go. Everywhere my father sent him, the different chairmen thought the most important place for Onion John was somewhere else. And John was anxious to get there. The truth is Onion John was a waste of time on a job, and material. It took time to explain to him what to do. And when he got started, he broke things. Even the two-inch galvanized water main couldn't stand up to Onion John. It split like a hickory nut soon as John put a Stilson wrench to it.

It would've been better for everybody if he didn't try

so hard, to change. First, he wasn't very good at it. And second, I didn't see anything wrong with the way he was.

At 9:17, my father said, "Plumbing. Make all your water and sewer connections into the cellar. We're waiting on you."

At 9:42, my father said, "Ditching. You'll find the cesspool marked out for you at the northeast corner."

At 9:53, my father said, "Masonry and Cement. Start your mixer. The foundation will be ready for you in exactly seven minutes."

And at 10:07, Onion John said, "Stop!"

It was clear enough for everybody to understand. Then the loud-speaker went garbled with shouting and yelling, until my father hollered for me to come over.

There was a crowd around the loud-speaker truck. John explained to me, he came there looking for my father because we were all in danger. My father wasn't around the truck and John took a chance at talking into the microphone himself.

"What danger?" asked my father. "What's wrong?"

All I started to get from Onion John was how beautiful the day turned out. That was true. The sun was way up, straight above the hills where the Musconetty comes from. And without clouds, the sky looked clean as a stretch of washed blue slate that was waiting to be written on. It was a little warm for November. But that didn't take away from how beautiful the day was.

"But what's the danger," asked my father, "in a pretty day?"

"Because the sun's shining," soon as I understood I told my father, "John says everyone has to work on the west wall in the morning, and on the east wall in the afternoon. To keep their shadows from falling into the foundation." I listened some more and it sounded a lot like Onion John, before he started changing. "If they let their shadows fall in, John says, they could get crippled, or sick. Or killed."

My father relaxed. Over the loud-speaker he said, "The alert's over. This is the all clear. Everybody carry on." By then I had the rest of the story from Onion John.

Years ago, he told me, anyone building a house or a castle, if they wanted it durable, would cement a live person up into the walls. Then they found that closing over a spot where someone's shadow fell was as good as having an actual man or woman built-in. As far as durability went. And it was just as hard on the person who's shadow it was. He'd be doomed and get feverish, sooner or later, or have a bad accident and die or get killed. John didn't want anything like that to happen, not to anyone who was kind enough to come up and help him.

"John, you can stop worrying," my father put his arm around John's shoulder. "Nothing like that can happen here. We're protected."

John waited to hear how.

"We're covered." John followed my father's arm sweeping across the top of Hessian Hill. "Completely protected by insurance. Comprehensive Liability and Workmen's Compensation."

Protected even against shadows in the cellar, John wanted to know.

"It's the fullest protection there is," said my father. "Against anything!"

John tried the word. "Compranshy," was as far as he got. The words had a powerful sound to them, he thought, like a very strong charm. He was glad to stop worrying, with everyone protected by Comprehensive Liability and Workmen's Compensation.

"And from now on," said my father, "why don't you stick around and help me." He gave John a clipboard to carry, full of lists and plans. "That way I can explain things as we go along and we won't run into any more trouble."

I watched them go off together. Over at the house they spoke to the man who was working the chute at the back end of the cement truck. My father and Onion John walked around the foundation watching how the stuff poured. They ended up at the east end, with the sun at their backs. They were tall men, the two of them, and their shadows stretched far across the wet cement on the cellar floor.

I went back to Carpentry where I was a junior helper.

At 11:02, the cement work in the cellar was done.

And ten minutes later, at 11:12, the frame of the four walls went up. It had taken a couple of hours to assemble these on the ground, two-by-fours nailed together and braced. But setting the frames up took only a few seconds. There was a cheer went up with them because all of a sudden the skeleton of a house appeared and for the first time it looked as if Onion John's new home was taking shape.

At 11:52, Onion John got a new name. This was at a conference Press and Publicity had, over at the loudspeaker truck, and I was asked to show up.

I'd never been to a press conference before. All there is to it is people standing around and talking. My father was there with Onion John, and so was Ernie Miller and Mayor Weltershot and a couple of others who were on Press and Publicity, including Ed Maibee. He was standing by, I guess, in case someone had an envelope to lick. There were editors from the weekly papers in the towns around. And one reporter, from the daily paper in Easton, *The Globe*, who took notes from what my father was telling him.

This was mostly about the number of people on the job. Close to two hundred and fifty, my father said, including women and musicians. The reporter, whose name was Mr. Jonah Davis, thought there had to be twice that from the look of the crowd. The extras though were only spectators, people who drove over special to watch. Or cars passing by that stopped to see what was going on. There was an ice cream man, to take care of spectators, and another fellow selling balloons.

"Did you ever expect this kind of circus," the reporter asked my father, "when you started out to build Mr. Claiblin his house?"

"Mr. Claiblin?"

My father looked around to where I'd been standing since I showed up. "Here's Andy now." The reporter nodded as if he were expecting me.

"Who's Mr. Claiblin? Not Onion John?"

"According to your father."

"We found out in New York," said my father. "Through the immigration office there."

"Mr. Claiblin?" I asked John.

John shrugged to say, No, and he nodded to say, Yes, both at the same time. He circled his fingers in the air to show that the name was close enough to be right. We shook hands, as if we were introduced.

"Pretty warm for November." I didn't know what else to say, getting introduced to someone I knew all my life.

John thought it was warm. And I kept studying him, how he looked in his new name, while Mr. Davis and I sat down on the running board of Mr. Berry's truck to have an interview.

"Just to get settled about you first." Mr. Davis looked at his notes. "You're in the seventh grade and you're going to major in mathematics. You're interested in science. And you're headed for the Massachusetts Institute of Technology."

"How'd you know?" I always thought an interview was where they asked you questions instead of telling you.

"Your father. That's correct isn't it? You're going into physics?"

"Years from now. But what's this got to do with me? What's happening here. I'm not what you're going to write about, are you?"

"You're part of it. I want to be able to tell who you are. I understand you know Mr. Claiblin about as well as anybody in town."

"Onion John?" I still couldn't connect him with a brand new name.

"Mr. Claiblin." He waggled his hand. "Onion John. It's the same thing."

"I guess it is." I watched Onion John under his fedora hat, standing with my father for a picture. "Except he is changing. There's no telling how he'll end up."

"Changing?" Mr. Davis crushed his paper inside out to find a clean side. "From what? How was he before?"

"Just fine," I told Mr. Davis. "There was no one else around who was like him. With his ideas. That's as far as I'm concerned."

"Well, you ought to know, you're his best friend."

"I guess I am," I said and that was the end of the interview. I couldn't see where anything I told Mr. Davis was worth writing up. But at least, I knew, I gave him the facts straight.

Onion John's name was what everybody talked about over lunch; fried chicken and cole slaw, baked lima beans, sweet potatoes and fresh cider, pumpkin pie and ice cream.

"What name does he use for his autograph?" asked Bitsy. There were a lot of spectators asking John to sign a copy of their program. "Onion John or Mr. Claiblin?"

"He signs an X," I said. "That could mean either one."

"And faster," said Eechee. "And easier, for him anyway, to keep up to schedule."

By early afternoon the schedule got to be a problem. Because of the crowds. The hills around and the fields were mobbed and more and more people kept coming. There was a big sign on Route 96 below Hessian Hill that read "Onion John Day" with an arrow, pointing. And up they came, those out for a drive on such a nice Sunday, with license plates from all over the state and from other states as well. Most of them, with their sticks of ice cream and balloons and hot dogs and picnic lunches, didn't think we could make it. They said we couldn't build the house in one day the way we planned.

On our own, it wouldn't make too much difference for some of us to come back on Monday to finish up. But with a big audience, what we had to do was make good. Onion John Day became like a championship. And to win, the committees broke apart and everyone worked at whatever job was going. A lot of times there weren't enough tools. And once even, the loud-speaker had to warn half of us to get off the roof where we were shingling on account of the house might cave in.

It gave my father and Ben Wolf a lot of extra work,

sorting things and moving help around where it was needed. And right behind them, everywhere they went, Onion John kept up with the clipboard he was carrying. Onion John or Mr. Claiblin, that is.

Whoever he was, it didn't change how he got along with my father. From up on the roof where I was shingling I saw them all over the place, the two of them together.

My father called me over, around 3:11 or so, and asked me if I wouldn't mind teaching Onion John a short speech in English, where he would accept the new house. It wasn't going to happen yet for four days. After the inside got fixed up with furniture and curtains, there was going to be a ceremony on Thanksgiving morning to give John the key.

"And it would be nice for him to say something everyone could understand." My father handed me a paper. "We wrote a couple of lines. I thought this would be a good time to go off with Onion John someplace, to help him memorize it."

I took the paper. "Where do you want to go?"

"Not me. I can't get away. You and John don't need me."

"Well sure, we could work it out together." The speech was only three lines. I showed it to John. He didn't think it would take him very long to learn. "We could get back in an hour."

"No, no, take your time. Get out of here and go off by yourself. Take the rest of the afternoon, you two!"

I could see my father was in the same fix as the other chairmen, as far as trying to work with Onion John around.

"The whole afternoon?" I asked him.

"Please, Andy. This whole deal's liable to fall to pieces if we can't keep it organized. Until we call you. Keep going until we've got this job licked."

John and I went off to find a quiet place to study. And there wasn't any, not until we got way in back of John's garden where we found the sheepnose tree was empty. We climbed up into that.

Dressed the way he was and with a new name, it was a little strange being back in the sheepnose tree with John. I asked him how he felt. He said he'd never worked so hard in his life.

"Just going around carrying a little clipboard?"

It wasn't the carrying, he said, it was trying to understand so many new things wore him out.

"Do you have to try so hard?"

Yes, John said, he had to do his best, with everyone else getting exhausted.

"Well, at least," I opened the paper, "this shouldn't be so bad." I read the speech off to him. "I feel happy and very proud that the people of Serenity have fixed me up in this fine new house. This is a good day to give thanks. But it is hard for me to say how much I appreciate all that you've done." That's all there was.

We sat in the tree and John learned the words, syllable

by syllable. The only problem was to keep John from putting in his own syllables, like *ovitch* or *owsky*. John tried hard. It didn't take long before the words started to come out clean with only a few extra grunts here and there and a couple of odd *z*'s. Tidying those up, in little more than an hour he was saying the whole speech so anyone could understand him.

From all the yelling that came over the loud-speaker, though, it sounded as if my father was still pretty busy. So I started all over to teach John the expressions he ought to use for his speech. "I feel happy," I taught him, "that's with your chin up and your arms stretched out wide."

"And very proud, is with a big smile."

To give him a start, I made out as if I were the speaker. "It gives me great pleasure to present these keys to Onion John—or," I asked him, "which is it, Onion John or Mr. Claiblin?"

There was an apple next to John, brown and shriveled from getting caught with frost. John picked the apple and turned it over in his hands, thinking, then he threw it away. The best thing he said was to ask my father. John thought Mr. Rusch would know best.

"But your own name! A thing like that, it's up to you."

He shook his head, none of them were his right name, not Onion, or John, or Claiblin either. His right name, when he pronounced it, was two blocks long. So it didn't make any difference what name was used, he shrugged, as long as it fitted the occasion. And who would know that better than his best friend, John asked me, Mr. Rusch.

John repeated about his best friend, Mr. Rusch. So there wasn't any mistake in the way I heard it. This was the biggest change that came along on Onion John Day. How my father was John's best friend. And this was one change I had to do something about. I had to get hold of the reporter from Easton, who's name was Jonah Davis.

I got the promise from John that he'd stay in the tree, to rehearse by himself. I climbed down and I searched all over Hessian Hill, where they were working at the house and all through the crowds that stood and watched. Mr. Jonah Davis wasn't anywhere. And no one I asked had seen him.

It looked as if he collected enough for his paper and he was gone. I thought to call him, but there wasn't any phone around. The best I could do was wait, until that night when I got to a phone. I only hoped that wouldn't be too late. I went back out to the tree where John was speaking his speech in a good loud voice and I went to teaching him the rest of his expressions.

By then, every time my father made an announcement there were cheers. There was a roar at 4:42 when the prime coat of white paint was done.

And another roar at 5:07 when the little roof over the front doorstep went up.

There was a roar at 5:32 when the last brick went into

the chimney. I don't know what the roar was about that came at 5:36. I didn't catch what my father said and what happened was inside the house. At 5:42 there was a rush for people to get into their cars. All the automobiles were shifted to make a wide circle around the house and they put on their headlights. From the tree the place looked fine, all lit up in the night that was coming, solid and white with a red chimney on top and a dormer window that was just for show because there wasn't any second floor.

In a little while the electricity came on inside the house, without any announcement, and there was another cheer.

In the dark, I couldn't see any of the expressions John was using or gestures. And I'd just as soon have heard from my father that we could come down. I listened to the words, so the time wouldn't be wasted, and to the wind that blew. After a while John's speech didn't sound so clear anymore because his teeth went to chattering with the cold. I figured if I couldn't see him, or hear him neither, he and I didn't have any other particular reason to sit around in a tree together. We started to climb down.

And my father said, "6:32. Right on schedule. Where's John? We're ready for John! Bring him in!" The house was finished.

The band played, "Mountain Majesty." They went through it once by the time we reached the house and had to start all over again. Walking through the two lines of people, I stayed with John. Everyone applauded. We stopped at Mr. Kinnoy's wagon to get John's valuables. And then we stepped into the house.

There was nothing to see. Except people. All of Serenity was jampacked inside, Mayor Weltershot and Judge Brandstetter and Mr. Weems from the bank, and Kinnoy, Donahue, Ries, Ben Wolf, my father, so many people there was no house to look at except the ceiling. The ceiling was painted blue.

Onion John looked up at the ceiling while everyone applauded. Then they held off and waited to hear what he'd say.

No words came out of him. I knew what to expect, no matter how much he was trying to change. And that's what happened. He stood there and cried. The house kept still and everyone watched him cry, until Onion John reached out and took my father's hand. Then the applause came back. Soon the clapping was drowned out by cheers. And the storm really broke when those outside joined in. The auto horns picked up, hundreds of them, and it sounded like the top of Hessian Hill was blowing off.

Everyone who could reach John shook his hand. He kept up crying. With his arms going and the tears rolling, he looked like he might get himself pumped dry. He was still crying though, when the room went white with the explosion of a flash bulb. It was Mr. Jonah Davis from *The Globe.* I reached through the crowd for him.

"Hold it." He pushed me aside and studied through the

wire square he had on top of his camera. "Out of the way, please. One more!" He shot off another blinding glare and he bent down in the noise so he could hear me. "What's up?"

"The interview we had. One of the facts I gave you is wrong."

"Which one?" he asked me.

"Where I told you I was Onion John's best friend. The fact is, I'm not."

"No?"

"Not anymore."

"Thanks," said Mr. Davis. He promised to print the story the way it should be, how it was my father instead. That was the last I had to do about Onion John Day. I caught a ride on a car that was going back to town, with some people who weren't going to stay for the barbecue supper either.

Chapter 12

My regular hours at the hardware store are Wednesday and Friday afternoons, and Friday nights when Rusch's stays open along with everyone else in town. But I came down to the store from school that Monday after Onion John Day, special. Christmas was coming. And Rusch's was always the first to be set for the holidays. Our decorations are up by Thanksgiving and that causes a lot of comment from people.

So I thought I'd help to get started on the decorations. All that Bits and Eech and George Connors and the rest at school could talk about was what happened on Onion John Day, how good it was. And long before the three o'clock bell everyone had told everyone else, as far as I could see, all they could remember that went on. With the exception, maybe, of me. I didn't tell all that went on, not everything. It wasn't that I was trying to protect any reputation about being John's best friend. There was just no sense to it, hashing over and over again the same things. I'd just as soon get busy with what was coming, like Christmas, and lay off after awhile what already happened.

Besides, there's a lot to dressing up a hardware store that's like getting set for a party. It's exciting. I don't get a chance at the windows, they're for my father to do or the different salesmen who put up their own displays. But inside where we have columns, we wrap those in red brick paper so they look like chimneys. I help with those. Then there's a fifteen-foot string of letters that spells MERRY XMAS I hang over the front counter, with two big red paper bells at each end. It's tricky, getting them up, but that's one of the things you learn in the hardware business.

I was on the ladder getting started when there was a thud at the front door. We'd been waiting for the afternoon *Globe* and when it hit, my father brought the paper in. He cussed Arnie Burke out, same as he does every day. Arnie rides route for the Easton *Globe* and he's phenomenal the tight weave he works into a newspaper. After my father got the knot untied and had a look at the front page, he whistled.

"Holy Hannah!"

"What's it got there?"

My father didn't answer. Reading the first page he walked back to where his desk was. I slid down the ladder and took off after him. But I couldn't see where it said anything about Onion John on the front page. All it had was, MOON ATTEMPT ASSURED BY NEXT SUMMER.

"What's so Holy Hannah?" I asked him. "Where does it have about Serenity?"

I helped him turn the page and there it was, right inside, three pictures and a big wide story. One picture showed Onion John getting pumped dry, near the end. One picture was from the morning, with John and my father and the mayor and the others. I was in the third picture. This was a full view of the house showing all the cars parked. I was one of those on the roof because you could see where the shingling was half done, and I was up there at the time.

Elbow to elbow, my father and I read the story and I was through first. I skipped till I saw the name Rusch. "A prime organizer of the event," the write-up said, "was Andrew J. Rusch, prominent merchant and Rotarian, who is John's closest friend in town." Mr. Davis had it the way I told him.

Then it said where the Onion John situation was brought to the attention of the town by me, "Andy Rusch, Jr." which was right enough. I was the one who brought it to the attention of my father how he and John might come to be friends, and that was the start.

"Nothing wrong there," I said.

"Wrong?" My father kept reading. "I'd say this was pretty good." He finished reading the write-up out loud. " 'For the next few days the house will be in the hands of various committees, mostly ladies, applying the finishing touches to the interior. On Thanksgiving, Mr. John Claiblin will formally take up residence in a home that will only seem to be built out of sticks and stones. In reality, its basic material is the warm hearted good will and the generosity of the town of Serenity.' "

"Certainly is a nice end to the story." I got up from leaning on the desk.

"But this one," my father turned back to the first page where it had about the moon. "I never thought this story would ever start so soon. As early as next summer."

I left my father reading about the moon and picked up a full box of thumbtacks. I climbed the ladder again and went back to hanging Merry Xmas.

"Twenty-four thousand miles an hour," he said that's how fast the rocket'd go. "Think of that." When I put my mind to it all I could think of was—whoosh. "And in two years, Andy, after they land their first rocket, they expect to send a human being up there. A man!" He looked from the paper up to where I was on the top of the ladder. "Man alive, it's coming a lot faster than anyone ever expected. If you want to be in on it, Andy, you'd better grow up fast."

It was a joke the way he said it, so I patted the ceiling right over my head. "I don't have too much room left, not here."

My father laughed at the way I picked him up. "You're right. Not around here." He came over to the glass counter at the foot of the ladder. "You know, next summer. I've been thinking about next summer."

"About going to the moon?"

"About General Magneto. I was talking to Ben Wolf yesterday. He works there."

"I know."

"Ben Wolf was telling me, down there at General Magneto, that to run errands and in the stock room they make a place for boys that are interested. They let three or four have summer jobs, Ben was saying."

The thumbtack bent, the one I was using for the letter X. I tried with another thumbtack. "Is this okay?" I asked him. "The space between Merry and X?"

My father said the space looked good. "Ben drives it alone," he went on, "down to General Magneto everyday. He has plenty of room in his car. In case anyone took a summer job, there'd be no trouble getting back and forth."

I had the X hung up. For the next letter, M, I had to get down and move the ladder. But I stayed where I was.

"I thought it might be a good idea for you, to take a job next summer down at General Magneto."

"Me?" I was careful, turning around to face my father below, and I kept my balance. "Why would I want to go down to General Magneto? What for?"

"Considering the plans you have, Andy, where you're headed, it's certainly something to think about. To see what goes on inside a big industrial plant like that. You'd start

getting into the atmosphere, that way, of what you're going to do. It might be a good way to spend the summer, don't you think?"

"But summers, where I work is here," I told my father. "With you, in the hardware store."

My father stepped back from the counter so he could look at me better. He leaned against a table full of kitchenware. "I know, Andy. But this isn't where your future is going to be. A one-horse business like this."

"One horse." I sat down on the top step of the ladder. That didn't seem like anyway to talk about the thousands of different items below. Every one of them was useful. "What's wrong with Rusch's Hardware Store?"

"It's not this store." My father looked around. "The whole business is old fashioned. Every customer comes into a hardware store, you've got to find out what his problem is and figure out what to do about it. You've got to talk to each one personally."

"Why not? Most of them are friends of ours."

"Yes, but it's the super market, that's the big way to operate today, where the customer takes care of himself. What's new, modern, the thing that's up to date is self service. And it's never going to happen in the hardware business. There's no future here."

I had to come down anyway. I took it one step at a time. "I'm not talking about the future," I told my father. "When it comes to what's way ahead, like Technology or the Institute, I'm all for that. And the moon, too, everything that's in the future. That's fine. All I had in mind was to keep on in Serenity, and help in the store the same as always, with you. For next summer."

I waited for my father to answer.

"It's only a couple of months away," I pointed out. "No more than six or seven. You couldn't call that the future, anything so close."

"Well." My father came over and pulled the ladder into position for the next two letters, M and A. "General Magneto's nothing we have to decide right this minute. It's just a thought."

"Can't we stop thinking about it? The thought it is? Just forget it?"

He went back to the desk to get his coat. "At least, we can stop talking about it." He folded the newspaper. "I'll see you at home, Andy. I've got to drop by and speak to Ben Wolf."

"Not about General Magneto?"

"Stop worrying." He laughed. "Ben and I have a lot of paper work left over from yesterday, invoices and the rest to straighten out." He stopped by the counter. "As far as General Magneto goes, Andy, the whole thing's only a possibility. A vague possibility."

That didn't sound so bad. I watched my father go out the door. A possibility is where anything can happen, even nothing. It's not like a fact, where it's all over with and you can't do anything about it. I took my father's suggestion not to worry, too much. I put all my attention back into the thumbtacks, getting them up straight into the ceiling. The bell over the door let go again, and it was Onion John.

He was still dressed in the coat with the velvet collar and the fedora hat. He was wearing his sneakers though. I guess the other shoes were too pointed for comfort.

I came down off the ladder and we stood at the counter. Even though I understood him as well as ever, I didn't know what to talk to him about after all the changes that came out of Onion John Day. I asked him how he liked his house, the first night he spent in it. He said fine. He asked me how I liked the house.

"The blue on the ceiling," I told him, "that's pretty."

He took the strap hinges out of his pocket, the ones he bought at the beginning. He was going to ask my father if we'd take them back because he might as well get his twenty-seven cents.

"I can take care of that." I took the hinges. "Rusch's always refunds anybody's money." I took a quarter and two pennies out of the cash register and remarked, "I'm sorry they didn't work out."

It's the kind of remark you have to make when you give a refund, how sorry you are. But John didn't take it that way. He told me I didn't have to be sorry. It's true there never would have been a new house if it weren't for me, and the hinges and my father. But that was nothing for me to be sorry about. He patted my hand. He didn't think it would take very long before he got used to the place. It was going to turn out fine, once the new house got to seem more like home and not just somewhere he was visiting.

The more he tried to make me feel better, the worse I began to feel that the hinges didn't work. From the way John sounded and the way I felt, it would have been a lot better if we'd just fixed the door somehow and let it go at that. There was no use talking about it, though. I didn't say anything, once John got finished cheering me up.

He sat down on a stack of paint cans and took out his purse to put away the twenty-seven cents. Now the business part was finished I couldn't see what else we had to go into. John sat and I stood with my elbows on the glass case, and we put in the longest time we'd ever been together without John talking. After a while he took some papers out of his inside pocket and he asked how much longer I thought it would be, before my father got back.

"He's not coming back. He went over to see Mr. Wolf, the one who works down at General Magneto."

John didn't know about General Magneto and there was no use going into the possibility that was. He handed me the papers. They were left with him the night before and he wanted to ask my father about them, what they were. They were fancy looking papers with a design on the top page, where it was folded over. It was the insurance policy,

Comprehensive Liability and Workmen's Compensation.

"Compranshy?" John tried to repeat the name. He didn't know "Compranshy" was papers. He thought it was a charm, the way my father talked about it, a spell. My father never did clear up for him what insurance was. He asked me.

"It's like a bet you make," I explained. "If you have a car you bet this company, say, fifty dollars you're going to have a wreck. And if you do, then the company has to pay you what the wreck is worth, whether it's five hundred or even a thousand dollars. But if you don't, then you lose the fifty dollars you put in. That's all insurance is."

John worked one hand over his face like he was checking to see if he needed a shave. He couldn't understand, he said, why my father should want to play betting games with him. Why did Mr. Rusch say everyone was protected?

"They are in a way. If they get their back broke or they get killed, then they're protected."

John held his ears to the side of his head. The way things stood, he told me, everyone who worked on the building was doomed. He studied the floor. There had to be a way to protect the people of Serenity from accidents and plagues. After searching around on the floor, he came up with it. A goat! There had to be a special kind of housewarming, he explained, with a goat as the chief guest. The goat had to be brought into the house for what sounded like a barn dance.

The house had to be filled with friends. He asked me if I'd come up the next afternoon. Me? He wanted me to bring Eechee and Bits and Hemmendinger. Me, he asked, would I come?

"How about my Pa? Don't you want him?"

John went back to looking at the floor. He didn't think my father would like so much to see a goat in the new house. I didn't think so either. Besides, John asked, out of everybody, including my father, wasn't I his oldest friend?

"If you think of it that way," I told him, "I guess I am." It was certainly a fact. It was more of a fact than any other kind of friend. It was one you couldn't change. "If you really want me to come, I'll be glad to come."

John couldn't think of anything that was more important.

"Then I will. And I can promise you the others will come too."

John picked up speed. He told me where he was going to get the goat and all the other preparations that went into the housewarming. I leaned on my hand and listened to him, all the different words coming out of the clatter. He didn't seem so changed. Not when he let out some of the things were going to happen up at his house the next afternoon. Except by the next afternoon, it was too late to visit Onion John in his new house.

Chapter 13

A fire in Serenity starts with a call to Ollie's Diner, which is on Water Street right next to the Good Will Fire Company, No. 1. Not that there's any number two fire company, or three or four. Though someday there may be and then you'll be able to tell which was the first.

The reason you call the Diner to report a fire is someone's always there. The place is open to all hours and Ollie sleeps out back. Whereas the firehouse, usually it's locked and empty because it's volunteer and no one gets paid to sit around and play checkers or lean against it, the way I've seen them in Easton where they make a steady job of being a fireman.

So the number that's written over everyone's telephone, for an emergency, is Ollie's. When someone calls about a fire, Ollie does four things. He goes to the firehouse and hoists up the doors. He presses the button that works the alarm. He calls Dusek, Mantini and Kay. These are three farmers who live in different directions out of town, and when they hear from Ollie where the fire is they tell their neighbors so they're saved from the trip downtown. While he's on the phone, Ollie writes on a blackboard the location of the fire. That way, anyone who shows up late knows where to go.

The next thing Ollie does is only sometimes. And that is to call the *Globe* if he thinks the paper would be interested in the fire. The *Globe* pays Ollie two dollars for every fire that they print. Ollie's the only one who makes any money out of a fire in Serenity but considering all the extra work he does, for free, no one begrudges him. By the time anyone shows up Ollie already has his fire hat on and he's at the wheel of the engine and he's moving out.

Ollie was serving a truck driver his breakfast that Tuesday morning when the call came in. It was from Mr. Tracy who runs an orchard on the other side of Hessian Hill. "All I said to Tracy was 'No!'," Ollie told us. "I couldn't believe it. Good grief, a terrible thing like that was hard to believe."

Just about the time the phone was getting ready to go in Ollie's, I was on DuBrock Street on my way to school. I was figuring out in my head how many days were left until the end of June and it amounted to two hundred and seventeen days. That seemed a pretty good stretch before I had to face any vague possibilities like General Magneto. Two hundred and seventeen days in Serenity with nothing to worry about and with John my oldest friend, that seemed like a lot to look forward to. I'd just picked up a leaf. It was sugar maple. There were hardly any leaves around, with any gold in them or red. And the ones were left, you noticed.

When a cow, a cow that had to be as big as a cloud, began to bawl. All of a sudden Serenity was like an empty barn with a cow in it struck down by colic. It stopped me dead. Until I remembered. It was the new alarm the Fire Department put in, instead of a siren. They called it a squawker. But the noise it made sounded like a hurt cow, big as any you can imagine, bawling.

I ran. All along DuBrock Street doors opened. Women stood. And men rushed out, fighting into their coats. From between houses, cars rolled back. They hit the street with a bump and let off downhill. The cow bawled and you could hear yells now, too. From all over. And then a regular siren came on and steadied into short blasts. It was the alarm for the ambulance corps. A bunch of kids rounded out of DePew Street, heading back from school. They pounded downhill. A lot of the yelling came from them. Eechee was at the end of the mob. He saw me and he hollered, "Who is it?"

"I don't know!" I yelled. But I did, I did know. Somehow it came when I was running, like a breath that I took. But it didn't leave, the idea, when I let go of the air that was in me and went empty and had to pull for some more.

I knew. Even before the engine went by, at the end of DuBrock Street.

Ollie was at the wheel. My father hung off the back. There were better than a dozen firemen crowding the top of the engine and hugging the sides.

"It's Onion John!" The engine flashed past. "Onion John!"

"Onion John!" It came from behind me now. From all over. "Onion John!" A couple of men stopped running. They turned back to their cars, now they knew where the fire was. The tank truck went by, down below, with its howler going. It carried even more firemen than the engine ahead. "Onion John!" was the yell you heard from anyone who looked at you.

The ambulance swept past down the hill and swayed into Water Street. By the time I came to the corner, Water Street was crowded with people running out of town. No one in his right mind would set out to run all the way to Hessian Hill, six miles! But they ran anyway because what else was there to do? I ran.

A horn honked behind me. It was Mr. Kinnoy's station wagon pulling into the curb, its door swinging open. Eech ran back to crowd in after me. The wagon was jammed.

"John's place, it's a total wreck."

"It exploded. Boom!"

"The body was thrown clear with the first blast."

I tried not to listen. Every fire you go to, you hear stories on the way. The worse they are, the more attention they get. Until it's a race who can tell the most awful. But not listening, you start thinking on your own how bad it could be. I didn't know what to do, listen or think, on the way up to Hessian Hill in Mr. Kinnoy's station wagon.

He wasn't dead. He was running from the brook with a pail of water when we pulled in. Onion John wasn't even hurt.

But the whole west wall of the house was climbing with flame. And the smoke poured off the top of Hessian Hill like it was a volcano.

Across the field in back of John's house the fire engine bumped its way toward Onion John's brook, paying out hose as it went. There was a good hundred and fifty feet to go but the distance wasn't the problem. The Serenity pumper carries fifteen hundred feet of two and a half inch hose. The problem was water. There wasn't enough water in the little trough Onion John used for his house supply. By the time we got there they were damming up the stream, fifteen men with picks and shovels, so there'd be a decent pool of water to draw from.

The tank truck was in front of the house. It carries seven hundred and fifty gallons of water and its own pump, so it can start before the engine is ready to go. The first stream that came off the hose of the tank truck was solid water with Barney McSwain the lead man at the nozzle.

"No, Barney. Spread it!" Mr. Kinnoy is an ex-fire chief

and one of the best firemen in town. He grabbed the nozzle and worked a valve to one side. The solid water spread out and started to fog and Mr. Kinnoy moved in to throw a curtain of water around the west wall. It could've been gasoline, for all the good it did. The flames held high and a red cloud tore out the front door. The second hose, the one from the engine, whipped out just about then and went to work on the door. For a couple of minutes, it looked hopeless. The water poured in and the red boiled out. But after the hose from the engine moved closer, the fire bellied back from the door. In that one spot, at least, the fire turned into smoke and steam.

The crowd of us cheered, for something to do. There were almost as many as on Sunday. And except for the firemen, we could only stand. And watch the house we built burn down. It was like watching your own home go. Because everyone did have a hand in the place and was proud of it, how it was built all in one day and on schedule.

Onion John ran for the steaming front door and the crowd hushed. The men at the hose grabbed John. He fought to break away, to get into the house where it was still a furnace. They pulled Onion John back and sat him down on the running board of the tank truck.

"*Stepan*" was all I could understand when they let me through the people around Onion John. He rubbed the smears on his face blacker and blacker, breathing heavy and crying and talking all at the same time.

"It's his valuables," I told the others. "The picture of *Saint Stepan* and the fiddle. There's other things. He wants to get them."

They wouldn't let John go. "How'd it start?" Mr. Ries yelled from the back of the truck where he watched the pump. "Ask him what started it." The crowd pressed in, asking how it started, as if the answei were the most important thing they needed to put the fire out.

John put his face in his hands. To hear him I had to get down on my knees and I listened at his hands like they were a closed door.

"He says he started it." I looked at all the people above. "Because he's dumb like an ox. And he's thick like a rock, he says. He's the one who started it."

"But how?"

It took a little while to get. It was the stove, John told me, all white and shiny and electric. How could a stupid fool like himself live with such a stove, he asked me, so magnificent. He brought it newspapers, to light it up that morning the same as he'd been doing all his life when he started a fire. And then in his terrible bonelike head, he remembered. All he had to do was turn a switch. So he put the newspapers on the stove and turned a switch and he went off to get water for his coffee. And that wasn't all. In his dumbness, he looked out the door at the morning, at the beautiful sun and he came out to smell the fine day. When he looked back there was blood red streaking through the smoke, jumping off the stove where the newspapers had caught. The wall was on fire. John threw the water that was in his hand through the door and he ran. That's how the fire started, John explained, because he was a numbskull.

All anyone did, when I finished, was nod. The crush around John loosened up. They went back to helping with the fire. Or they went to tell those who hadn't heard how the fire started. I sat there with John, on the ground next to the running board, and I told him, "It wasn't you're a numbskull. Some of these appliances are fierce, catching on to them."

No good, John stared at a rock between his feet. No good, he rapped with his knuckles on his own forehead as if he were coming to pay himself a visit. It was no good, he said. He could spend the rest of his life trying to change, but it was no good. He couldn't. He was too dumb, too stupid, too much of an ox, a mule, a buffalo, to be like anyone else. He had tried with all his might to make himself different. It was no good. He was the same as always.

"Onion John."

He looked at me, his eyes red and almost floating, his face ragged.

"That's not so bad, you're the same as always. It was pretty good, the way you were."

He started to smile but he didn't get very far with it. He started back behind his hands. There was another cheer.

We looked past the edge of the tank truck. The fire was brought under control. Part of the shingled roof was caved in but the walls stood, dripping, and there were only sparks inside, instead of fire. The place was drenched.

John was gone. He rounded the corner of the tank truck. He headed for the house. It was a last dash to find what was left of his valuables. It was a surprise and he got away with it. None of the crew on the hose laid a hand on him as he went past. It was only after he was inside, hopping across the black and crumbling beams of the floor that Mr. Kinnoy took after him, yelling, "Onion John."

Kinnoy stopped and turned away from the house. He and the gang at the hose started running. The house sagged. There was a scream. It was a wooden board slowly being ripped. Another sag and the house caved in with a long drawn out wrench and a groan. If John made any sound you couldn't hear him in the roar. The burnt out frame of the house balanced and folded into the cellar. In seconds, John's place was nothing but a hole in the ground with broken, twisted ends of lumber sticking out of it and smoke rising and dust.

I got caught in the charge, in the shrieking and running that started from everywhere to get into that hole of black rubbish and tear it apart. There was a push and I stumbled. I got slammed and I tripped and went down. I was on my knees, scrambling up to follow the crowd when the back of my neck was caught. It was Mr. Jonah Davis up from

Easton because of the call Ollie made at the first alarm.

"Where is he?"

I didn't stop to answer Mr. Jonah Davis. He stayed with me and we pushed our way into the wreck, down into the smoke and the heaving bodies and the swinging arms where everyone dug and pulled to get at Onion John. My jacket caught and I tore it loose.

"Where is he?" Mr. Davis kept asking.

"No!" yelled my father. "This is no time for reporters."

"You were glad to have me here on Sunday." Mr. Davis blocked his way past my father. "And this is just as big a story. Bigger! Where is he?"

There were too many of us bellowing for the next one to get out of the way. My father, Kinnoy and some of the firemen went to work on people, getting them out of the cellar. They organized a line, grabbing junk and passing it behind them up to the people who were on top. Davis went yanking at whatever he could lay his hands on, working as wild as anyone else. Down below me, at the bottom of the twisted heap, Davis was the first person to reach Onion John.

I managed to see him through the people and Onion John turned out to be the quietest person on Hessian Hill. He sat under a blackened beam that was part of the ridge pole of the house, resting with his eyes closed, waiting. And the miracle was his face. It wasn't even scratched. It was caked with charcoal and gray with ash but without a sign of blood. He opened his eyes when Davis reached him and nodded as if to say, hello. At the sight of John everyone started to work twice as hard as before, to get the rest of the stuff off him.

Except Mr. Davis. "How are you?" he leaned over John, yelling at him. "What do you think about this?"

I didn't wait to hear what Onion John had to say, working where I could.

"English!" Mr. Davis yelled. "Can't you say something in English? Please, John! Something we can print!"

I must've been six or eight feet away but I heard the words very clear.

"I feel happy."

I stopped to turn and look at Onion John. I didn't believe what I was hearing. But what other way did John have, to give Davis what he wanted? John went ahead with it. He took a long breath and kept going.

"I feel happy and very proud."

The only stretch of clear English that Onion John knew was the speech that I taught him. He recited it now for the reporter. He spoke each word of the speech clear and separate the way we rehearsed it.

"Very proud that the people of Serenity," John spoke slowly, word by word, "have fixed me up in this fine new house."

"That's Onion John!" said Eechee Ries right behind me. "He's talking!"

All around as they heard Onion John for the first time, heard him so they could understand, first one then another stopped working and straightened up.

"This is a good day," said Onion John, "to give thanks."

In the surprise of hearing Onion John talk, everyone held still. It was as if a tree they were used to hearing, when the wind passed through, or the noise of a brook suddenly made sense and turned into words and the tree talked, or the brook, in a plain and simple way.

"But it is hard for me to say," Onion John took a long breath and he looked up at us, "how much I appreciate all that you've done."

Onion John could hardly move, wedged like in a vise the way he was. So he couldn't, even if he wanted to, give any of the gestures we rehearsed.

He coughed and there was blood on his chin.

Chapter 14

Everyone stayed still, where they were when the first words caught them.

"Is that all you've got to say?" asked Mr. Davis.

It was like Davis pulled a trigger, of a starting gun.

"All?" yelled Mr. Kinnoy. "Isn't that enough?"

"Out of the way, Davis!" yelled my father. "Let's get to him."

"Ease that beam," yelled Mr. Ries, "the one to the right."

"Let's get him out of here!"

The crowd went frantic again, trying to clear a way for Onion John. He saw me. Onion John rolled his head for me to come to where he was pinned under the beam. I crawled down past the legs of the ones closest to him.

"Compranshy," John whispered. It was the insurance, he told me. It was the curse, and the curse had caught up with him. There was only one way he'd be saved and John asked me to help him.

"Andy! Out of there!"

The only way was to go ahead with the housewarming we'd planned. The goat, John whispered, first I had to bring a goat down into the wreck and then—.

"For Heaven's sakes, Andy. Come up here!"

I didn't turn around. "He's telling me what to do."

Then when I had the goat there, Onion John coughed.

Someone picked me up. Two arms came around my belly and I was lifted clear off the ground. I couldn't move my arms and I couldn't kick loose. I was put to one side. The someone who had me was Ben Wolf. He was wearing an ambulance corps hat.

"What do you want?" I asked him. "What are you doing to me?"

"There isn't any time." Ben pushed his eyeglasses back on his nose. "We've got to get that man out of here."

I was lifted again by Mr. Kinnoy up to Mr. Maibee and then to Mr. Schwarz who was on top. As soon as they let me go, I jumped back down and my father grabbed my arm.

"He was telling me what to do!" I said.

"We know what to do."

"Not about the housewarming!"

"Housewarming? Are you insane? How much warmer d'you think this place ought to be? Get back up, Andy. Stay out of this!"

All I could do was watch them pull the wreck clear. Then

Dr. Wallace climbed down to examine John before he was moved. He stayed down there, Dr. Wallace did, talking to the men around him while Ben Wolf and three others from the ambulance corps got John carefully, very slowly, on to a stretcher. Dr. Wallace shook his head as he talked. And those that listened to him, those men shook their heads too. The stretcher was carried to the ambulance and Ben Wolf jumped out of the back door and rushed around to the driver's seat. The motor started.

They were taking Onion John away before I knew what to do. But my father stopped me from getting to the ambulance.

"A half a minute!" I asked my father. "So he tells me what to do with the goat."

"This is no time for goats." My father sat on his heels in front of me and he held on to my shoulders. "This may be very serious. There's a cracked rib, on his left side. That's not so bad. But Dr. Wallace is afraid of the cough and the blood, he's afraid of a punctured lung."

"But John knows what to do for himself!"

"There's nothing to do until he's X-rayed."

The ambulance carefully bumped its way out of John's place and settled into the smooth road.

"A punctured lung, Andy," my father tightened the grip he had, "can be fatal. Often it is. We can hope, that's all, the X-ray shows that the lung is all right. There's nothing else we can do."

The ambulance took on speed and the dust from it waved a slow goodbye over Hessian Hill. I looked down to where I'd torn the pocket of my mackinaw away. It was hanging and I folded the cloth back on itself so the look of it was neater. Maybe on account of the fire I hadn't noticed how frosty the morning was, the chill. I buttoned my coat while my father watched. He buttoned the top button.

"If there's any chance of fatal," I asked my father, "then oughtn't we try everything. Even a goat?"

"What we ought to try for," he lifted my chin, "is self-control. All of us." He looked my face over. I felt all right, as far as control went. A couple of breaths came choppy, until I let go all the way and then hauled in. It went smooth from then on.

"The best thing you can do for the next couple of hours," my father said, "is get back to school. The lot of you. To get your mind going on something."

Back in the seat I had in class near the window, after the cars brought us down from Hessian Hill, I got my mind going on *3x over 8 plus 2 equals 11.* That's the problem we were given to solve. I didn't get very far with it. If it was going to be fatal with John, fatal meant dead. So why was I trying to find out what *x* equals? The *x*'s and *pluses* that covered my paper, all they amounted to was something like the picture of a cemetery. I drew a goat, instead. I put eyeglasses on him, the sort Ben Wolf wears. And the goat turned out to be a very smart looking animal. A smart goat, once I brought him up to John's place, might know what to do by himself.

At least, getting a goat up there, that'd be something along the lines of what John had in mind. At least, there was a chance with a goat where with *3x over 8 plus 2 equals 11*, there was no chance at all.

I tore up the sheet of paper into four small parts. On the back of each little square I wrote the word, *Hemarzrich.* It was the first time since Halloween anyone of us had used the secret code that meant the others had to help. I passed the notes along to Ries and Hemmendinger and Schwarz. Then I raised my hand to be excused.

Eechee was the first one after me, into the BOYS. Schwarz showed up with a handful of pencils he was supposed to sharpen. By the time Bo made it, I was already explaining how for land sakes alive we had to get out of there, out of school and back to Hessian Hill and hold the housewarming ourselves.

"How?" asked Bitsy. "What do we do with the goat?"

"I don't know. We'll have to see. But just sitting around here, that could be fatal for Onion John. And it'll be on our heads. On us."

"Why?" asked Bo. "Why's it our heads?"

"All it is," said Eech, "it's a terrible accident."

"It's no accident. It was the stove! They never should've put one in."

"Then why's it us?" said Bo. "It's the town's, your

father and everybody; it was their fault putting in the new stove."

"It wasn't them." I shook my head. "Everybody and my father were doing the best they knew how for Onion John."

"Then why's it our fault? Us?" asked Eech.

"I guess it isn't." I looked around to one of the wash bowls and turned on the hot water. The faucet works on a spring so that water only runs when you hold it. I spurted the water a couple of times before I made up my mind to tell them who's fault it was. "If you heard John, the speech he made when he thanked everybody?"

They nodded.

"The one he had most to thank was me." I held the water till it steamed. "When it comes down to anybody, it was my fault. If I wasn't John's oldest friend, the one who understood him, my father wouldn't ever have gone up there to Hessian Hill. That's so and it was even in the paper there wouldn't be any new house, if not for me. So that's whose fault it is. And when I say we got to do something, I mean me. And you have to help." I couldn't stand around all day waiting for them to answer. "Why are you looking at me like I was crazy?"

"I'm ready to help." Eech took a twist out of one of the faucets. "Except who're you to take the blame for everything?"

"Because I am, that's all. John said so himself. There's no point talking about blame. You can forget it. And you can forget about *Hemarzrich,* too, if you want. If that's the way the three of you feel, then what's the use of talking?"

"What're you getting sore about?" Eech let go of the faucet. "I said I was ready to help."

"Just because I asked what to do with the goat," Bitsy explained, "that doesn't mean I'm not ready, does it?"

"Me too!" said Bo.

I didn't know what there was I could do, but at least I had help. At least, we were on our way. The three of them followed me. To get out of school we took a chance on the front door instead of the basement, because the janitor's usually somewhere around down there. The stairs weren't any problem, we took them two at a time. It was the front hall, past the principal's office, we had to look out for.

We handled it like we were on TV, sliding along the walls and ducking past the doors, under where the glass was. We made it to the big main door without anyone seeing us. Except it wasn't necessary to sneak out of school. The lunch bell sounded. All we had to do was straighten up and walk out the big main door, with a flood of first and second graders tearing around us.

And even getting up to Hessian Hill, that wasn't necessary. From the back way we were taking out of town, we looked down an alley to the hardware store and there were a lot of cars parked in front. Including the ambulance.

"Wolf's back." Eech pointed. "He'd know, wouldn't he?

What happened at the hospital? How Onion John is?"

We headed down the alley and the closer we came to the hardware store, the better it looked. Through the windows we could see the store was crowded and we could see the men laughing. And no more than we opened the door, my father shouted, "It's okay, Andy. He's out of danger! Onion John is all right!"

Eech yipped. He and Bo and Bitsy went charging into the bunch around Ben Wolf who had all the news. I closed the door behind me and leaned against it until the bell up top stopped jangling. The hardware store is always worth smelling when you come in, a little sweet and oily and old. I took time for self-control, too, with my back and different joints and in my knees.

He was all right and I could take the time now. Even if everything that did happen was my fault, at least none of it was fatal. And when you stopped for a second, to think, John's new house wasn't my fault either, not anymore. Now that it was gone. Onion John could go back to living the way he wanted to. Except for his valuables, *Stepan* and the fiddle. They were my fault. But a picture of an old saint, anyone good at drawing could work that out. And there were plenty of old fiddles around and Rusch's stocked friction tape, all we'd need. When you came to look at it the fire might be the best thing could've happened to John as long as the rest of him was okay.

And from the way Ben Wolf talked, there didn't seem

to be any question of that. "They had John in a bath when I left," he said. "The nurse figured it would take two or three hours soaking to get through to him. What with the fire and just generally."

"But they're sure about it?" I pushed through to my father. "The X-ray?"

"His lung wasn't touched." Ben Wolf answered me.

"And the rib isn't so bad?" I asked my father.

"It's strapped," Ben answered me again. "It'll heal in no time."

"How long," I asked my father, "before they let John come back?"

"Why don't you ask Ben Wolf?" said my father. "He's the one who was there."

It was just I didn't feel like talking to Ben Wolf, right then. He was part of what no one had to think about for months to come, not until next summer. It was Eech told me that the hospital was going to keep John for about a week, to observe him.

"So it's all off," said Bitsy. "No use messing around with a goat now, is there?"

"What goat?" asked Ernie Miller, from the *Lamp*, behind me.

"Yes," said my father. "What was that all about, Andy, in the middle of everything?"

"John thought a goat would help him." I told about John's plans for the housewarming. "He couldn't see any use you get out of being protected with Compranshy. That's the insurance, he meant. You know, Comprehensive."

"He couldn't see any use?" My father shook his head. A couple of men laughed and my father laughed too. "It's only a life saver that's all it is. If it weren't for that policy we'd never be able to rebuild his house."

"What house?"

"John's new house."

Eechee looked at me. And so did Bo Hemmendinger and Bitsy Schwarz. "You're going to rebuild the whole house? That is, the same as it was?" I asked my father.

"Of course, Andy. That's the good of insurance. John's not going to lose out just because of the fire. We're putting him right back into it, the identical place, nail for nail."

"But you can't," I told my father.

"Can't what?"

"You can't do that. The thing is, you can't do that to me. I was lucky enough it wasn't fatal for Onion John. But a whole new house, that would be my fault too. Anything that happens, I'd be the one to blame."

"What's all this about you?" asked my father. "We're concerned with Onion John, getting a home for him. A proper place for Onion John to live in."

"But he can't live that way. He says it's no use trying. Wouldn't it be just as good, as far as Onion John goes, to leave him alone?"

My father started to smile at me, shaking his head. But when Ernie Miller from the *Lamp* interrupted, my father seemed to forget what he was going to say to me. He stopped smiling, too.

"The boy's right," said Ernie. "I think we've done enough for Onion John."

My father lifted up from leaning on the counter. He went up straight and his arms crossed. He held his elbows. The others around quieted too, looking at Ernie.

"Hasn't it become pretty obvious?" asked Ernie. "What we think is proper and what John thinks is proper, they're two different things. What are we trying to prove to him, that he's wrong?"

"Now, Ernie. We went all through this with you at the first Rotary meeting." My father waited until a couple of men nodded. "We're not going to rehash that discussion all over again. Not now."

"A lot's happened. We almost killed the man, doing him good. I think he's had it. I think we ought to forget the new house."

"That's what I think," I told my father.

"Not now, Andy. We'll go into this later." My father came out from behind the counter until I couldn't see his face anymore, the way he stood facing Mr. Miller. "This town took on an obligation, Ernie. To Onion John. And to ourselves. We've had a setback. All right. We didn't look for this to happen, but we're not going to let it stop us."

"We'd look foolish," said Mr. Ries, "backing out now."

"Onion John's our responsibility," said my father. "We decided to help him. And he needs our help more, right now, than he ever did before."

Most everybody agreed with my father. It came to sound like politics. Democracy came into it, which is what you hear about when there's going to be a vote or an election. Ernie said that no one's private rights ought to get invaded even if it's with kindness. And my father said that democracy didn't mean we ought to leave the next fellow go hang and not care how he got along. It went too fast for me to follow, and too loud. Judge Brandstetter said the question ought to be argued out in a regular way by the town council because Onion John had become a town matter by then. They all agreed, there ought to be a meeting. But it went on anyway, Ernie and my father and Ries and Brandstetter and Wolf and the crowd of them.

I left. Even though a good stiff argument with a lot of men lambasting each other can lead almost anywhere. And usually it's worthwhile staying around to watch what develops.

But this time I thought I might as well leave. My father said we'd go into it later, anyway. And now that I was going back to school, after all it was my lunch hour. And this time, besides all that, for the first time in my life I wasn't on my father's side. So there wasn't much use in sticking around.

Chapter 15

But it certainly didn't mean I had to run away from home. Just because we weren't on the same side together, me and my father.

All the running away I ever thought about was when I wanted to join the Third Cavalry Detachment in Fort Laramie and practiced drumming until I found there wasn't any more cavalry. Or any Fort Laramie either, except it's a town in Kansas. And of course, pirates. I put in a couple of days thinking I ought to ship out for one of those. But all that was when I was six. I haven't had any of those ideas since.

So it wasn't as if I was looking for an excuse to leave town, my father and mother and Serenity for good. It was just that there didn't seem to be any other chance for me to help Onion John.

I couldn't let him be moved back into a completely rebuilt new house. Where anything that happened would be my fault. And I couldn't side with Ernie Miller. Because how would I feel if I got into an argument with George Connors, who usually ends up sitting on your head when he argues. And my father came along? And he sided with George? I'd feel awful. It was bad enough I couldn't be on my father's side. I couldn't go lining up with Ernie Miller against him.

Especially after what Ernie wrote in the *Lamp*. In the paper he put out Wednesday, because Thursday was Thanksgiving, you could see he was talking about my father. "Let our knights in shining hardware spare Onion John," it said, "not spear him with their good intentions." Seeing how Rusch's is the only hardware store in Serenity, my father had every reason to take that personally. He put in the whole week end winding up to get back at Ernie. By talking to people about the council meeting that was coming, until it looked like everybody was going to vote with my father. And by writing the speech he was going to make.

My mother and I heard the speech right through the week end, in bits and pieces as my father made it up. And at breakfast on Monday we heard the whole thing through. By then, it sounded fine. Except it was just the opposite of what I wished my father was saying.

My mother applauded and I couldn't help but join in, to show how good the speech was. "That new gesture," she said, "where you clench your fist with your thumb up," she jabbed away as if she were ringing a doorbell. "That looks stunning."

"I didn't even realize I was doing it." My father was pleased. "It came out of the way I feel, I guess." He squared up the papers he had. "Anyway, I'm all set for tomorrow night."

There wasn't much time left if ever I was going to help Onion John. When my father finished his coffee, he looked at me and he asked, "How about it, Andy, does the speech convince you?" I figured the time had come when I ought to go into it, to do what I could.

"It certainly does," I said. "I don't see how Ernie Miller's going to argue against a speech like that."

"Well, I'm glad you're convinced. After what you said down at the hardware store."

"Me? I wasn't trying to argue with you, not like Ernie Miller. All I want to do is ask you a favor."

"What?"

"I want to ask you please not to build Onion John a new house again."

My father waited for whatever else I had in mind. There was nothing else I wanted except to ask him the favor. He picked up his speech from the table. "Didn't you hear any of this?" It was quiet the way he spoke. "The reasons why we're going ahead."

"I think they're fine," I told him. "All those reasons. Except Onion John doesn't want any new house."

My father nodded seriously when I told him that. He thought it over, squaring up the papers again on the table. He looked at my mother drinking her coffee and then he laid the speech down carefully, so the papers stayed neat. "Maybe you're right, Andy. Maybe Onion John doesn't want a new house."

"Then why build it up again?"

"Take you," said my father.

"Me?" I couldn't see why he was changing the subject so fast. "I wanted to talk about Onion John."

"You're the one who's important here," said my father. "And tell me, Andy, how much did you know a year ago about some of the plans we've been talking about? The things you're going to do?"

"Like the Institute? The way we've been talking about Technology? What've they got to do with Onion John?"

With only one day left to get John settled, I didn't see why we were talking about what didn't have to happen for years yet, to me.

"It all fits in, Andy. You couldn't have made any of those plans by yourself. You didn't know enough. Those were matters too strange and too new for you to even think about. And maybe the whole idea didn't sound too good to begin with. But as time goes by, you're beginning to see the possibilities there are, the kind of life it'll be. Isn't that so?"

"Well, I understand a lot more about it, sure."

"And the chances are, a dozen years from now, you'll thank your lucky stars for the career you're in. But no matter how far you go, Andy, the start was something you couldn't decide for yourself. You wouldn't know how to go about it. Someone had to make up your mind for you, what you wanted to do and how to live. And it's the same with Onion John."

I was glad we were back to Onion John and I nodded.

"He doesn't know what it means to live decently. All we're doing is to give him the chance to find out. He'd never know if he kept on living the way he was. And if he's a little unhappy at the start, well, that's part of it, part of getting used to a new idea. It's no more than the gripe you might feel, first off, about putting in next summer down at General Magneto."

I felt like a drink. Not milk, because there was a pitcher of that on the table. I felt like a glass of water. And I went over to the sink to get it.

But even at the faucet, with my back to my father so that I didn't have to look at him, I couldn't decide what my father was trying to say about General Magneto. I could see about Onion John. It was clear, it was very clear I wasn't helping him to get left alone. But me and General Magneto, that sounded like it was all settled too. Except the last time we talked there were two hundred and seventeen days before anyone had to think about General Magneto. And all those days I had to look forward to, they couldn't come to an end right this morning. I was pretty sure my father wasn't trying to say anything like that. But I thought I'd better stop drinking water and find out.

"It's not the same, is it?" I held on to my glass. "Because Ben Wolf and General Magneto are vague. After all, they're no more than possibilities to think over."

"No." My father shook his head at me when I turned. "I asked Ben to fix it. And he has." There wasn't any more doubt about what my father was trying to say. He just said it. "It's all arranged. There's a job waiting for you at General Magneto. That's what you're going to do. Why waste another summer down at the hardware store?"

I didn't answer him right off. Because that's when the thought struck me. How there was one more, last way that I could help Onion John. It came to me right out of the blue and I went back to drinking water. I could run away with Onion John. It was a surprise, even to me, how simple the idea was. But before I put my mind to it, I wanted to make sure.

"It's all arranged?" I sounded hollow from talking into the glass.

My father shook his head, once, to say yes. "Ben's set up an interview down there and I thought one of these days—"

My mother interrupted. "Andrew," she told my father, "you'd better get going. It's late."

According to the alarm clock on the window sill above the sink it wasn't so late. But my mother insisted. "We've gone far enough, Andrew, for the moment. It's late. We can leave this for some other time."

My father took another look at the clock and remembered he had to be down at the store early. "See you, Andy," he said. I nodded to him as he left the kitchen, without talking, because the glass was clamped between my teeth. And besides my new idea was spreading out and I was beginning to see how good it was. Why it never came into my head before, that's the only part I couldn't figure.

"What's the idea of all the water?" my mother asked me. "If you're thirsty, sit down and have some milk."

I got the glass from between my teeth. And I sat down. It was absolutely clear. If they couldn't leave Onion John alone, my father and the town, then what was more natural. Onion John could leave them alone. If he wanted to stay the way he was, John's only chance was somewhere else. It was that simple.

"Andy," said my mother.

"Yes ma'am."

"I want you to understand your father."

"There's nothing so hard about it. Onion John's going to get built up again. And I'm going down to General Magneto."

"Let's leave Onion John out of this. It's your Pa I want you to understand, the plans he's making for you."

There was nothing else to think about, for me, except Onion John. The idea was only the beginning. To get set to run away, there's a lot to decide on. For instance, how soon? And then, where to?

"It might help you to know this, Andy. There's one thing your father's never told you about your career. It's a lot older than you are. It used to belong to him."

And a third was, what to take along?

"Andy."

"I'm listening."

"Does it help you to understand, that your father wanted to be an engineer? It was radio in his time. But all the plans he has for you, those were the things he was going to do himself. He was going to leave Serenity. And he was going up to M. I. T. And on, from there. That used to be his career, Andy."

"What happened?"

"Well, there were circumstances. And you happened, you were one of them. Anyway, he never made it. But your father held to that plan, he's kept it bright and new with the thought he's put into it year after year. And now he's giving it to you. You mightn't think much of it, at the moment. But no matter how you feel about that career, Andy, I want you to remember it's about the most valuable possession your father has."

"I'll remember," I said.

My mother made a pile out of three or four dishes. She started to collect the silverware too and had a fistful before she stopped.

"Not only remember it. But consider it. Try to understand how your father feels about it."

"I'll try." I figured we'd have a lot of time once we left town to consider how my father wanted to be an engineer. South was where we'd probably head, now it was December. Out in the desert or under a palm tree, we'd have plenty of time. "I'll certainly try," I told her.

"Andy!" It was Eechee Ries outside, come to pick me up on the way to school. He banged at the door and opened it. He stared at me, surprised, as if I'd already told him what I was going to do. "Wait'll you hear!" he said.

"Wait'll you hear!" I told him. I could just see Ries keel over when he heard I was going to run away.

"Onion John's gone," said Eech. "He's skipped the hospital. He's run away."

"By himself?" I asked.

"Yes," said Eech.

Chapter 16

The door closed. Eech bumped it with his backside and it closed.

There wasn't much more he had to tell us about Onion John running away. Just that he did. Ben Wolf heard the report from the hospital that Onion John's bed wasn't even slept in. Eech heard it from Mr. Kinnoy, not two minutes before, just around the corner. For all the questions my mother asked, that's all there was to find out. Onion John had run away. That was enough, it seemed to me, and I listened without asking any questions.

I listened and I looked at the door behind Eech. It has four panels, the door in our kitchen, two long ones at the bottom and square ones on top. It has an Erwin lock that's mortised in, not screwed on the outside, and a pair of heavy brass knobs. The door has a nice balance to it. One touch and it closes solid with a loud click when the latch springs home.

The door's been around as long as I have. But I never

came to notice all the things about it the way I did that morning. And the reason is, that's how I felt when Eech said, "He's run away!" Like a door closed. And watching a real door actually close, a second later, I suppose that's what made me notice.

I saw I couldn't leave Serenity, not with Onion John. Because he was gone. And I couldn't stay, not with my father. Because I was on my way to General Magneto. And in four more years I was on my way out of Serenity for good. Both ways, it was like a door closed.

And there was nothing to do, nothing at all, except to go to school and study about World War I in history. And *Ivanhoe* in English. And the isosceles triangle. And in geography, Brazil, its resources. I found out about Woodrow Wilson, all his problems. And about knights with their battle axes. And 130 degree angles. And the coffee bean. But I didn't find out how it happened with me. How it ever happened that anyone could start out with as good a friend as Onion John, and as good a father as the one I had, and end up nowhere. Behind a closed door.

The only decent thing about that Monday was the kind of day it was. If you felt mean and miserable and hopeless, it was a great day for that. It was cold and gray and the damp cut into you, and it felt like snow. It was a great day to go no place but home and to stay behind closed doors. But I didn't go home from school. On account of Eech, again.

He has ears like an elephant. Whatever's going around, he's likely to hear it soon. Like that morning, how Onion John had run away. And that afternoon, how Onion John was seen up on Hessian Hill digging in his garden. It was Mr. Tracy who saw him. When Tracy yelled, Onion John dropped what he was doing and headed for the woods. A car, full of men, had gone up to Hessian Hill to find John and take him back to the hospital. Eech heard it all from the janitor, down in the basement during afternoon recess.

It was a hope. It meant that Onion John hadn't lit out for west of the Rockies, somewhere. It could mean he was still around.

"We could be the ones to find him," I told Eech. "Instead of whoever it was that went up to Hessian Hill."

"What for? To send him back to the hospital?"

"No." I didn't want to let Eech in on my plan to run away with John. "Maybe we could help him stay out of sight. They might vote different at the meeting tomorrow night, if they think John's gone. Besides," I told Eech, "*Hemarzrich.*"

"Sure," said Eech. "I'm ready to go look."

Hessian Hill's to the east of Serenity. There was no use going there, long as the place was covered. We headed west. We knew most of John's favorite spots on the Musconetty and we checked down the creek until we came to Mantini's meadows where we cut across to look along the big river. It was Eech who thought of McKardle's cave.

This isn't a real cave, just an old foundation dug into a slope high over the river, in back of where the Duseks farmed. Part of it was covered over, so you could think of it as a cave, and John talked of the place as ideal to settle in for anyone who was looking around. We hauled ourselves up there.

The day it was, you didn't know whether it was over with and night was coming or whether it was hours yet until supper. Either way, McKardle's cave was the last chance we had. We couldn't make any time wading up through the fallen leaves, pulling ourselves past the wet empty trees and climbing over one ledge of stone then another. If there was nothing to see in McKardle's cave, all we had left was to head back to town.

He was there! When we came over the crest of the hill and looked down the river side to the cave below, there sat Onion John in front of a little fire.

All he had on was a nightgown, a hospital nightgown for a shirt and a pair of pants pulled over it. But to me he looked better than I ever saw him in all my life. He looked wonderful.

"Onion John!" Eech and I didn't care if they heard us back in Serenity. We jumped and we landed on the floor of the foundation in a dead heat, the two of us.

John jumped too. He headed straight out of sight. He disappeared behind the stone wall that was part of the old cellar.

"John!" I yelled. "It's only us. It's me, Andy. And Eechee Ries."

John peeked back around the edge of the stone.

"Only us!"

John made the trip back as fast as he left. He came down to his knees and threw an arm around Eech and one around me, like we were a couple of ball carriers he was tackling. We yelled at the squeeze he put on.

"You look great," I told him. "How do you feel?"

John let go and he moaned. The trouble was he felt fine. His rib and all the rest of him was just fine. And still they insisted on keeping him in the hospital. All they did was bathe him, he complained, once every day. That was one of the reasons he ran away, to escape from all the baths. Another reason was to get to his garden before the cold froze it solid, so he could spade it up for a winter crop of rye. But the big reason was the meeting. He'd heard they were going to vote him back into the new house.

"It's practically certain," I told Onion John. "Especially after they hear my father's speech. It convinced me."

John nodded. That's what he was afraid of, and sitting in a tub of hot water there was nothing he could do about it. But now he was out he certainly didn't intend to let the house be voted up again.

"Don't you worry," I told him. "I know how to stop them. A plain, easy, simple way."

John wasn't worried. He had plans of his own, to keep

them from building any more houses. He brought us over to the fire to listen.

And then he came out with the most ridiculous, the dog-awfulest notion I ever heard of. He said he was going to fumigate the whole town of Serenity, just the way he smoked the evil spirits out of my cellar on Halloween eve. John had the idea that if he collected a pile of oak and got a fire started with a twirling stick when the wind was in the right direction, that would solve his problem. He actually believed that if the people around town breathed in the smoke, it would get rid of the evil spirits that were in them.

He went on that way, explaining it all as if it were the most sensible idea in the world. He said it was the evil spirits in the people of Serenity that plagued them into building the new house. And he was positive, once the smoke drifted through the town it would carry the evil spirits away. And then everyone would forget about the vote. And they'd all go back to being ordinary good friends of his again, with no more on their mind than to wish him, "Good day."

"Onion John," I said when he finished and stood by the fire smiling at Eechee and me, "if you ask me, that's not such a good idea. I don't think it'll get you anywhere."

John stood there a little bewildered, pleased as he was with the plan he figured out.

"There's only one way you're going to stop them," I

said. "Only one, sure, practical way. And that is, you've got to leave town. You have got to run away from Serenity."

John leaned way back with his palms out. He couldn't see that at all. He liked Serenity. He shook his head. Why should he run away?

"It doesn't look as if they're ever going to leave you alone, John. So, you've got to leave them alone. It's the only way!"

John picked up a branch from a pile of wood he'd gathered. He broke it over his knee and he tossed the pieces on the fire. Onion John asked me to please explain to him what was wrong with the oak fire, the notion he had.

"It won't work." I didn't just want to tell him how mixed-up and far-fetched it was. I thought I'd prove it to him. "When you say evil spirits, there's none of those in Serenity. Those people, they're filled with good spirits. Look, John, they want to do the best they can for you. There's no evil spirits in that. Every one of them is out to make you happy. And if you fill them with smoke that's meant for evil spirits, then no one's going to notice it. Except to sneeze, maybe."

John smiled to quiet me down. He had a theory. It was just about as sensible as the rest of it. He told how a spirit gets into a person, sometimes, hiding behind a thought that's very nice, and gentle and kind. But once inside the spirit turns out to be evil the way a crock of milk goes sour on an August afternoon. He was sure that's what happened in Serenity, to everybody. What started out nice ended up, without anyone knowing, bad.

I gave up. "Onion John, what's the use arguing." This was real, the trouble he was in, and he couldn't go playing around with it like it was a fairy tale. "Trying to fumigate the evil spirits out of Serenity is just plain foolish. And that's all it is, foolish."

Onion John worked it around a couple of times, his lips moving, and then he got the word out. "Foolish?" He sat down at the fire and looked across at me, as if to check whether he had it right. He made it again, very clear. "Foolish?"

"I mean impractical." I got down on my hands and knees across from where he sat. "There's no logic to it. No rhyme or reason! Ask Eechee."

John looked behind him, to Eech. Eech sat down and picked up a piece of wood to juggle. "I don't know," he said. "It sounds just as good as a lot of other ideas that Onion John's had."

"But Eechee!" I had to get them to listen very carefully. "And John!" I waved away the smoke from between us. "This is serious, a serious situation. It's nothing you can take a chance on. And the oak fire, let's just say that it can work. For the sake of argument, let's say that. But maybe it won't work! Maybe John drowns this whole valley in smoke and still and all, the first time anyone sees him, klunk, in he goes to the hospital and up goes the house. That can happen, couldn't it?"

"Of course," said Eech. "It's possible. It could happen."

"But if he runs away, it can't happen. That's the difference. Nothing like that's possible. It just isn't!"

Eech hefted the stick in his hand. "I see what you mean." Onion John sat studying the fire, quiet as ever.

"It stands to reason, they'll never build that house for Onion John if he's not around to build it for."

Onion John left off with the fire and took to studying me. I could see he was getting the drift of it now.

"That's all I want to point out. One way's sure. There's sense to it. It can't help but work. And the other way is only maybe."

"And between the two," Eech used his stick for a poker, "I think you're right. Your way is sure."

John nodded. He held his hands out to the fire and bathed his face in the warmth he collected. When he started to talk, it was in low gear, not pushing sixty the way he usually went. My way was sure, he agreed. Except, he shrugged, he didn't want to leave Serenity. And even if his idea wasn't so sure, maybe it would root a lot of evil spirits out of the town. Maybe his way, everyone would be better off.

"Well, I don't know." I looked at the fire and Eech shifted a stick where the draft was blocked. The spot blazed up. "It's up to you to decide, Onion John. Whether you want to fix up the town or get yourself saved. It seems to me you're the one's most in trouble. And if you want to get out of it, well, you have to get out. That's about it!"

John took a long time to make up his mind. I watched him and then I watched the smoke from the fire go up, to stop and dip and circle up again until it spread into nothing, a part of the heavy gray day that was ending.

The first part of what Onion John had to say was in his own language and it sounded like the longest string of slow riding cuss words I ever heard. And then it turned out he was agreeing with me. My way was sure. It was sensible. It was the only thing he could do.

"He's going to run away, Eech!" I was on my feet looking down at them. "He's going to do it!"

"Are you, John?" asked Eech. Slowly, John nodded.

"And now!" I walked around the fire. "Wait'll you hear!"

"Something else?" Eech followed me, with his eyes.

"Maybe the best part. I didn't have in mind, John, to see you go off by yourself. On your own. Do you know what I'm going to do?" I let them wait for a couple of seconds to find out what I was smiling at. "I'm going to run away with you."

"Who?" asked Eech.

"Me."

"Why?"

"John's my fault, isn't he? Wasn't I the one had to help

him? I've had it ever since this morning, how I could. I'm going to help him run away. Do you understand, John? I'm going with you!"

The least I thought he'd be was pleased. John didn't move. As if he didn't even hear me. He sat and watched the fire. I told him again, I was going to help him. He started to shake his head. Then a rumble came out and soon he was breaking his own speed limit. It all ended up, No! He wasn't going to let me help him. And why? Because that's how all the trouble started, the help that was piled on to him. He wasn't going to take any more help. From no one. Not even me. He saw he had to run away. It was the only sure thing. But he was going by himself. Without any help.

He threw a knot of wood into the flame and the fire scattered.

"But, John," I started. "The thing is—"

And right then and there I stopped. I stopped lying. Because I could see that's all it was. Me wanting to help John run away, that was a lie. If all I wanted was for John to run away, I would've cheered that morning when Eech came through the door. When I heard John was gone. And I didn't cheer. I didn't even feel happy about it. I felt sad. A good many lies, there's at least two sides to them and you can take a point of view. But this was a flat lie. You couldn't get around it.

I sat down and I told him the honest truth. "If you want to know, John, I'm in the same fix you are. And when it comes to any help, the truth is I'm asking you to help me. For you to please let me go away with you."

"Why?" Eech was shocked. "What's the matter with you, Andy?"

"Nothing, except I'd like to stay in Serenity."

"That's why you want to run away? Where's the sense to it?"

"It's not a question what I want. I'd just as soon stay on here, down at the store, with my father. But I can't. I have to go. And I'd rather go with John, if he'll only let me, than down to General Magneto." I told them all about it, how it was settled for next summer. And then how I was going up to Technology and up to the moon, for all I knew, before I stopped going. "Unless it's okay to go with you, John."

The look of disgust came over John's face, you'd think he bit into a mildewed onion. He told me to stop lying.

"But I have. Didn't you hear, I want you to help me. That's no lie! What I'm telling you now is the absolute truth."

Not about the moon, John shook his head. There couldn't be any truth in that. Whoever heard of any one going to the moon, he asked, least of all me?

"But it is true," said Eech. "That part."

"In only a couple of years, John. There's men going to the moon. Ask anybody!"

It took us a while before John would even listen. Eech

remembered about orbits and intercontinental ballistic missiles. And I remembered about LOX, the fuel they use in rockets, and twenty-four thousand miles an hour. But it was impossible to get John to believe in a simple, ordinary, everyday fact. It was only when we swore on the name of *Stepan,* the saint from his hometown, that he began to put any trust in us. We swore three times and then he believed us.

It veered his attitude into a complete about face. He took me by the arm and held it tight. He patted me on the shoulder. I was in worse trouble, he said, than anything was happening to him. Worse trouble than anyone he ever heard about, as far back in history as he could remember.

"Then look, John, can I go with you?"

Onion John said yes.

I shot up to my feet.

"You're going?" yelled Eech. "Really, Andy?"

"We're on our way!" I swung at Eech and he belted me, harder than he had to for a celebration. I let him have one just as hard. He pushed and I sprawled, clipping him in back of the knees so he went down too. We ended up on the other side of the fire. When we looked around to John, there wasn't much of a smile on his face. He sat there quiet.

"When are you taking off?" asked Eech.

John looked up beyond the trees, studying the sky and sniffing at it. It was going to snow. But snow or not, John thought, we'd better leave that night. To put an end to anyone looking for him. And the snow wasn't so bad. When he came to Serenity, twenty-five years before, it snowed. And he'd just as soon go out of Serenity the way he came in. It was suitable, he thought. If I could get ready—

There wasn't much I needed. John was the problem, getting him outfitted. That's when *Hemarzrich* turned out to be such a good code, again. Eech promised to rustle up a couple of overcoats for John and bring them up to McKardle's cave with whatever other clothes he could lay his hands on. The food and groceries were left up to me.

"It won't take long to get ready," I said. "Except I'll have to wait until we're all asleep in our house."

"Midnight," said Eech. "That's when you ought to leave. You could meet behind the piano factory at midnight."

"Why then?"

"Think of the way it sounds. When I tell the story how the two of you left Serenity, I can say—they left at midnight."

John didn't have any objections to midnight. And neither did I. As long as it gave Eech a better story to tell. John and I shook hands. There was a wet spot on my cheek, a flake of snow. It was starting. "Midnight," I said. "Behind the piano factory."

Chapter 17

My mother looks like a very beautiful woman. She has a round face and a nose that's undersized and straight back shiny hair that rolls together behind her neck. She's not the kind of beautiful you see on TV. There's a picture we have of a beautiful woman down at the hardware store, inside the cover of a cigar box where we keep off-standard screws and nuts. My mother is beautiful the way that picture is.

I checked her over at supper that night. And my father too. I hadn't much of a chance to study either one since that morning when I decided to run away. And supper was getting close to the last chance for a good look. I could see there was nothing wrong with my father's ears. He jokes about the way they stick out. They're pretty good looking ears as far as I'm concerned. Everything else on my father's face is long, his nose and his chin and his eyebrows, the way they close in on each other.

All through the thick pea soup that was made out of the

carcass of the Thanksgiving turkey, with dumplings in it, I had the view of them pretty much to myself. Most of that time they put in on Onion John, without any need for me to join in. They wondered where he might be. My father was one of those who went up to scour Hessian Hill, and he thought it was terrible that Onion John had disappeared. He and my mother wondered how it would affect the council meeting the next night. Or whether there'd be any meeting at all. My mother had a string of pearl beads on and my father, a bow tie. The sight they made across the table, I knew I'd never forget it no matter how far away I went.

I had an extra plate of the thick pea soup. Besides being a favorite of mine, there was no way of telling how lucky we'd be getting a hitch out of town and when we'd hit a diner to get something hot. It was going to be a long night, with the wind coming up and the snow. I reminded myself how that was something I had to take along, something hot, in a thermos.

I stayed on at the dining room table with my school books and, to be sure I remembered everything, I worked on a list of what I had to take. The two went on to the living room where my mother was embroidering a pillow slip and they watched a quiz program. There was a question came up about Woodrow Wilson I knew the answer to myself. Only the lady on the program got a hundred and twenty eight thousand dollars for it.

On my own, I had a dollar and a half saved. It wasn't

much to run away on. But John had his pocketbook. And there was the snow. It made traveling worse but the snow was something to shovel to bring in a little extra.

After the quiz I heard them talk over about the late show, whether it was worth losing any sleep over. For a second I was worried because that'd keep them up until twelve thirty. My mother thought it wasn't worth going back twenty years, just to look at a picture. So the set went off. I put away my school books, in the broom closet where they'd be out of the way from now on.

I was the first one up and I was in the bottoms of my pajamas when they came to the top of the stairs. Ordinarily I yell out, but this time I went into the hall special to say good night. It was for the last time. I would've liked to say something more than usual, the occasion it was. But there's not too many different ways of saying good night, without raising suspicion. We said, "Good night, sleep tight," same as always and I went back into my bedroom and got dressed again.

I had an hour and a half to get ready.

I worked with a flashlight, picking out the clothes to put in the knapsack I had. Keeping quiet, working with that small circle of light, my breath grew shorter and shorter until I found it was stopped all together. I sat down on the bed and reasoned there was nothing to get winded about. As long as I kept very quiet. I didn't take many clothes. And there was nothing else out of my bedroom, to go, except that copy of the *Lamp* from the summer with the picture of the ball team in it.

I needed all the room there was in the knapsack for food. I found a lot of turkey wrapped in wax paper in the refrigerator. It made five sandwiches. Thick and not so neat, the sandwiches used up space. And when I piled in a jar of pickles and two cans of peaches, an extra loaf of bread, all the onions there were for John, and two boxes of sweet crackers, the knapsack was stuffed. Without even room for the thermos. A jar of pickles went back, a can of peaches and a box of crackers.

I thought I was ruined, boiling up a pot of instant cocoa. I banged the pot. For five minutes I stood still as a chair in the dark kitchen. There wasn't any other sound. I boiled the cocoa and filled the thermos. And I was ready.

I ran the light around the kitchen for a last look. I noticed the door again with its four panels. I tiptoed upstairs to my bedroom for the scout knife I remembered about. It was in the top drawer of my dresser. I took a last look at the bedroom. I noticed the pennant my father gave me, over the bed, Massachusetts Institute of Technology. Onion John and I would take a walk past the Institute, someday, I thought, to see what it was like.

The numbers on my alarm clock were dim in the dark. It was eleven thirty. That gave me a half hour to get out to the piano factory. There was time to spare. And I didn't think so much of waiting around for Onion John in back of the piano factory, blowing the way it was outside and the curve growing in the corner of my window from the snow. But there was nothing to keep me any longer. Nothing more to do. And no reason why I shouldn't get started. This was one night I was going to be out in, anyway, for as long as it lasted. Ten minutes more wasn't going to make any difference.

I went down a step at a time. I felt carefully, one foot after another, on each stair before I let my weight go. One of them squeaks, depending on the weather. None did, this time. At least none of the upper stairs did. I never did get to find out about the last eight steps.

Because the front doorbell rang. I stood still in the dark that was turned into a boiler factory, with the doorbell ringing. The whole house shook, or I did, and shivered with the machine gun clang that came up. The light went on behind me and my father was at the top of the stairs with one arm in his bathrobe.

"Andy! What are you doing, up?" He came to where I was. "With your mackinaw on?" He didn't give me a chance to answer, rushing past to get to the doorbell ringing. I couldn't anyway, being choked. And I didn't have to answer my mother either when she showed up in her dressing gown. "Good grief!" She came down the steps. "Great heavens, Andy, look at you!" There was nothing you had to say to those remarks.

By that time my father had the door open.

And there stood Onion John. He stood with a heavy bag over his shoulder and he was embroidered in snow. Eechee had him fixed up fine. He had an army coat again, a long one. And a stocking cap, a blue one that came up to a ball instead of a point. There were heavy shoes on his feet, good ones for walking, and around his pants he'd wrapped a pair of puttees made out of burlap. He couldn't be dressed any better for a trip.

He stood in the door with the fingers of his left hand pinned together and he circled them, talking away.

My father wrung his head as if to get the water out of his ears. "What's this all about?" He turned to me. "What's he saying?"

"On account of it's a cold night, he thinks if you don't want to get the house chilled it would be better if he could close the door. That is, if you don't mind for him to come in to the hall." I got it out before my voice twisted up. I didn't have any more control over it than a busted radio.

My father didn't make me out too well, either. He squinted up the staircase. "And you?" he threw off another shake of the head. "What is this?"

"Yes, Andy," my mother had me tight around the shoulders, "what is this?"

"I don't know," I tuned myself down. "Whatever it is, I guess it's all off. Except Onion John wants to know can he come in?"

"Of course, John. Get in here!" My father pulled the

door wide. John dropped his bag. He unbuttoned his overcoat and ruffled it to get the snow off. Underneath he was wearing a nice tan raincoat that had a belt around it. It was a new looking raincoat so he was wearing it inside, I imagine, to protect it from the weather. He stamped his feet. And all the while he looked at me, serious, as if he couldn't wait to tell me what he had in mind.

I couldn't wait, either, watching him come in. Except my father kept piling him with questions. Where'd he been? What did he think he was doing? Didn't he realize the whole town was looking for him, with everybody worried? And my mother had another pile to ask me. How come I was all dressed up? Did I know what time of the night it was? And where was I going?

John stood at the foot of the staircase and I sat down. We stared at each other, waiting for the chance that my father and mother would get through. My father stopped first. Onion John told my father that he'd come to see me.

"Why?" I asked him. "Why did you have to call it off? You're not going back to fumigating, don't tell me that!"

John got as far as to say, no, he'd given that up. When my father came in again.

"If you'd only give him half a minute?" I asked my father.

"What's called off?" asked my mother.

"Andy, I want to know what goes on here?"

"I don't know. I mean it. If you'd only let me find out,

I'd be glad to tell you. Just half a minute is all." My father held still. My mother sat down beside me. The three of us waited on Onion John. He came around the bottom of the staircase and he talked to me through the banisters.

He told me nothing was called off, as far as leaving Serenity went. That was still the idea.

"Except can't you see, John, it's wrecked. With you coming here! What was wrong with the piano factory? For Heaven's sakes, John, the way we planned."

"What plans?"

"Let them be, Andrew," said my mother.

Onion John told me, then, that he was going to leave Serenity without me. He told me that I couldn't go with him. He told me he sat up in McKardle's cave and that many hours went by with him looking at the fire. And after all that time, when he had nothing more to look at except red coals, he decided. He came to the place where he changed his mind about me. He decided he would run away alone. I couldn't come with him. He said he was sorry.

"What's the matter with me?" I asked him. "Why?"

Onion John told me I was grown up.

"What?" I looked over the rail at him. "What're you talking about?"

John nodded very slowly, like a principal in school. He was pretty sure, he said. He looked at it from every angle before he decided. And there wasn't any doubt in his mind what happened to me.

"Andy? What's the trouble?" asked my mother. With one finger under my chin, she closed my mouth.

My father came up the stairs and kneeled on the step below us. "What'd John say?"

"He said I was grown up."

My father and mother examined each other for a second, very surprised. "When did it happen?" asked my father.

"John says this afternoon."

"How does he know?"

John shrugged and told me he'd had enough experience. After twenty-five years in Serenity, he pointed out where he'd become an expert in small boys. They were the only ones he got along with when it came to doing things together. And the day always came, he noticed, with every one of them, when they stopped believing in him. When they just didn't see any more sense in the things he did. All through those twenty-five years in Serenity it happened over and over again. As one, then another, grew up.

And that afternoon, John nodded his head at me through the banisters, it happened to me.

"Good grief," I said. "When?"

"Foolish." John spoke the word clearer than that afternoon, as if he'd been rehearsing it. It was because of what I thought about that far-fetched idea he had, with the oak fire, how it would never work. That was it. That's why he changed his mind. If I didn't believe him anymore, how was it possible for us to get along together? We couldn't.

It was too late, John shook his head. I was too far gone to run away with.

"It just isn't so," I told him. I raised myself up a step. "I don't care how many angles you looked at." I lifted back another step. "It isn't, John, it just isn't so!"

"What isn't so?" My mother watched me climb the stairs backwards.

"I'm not grown up," I yelled at John through the posts. "The whole idea you had, it wasn't practical. It wouldn't ever work."

"What wouldn't?" asked my mother.

"Andy, can't you let us in on this?" My father followed me up a couple of steps.

"All right, John, you listen to my father. He'll tell you himself." I pointed to a flower in the stair carpet, just for something to point at. "If you got up tomorrow morning," I asked my father, "and you breathed some smoke from an oak fire, would that make any difference to you?"

"How, Andy? In what way?"

"Would it get rid of any of the evil spirits in you?"

"Evil who?" My father caught at the rail and straightened up. After a second, he passed the question along to my mother. "In me?"

She looked puzzled too. "Is that the way you think of your father, Andy? You think he's evil?"

"No, I'm not saying that." I pointed to the flower and made it clear for them. "Pa's great. There's no doubt about it. He thinks only kind thoughts. And all he's out to do is what's best, for the best reasons, and the best arguments. Like he wants to build a new house to make John happy. And me. He wants me to go to the moon so I'll have the best career. It's only the way the thought works out. What happens to it. It don't make John happy. And me neither, not about General Magneto. The only one it makes happy is the evil spirit that's turned up in Pa. And all I'm asking—"

"Whoa, Andy! Hold it!" My father felt around with his knee and he shifted to sit down on the step where he was. "We can't take all that for granted! That there are evil spirits in me!"

"We don't have to. All it gets down to is this. Yes or no. Would an oak fire, the smell of it, stop you from building John's house again?"

I don't know why it took my father so long. His attention was caught by the carpet in front of him, by the design of it.

"It's a simple enough question."

"As far as it goes," my father sighed, "I guess it wouldn't stop me. No."

"There, did you hear that?" I yelled at John. I threw one leg over the rail and slid half way. I jumped the last four steps into the hall. "The whole idea of fumigating, John, it was useless. That's why I said foolish. It doesn't have anything to do with how old I am. Any baby in a cradle would tell you the same thing."

John acted like I had temperature. He smoothed my shoulder. It didn't make any difference, he said, the way my father agreed with me. It was only more proof, even, I was grown up. He pulled the top button of his overcoat closed.

"But, John!" I raised my hand. And I looked at it, at my hand. What was it doing up there? What was the point of arguing? Even if I convinced Onion John I was the same as always, I couldn't walk out of the house past my father and mother and go along with him. "Can't you see," I let my hand down, " how things are?"

John closed his eyes to show how sorry he was for me. Never in his life, he said, had he heard of anyone who was in more trouble than I. But there was nothing he could do about it. And now it was time he got started.

"Not tonight!" I walked backwards, ahead of him down the hall. He had to give me another chance. He had to wait until we could get off somewhere, just the two of us and we could talk. So I could get him to understand we were still good friends and nothing was changed. "Please!"

The way he went about it was very gentle. There wasn't any push to it, or shove. But I was like a stranger he met who was blocking the sidewalk. He took me by the shoulders and he set me over to one side, out of his way. It was as if we were passing by somewhere, the way he acted, and he was going one way and me another.

"Where's he going?" asked my mother.

For the life of me I couldn't see what I'd done, so wrong, for us to end up strangers this way.

"Andy?"

"I don't know where he's going. Except he's running away from Serenity, by himself."

"By himself? You mean that's what you were up to, Andy?" My mother was right behind. She pulled me around. "Andy, you were running away from home?"

She looked even more beautiful than at supper because her face, the color of it, was like she'd been walking through the wind.

"Not anymore," I told her. "I'm too old for it. That's what John says."

My mother took the black and white hunting hat off my head and held it to her dressing gown. "Onion John, I don't know how to thank you for coming here tonight."

"That was very wise and helpful of you, John. Once a boy grows up, you're right, he can't run away from home. That's no way for him to get anywhere!" My father put a hand on John's arm, to keep him from buttoning his overcoat. "And you can't either. You can't run away from Serenity. Your home's here. We're your friends. We want to help you."

John shook his head. "That sounds like another lie," I told my father.

"Another what?" The fists my father made, he put into the pockets of his bathrobe.

"It's something like what I told John this afternoon. I said I wanted to help him. Then I saw I was trying to work things out for myself. More than to help just him. It was too big a lie for me to handle. I don't know about you. Anyway, John says he can't use any more help."

John nodded to show that's the way he felt about it. He finished with his overcoat and went to work on the big collar it had, tucking himself in. Which was just as well, from the noise the wind made in the quiet of the hall.

"John," my father's hands were open again. "I won't ask you to believe me. But one thing you can see is true, beyond question. You can help us. The town. It's not only how ridiculous we'll feel, if you leave. Though that's part of it, to be honest with you. We're proud of what we tried to do. And it will be a blow, to our self-respect, if you throw it all back at us and walk out. John, would you listen to me?"

It was a tough collar to close. John was bent half backwards, looking at the ceiling, trying to get the loop over a button. With his elbows out, stiff, he looked to be strangling himself.

"It won't do you any good, asking John for his help." I didn't want to see my father go to all that trouble. "I asked him too. He just won't."

My father went to John's rescue and the two of them got the collar, at least, straightened out.

"But it isn't only our pride, John, that's not why I'm

asking you to help. It's a great deal more important than pride. If you leave Serenity, the people here will be shy of every kind hearted thought that comes along. The next time there's a real need, no matter what, we'll hesitate. We'll get suspicious of ourselves. On account of what's happened to you. If you leave, John, you'll leave this town cold. And scared to make even the smallest move that's friendly. That's why you have to stay and help us."

John listened, now he was dressed snug, till my father finished. Then he put his hands to his chest and he shrugged. He explained how he felt.

"He won't stay?" asked my father.

"He can't help. He's tried. Up at the house he tried his best to do everything you wanted. He can't manage it. And he's not going to try anymore."

"And the rest? What else was he saying?"

"Nothing. Except if he could help anyone, he would like to help me."

"What else, Andy?"

"Well, it's only his way of talking."

"Tell me."

"Well, he said he never heard of any father who would send his only son to the moon. He heard of kings putting their boy on top of a castle. Or in a cave with a dragon outside. But I was the first he ever came across, getting shipped to the moon. And he was interested to help me, if he could. The only chance though, he thinks, is fumigating."

"Good night!" My father rubbed his eyes, tired as he was, considering the time and all his hard talking. "Doesn't he know how foolish that is?"

"Well, I did try to tell him that."

"So you did." My father's smile, when he took his hand away from his mouth, was tired too. "I never thought," he said to my mother, "we'd ever hear Andy call an idea of Onion John's foolish. If nothing else comes out of this, I think maybe your son has grown up."

He pulled the cord of his bathrobe tighter. His arms crossed and he held on to his elbows, but this time it was like he was holding himself together in front of Onion John. "All right, John. Maybe I am filled with evil spirits. And maybe we did try to lie to you, Andy and I. But all that's over with. You win."

What was win? John wanted to know.

"We're going to forget the house. We'll call it off. At the meeting tomorrow night. Let Ernie Miller get up on his hind legs and crow. But there won't be any new house, Onion John. We'll vote it down."

Onion John had his head twisted, listening with his right ear. "My father's trying to tell you," I went to him, "you don't have to run away. It's going to be the way you want. No house. You can stay here in Serenity."

Onion John stood there in our hall, buttoned up in his overcoats, and along with the wind piling around the corner outside, my father and mother and I listened to Onion John.

He thought the best thing he could do was leave. He was going.

"But I promise you," said my father. "We'll vote it down. Believe me."

Onion John told me what to say. "He believes you. But votes, he doesn't know so much about them. The good they are for getting people cleaned up. This week's vote is No, could be, and next week it turns out to be Yes. You never know. And besides, votes only go so far."

"Yes, Andy?"

"He mentioned, you vote about a house and that's as far as it goes."

"What else is there?"

"He sees where lots of different things can happen and there's no vote to them."

"Like what, Andy? Do we have to pull teeth?"

"What he had in mind, was the moon. How's a vote, he wants to know, going to keep anyone from being shipped to the moon."

"Andy! Tell him, Andy, can't you get him to see we're talking about him. Only him. You're no part of this anymore. You're grown up. Whatever concerns you, that's your affair and it's for you to decide, for yourself."

"Me?" That hall was no place for anyone wearing a mackinaw. It was warm. I took the time to pull down my zipper. "I'm the one to decide? Even about General Magneto?"

"Yes." My mother slipped the coat off and she held it. "That's what your father means." And my father said exactly the same thing. "Yes. That's right."

What I probably did was, I sat down. Anyway there I was on the bottom step looking up at them. I don't know what the three of them expected, watching me so close. Maybe that I'd dash upstairs for the bathroom, now I was grown up, to start shaving. John gave me a nice smile, as long as everybody agreed with him how much I'd aged. He turned slowly and started for the door.

I jumped for him and I grabbed him. "Not now, Onion John! Why? Nothing's going to happen to you. Or to me either. It's all going to be the same. If you'll only stick around, the same as always."

Still smiling John picked me off from his left arm where I had a hammer lock, like I was a bramble he was caught in.

"Please," said my mother. "There's an extra bed. In this storm, it's a terrible night for running away."

"Don't leave Serenity?" asked my father.

Onion John spread the fingers of one hand to wipe down his mustache. They went on to circle his chin. He talked slowly.

"He says he's got to go except—the only way he could ever stay in Serenity," I told my father and mother, "is to fumigate. To burn an oak fire up at McKardle's cave. If it ever worked, there wouldn't have to be any votes. The town would be swept clean again and tidy. No one would have to be afraid of any nice thoughts or good feelings. But he doesn't suppose it's very practical from all we tell him. And he'd like to ask us just once more. Do we honestly think there's no use to it at all?"

I waited for my father to answer first. He thought it over and he said, "I'm afraid not." Even if it would keep Onion John in Serenity, it was too much for me to handle to say anything else but, "No." My mother said, "No, John, I don't think so." Onion John nodded as if he hadn't heard anything other than what he expected, and he might as well be on his way.

A couple of snowflakes whirled in, when the door opened, and they slowed to settle down and disappear. Ours is a big deep porch so it had to be snowing heavy and blowing hard for snowflakes to carry across. Once the door went wide you could see how heavy and hard the storm was. In the small light of the street lamp outside, it looked as if Serenity was filled with smoke. Until another gust hit, like the muffled crack of a wave breaking, and the wind carried the snow into a steady slant. There was a drift against the burlap bag as it lay on the porch. The pile broke and the snow scattered off the bag as it swung to John's shoulder.

Onion John stood in the light of the door and he smiled to the three of us in the hall. He felt on the top of his hat. "Well, good day," he lifted the little ball. The door closed and Onion John was gone.

Chapter 18

It was hard to believe. It was something awful and it was wonderful, there were two sides to what happened. And both were hard to believe.

When the shovels starting scraping the next morning and I went to the window for a look at the Rorty's down the street, where Onion John is always the first one shoveling snow, I remembered the worse part. He was gone.

And when I went back to reach under the bed for my socks, I remembered the wonderful part that was left. How I was still in Serenity and the only one it was up to for next summer and always, was me.

It seemed too good to be true, what happened, and too bad.

I went to find my father and he was down in the cellar stoking up the furnace before breakfast. I checked both sides of how things stood. There wasn't any doubt about Onion John. My father only hoped John didn't have to wait too long, heavy as the storm had been all night, until he got a hitch. My father closed the furnace door and looked around where he left the snow shovel way back last spring, so we could clean off the walks before we went up to eat. It was then I asked about the good part, whether he really meant what he said about me the night before.

My father found the snow shovel and he handed it to me. It was the same as an answer. I always get the coal shovel when we dig out after a storm. It's smaller. When he gave me the big one, it meant there wasn't any doubt that I was grown up.

"And I'm the one to decide about myself?" I was halfway down the driveway, right behind him, cutting a narrow path alongside the house.

He said, "Yes," same as the night before.

"Well, I've decided," I told him when we reached the sidewalk out front.

"No, you haven't." He heaved the shovelful he had and turned around. "You haven't had time to think about it."

"All the way out here," I told him. "I've had the last ten, twelve minutes to think about it."

"It's the rest of your life you're deciding on. Don't you figure you ought to give it a little more time?"

"That's so!" I leaned on my shovel. "I suppose I ought."

I gave it until afternoon, when I could get down to the hardware store. Even though in between, I didn't have much time to myself for thinking, the shock there was at school that Onion John had run away from Serenity. The only one not shocked was Eech. And he was surprised that I was still around. When I described how I could stay in Serenity now, I got a promise from Eech. Not to mention about McKardle's cave. Everyone was asking, why? Why did Onion John leave town? I didn't especially want them to know it was on account of me, because I told him he shouldn't fumigate.

When I did show up at the hardware store there was a gang, men, and they were discussing Onion John, too. I asked my father if he wouldn't mind stepping over to the desk, away from the others.

"I've decided," I told him, "about General Magneto next summer and M.I.T. and, you know, going to the moon. What I want to do the rest of my life. And I think the best thing—"

"No, Andy. Hold it." He lifted me up and sat me on the desk. "I don't want to hear your decision, not yet. Not until you've really considered it. Thought it through."

"I've had all day."

"It's the most important decision you'll ever make. Give it time."

"Until tomorrow?"

"Give it months. Years, even."

What was the use of being the one who was going to decide if it took that long? "Why wait? You were the one, I thought you wanted to get it settled so quick."

"I know. Maybe that was a very big mistake."

"I don't see any mistake to it. Wouldn't it be better if we knew how things stood? What's the use for such a long time?"

"Look, Andy." My father slammed the carriage of the typewriter and the bell went. "We're trying to figure out if there's anything we can do about Onion John. There's the meeting tonight. No one really believes Onion John's gone for good. The least we can do is fix things so he'll want to come back. Let's see what happens to Onion John first."

"Before I tell you my decision? But that could be as long as what you said, months or years. He may never come back."

"On the other hand," my father nodded over to the men, "a lot of them believe he'll be coming back in a day or so. Mr. Donahue does, and Herm Ries. Anyway, for the fish drive. He hasn't missed one of those in twenty years. They're sure he'll be back for that. Let's wait, at least until the fish drive."

"All right. I'll tell you what I decide, then."

The fish drive could come along almost any time. It didn't depend on the calendar, only on the weather. When it turned cold enough. The fish drive was always the first Saturday after the Musconetty froze over. That couldn't be very long, the early winter we were having. And if the hunch Donahue had was right, or Mr. Ries, Onion John might be back even before. And then there wouldn't be any more bad to what happened, it would all be good.

I certainly hoped everybody was right, the way they looked for Onion John to come walking along Route 96, some morning, with that burlap bag over his shoulder.

To listen to them all, you'd think they were talking about the courthouse. Onion John could no more disappear out of Serenity, everybody agreed, than the courthouse could get up and wander off into the night. One was as much a fixed and regular part of town as the other. And everybody had a different part to remember about Onion John, that only he knew about.

It could be only the nickel John gave them when they were six. Or the way he showed them how to spit on bait to make it better for eels. Or the figure he drew, maybe, on a kite to make it fly higher. Or no more than a walk they took with him along toward dark, through the wind and past the shadows when Onion John scared them with the noises he made and then got them to laughing with the faces he put on. Each one had something to recall, whenever they saw Onion John, about long ago. Something good they might forget, now he wasn't around to remind them.

So they all asked, why? Why did he ever take it into his head he had to leave Serenity at all, much less for good? That was the big question at the council meeting that night.

If Onion John was so hard rock set against the house, everyone argued, that didn't mean he had to run away. It was easy enough getting rid of the house. All anyone had to do about that was raise their hand, when the time came.

And that's what did happen that night. After my father let Ernie Miller get up on the platform and roam around for a half an hour, going into politics and democracy and whatever, all my father had to do was get up and say he agreed with Ernie, one hundred percent. And with just a couple of words, he made a bigger fuss at the meeting than Ernie did with his whole speech.

When my father announced that Serenity was wrong, the way it went at Onion John, and the worst one wrong was himself, there wasn't any argument. The assembly hall at the courthouse looked like a field of sprouting corn when the vote was called. It was against the new house, building it for Onion John when he came back.

Except the vote didn't answer anyone's main question, why did he have to run away at all? We were the only ones who knew, my father and I, the whole reason.

"Do you think we have to tell them?"

"Tell them what?" My father went ahead of me through the paths on the sidewalk, on the way home from the meeting.

"Why Onion John left." Walking on the dry stiff snow, my father squeaked out ahead like a cork in a bottle. "I'd hate for everyone to know it was because of you and me. Because we told him an oak fire was senseless and that's why he left."

My father pulled up for a drifted stretch and I bumped into him. He turned. "Is that the reason?"

"It was on account of us, wasn't it?"

"It was on account of us, all right!" My father took into the deep snow and plowed through in his galoshes. "And I guess we'll have to admit it. Unless we're lucky and he does come back." He pounded the snow off his feet. "How about if we wait, Andy, before we tell anybody why Onion John left. Anyway, until the fish drive."

There was a lot getting hung up on that fish drive to wait for. It's a thing that goes on every year and it's been going on for a long time, the last hundred years or so. Soon as the ice gets thick enough on the Musconetty, a crowd shows up to drive fish. What happens is, there's a net gets sunk across the creek and then a mob of maybe eighty or ninety back off about a half a mile and chase the fish, whooping and banging on the ice, downstream into the net.

The fish drive doesn't happen on schedule. There's never any announcement about it, any posters in the window like for a covered dish supper at the Methodists, or any committees to organize what's coming. It happens naturally. When the temperature goes down close to zero and hangs down there for three or four days, in the still hard cold that's come, you naturally get ready for next Saturday.

And even though there isn't any plan to it, or very much talk, everyone you expect shows up early that morning somewhere below Conroy's Bend fattened out in their extra sweaters and mufflers and overshoes and gloves. Each one brings his own lunch and his own tools for chopping and banging. Farmer Dusek brings the net, a special one made out of Irish linen with two inch mesh. It's about twelve feet deep and sixty feet wide, enough to reach across the creek from bank to bank. Marty Bemeth brings a chain saw. He uses it to cut a path across the creek, a stretch of open water three feet wide. On the downstream side of this cut, the net is hung on a half dozen posts that stand on the bed of the stream. It blocks the creek from shore to shore.

Everything about a fish drive happens in a set and natural way. A fire starts up near the net and everyone stands around it, before they get going, to have a last drink out of what they brought for lunch, of something hot. Or the first drink, for some of the men, of hard cider or applejack. You need bolstering up inside, cold as it always is.

Then one or two wander off upstream and pretty soon we're all on our way, taking down saplings for clubs or cutting branches as we go. There's usually a wait at the place the drive commences until everyone collects. And then someone flips his cigarette and says, "Well," and the first wave takes off.

These are the choppers. There's ten or twelve of them with axes and they go downstream in a line, cutting holes across the creek about two yards apart every twenty feet or so. After them come the stirrers who carry long poles to put down through the holes to stir up a commotion that will get the fish moving. And then come all the rest of us, we're the beaters, with axes and clubs and sledgehammers, jumping and yelling and banging, to chase the stirred up fish downstream ahead of us.

There's plenty of noise to it, even when the first line of choppers move out. And by the time the beaters join in, the whole winding silvery creek sounds like Serenity was going over for one long continuous touchdown. Cold as it is, the morning's right for jumping and yelling as well as, for some of the men, more hard cider and applejack. To the fish below, it must sound like the world's come to an end.

And for about fifteen hundred pounds of them, the world does come to an end, their world at least. We usually haul six to eight hundred fish, averaging two pounds apiece. It takes a lot of weight and muscle to pull in the ropes that roll the net over that dark and wriggling catch from down below.

Most of them are suckers. There oughtn't to be any trout or bass because the season on those fish is closed. That's the reason we use such a big mesh, two inches, to let the game fish through. But if the trout and the others are so big they get caught anyway, then every year we decide it's their fault, not ours, and we divide them up with the rest. A trout or a bass isn't any better, really, than a midwinter sucker. Summers, a sucker that you take out of water that's warm and muddy isn't worth the trouble. But in the winter, a sucker is firm and clean as any fish you'd want on your table.

The fish get divided up while we eat. Lunch takes a long time because of all the food everyone brings and all the hard cider there is, for some of the men, and applejack. And because there's a lot to talk over about the fish drive that's finished and the fish dinner that's coming.

For the sport it is, a lot of people judge the fish drive to be the best thing that happens in Serenity every year. Onion John thought so. He was the most important man to show up for a fish drive.

Because even though no one's in charge, there's always one second when someone has to say, "Now!" When to haul in the net. The exact second has to be figured to the hair. It can't be too soon, before the fish are all crowded in. And it can't be too late, after the beaters come too close, because they'll drive the fish back from the net, upstream. "Now!" —the time to lay hold of the net—has to be said just right.

And somehow, Onion John never missed. He'd stand there on the ice with his head cocked and his eyes closed and his hand up. You'd think he had some way of knowing what went on in the deep dark, below. The message would come and his hand would drop, some years early and some years "Now!" came long after anyone thought was right. But year after year the haul we'd get with Onion John was always half again better, according to some of the older men, than the fish they caught before John showed up.

It was only natural, Onion John never missed a fish drive. And that's why everyone was sure he'd be coming back to Serenity, at the very latest, for the one this year.

But when the temperature went to six degrees of cold right before Christmas, and the next day it held and the next one and the one after that stayed steely and bitter and hard to breathe, and when for two nights after it dipped to eight below zero until a row of white wicked teeth stretched across the falls on High Street and the Musconetty was ten inches solid with ice and when Saturday morning came and the fish drive and we waited for Onion John, he never showed up. And then we knew, hard as it was to believe, that he was gone from Serenity for good.

Chapter 19

We did it."

"What?" I asked my father.

"I'm afraid we've chased Onion John out of Serenity. He's disappeared."

"He might still be coming. And got held up. In traffic maybe."

My father shook his head. He dropped the edge of his axe, a four pound Widgecomb, down to the ice. He was dressed in his navy pea jacket and a heavy blue muffler and a blue hunting cap, too, all dark. It could've been church he was ready for, or someone coming to dinner and not for a fish drive.

We stood with about a hundred others down from the bridge across the Musconetty, where the road leaves Route 96 to go up to Hessian Hill. The crowd of us stood around and waited like the stretch of creek we were on was a depot, and there was a train coming. Now and then, there'd be someone who'd have another cigarette or more coffee or whatever it was they brought along. You didn't hear much talk. You saw it instead, little clouds that went from one to the other. In the quiet and in the cold we didn't move much as the time went and the sun came through the solid sky to spread a net of shadows on the Musconetty where we were bunched. In the trees along the creek there were lights the sun made, along the branches hung with snow, points that came on and went out.

"Traffic, maybe. Or else trouble getting a hitch."

"He's not coming," said my father.

"Let's face it," said someone on the other side of the crowd, "Onion John's not going to get here. How about moving?"

But there wasn't any answer and, instead, a couple of men lighted up to have one more cigarette and they stood still as chimneys with the smoke coming out along with the fog.

"You don't think there's any more chance at all?" I asked my father.

"I'm afraid not."

"And the time's come when we got to admit why he left?"

"At least to ourselves."

"And not tell the others?"

"I suppose so, Andy. I guess we should." My father didn't seem too anxious. I wasn't either. Except it was one of the things we promised to do when the fish drive came.

"Unless we have to make an announcement about it, I figured another way." I slipped the knapsack with our lunch off my back. "If I tell Ries and let him go, it'll be all over the place in ten or fifteen minutes. That might be a lot better than an announcement, less fuss."

"Go ahead." My father nodded. "Your way."

"Eechee Ries!" I yelled. He came over carrying a piece of locust he was going to use for a club. "You don't have to keep it a secret anymore, why Onion John left."

"Why did he?"

"Don't you remember? When I told him it was no use fumigating. That's why. And my father was in it too. He said the same thing. It was because of us."

"I see," said Eech. "What do you want me to do about it?"

"Do? Anything you feel like doing. I just want to let you out of the secret."

Eech didn't act as if it were too big a secret to tell about. He stopped to make a remark to George Connors. If anyone, Connors would be interested in news about me that was bad. He took a look over to where we stood, me and my father, but that's all. Watching Ries walk back into the crowd it didn't seem anyone was too interested in why Onion John left, anymore. Now they knew he was gone for good.

But at least I kept one of the promises we made for the fish drive, the hard one.

The talk came up louder. "Let's go!" And, "What's the use?" And, "This is it! He's gone." And, "What are we waiting for?" Cigarettes got tossed and axes and clubs picked up. And without any signal, the choppers walked out in a line.

The only noise was the crack and splinter of the ice as they drove the first string of holes across the creek. Without any more to do, the stirrers moved off and they stood, legs apart, across the Musconetty and worked the long poles quietly back and forth, around and around, in the water below. There was a lot more noise, naturally, when all the rest followed, as beaters. But it didn't sound like sport. Most of the noise was clubbing and hammering on the ice, without too much whooping and hollering.

I hung back. My father took a heavy swing and pounded the ice once.

That's when I asked him, "How about the other promise? Is it time?"

He straightened up and looked back at me.

"Do you want to hear now, what I've decided. About General Magneto and Technology? Or does that come later?"

"If you don't mind, I'd like to hear about that later."

"After the drive?"

"Much, much later. After we've had a chance to forget about this drive."

"But all you said we had to wait for was today!"

"I know." That one swing of a four pound axe, it looked, had made my father tired. "I was counting on Onion John I guess, to show up. You were never in such a hurry to make up your mind, when he was around."

"But he's gone. And you said today."

"I said it was up to you, Andy. And it is. Any decision that's made, you're the one that's going to make it. Isn't that enough, for the moment. Can't you wait?"

"I suppose I could. But I don't know how fair it is. After we talked it over, it was going to be today. Myself, I thought you'd want to hear. I always thought you wanted to get things settled, without wasting any time."

"I've told you, that was a mistake. A big one. I don't want you to make the same kind of mistake. To be in such a hurry."

"It isn't fair, though."

"Maybe not." My father looked at the blade of his axe and tested it with his thumb. "I think you ought to know, Andy." He stopped and forgot his axe. He watched the beaters hammering their way downstream. We were left behind. The two of us stood out on the ice alone in the middle of the creek. He turned back to me. "What I think you ought to know is, I'd like another cup of cocoa."

He picked up my knapsack and he went in to shore. He sat down in the overstuffed bankful of snow as if he'd just come in from a day at the store and was settling to have a look at the *Lamp*. He forced his elbows back, to get a stretch into his shoulders and then rummaged around in the knapsack to find the thermos. It had two cups on top, nested together, and he poured one to hold out to me. The steam of it floated away from his hand.

I didn't feel so much like cocoa, not with everything so undecided and getting hung up until who knows when. But it seemed like such a good idea to my father, the way he held the cup out, I took a couple of steps and slid into shore. The bank was soft as a sofa and the cup felt as if you were holding your hands out to a stove. You could trail the cocoa all the way down inside, the heat of it. My father's voice was quiet.

"What I think you ought to know about your father is this. He's nothing but a hardware storekeeper in a small town in New Jersey."

That's all he said, looking over the top of his cup, out across the ice. It sounded very important, the way he put it.

"What's there I ought to know, I mean about that?"

"Only that he wanted to be an engineer, somewhere else."

"Well, I do. I do know about that."

He leaned back and took a drink of cocoa. "How?"

"Mom told me."

"I see. Then that makes it a lot easier. As long as you know, I don't have to go into it, the kind of a failure I am. Or was, until you started coming along. And I thought I'd get there yet, up to M.I.T. and out into the world where the big things happen—I thought I'd get there yet through you." He looked into his cup. "That sounds pretty bad, doesn't it? Using you to make up for how I lost out. Like one of John's evil spirits who helps the next fellow so he can get what he wants for himself. But the worst of it—" He finished off his cocoa and swept what was left out across the ice, a circle of brown splotches and dots. "The worst, was how I wanted to be sure. How anxious I was to get you started. The hurry I was in. Someone was bound to get run over in the rush. And that's why I say, now, I think we ought to slow down a bit and wait, take it easy. Before anyone else gets hurt."

"Anyone else?"

My father looked around as if he was surprised I was still there, sitting next to him on the bank.

"Besides Onion John! We have to admit that we wrecked him bad enough. Once you took off to hide behind him, once I came chasing after you, before we got finished, well, not even Dick Ries thought it was much of a secret any more, why Onion John disappeared."

"No."

I handed my father the empty cup. He twisted it back on top of the thermos along with his own.

"So let's wait, Andy, before we make any big decisions. Don't you make the same mistake I did. There's school. And all the rest that goes on around town. If you keep up in your studies, all of them, when the time comes you can go whichever way you want. But for a while, forget you're grown up."

"How can I? It's happened."

"Well, then, get used to it. See how it feels before you decide what kind of grownup to be."

My father threw the thermos into the knapsack, only he missed. He caught the bottle before it slid too far and then he packed it carefully away.

"Let's get started. This is no way to spend the morning, sitting in the snow here and talking about mistakes and about failures. And all you've got to tell me, all it would amount to is one more failure. The point is, Andy, I don't want to hear what you have to tell me. Please, let it wait."

The only other time I ever heard my father want a favor so bad was in the hall, that night, with Onion John when there was nothing I could do about it.

"I'll wait," I told him. "Until whenever you want to hear about what I decide."

"Thanks." He shoved the knapsack over to me so I'd put it on. He picked up his axe. As if it were all over and there was nothing left except to catch up with the others. They were far downstream, near a bend, where a lot of sunlight came through to the ice. There was plenty of yelling by now. It sounded more like a fish drive. I expected by this time of the morning when the fish drive came, I'd have everything said to my father so he'd know what I had in mind. And I'd know what he thought about it.

"It's only I'd like to tell you how I've been turning things over. Not a decision about anything. Just the general idea I have."

"Don't you think we ought to get going?"

I started to buckle up the knapsack. "Just another half minute."

The *Lamp* was stuck in the outside pocket where I'd put it the night I was going to run away. It reminded me of when it was hot and it was noontime back in August and I asked my father about the ball club picture, "Who am I?" I should've stopped when he answered me and then none of this would have happened. When he told me to look from left to right and I saw I was "Andrew J. Rusch, Jr." My father was right, then, and that's what I told him now.

"I'm the same as you. The same name and all. And I'd just as soon go on being you, as much as anyone I've ever met. I'm not talking about Woodrow Wilson and those, who are supposed to be great. I'm saying the only one I ever come across, who's anything great, is you. It was along those lines what I had in mind."

He stopped from getting up at least. He eased back into the snow and the axe dropped, so it rested on the ice between his knees. He seemed comfortable enough, watching a boulder across the way that was coated up and shining in the sun. As long as he didn't mind listening, I thought I'd get a little more in.

"I don't know about General Magneto, if there's any one

great down there. Maybe there is, but why waste a whole summer looking around. Because it's not a question of failure. I don't see how you can say that. The thing is if you were an engineer, well, that's what I'd like to be. And if you were going to the moon, I'd go there. But as long as you're in the hardware business, all I'm trying to say is I don't want to be anything special in particular. Except you. Seeing the start I have in that direction anyway. And what I thought." He seemed to be resting easy. "If you don't mind just another second?"

"Go ahead."

"Not that it's any decision. I'll wait about that. But just as a matter of judgment I thought the best thing I could do was to look over the possibilities in Serenity, down with you at the hardware store. That seems sensible."

Walking a fence wasn't any worse than showing my father what I had in mind without saying it right out, positively. I don't know whether I went too far before I quit.

When I did it was quiet. The racket from the fish drive below was a faraway noise you couldn't tell about, whether it was yelling or traffic or trees in a storm. A breeze did come from downstream and the snow shook off the branches like it was a celebration, and it was confetti coming down. Except there was nothing to celebrate until I heard my father's opinion about what I mentioned. I couldn't see anything in that boulder he was looking at, worth all the time he gave it.

"You don't mind I went into it so far?"

"I don't mind."

We sat and got nowhere. After a while my father put his hands behind his head and leaned back till you'd think he was in his reading chair at home, with his feet stretched out. The boulder across the way must have turned into a shape, the way a rock does when you stare at it, like a face or an animal. My father smiled at whatever he saw.

"After all, it's not as if you've arrived at any decision."

"No. I promised you about that."

"Well, just as a general point of view I'd say it was about as interesting as anything I've heard for a long time, in years."

"You don't see anything wrong about it?"

"I wouldn't go so far as to say whether it was right or wrong, Andy. But interesting, there's no question."

"So that, you could almost say you agree with me. That it's all right."

"Better than that. It's like the time we went out for pheasant with Onion John. I don't know if I agree with him to this day, about what happened. But it was wonderful, wasn't it?"

"I remember."

"It's like that here, this morning, with you."

The position he was in, bent way over backwards, seemed all right for smiling. But when it came to laughing, my father had to sit up. It wasn't a big laugh, the kind there is after a joke. It was a deep one, covered up, and the only part to see was what escaped. This was everything I'd ever waited until the fish drive for. I'd said what I had in mind, most of it. My father listened. He did better than agree with me. He laughed.

"But don't forget," he leaned on his knees. "This is not your final decision."

"Certainly not."

"Promise me one thing, Andy. In the next two or three years you'll be hearing a lot of new things. There'll be a good deal to learn and to see you never knew existed. Promise me you'll keep an open mind, whatever you run into. So that when the time does come to decide, you might want to change it, change your mind."

"Is that what you want?"

"Frankly, that's what I want."

"That I should change my mind about you?"

"No!" It was a shout, a loud one.

He looked at me sideways. He shook his head in a slant. "No, I'm not saying that."

His look slid away and went out over the creek. He saw where there was a knob of ice, almost a mushroom, about five feet out. He got up to go over to that. He kicked it, one boot that broke it into chips, slithering across the ice.

"All I'm saying is, when the time comes you make up your own mind."

"You said that."

"I guess I did. I guess the truth is, there's nothing more I can say."

My father held up my knapsack like a coat. I slipped into it. He picked up his axe. There was a hemlock branch I'd cut for a club, and it lay out on the ice. I picked it up and we took off, me and my father, to catch up with the others far down the creek.

I thought I knew what a great day was. It had to be a day with a band in it some place and a majorette out front lifting her knees. Crowds had to be a part of it, waving over each other's heads and applauding at the same time. And cheering, plenty of that, with yell leaders out front wearing tight sweaters they had to pull down. And a speech where every fifth word was your own name. And getting punched and shoved and pounded on the back until you ached. And laughing, everyone bent over. That was my idea.

But this was a great day. The greatest, for me, yet. It was nothing like what I thought. All we did was to walk down the Musconetty, slicked over with a shine across it.

Far from any bands, they would've been out of place. The creek was more like a long church, with the frosted trees arched over and the branches tangled so you'd think of windows with pictures in them that you see in church. The cheering and yelling there was from the fish drive was too far off, now, to amount to more than a quiet, heavy beat. It could've been a choir going through a low part.

There weren't any speeches. Or even talk. My father didn't have anything more to say. And neither did I. We understood what each of us wanted the other to know.

There wasn't any laughing. Except once when my father pulled up for a couple of seconds and he looked overhead, to laugh at nothing in particular.

We did a good deal of smiling when we happened to turn to each other. Which is the least you'd expect, considering the great day it turned out to be.

There was, though, a good deal of pounding. It began with my father when we came up to the first big bend. I thought he was struck with a thought when he stopped. But he let heave a full circle swing with his axe and he brought it, hammer side down, on the ice. The creek boomed and a crack snaked across stream.

I tried the best I could for an answer. But a hemlock branch can't compare to a four pound Widgecomb axe, not to mention my heft when compared to my father. The place I clubbed was near a stirring hole and the water jumped. At least, it was a different kind of an effect. Good enough for my father to let go again and answer me. And I answered him. We took to pounding, first him then me, and that's the way we went around the bend. It was one way to let off steam and useful for getting a move into any fish that were left behind, stragglers.

Just before we took the last of the bend, I looked back to where we'd been sitting.

You could see the spot from the way the snow was bunched, where we shoved back into it. It had the shape we were, the head and shoulders. Mine anyway. My father's was hid behind a tree. I remembered the song of Onion John's, the one he sang on Halloween, because this sight was something like in the song. Where the fellow goes floating down the river and he sees himself getting left behind on the bank. And he hears goodbye. Or the way Onion John would say it, farewell.

One step further and I couldn't see the shape, anymore. It was around the bend.

The End

Chapter 20

Two minutes after Andrew J. Rusch, Jr. and his father turned the bend of Musconetty Creek, a thin column of smoke rose above the hill west of Serenity where McKardle's cave is located. The prevailing breeze was from the west and the smoke drifted toward the town. From the smell of the smoke, it was an oak fire that was burning.

J. K.

ABOUT THE AUTHOR

Joseph Krumgold was the first writer to receive the Newbery Medal twice. He was awarded the medal, which is given for the most distinguished contribution to literature for children, in 1954 for ... AND NOW MIGUEL and again in 1960 for ONION JOHN.

Mr. Krumgold began his writing career in Hollywood. For more than twelve years he wrote and produced screenplays for several major studios. He then worked away from Hollywood on documentary films in which the story was given as much emphasis as the fact. These films earned the author first prizes at the Venice, Prague, and Edinburgh Film Festivals, a nomination for the Academy Award, and wide approval both in the United States and abroad.

Mr. Krumgold grew up near New York City, although he traveled extensively and lived in a variety of places, including California, Paris, and Rome. From 1947 to 1951 he spent most of his time in Israel, where he made movies throughout the conflicts that marked the founding of the Israeli nation.

"A rarely beautiful, understated novel about a black sharecropper and his family in the 19th-century American South. . . . the human characters' namelessness lends them universality as oppressed people, while the author's authentic, detailed descriptions . . . assure their individuality. An extraordinarily sensitive book . . ."—*School Library Journal*

". . . written with quiet strength and taut with tragedy. Grim and honest, the book has a moving, elegaic quality that is reminiscent of the stark inevitability of Greek tragedy."—*Bulletin of the Center for Children's Books*

"There is an epic quality in the deeply moving, long-ago story of cruelty, loneliness, and silent suffering. The power of the writing lies in its combination of subtlety and strength."—*The Horn Book*

"The writing is simple, timeless, and extraordinarily moving. An outstanding book."—*Commonweal*

"The main characters, though nameless, are sharply etched and the portrayal of the quiet dignity with which the boy and his parents face adversities not of their own making is powerfully moving."—*The Booklist*

Also by William H. Armstrong

SOUR LAND

SOUNDER

BY WILLIAM H. ARMSTRONG

Illustrations by James Barkley

HarperTrophy
A Division of HarperCollins*Publishers*

To Kip, Dave, and Mary

Sounder

LC Number 70-85030
Trophy ISBN 0-06-440020-4
First Harper Trophy edition, 1972.

"A man keeps, like his love, his courage dark."
—Antoine de Saint Exupéry

Author's Note

FIFTY YEARS AGO I learned to read at a round table in the center of a large, sweet-smelling, steam-softened kitchen. My teacher was a gray-haired black man who taught the one-room Negro school several miles away from where we lived in the Green Hill district of the county. He worked for my father after school and in the summer. There were no radios or television sets, so when our lessons were finished he told us stories. His stories came from Aesop, the Old Testament, Homer, and history.

There was a lasting, magnificent intoxication about the man that has remained after half a century. There was seldom a preacher at the whitewashed, clapboard Baptist church in the Green Hill district, so he came often to our white man's church and sat alone in the balcony. Sometimes the minister would call on this eloquent, humble man to lead the congregation in prayer. He would move quietly to the foot of the balcony steps, pray with the simplicity of the Carpenter of Nazareth, and then return to where he sat alone, for no other black people ever came to join him.

He had come to our community from farther south, already old when he came. He talked little, or not at all, about his past. But one night at the great center table after he had told the story of Argus, the faithful dog of Odysseus, he told the story of Sounder, a coon dog.

It is the black man's story, not mine. It was not from Aesop, the Old Testament, or Homer. It was history—*his* history.

That world of long ago has almost totally changed. The church balcony is gone. The table is gone from the kitchen. But the story remains.

W. H. ARMSTRONG

SOUNDER

I

THE TALL MAN stood at the edge of the porch. The roof sagged from the two rough posts which held it, almost closing the gap between his head and the rafters. The dim light from the cabin window cast long equal shadows from man and posts. A boy stood nearby shivering in the cold October wind. He ran his fingers back and forth over the broad crown of the head of a coon dog named Sounder.

"Where did you first get Sounder?" the boy asked.

"I never got him. He came to me along the road when he wasn't more'n a pup."

The father turned to the cabin door. It was ajar. Three small children, none as high as the level of the latch, were peering out into the dark. "We just want to pet Sounder," the three all said at once.

"It's too cold. Shut the door."

"Sounder and me must be about the same age," the boy said, tugging gently at one of the coon dog's ears, and then the other. He felt the importance of the years—as a child measures age—which separated him from the younger children. He was old enough to stand out in the cold and run his fingers over Sounder's head.

No dim lights from other cabins punctuated the night. The white man who owned the vast endless fields had scattered the cabins of his Negro sharecroppers far apart, like flyspecks on a whitewashed ceiling. Sometimes on Sundays the boy walked with his parents to set awhile at one of the distant cabins. Sometimes they went to the meetin' house. And there was school too. But it was far away at the edge of town. Its term began after harvest and ended before planting time.

Two successive Octobers the boy had started, walking the eight miles morning and evening. But after a few weeks when cold winds and winter sickness came, his mother had said, "Give it up, child. It's too long and too cold." And the boy, remembering how he was always laughed at for getting to school so late, had agreed. Besides, he thought, next year he would be bigger and could walk faster and get to school before it started and wouldn't be laughed at. And when he wasn't dead-tired from walking home from school, his father would let him hunt with Sounder. Having both school and Sounder would be mighty good, but if he couldn't have school, he could always have Sounder.

"There ain't no dog like Sounder," the boy said. But his father did not take up the conversation. The boy wished he would. His father stood silent and motionless. He was looking past the rim of half-light that came from the cabin window and pushed back the darkness in a circle that lost itself around the ends of the cabin. The man seemed to be listening. But no sounds came to the boy.

Sounder was well named. When he treed a coon or possum in a persimmon tree or on a wild-grape vine, his voice would roll across the flatlands. It wavered through the foothills, louder than any other dog's in the whole countryside.

What the boy saw in Sounder would have been totally missed by an outsider. The dog was not much to look at—a mixture of Georgia redbone hound and bulldog. His ears, nose, and color were those of a redbone. The great square jaws and head, his muscular neck and broad chest showed his bulldog blood. When a possum or coon was shaken from a tree, like a flash Sounder would clamp and set his jaw-vise just behind the animal's head. Then he would spread his front paws, lock his shoulder joints, and let the bulging neck muscles fly from left to right. And that was all. The limp body, with not a torn spot or a tooth puncture in the skin, would be laid at his master's feet. His master's calloused hand would rub the great neck, and he'd say "Good Sounder, good Sounder." In the winter when there were no crops and no pay, fifty cents for a possum and two dollars for a coonhide bought flour and overall jackets with blanket linings.

But there was no price that could be put on Sounder's voice. It came out of the great chest cavity and broad jaws as though it had bounced off the walls of a cave. It mellowed into half-echo before it touched the air. The mists of the flatlands strained out whatever coarseness was left over from his bulldog heritage, and only flutelike redbone mellowness came to the listener. But it was louder and clearer than any purebred redbone. The trail barks seemed to be spaced with the precision of a juggler. Each bark bounced from slope to slope in the foothills like a rubber ball. But it was not an ordinary bark. It filled up the night and made music as though the branches of all the trees were being pulled across silver strings.

While Sounder trailed the path the hunted had taken in search of food, the high excited voice was quiet. The warmer the trail grew, the longer the silences, for, by nature, the coon dog would try to surprise his quarry and catch him on the ground, if possible. But the great voice box of Sounder would have burst if he had tried to trail too long in silence. After a last, long-sustained stillness which allowed the great dog to close in on his quarry, the voice would burst forth so fast it overflowed itself and became a melody.

A stranger hearing Sounder's treed bark suddenly fill the night might have thought there were six dogs at the foot of one tree. But all over the countryside, neighbors, leaning against slanting porch posts or standing in open cabin doorways and listening, knew that it was Sounder.

"If the wind does not rise, I'll let you go hunting with me tonight." The father spoke quietly as he glanced down at boy and dog. "Animals don't like to move much when it's windy."

"Why?" the boy asked.

"There are too many noises, and they can't hear a killer slipping up on them. So they stay in their dens, especially possums, because they can't smell much."

The father left the porch and went to the woodpile at the edge of the rim of light. The boy followed, and each gathered a chunk-stick for the cabin stove. At the door, the father took down a lantern that hung on the wall beside a possum sack and shook it. "There's plenty of coal oil," he said.

The boy closed the door quickly. He had heard leaves rattling across the frozen ground. He hoped his father didn't hear it. But he knew the door wouldn't shut it out. His father could sense the rising wind, and besides, it would shake the loose windowpanes.

Inside the cabin, the boy's mother was cutting wedge-shaped pieces of corn mush from an iron pot that stood on the back of the stove. She browned them in a skillet and put them on the tin-topped table in the middle of the room. The boy and the three younger children ate their supper in silence. The father and mother talked a little about ordinary things, talk the boy had heard so many times he no longer listened. "The crop will be better next year. There'll be more day work. The hunting was better last year."

This winter the hunting was getting worse and worse. The wind came stronger and colder than last year. Sometimes Sounder and his master hunted in the wind. But night after night they came home with an empty brown sack. Coons were scarcely seen at all. People said they had moved south to the big water. There were few scraps and bones for Sounder. Inside the cabin, they were hungry for solid food too. Corn mush had to take the place of stewed possum, dumplings, and potatoes.

Not long after supper, Sounder's master went out of the cabin and stood listening, as he always did, to see if he could hear the cold winter wind beginning to rise in the hills. When he came back into the cabin, he took off his blanket-lined overall jacket and sat behind the stove for a long time. Sounder whined at the door as if he were asking if someone had forgotten to light the lantern and start across the fields of dead stalks to the lowlands or past the cottonwoods and jack oaks to the hills. The boy took Sounder some table scraps in a tin pan. As Sounder licked the bottom of the pan it rattled against a loose board in the porch as if somebody were walking across the floor.

Later, when it was time for the smaller children in the cabin to go to bed, Sounder's master got up, put on his overall jacket, and went outside. He did not take the lantern or Sounder or the boy with him. The stern order to the coon hound to go back under the porch came in through the cabin door, and Sounder's whining continued long after the footsteps on the frozen path had died out.

Inside the cabin, the boy's mother sat by the stove, picking kernels of walnuts with a bent hairpin. The woman watched each year for the walnuts to fall after the first hard frost. Each day she went with the children and gathered all that had fallen. The brownish-green husks, oozing their dark purple stain, were beaten off on a flat rock outside the cabin. On the same rock, the nuts were cracked after they had dried for several weeks in a tin box under the stove. When kernel-picking time came, before it was dark each day, the boy or the father took a hammer with a home-made handle, went to the flat rock, and cracked as many as could be kerneled in a night.

The troubled whimper of a child came through the little door that led to the shed-room where the children slept.

"You must go to bed soon," the mother said. "Your little brother gets addled in his sleep when you ain't in bed with him."

The boy reached into his mother's lap, where the golden half-kernels lay in the folds of her apron. She slapped his hand away. "You eat the crumbs from the bottom of the hull basket," she said. "I try to pick two pounds a night. That's thirty cents' worth. Fifteen cents a pound at the store if they're mostly half-kernels and dry. The man won't pay if they're all in crumbs."

Sometimes the woman told the boy stories she had heard at the meetin' house. "The Lord do powerful things" she would say. The boy liked it when she told her stories. They took away night loneliness. Night loneliness was always bad when the younger children had gone to bed, or when the father was not in the cabin. "Night loneliness is part fearing," the boy's mother had once said to him. But the boy was never afraid when his father was near.

Perhaps she too felt the loneliness that came with the wind as it passed the cabin outside, and the closeness of a world whose farthest border in the night was the place where the lamp light ended, at the edge of the cabin walls. So she told the boy a story of a mighty flood which the Lord had sent to wash away all the evil in the world. When the story was over, she sent the boy to bed and continued picking out kernels and adding them to the neat mound in the folds of her apron.

The boy pressed his head deep into his straw pillow. The pillow was cold, but it felt smooth, and it smelled fresh. He had the same feeling he got when he rubbed his face against the sheets that hung on the clothesline every Monday. His mother washed his pillowcase and sheet every week, just like she did for the people who lived in the big house down the road. He buried himself deep in his side of the straw tick; he felt where the wooden slats of the bed crossed under his body. He rolled close to his little brother and tucked the edge of the coverlet under his body to keep out the cold that seeped up through the straw ticking. His little brother's body warmed him.

He heard Sounder whimpering under the porch. But Sounder was warm because the boy's father had put two burlap sacks under the porch for the time when the hard frosts came. The boy thought there must be two pounds of nuts in the pile on his mother's lap. His mother always said "Two pounds is a good night's work if you can start early and there ain't a sick child to rock."

He wondered where his father had gone without Sounder; they always went together at night. He heard the thump, thump, thump of Sounder's paw hitting the underneath side of the porch floor as he scratched at a flea in his short tan hair.

The boy dreamed of the stalk land covered by the Lord's mighty flood. He wondered where the animals would go if the water rose over the foothills. "Cabins built on posts would just float like boats, porch and all," he assured himself in a whisper. If they floated from the far ends of the land and all came together, that would be a town, and he wouldn't be lonely anymore . . .

* * *

When the boy awoke in the morning, he went to the window. He remembered his dream of the flood covering the stalk land. He called the younger children. His breath steamed up the windowpane. He wiped the steam away with the bottom of his fist. His dream had not come true. There was no floodwater rising in the bottomland. Except for frost on the ground, everything looked just the same as it had yesterday. The younger children looked, saw nothing, and asked, "What is it?"

The big blue-enameled possum kettle was boiling on top of the chunk stove. It had two lids and doubled for cooking and heating. The boy felt the brown paper bag of walnut kernels on the shelf behind the stove. "Yes," he said to his mother, "I think there are two pounds."

He stood close to the warm stovepipe, turning one cheek and then the other to its glowing warmth. He circled his arms in a wide embrace around the pipe and rubbed his hands together. The warmth ran up his sleeves and down over his ribs inside his shirt and soaked inward through his whole body. He pulled in deep breaths from above the stove to catch the steam escaping from under the kettle's lid as it bounced up and down, breaking the rhythm of the bubbles that went *lob, lob, lob* on the surface of the fast-boiling pot.

In a skillet on the second stove lid there were pork sausages! He sniffed the thin lines of smoke curling up from under the edges of each of them. Pork sausage was for Christmas. But he knew it wasn't Christmas yet. His mother put a pan of cold biscuits on the lid of the possum kettle to warm. She was humming to herself. The lid stopped jumping up and down, and the steam began to whistle softly as it squeezed from under the lid.

The smell that came from under the lid wasn't possum. It was ham bone. The boy had only smelled it twice in his life, once before in his own cabin, and once when he was walking past the big house down the road. The sausage and hambone smells filled up the cabin and leaked out through the cracks in the floor and around the door. They excited Sounder, and now he was scratching at the door.

Sounder hadn't had much to eat yesterday. Besides a few scraps, he had had one cold biscuit. When flour was scarce, the boy's mother would wrap the leftover biscuits in a clean flour sack and put them away for the next meal. Then they would be put in a pan, sprinkled with a little water to keep them soft, and warmed over. The boy called to Sounder to stop and go away. His mother stopped her humming and said, "Shush, child, you'll wake your father."

Then she went back to her humming. His mother always hummed when she was worried. When she held a well child on her lap and rocked back and forth, she sang. But when she held a sick child close in her arms and the rocker moved just enough to squeak a little, she would hum. Sometimes she hummed so softly that the child heard the deep concerned breathing of terror above the sound of the humming. The boy always thought her lips looked as though they were glued together when she hummed. They seemed to be rolled inward and drawn long and thin. Once when she kissed him good night when he was sick, they were cold, he remembered. But when she sang or told stories, her lips were rolled out, big and warm and soft.

Outside, the wind still blew, the sun was weak, and the earth was gray. Several times the boy went out to bring wood for his mother. He ate sausage and biscuits at the tin-topped table with the other children.

When his father got up, he chopped some wood and sat by the fire. The top of the possum kettle bounced up and down again because the biscuit pan had been moved. The father lifted the lid now and then. With the big wire fork that had a wooden handle, he pulled the ham half out of the water and turned it over. The boy felt warm and proud inside when he saw his father's great hand take hold of the handle of the hot lid without using a pot rag the way his mother always did. Finally his father took from the shelf a flat oak slab, bigger than any of the pans or dishes, and put it on the table.

The boy liked to smell the oak slab. It smelled like the Mercy Seat meetin'-house picnic held every summer. He also liked to rub his fingers on the edge of the slab, for it was soft and smooth where the grease had soaked it. His father had hollowed it out during long winter evenings as he sat by the stove. The boy had cleaned up the shavings and slipped them under the door of the stove when the draft was open. They burned with a bright flame, and they made a great mystery for the boy: The curled ones straightened out as they burned, but the straight ones curled up.

The boy remembered when the oak slab had had ham on it before. One year his father had won a pig in a shooting match and raised it to a hog. They had eaten one ham and traded one for beans and flour at the store. That year they had spareribs and chitlins and pan scrapple. Sometimes when the boy's father helped butcher hogs down at the big house, he would bring home spareribs and sowbelly—lots of sowbelly, but not much spareribs.

The boy's father took the ham from the kettle and put it on the oak slab. "Save the ham-boilin' for Sounder," he reminded the boy's mother.

"Sounder will eat good now," the boy said.

The father sharpened the butcher knife with the whetstone he used to whet his scythe and his goose-necked brier hook in the summer when he cut brambles and young sumac in the fencerows. He cut big pieces of ham, and they stuck out from under the brown tops of the biscuits. It was like a Christmas bigger than a pork-sausage Christmas. The boy slipped a piece of the fat rind into a biscuit and took it out to Sounder. When the ham-boiling had cooled, he filled Sounder's pan and ran his fingers up and down the great dog's back as he lapped it up.

The windows of the cabin stayed steamed up almost all day, the kettle had boiled so long. The cold wind continued to blow outside. Nothing moved except what the wind moved—dead leaves under the cabin, brown blades and stalks from the fields which were dead and ready to be blown away, bare branches of poplars, and the spires of tall pines. Toward evening the father wiped the steam away from the glass and looked out a couple of times. The dry cottonwood chunks burned like gunpowder in the stove. In one or two spots the side of the stove gave off a red glow.

With the flavor of ham and biscuit still in his mouth, the boy felt good. He watched his mother as she patched his father's overalls with a piece of ticking. The combination of faded blue overall cloth and gray-and-white-striped ticking looked odd. One time at the meetin'-house picnic, boys with patches the same color as their overalls had laughed at him and pointed to the checkered gingham on the knees of his overalls. He had felt mad and hurt. But his mother had said, "Pay no mind, child," and had led him away. He hoped no one would laugh at his father. His father wouldn't be hurt. He didn't get hurt. He would get mad and fight back, and the boy was always afraid when his father got mad.

When the woman had patched the torn place, she got the walnut basket, folded her apron in her lap, and began to pick out the golden-brown kernels. The boy thought she would sing, but the rocker only moved enough to squeak. She hummed softly, and her lips looked glued together. "Look down, look down that lonesome road." The boy wished she would stop humming and tell a story about the Lord or King David, but she kept humming "That Lonesome Road."

The boy decided it was lonesomer in bed in the dark than it was staying up. He was glad he could set a long time after the young children had gone to bed. Once he had been gathering weeds which his father had cut at the edge of a lawn. On the lawn a lady sat under a tree reading a story aloud to some children. He wished his mother or father could read. And if they had a book, he would hold the lamp by the chair so they could see the words and never get tired. "One day I will learn to read," he said to himself. He would have a book with stories in it, then he wouldn't be lonesome even if his mother didn't sing.

II

THE ROAD WHICH passed the cabin lay like a thread dropped on a patchwork quilt. Stalk land, fallow fields, and brushland, all appeared to be sewn together by wide fencerow stitches of trees. Their bare branches spread out to join together the separate patches of land. Weeds grew on either side of the road in summer, and a thin strip of green clung to life between the dusty tracks. In summer a horse and wagon made almost no noise in the soft earth. In winter when the ground was frozen, the rattle of wheels and each distinct hoofbeat punctuated the winter quiet. When the wind blew, little clouds of dust would rise in the road and follow the wind tracks across the fields.

The boy was allowed to go as far as he wanted to on the road. But the younger children couldn't go past the pine clump toward the big house and the town, or the bramble patch where they picked blackberries in summer in the other direction. Almost no one passed on the road in winter except to buy flour at the store far down the road or to go to the town of a Saturday. Even in summer a speck on the horizon was a curiosity. People sitting on cabin porches would wonder whether the speck would take the form of man, woman, or child.

The third day after the boy had awakened to the smell of ham bone and pork sausage, it was still cold and the wind still blew. But the cabin still smelled good, and there was plenty to eat. Just as dark was gathering, the boy started to go to the woodpile to bring in wood for the night. The dim light of the lamp ran past the boy as he stood motionless in the open cabin door.

"Shut the door," the boy's father called from where he sat near the stove. But the boy did not move.

Just past the edge of the porch three white men stood in the dim light. Their heavy boots rattled the porch floor, and the boy backed quickly into the cabin as they pushed their way in.

"There are two things I can smell a mile," the first man said in a loud voice. "One's a ham cookin' and the other's a thievin' nigger."

"Get up," the second man ordered. The warm, but frozen circle of man, woman, and three small children around the stove jumped to their feet. A stool on which a child had been sitting fell backward and made a loud noise. One of the men kicked it across the room. The boy did not move from his place just inside the door.

"Here's the evidence," said the first man. He jerked at the grease-spotted cloth on the tin-topped table. The oak slab and the half-eaten ham fell to the floor with a great thud and slid against the wall.

"You know who I am," said the first man as he unbuttoned his heavy brown coat and pulled it back to show a shiny metal star pinned to his vest. "These are my deputies." The stranger nearest the door kicked it shut and swore about the cold.

"Stick out your hands, boy," ordered the second man. The boy started to raise his hands, but the man was already reaching over the stove, snapping handcuffs on the outstretched wrists of his father.

The click of the handcuffs was like the click of a gate latch at the big house where the boy had once gone with his father to work. He had swung on the gate and played with the latch until someone had called out from the house, "If you want to swing on a gate, boy, swing on the one behind the house. Get away from the front."

The third stranger, who had not spoken, turned toward the door. "I'll bring up the wagon." But he did not open the door.

Suddenly the voice of the great dog shattered the heavy, seemingly endless silence that came between the gruff words of the sheriff and those of his men. Sounder was racing toward the cabin from the fields. He had grown restless from waiting to go hunting with his master and had wandered away to hunt alone. That's why he hadn't warned them. He always barked and sometimes, even in daytime, he would start from under the porch, the hair on his back straightening before anyone had sighted a moving speck at the far end of the road. "Somebody's comin' or a creature's movin' " the boy's mother would say.

Now he was growling and scratching at the door. The noise seemed to undo the fearful shock that had held the smaller children ashen and motionless. "The youngest child began to cry and hid behind his mother. He tugged at her apron, but the woman did not move.

The men were speaking roughly to Sounder's master. "That tear in your overalls where the striped ticking is—that's where you tore them on the door hook of the smokehouse. We found threads of torn cloth in the hook. You gonna wear nothing but stripes pretty soon. Big, wide black and white stripes. Easy to hit with a shotgun."

The deputy who had started out to bring up the wagon kicked the closed door and swore at the dog on the other side.

"Go out and hold that mongrel if you don't want him shot." He held the door ajar the width of the boy's body and thrust him out. The boy fell on the back of the dog, whose snarling jaws had pushed into the light between the boy's legs. A heavy boot half pushed, half kicked the entangled feet of the sprawled boy and the nose of the dog and slammed the door. "Get that dog out of the way and hold him if you don't want him dead."

The boy, regaining his balance, dragged Sounder off the porch and to the corner of the cabin. Then the deputy, hearing the barking move back from the door, opened it and came out. He walked out of the circle of light but returned soon leading a horse hitched to a spring wagon. A saddled horse followed behind the wagon.

The appearance of the horses and the added confusion of people coming from the cabin roused Sounder to new fury. The boy felt his knees give. His arms ached, and his grip on the dog's collar was beginning to feel clammy and wet. But he held on.

"Chain him up," said the sheriff.

The boy thought they were telling him to chain up Sounder, but then he saw that one of the men had snapped a long chain on the handcuffs on his father's wrists. As the men pushed his father into the back of the wagon his overalls caught on the end of the tail-gate bolt, and he tore a long hole in his overalls. The bolt took one side of the ticking patch with it. The man holding the chain jerked it, and the boy's father fell backward into the wagon. The man swung the loose end of the chain, and it struck the boy's father across the face. One of the deputies pulled the chain tight and tied it to the wagon seat. The two deputies climbed on the wagon seat; the sheriff mounted the saddled horse. The cabin door was open; the boy's mother was standing in the doorway. He did not see his brother and sisters.

Sounder was making an awful noise, a half-strangled mixture of growl and bark. The boy spoke to him, but the great paws only dug harder to grip the frozen earth. Inch by inch the boy was losing his footing. Numbness was beginning to creep up his arms and legs, and he was being dragged away from the corner of the house.

The wagon started, and the sheriff rode behind it on his horse. Sounder made a great lunge forward, and the boy fell against the corner of the porch. Sounder raced after the wagon. No one yelled after him. The mother stood still in the doorway. The deputy who wasn't holding the reins turned on the seat, aimed his shotgun at the dog jumping at the side of the wagon, and fired. Sounder fell in the road, and the sheriff rode around him. Sounder's master was still on his back in the wagon, but he did not raise his head to look back.

The boy struggled to his feet. His head hurt where he had hit it against the corner of the porch. Now his mother spoke for the first time since he had opened the door to bring in wood. "Come in, child, and bring some wood."

Sounder lay still in the road. The boy wanted to cry; he wanted to run to Sounder. His stomach felt sick; he didn't want to see Sounder. He sank to his knees at the woodpile. His foot hurt where the door had been slammed on it. He thought he would carry in two chunk-sticks. Maybe his mother would drag Sounder out of the road. Maybe she would drag him across the fields and bury him. Maybe if she laid him on the porch and put some soft rags under him tonight, he might rise from the dead, like Lazarus did in a meetin'-house story. Maybe his father didn't know Sounder was dead. Maybe his father was dead in the back of the sheriff's wagon now. Maybe his father had said it hurt to bounce over the rough road on his back, and the deputy had turned around on the seat and shot him.

The second chunk-stick was too big. It slipped out of the boy's arms. Two of his fingers were bruised under the falling wood.

Suddenly a sharp yelp came from the road. Just like when a bee stung Sounder under the porch or a brier caught his ear in the bramble, the boy thought. In an instant the boy was on his feet. Bruised foot and fingers, throbbing head were forgotten. He raced into the dark. Sounder tried to rise but fell again. There was another yelp, this one constrained and plaintive. The boy, trained in night-sight when the lantern was dimmed so as not to alert the wood's creatures, picked out a blurred shape in the dark.

Sounder was running, falling, floundering, rising. The hind part of his body stayed up and moved from side to side, trying to lift the front part from the earth. He twisted, fell, and heaved his great shoulders. His hind paws dug into the earth. He pushed himself up. He staggered forward, sideways, then fell again. One front leg did not touch the ground. A trail of blood, smeared and blotted, followed him. There was a large spot of mingled blood, hair, and naked flesh on one shoulder. His head swung from side to side. He fell again and pushed his body along with his hind legs. One side of his head was a mass of blood. The blast had torn off the whole side of his head and shoulder.

The boy was crying and calling Sounder's name. He ran backward in front of Sounder. He held out his hand. Sounder did not make a sign to stop. The boy followed the coon dog under the porch, but he went far back under the cabin. The boy was on his knees, crying and calling, "Sounder, Sounder, Sound . . ." His voice trailed off into a pleading whisper.

The cabin door opened, and the boy's mother stood in the door. The pale light of the lamp inside ran past the woman, over the edge of the porch, and picked out the figure of the boy on his hands and knees. "Come in, child," the woman said. "He is only dying."

Inside the cabin the younger children sat huddled together near the stove. The boy rubbed his hands together near the stovepipe to warm them. His bruised fingers began to throb again. His foot and his head hurt, and he felt a lump rising on the side of his head. If Sounder would whimper or yelp, I would know, the boy thought. But there was no sound, no thump, thump, thump of a paw scratching fleas and hitting the floor underneath.

"Creatures like to die alone," the mother said after a long time. "They like to crawl away where nobody can find them dead, especially dogs. He didn't want to be shot down like a dog in the road. Some creatures are like people."

The road, the boy thought. What would it be like? Did the shotgun blast a hole in the road?

"I ain't got the wood," the boy said at last. "I'll light the lantern and get it."

"You know where the wood is. You won't need the lantern," the woman said.

The boy paused in the doorway. Then he took the lantern from the nail where it hung beside the possum sack. He took the lantern to the stove, lit a splinter of kindling through the open door-draft, and held it to the lantern wick the way his father always did. His mother said nothing to him. She spoke to the younger children instead. "I ain't fed you yet."

When he got outside, the boy did not go to the woodpile. He followed the trail of blood in its zigzag path along the road. At the end of it there was a great wide spot, dark on the frozen ground. Little clumps of Sounder's hair lay in the blood. There was no hole where the shotgun had blasted. At the edge of the dark stain, the boy touched his finger to something. It was more than half of Sounder's long thin ear. The boy shivered and moved his finger away. He had seen dead lizards and possums and raccoons, but he'd never seen a human animal, like Sounder, dead.

It wouldn't work, he thought. But people always said to put things under your pillow when you go to bed, and if you make a wish, it will come true. He touched Sounder's ear again. It was cold. He picked it up. One edge of it was bloody, and jagged like the edge of a broken windowpane. He followed the zigzag trail back along the road, but he could scarcely see it now. He was crying again. At the corner of the porch he took the possum sack from the nail where it hung and wiped the ear. It gave him the shivers. He jumped down quickly, and holding the lantern near the ground, tried to see under the porch. He called Sounder. There was no sound. He went back to wiping the ear. His throat hurt. He put the ear in the pocket of his overall jacket. He was going to put it under his pillow and wish that Sounder wasn't dead.

The wind had stopped blowing. This would have been a good hunting night, he thought. Far away, a single lantern was moving into the foothills. The boy was still crying. He had not forgotten the wood. Now he put out the lantern and hung it against the wall. He went to the woodpile, picked up two chunk-sticks, and went into the cabin.

The loneliness that was always in the cabin, except when his mother was singing or telling a story about the Lord, was heavier than ever now. It made the boy's tongue heavy. It pressed against his eyes, and they burned. It rolled against his ears. His head seemed to be squeezed inward, and it hurt. He noticed grease spots on the floor where the oak slab and the ham had fallen. He knew his mother had picked them up. His father would be cold, he thought, with that great rip in his overalls.

His mother sat by the stove. "You must eat," the woman said. The boy had been outside a long time. His mother had fed the other children, and they were already in bed. She did not take down her walnut basket to begin the slow filling of her apron with fat kernels. She did not sing or even hum. "Child . . . child" she would say with long spaces between. Sometimes she would murmur to herself with her eyes closed. His little brother would murmur and be addled in his sleep tonight, the boy thought. He would set as long as his mother would let him. Maybe his mother would let him set and listen all night.

The boy listened for a yelp, a whine, a thump, thump, thump under the floor. There was no sound. His mother's rocker did not even move enough to squeak. One chunk-stick burning atop another in the stove rolled against the stove door with a slight thump. The boy started toward the cabin door.

"You know it was the stove," the mother said as she reached for the poker to push the wood back from the door.

"It sounded outside," the boy said as he pulled the door closed after him.

Soon he returned carrying the lantern. "I want to look more," he said. "I keep hearin' things." He lit the lantern from the stove as he had done before. His mother said nothing. He had thought she might say "Hang it back, child" as she often did when he wanted to go along the fencerows and hunt with Sounder after dark.

Outside, he murmured to himself, "That was

the stove, I reckon." He put the lantern on the ground and tried to see under the cabin. Nothing moved in the dim light. He wished the light would shine in Sounder's eyes and he would see them in the dark, but it didn't. Backing from under the porch on his hands and knees, he touched the lantern and tipped it over. He grabbed it by the wire rim that held the top of the globe and burned his hand. "Don't let it fall over; it'll explode" his father had said to him so many times when they hunted together. He sucked his burned fingers to draw out the fire. Sounder's pan was on the ground, and someone had stepped on it. The mean man who had kicked him with his big boot, the boy thought. He straightened it as best he could with his hurt fingers and put it on the porch.

He blew out the lantern and hung it by the possum sack. He stood on the porch and listened to the faraway. The lantern he had seen going into the foothills had disappeared. There were gravestones behind the meetin' house. Some were almost hidden in the brambles. If the deputy sheriff had turned around on the seat of the wagon and shot his father, the visiting preacher and somebody would bring him back and bury him behind the meetin' house, the boy thought. And if Sounder dies, I won't drag him over the hard earth. I'll carry him. I know I can carry him if I try hard enough, and I will bury him across the field, near the fencerow, under the big jack oak tree.

The boy picked up Sounder's bent tin pan and carried it into the cabin. The woman pushed back in her chair for a brief second in surprise and half opened her mouth. But, seeing the boy's face in the lamplight, she closed her mouth, and the rocker came slowly back to its standing position—her head tilted forward again, her eyes fixed on the boy's uneaten supper, still warming on the back of the stove.

In the corner of the room next to the dish cupboard, the boy filled Sounder's tin with cold hamboiling from the possum kettle. "What's that for, child?" asked the mother slowly, as though she were sorry she had asked and would like to take it back.

"For if he comes out."

"You're hungry, child. Feed yourself."

The boy put Sounder's tin under the porch, closed the door, pushed the night latch, sat down behind the stove, and began to eat his supper.

III

IN THE MORNING the boy's mother did not cook any pork sausage for breakfast. The ham was on the tin-topped table, but she did not uncover it. Everybody had biscuits and milk gravy. There was still a faint smell of ham, but the boy missed the scent of sausage coming up to him as he stood warming himself. He had hurried out and called Sounder and looked under the house before he had finished buttoning his shirt, but his mother had made him come in. She knew he would be crawling under the cabin, so she made him put on last year's worn-out overalls and a ragged jacket of his father's that came down to his knees. It wouldn't keep out much cold because it was full of holes.

The boy's mother put what was left of the pork sausage and the ham in a meal sack. When she had wrapped her walnut kernels in brown paper and tied them with string, she tied a scarf around her head and put on a heavy brown sweater that had pink flannel-outing patches on the elbows. She put the brown package in the basket she always carried when she went to the store. She put the meal sack over her shoulder.

"I'm taking the kernels to the store to sell them," she said to the boy. She did not say where she was going with the meal sack she had swung over her shoulder.

"Watch the fire, child," she said. "Don't go out of hollerin' distance and leave the young ones. Don't let them out in the cold.

"Warm some mush in the skillet for you all to eat at dinnertime. I'll be home before suppertime.

"Whatever you do, child, don't leave the children with a roaring fire and go lookin' for Sounder.

You ain't gonna find him this day. If a stranger comes, don't say nothin'."

The boy had nodded each time she spoke. He thought he would say "Yes" or "Don't worry, I will," but he didn't. He pushed the younger children back out of the cold and closed the door.

As his mother stepped off the porch and started for the road she began to hum softly to herself. It was a song the boy had heard her sing many nights in the cabin:

You gotta walk that lonesome valley,
You gotta walk it by yourself,
Ain't nobody else gonna walk it for you.

The boy wanted to run after her. He watched as she became smaller and smaller, until the meal sack over her shoulder was just a white speck. The rest of her became a part of the brown road and the gray earth. When the white speck had faded into the earth, the boy looked up at the sky.

"No sun to thaw things out today," he said aloud to himself. His father always spoke aloud to the wind and the sky, and sometimes to the sun when he stood on the porch in the morning, especially when it rose out of the far lowland cottonwoods and pines like a great ball of fire. "Warmin' the cold bones" his father would say. And preparing for a hunt, his father would caution a full moon, hanging over the foothills, "Don't shine too bright, you'll make the creatures skittish." And Sounder too, settin' on his haunches, would speak to the moon in ghost-stirrin' tones of lonesome dog-talk.

People would be very mean to his mother today, the boy thought. He wondered if she would tell them that the ham had slid across the floor. If she told them, they might just throw it out and feed it to their dogs. They might let his mother keep it and bring it home again. They wouldn't let her keep the pork sausage, for it was wrapped in clean white paper and not cooked. They might push and pull his mother and put her in the back of a spring wagon and take her away too. She would spill the walnut kernels, and then she wouldn't be able to sell them to buy sowbelly and potatoes.

The boy had hoped the sun would shine. It would soften the frozen crust of earth and make it easier for him to dig a grave for Sounder—if he found Sounder. If Sounder was dead, he hoped no one would come along and see him carrying the grub hoe and shovel across the field to the big jack oak. They would ask what he was doing. If anybody passed while he was digging the grave, he would hide in the fencerow. If they saw him, they might run him off the land.

He felt like crying, but he didn't. Crying would only bother him. He would have his hands full of tools or be carrying Sounder's body. His nose would start dripping and be powerful troublesome because he wouldn't have a free hand to wipe it.

He took in an armload of wood and punched up the fire. "Don't open the stove door," he cautioned the younger children. "I have to go out some more." He went to his bed and took Sounder's ear from under the pillow. He would bury it with Sounder. He smelled his pillow. It still smelled clean and fresh. He put the ear in his pocket so the children wouldn't ask questions as he passed them on the way out. He smoothed his pillow. He was glad his mother washed his sheet and pillowcase every week, just like she did for the people who lived in the big houses with curtains on the windows. About twice a year his mother washed a lot of curtains. The clothesline was filled with them, and they were thin and light and ruffled and fluffy. It was more fun to rub your face against the curtains than on the clean sheets every Monday. The curtains, moving in the breeze, were like the sea's foam. The boy had never seen sea foam, but his mother had told him that when the Lord calmed the mighty Jordan for people to cross over, the water moved in little ripples like curtains in a breeze, and soft white foam made ruffles on top of the water.

The boy had never looked out of a window that had curtains on it. Whenever he passed houses with curtains on the windows, he remembered that if he put his face close against the curtains on the washline he could see through them. He thought there were always eyes, close against the curtains, looking out at him. He watched the windows out of the corner of his eye; he always felt scared until he had passed. Passing a cabin was different. In a cabin window there were just faces with real eyes looking out.

He could go out now, he thought. The wood in the stove had burned down some, and it would be safe. Besides, he would be close by for a while. Getting the body of Sounder from under the cabin wouldn't be easy. The younger children would bother him; they would ask a lot of questions like "Why is Sounder dead?" and "Will he stay dead?" and many more that he would not want to answer.

"When I'm out, don't be yellin' for me. I'll be through in a while," he said to the smallest child, who was looking out of the window, his chin barely high enough to rest on the sill.

There's no hurry, the boy thought. I have all day, and it's still early. And he looked out of the window too. "If you're inside you look out, and if you're outside you look in, but what looks both ways? That's a riddle; what's the answer?" He directed it to no child in particular. And no one answered. "What's the answer?" the boy repeated, and then he answered his own riddle. "The window is the answer; it looks both ways." None of the children paid any attention.

"I must go now," said the boy to his brother and sisters, "before it gets colder. The wind is starting up, so keep the door shut."

Sounder had not died in his favorite spot right behind the porch steps where he had a hole dug out and where the boy's father had put two coffee sacks for a pallet. His mother had said, "Sounder will crawl to the darkest, farthest part of the cabin." That's why she had made the boy put on his ragged clothes.

The boy could not see all the way under the cabin. At one time rats had lived there, and they had pushed up the earth in some places so that it almost touched the beams. They did this so they could gnaw through the floor from below.

He hurt his head and shoulders on nails sticking down from above as he crawled. He hurt his knees and elbows on broken glass, rusty sardine cans, and broken pieces of crockery and dishes. The dry dust got in his mouth and tasted like lime and grease. Under the cabin it smelled stale and dead, like old carcasses and snakes. The boy was glad it was winter because in summer there might have been dry-land moccasins and copperheads under the cabin. He crawled from front to back, looking along the spaces between the beams.

Sounder was not to be seen. The boy would have to go back and forth. Maybe Sounder had pushed with his hind feet and dug a hole into which he had settled. The threadbare knees of last year's overalls opened up, and his bare knees scraped the soil. His father's long jacket caught under his knees as he crawled and jerked his face down into the dust. Cobwebs drooped over his face and mouth. His mouth was so dry with dust that he could not spit them out.

He crawled over every spot under the cabin, but Sounder's body was not there. The boy felt in his pocket. He had lost Sounder's ear under the cabin. It made no difference. It could be buried there.

But where was Sounder's body? he wondered.

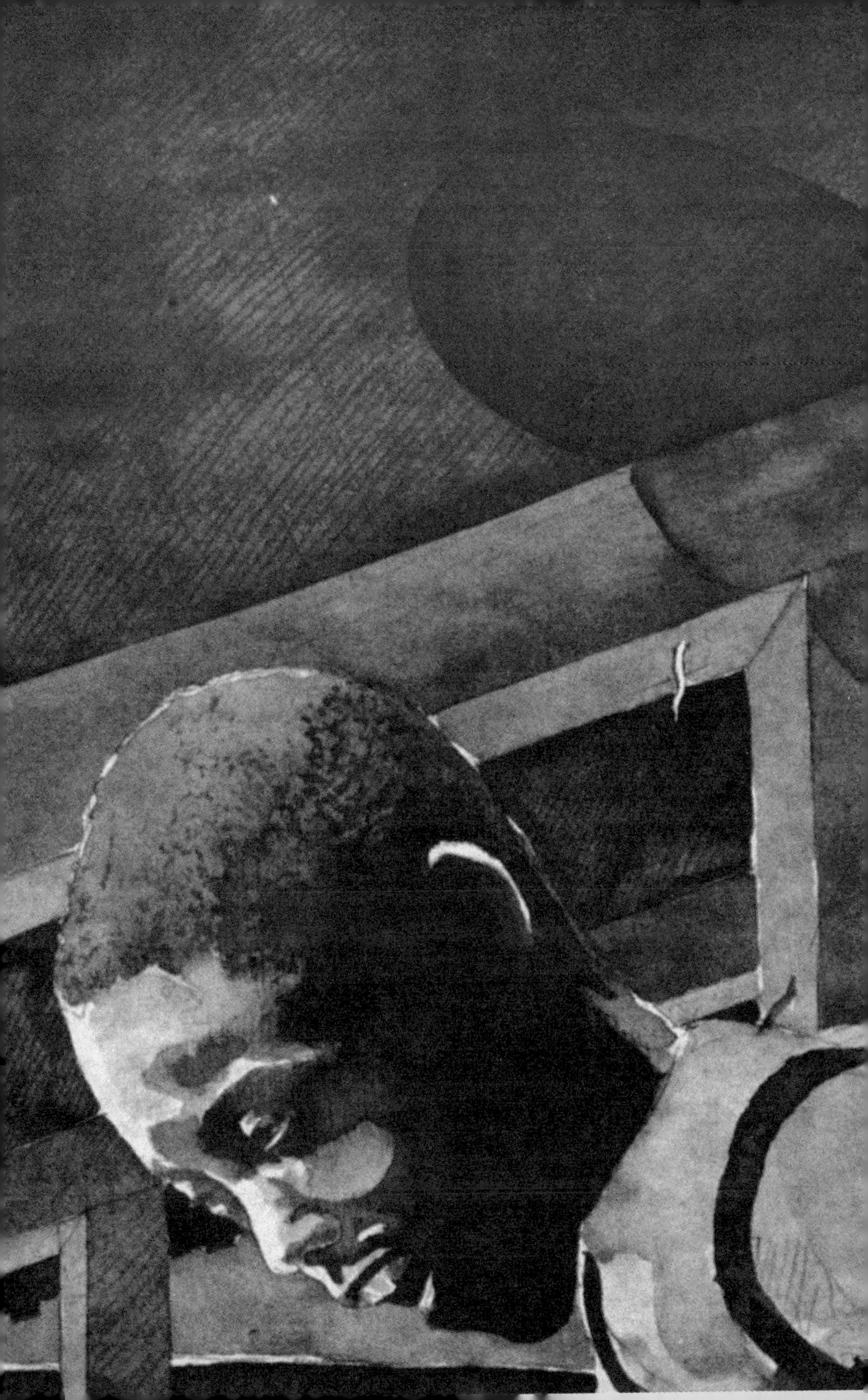

Perhaps the injuries in the side of his head and shoulder were only skin wounds. They looked so terrible, but maybe they were not bad after all. Perhaps Sounder had limped down the road, the way the wagon had taken his master, and died. Perhaps he had only been knocked senseless and that was why he zigzagged so crazily, running for the cabin.

No wild creature could have carried the dead body away. Foxes could carry off dead squirrels and possums. But no animal was big enough to drag Sounder's body away. Maybe the boy, looking under the cabin with the lantern, had caused Sounder to crawl out the other side and die in the brown stalk land.

The boy was crying now. Not that there was any new or sudden sorrow. There just seemed to be nothing else to fill up the vast lostness of the moment. His nose began to run and itch. The tears ran down through the cobwebs and dust that covered his face, making little rivulets. The boy rubbed his eyes with his dirty hands and mixed dust with tears. His eyes began to smart.

He followed the road the way the wagon had taken his father as far as he dared leave the fire and the children in the cabin, still in hollering distance. There was no sign of Sounder's body.

He spiraled the brown stalk land in ever-widening circles, searching the fencerows as he went. Under the jack oaks and the cottonwoods there was nothing. In the matted Scotch-broom tangle he visualized the great tan body as he carefully picked each step. But the dog was not there.

IV

AFTER THE BOY had fed the children and eaten something himself, he sat down by the warm stove and looked out of the window. There was nothing else to do. Now and then a cloud would cross the sun that had finally burned its way out of the gray. The boy watched the cloud shadows roll over the fields and pass over the cabin. They darkened the window as they passed.

He carried in wood for the night before the sun

began to weaken. Then he looked out of the window again to where his mother would appear. Finally he saw a speck moving on the road. He watched it grow.

"She's coming," he said to the younger children, and they crowded around him and pushed their faces against the window. "She's been gone long enough to walk to town and more," he added.

"What will she bring?" one of the children asked.

"She'll bring nothin', but maybe things to eat. She won't bring no stick candy. Don't ask her for none. Don't ask her nothin'."

Several times during the day the boy had said to himself, "Maybe they'll let him come home if she takes back the stuff. Some people might, but some won't." But his father was not with her.

"I gave the stuff back," she said when she got to the cabin.

The boy's throat hurt with a great lump, and when he swallowed, it would hurt more. If his father had come, it would have been easy. Together they could have found Sounder's body and buried him.

When the boy's mother heard that he had not found Sounder under the cabin, she stood in the doorway and thought for a long time. If one of the children had stood in the door that long, she would have said "Go in or out, child."

"Creatures like to die under somethin'," she said at last, "and there ain't nothin' else close to crawl under. He wasn't hit in his vitals, I reckon. He's got a flesh wound. He's gone into the woods to draw out the poison with oak-leaf acid."

Now she shut the door and put her basket on the tin-topped table. "Poke up the fire," she said to the boy. "Oak leaves has strong acid that toughens the skin, just like the oak bark that they use to tan leather in the tannery. The creature beds down with the wound against a heap of oak leaves. The leaves make a poultice that draws out the poison and heals the wound with a hard brown scab. That's why creatures head for the swampland around the big water when the mange hits. Wet leaves heals better."

"Sounder's blood would wettin the leaves," the boy said after he had stood a long time with the poker in his hand. His eyes were fixed on the open stove door, watching the yellow flame change shape and turn to blue and red.

"Sounder was jumping at the wagon and hard to hit," the boy's mother said. "I think maybe he was hit a glancing shot that tore off the hide on his head and shoulder. If he was, he's gone to the jack-oak woods to heal himself. The Lord shows

His creatures how to do. If he ain't dead now, he'll come limpin' home, powerful hungry, in time."

"Tomorrow or the day after?" the boy asked.

"Longer, maybe four days, or more like seven. But don't be all hope, child. If he had deep head wounds, he might be addled crazy and not know where he wandered off to die."

The boy's mother had brought home the empty meal sack. In her basket she had some fat meat, potatoes, and a small bottle of vanilla flavoring, which she had bought with the money she got for her walnut kernels. From the bottom of the basket she took the folded brown paper bag into which she poured each night's pickin's and put it on the shelf. She also brought home an empty cardboard box which the storekeeper had given her. She didn't say where she had been, besides the store, or what had happened. The boy could see that her eyes were filled with hurt and said nothing. The younger children remembered not to ask anything except, looking in the empty box, one said, "Nothin' in here?"

"I'm gonna use it to put a cake in," the mother said.

"Better go out and crack nuts for the night's pickin' before dark," she said to the boy.

The boy scooped up a tin pail of nuts from the

big box under the stove and went out to the flat cracking stone. With his knees still sore from crawling under the cabin, he hesitated a long time before he knelt on the frozen earth. Standing, he looked one way and then another, tracing the fencerows that had more oaks than other trees, the far lowland woods and the foothills. "I'll go there first tomorrow," he said to himself as he faced the foothills. "There's big patches of oak trees there. And whenever Sounder was given his head, he picked the hills for huntin'."

When night came, his mother hummed and picked kernels. She did not tell a story. The boy wanted to ask who carried in wood to keep the people in jail warm. He knew they had big stoves in big jails. Once his mother had told him a story about three people named Shadrach, Meshach, and Abed-nego who were in jail. Some mean governor or sheriff got mad and had them thrown right into the jail stove, big as a furnace, but the Lord blew out the fire and cooled the big stove in a second. And when the jail keeper opened the stove door, there stood Shadrach, Meshach, and Abed-nego singing:

Cool water, cool water;
The Lord's got green pastures and cool water.

"Tell me about Joseph in the jail and the stone

quarry in Egypt and chiselin' out rocks to make ole Pharaoh's gravestone," the boy asked. But his mother went on humming, and the boy went back to his thinking.

No stove could be that big, he thought. He watched the red coals through the open draft in the stove door brighten each time the wind blew loud enough to make a low whistling noise in the stovepipe. A burning chunk-stick fell against the inside of the stove, but the boy did not try to convince himself that it might be the thump of Sounder scratching fleas underneath the floor. He was thinking of tomorrow.

Tomorrow he would go into the woods and look for Sounder. "The wind whistlin' in the pipe is bothersome," he said. He hated the cold wind. It blew through his clothes and chilled his body inside and made him shiver. He hoped the wind would not be blowing in the woods tomorrow. The wind made the woods noisy. The boy liked the woods when they were quiet. He understood quiet. He could hear things in the quiet. But quiet was better in the woods than it was in the cabin. He didn't hear things in cabin quiet. Cabin quiet was long and sad.

"Turn the pipe-damper a little and the whistlin' will stop," his mother said at last.

The next day he walked the great woodlands,

calling Sounder's name. The wind blew through his clothes and chilled him inside. When he got home after dark, his clothes were torn. His throat hurt with a great lump choking him. His mother fed him and said, "Child, child, you must not go into the woods again. Sounder might come home again. But you must learn to lose, child. The Lord teaches the old to lose. The young don't know how to learn it. Some people is born to keep. Some is born to lose. We was born to lose, I reckon. But Sounder might come back."

But weeks went by, and Sounder did not come back.

* * *

One night the boy learned why his mother had brought home the bottle of vanilla flavoring. Now it was Christmas and she was making a cake. When the four layers were spread out on the tin-topped table and she began to ice them, the boy noticed that she put three together in a large cake and made a small one of the leftover layer.

"Why we having two cakes?" the boy asked. But she was humming to herself and did not answer him. When she had finished, she put the small cake on the top shelf of the dish cupboard. The big one she put in the cardboard box she had brought from the store.

The sweet smell of baking and vanilla had drawn the smaller children from the stove to the edge of the table. The woman reached over or walked around them as she worked. "I'm done," she finally said. "You can lick the pans."

The boy had not moved from his chair by the stove. Today he had searched the oak clumps along the far fencerows for Sounder. He never got the sweet pan till last, anyway. It always went from youngest to oldest, and there was never much left when his turn came.

"You're tired and worried poorly," his mother said. And she handed him the icing pan.

In the morning the woman told the boy that she wanted him to walk to town, to the jail behind the courthouse, and take the cake to his father. "It's a troublesome trip," she said. "But they won't let women in the jail. So you must go." She tied a string around the cardboard box and said, "Carry it flat if your hands don't get too cold. Then it'll look mighty pretty when you fetch it to him." She stood at the edge of the porch until he was far enough away not to be able to look back and see her crying, then called to him,

"Whatever you do, child, act perkish and don't grieve your father."

On the road, the boy felt afraid. He had been to the town at Christmastime before. Not on Christmas Day, but a few days before, to help his father carry mistletoe and bunches of bittersweet berries that his father sold by the wall in front of the courthouse or on the corner by the bank. And sometimes, when it was getting late and they still had trimmings to sell, his father would go to the back door of houses along the street and say "Ma'am, would you need some trimmin's?" and hold up the biggest sprig of mistletoe left in his grain sack. They usually sold most of the mistletoe, the boy remembered, but bunches of bittersweet that the boy had carried all day were always left over to be thrown in a fence corner on the way home. "Ain't no good for nothin' now" his father would say.

From early fall until gathering time, the father and boy kept their eyes peered for the golden-green clumps with white berries that grew high up in the forks of water elm and sycamore trees. Bittersweet was easy. "Pull down one vine and trim it, and you've got as much as a man can carry" his father always said. "But it takes a heap of fearful climbin' for mistletoe." They had already started gathering, and half a grain sack of mistletoe was still hanging against the side of the cabin. "If she hadn't had such a big load, she might have taken it," the boy said to himself.

The boy's fearful feeling increased as he got nearer town. There were big houses and behind the curtained windows there were eyes looking out at him. There would be more people now, and somebody might say "What you got in that box, boy?" or "Where you goin', boy?"

Church bells were ringing in the town. It was Christmas, and some people went to church on Christmas. In town the people he saw were laughing and talking. No one noticed him and he was glad. He looked at the store windows out of the corner of his eye. They were silvery and gold and green and red and sparkling. They were filled with toys and beautiful things. With the Christmas money from peddling, his father had bought what toys he could for the boy and his little brother and sisters. They had worn-out toys too. People in the big houses where his mother worked had given them to her to bring home.

He always wished they would give his mother an old book. He was sure he could learn to read if he had a book. He could read some of the town signs and the store signs. He could read price figures. He wanted to stop and stand and look straight at the windows, but he was afraid. A policeman would come after him. Perhaps the people had offered his mother old books, but she had said "No use, nobody can read in our cabin." Perhaps the people knew she couldn't read and thought her feelings would be hurt if they offered her the books their children had used up and worn out. The boy had heard once that some people had so many books they only read each book once. But the boy was sure there were not that many books in the world.

It was cold, but there were a few people standing or sitting along the wall in front of the courthouse. Winter or summer, there were always people there. The boy wondered if they knew it was Christmas. They didn't look happy like some of the people he had seen. He knew they were looking at him, so he hurried quickly past and around the corner to the back of the courthouse. The front of the courthouse was red brick with great white marble steps going up to a wide door. But the back was gray cement and three floors high, with iron bars over all the windows.

The only door that led into the jail had a small square of glass at about the height of a man, and there were iron bars over the glass. The boy was not tall enough to see through the glass. He

JAIL

clutched the box close to him. He felt that something was about to burst through the door. In the middle of the door there was a great iron knocker. The boy knew he had to knock at the door; he wished he could be back in the great woods. He could hear voices inside the windows with the iron bars. Somewhere a voice was singing "God's gonna trouble the water." From one of the windows there came the sound of laughter. Now and then a door slammed with the deep clash of iron on iron. There was a rattle of tin pans. The boy felt very lonely. The town was as lonely as the cabin, he thought.

A large red-faced man opened the door and said, "You'll have to wait. It ain't visitin' hours yet. Who do you want to see? You'll have to wait." And he slammed the door before the boy could speak.

It was cold on the gray side of the building, so the boy went to the corner near the wall where the people and visitors stood or sat. The sun was shining there. The boy had forgotten it was still Christmas, the waiting seemed so long. A drunk man staggered along the street in front of the courthouse wall, saying "Merry Christmas" to everyone. He said "Merry Christmas" to the boy, and he smiled at the boy too.

Finally the great clock on the roof of the courthouse struck twelve. It frightened the boy because it seemed to shake the town. Now the red-faced man opened the door and let several people in. Inside, the man lined everybody up and felt their clothes and pockets. He jerked the cardboard box from the boy and tore off the top. The boy could hear iron doors opening and closing. Long hallways, with iron bars from floor to ceiling, ran from the door into the dim center of the building. The man with the red face squeezed the cake in his hands and broke it into four pieces. "This could have a steel file or hacksaw blade in it," he said. Then he swore and threw the pieces back in the box. The boy had been very hungry. Now he was not hungry. He was afraid. The man shoved the box into the boy's hands and swore again. Part of the cake fell to the floor; it was only a box of crumbs now. The man swore again and made the boy pick up the crumbs from the floor.

The boy hated the man with the red face with the same total but helpless hatred he had felt when he saw his father chained, when he saw Sounder shot. He had thought how he would like to chain the deputy sheriff behind his own wagon and then scare the horse so that it would run faster than the cruel man could. The deputy would fall and bounce and drag on the frozen road. His fine leather jacket would be torn more than he had torn his father's overalls. He would yell and curse, and that would make the horse go faster. And the boy would just watch, not trying to stop the wagon. . . .

The boy would like to see the big red-faced man crumpled on the floor with the crumbs. Besides the red face, the boy had noticed the fat, bulging neck that folded down over the man's collar and pushed up in wrinkled circles under his chin. The bull neck of the man reminded the boy of the bull he had seen die in the cattle chute at the big house where his father worked. The horse doctor had been trying to vaccinate the bull in the neck, but the rope through the ring in the bull's nose didn't keep the bull from tossing his head from side to side, knocking the horse doctor against the side of the chute. Then the horse doctor had gotten mad and said, "Get a chain. I'll make him stand still."

When the chain was snapped around the bull's neck, the farm hands pulled it over the crossbar of the chute posts and hooked it. But when the horse doctor stuck the bull in the neck, he lunged backward, set his front feet with his whole weight against the chain, and choked himself to death before one of the farm hands could jab him with a pitchfork and make him slacken the chain. The legs of the bull folded under him and the chain buried itself in the fat of his neck. When the farm hands finally got the chain unhooked from the crossbar, the bull's head fell in the dirt, and blood oozed out of its mouth and nostrils. . . .

The bull-necked man would sag to his knees, the boy thought, and crumple into a heap on the floor. Just the way the bull did, the boy thought, and blood would ooze out of his mouth and nose.

"Get up," the red-faced man said, "you wanta take all day?" The boy stood up. He felt weak and his knees shook, but there were no more tears in his eyes.

The red-faced man took a big iron key on a ring as big around as the boy's head and unlocked one of the iron gates. He pushed the boy in and said, "Fourth door down." Passing the three doors, the boy could feel eyes following him. He saw men, some sitting on cots, some standing behind the iron gates with their hands on the bars, looking at him. Each step echoed against the iron ceiling and made him sound like a giant walking. Far down the long iron-grated corridor a sad voice was singing:

Far away on Judah's plains
The shepherds watched their sheep.

The boy's father stood with his hands on the bars. He did not have his hands and feet chained together. Seeing the hands that could handle a hot pot lid without a pot rag, open the stove door without using a poker, or skin a possum by holding the hind legs of the carcass with one hand and the hide with the other and just pulling, the boy knew his father could have choked the cruel man with the bull neck.

The father looked at the boy and said, "Child." On the way, the boy had thought about what he would say to his father. He had practiced talking about his mother selling kernels at the store and buying the cake makings, his little brother and sisters being all right, no strangers coming past, not finding Sounder's body. And he was going to ask his father where Sounder came to him along the road when he wasn't more'n a pup. He practiced saying them all over and over to get the quiver and the quiet spells out of his voice because his mother had said, "Whatever you do, child, act perkish and don't grieve your father."

But the boy was full of mixed hate and pity now, and it addled him. There was an opening in the bars with a flat, iron shelf attached on the inside. The boy had left the lid of the box on the floor. Now he pushed the box through the opening and said, "This was a cake, before—" But he couldn't finish. An awful quiet spell destroyed all his practice.

"Sounder might not be dead," the boy said. He knew his father was grieved, for he swallowed hard and the quiet spells came to him too.

"I'll be back 'fore long," said his father.

From somewhere down the corridor there came a loud belly laugh, and a loud voice called out, "Listen to the man talk."

"Tell her not to grieve." His father was almost whispering now.

"Sounder didn't die under the cabin." But the boy couldn't keep the quivering out of his voice.

"Tell her not to send you no more." The quiet spells were getting longer. The man stopped looking through the bars at the boy and looked down at the cake.

"If he wasn't shot in his vitals," the boy said, "he might get healed in the woods." Then there was a long quiet spell that was split in the middle by the loud clank of an iron door banging shut.

"Tell her I'll send word with the visitin' preacher."

The big red-faced man with the bull neck opened the corridor door and yelled, "Visitin' over." The boy felt numb and cold, like he had felt standing outside the jail door. He choked up. He had grieved his father. He hated the red-faced man, so he wouldn't cry until he got outside.

"Come on, boy," the man yelled, swinging the big key ring.

"Go, child," the father said. "Hurry, child."

The boy was the last person through the big iron door. The bull-necked man pushed him and said, "Git, boy, or next time you won't get in."

V

THE BOY MOVED quickly around the corner and out of sight of the iron door and the gray cement walls of the jail. At the wall in front of the court-house he stood for a while and looked back. When he had come, he was afraid, but he felt good in one way because he would see his father. He was bringing him a cake for Christmas. And he wasn't going to let his father know he was grieved. So his father *wouldn't* be grieved.

Now the sun had lost its strength. There were only a few people loafing around the courthouse wall, so the boy sat for a spell. He felt numb and tired. What would he say to his mother? He would tell her that the jailer was mean to visitors but didn't say nothing to the people in jail. He wouldn't tell her about the cake. When he told her his father had said she shouldn't send him again, that he would send word by the visiting preacher, she would say "You grieved him, child. I told you to be perk so you wouldn't grieve him."

Nobody came near where the boy sat or passed on the street in front of the wall. He had forgotten the most important thing, he thought. He hadn't asked his father where Sounder had come to him on the road when he wasn't more'n a pup. That didn't make any difference.

But along the road on the way to the jail, before the bull-necked man had ruined everything, the boy had thought his father would begin to think and say "If a stray ever follard you and it wasn't near a house, likely somebody's dropped it. So you could fetch it home and keep it for a dog."

"Wouldn't do no good now," the boy murmured to himself. Even if he found a stray on the way home, his mother would say "I'm afraid, child.

Don't bring it in the cabin. If it's still here when mornin' comes, you take it down the road and scold it and run so it won't foller you no more. If somebody come lookin', you'd be in awful trouble."

A great part of the way home the boy walked in darkness. In the big houses he saw beautiful lights and candles in the windows. Several times dogs rushed to the front gates and barked as he passed. But no stray pup came to him along the lonely, empty stretches of road. In the dark he thought of the bull-necked man crumpled on the floor in the cake crumbs, like the strangled bull in the cattle chute, and he walked faster. At one big house the mailbox by the road had a lighted lantern hanging on it. The boy walked on the far side of the road so he wouldn't show in the light. "People hangs 'em out when company is comin' at night," the boy's father had once told him.

When court was over, they would take his father to a road camp or a quarry or a state farm. Would his father send word with the visiting preacher where he had gone? Would they take his father away to the chain gang for a year or two years before he could tell the visiting preacher? How would the boy find him then? If he lived closer to the town, he could watch each day, and when they took his father away in the wagons where convicts were penned up in huge wooden crates, he could follow.

The younger children were already in bed when the boy got home. He was glad, for they would have asked a lot of questions that might make his mother feel bad, questions like "Is everybody chained up in jail? How long do people stay in jail at one time?"

The boy's mother did not ask hurtful questions. She asked if the boy got in all right and if it was warm in the jail. The boy told her that the jailer was mean to visitors but that he didn't say nothing to the people in jail. He told her he heard some people singing in the jail.

"Sounder ain't come home?" the boy said to his mother after he had talked about the jail. He had looked under the porch and called before he came into the cabin.

Now he went out, calling and looking around the whole cabin. He started to light the lantern to look more, but his mother said, "Hang it back, child. Ain't no use to fret yourself. Eat your supper, you must be famished."

"He said not to come no more," the boy finally said to his mother when he had finished his supper. "He said he'll send word by the visitin' preacher." He poked up the fire and waited for his mother to ask him if he had been perk and didn't grieve his father, but she didn't. He warmed himself and watched a patch of red glow the size of his hand at the bottom of the stove. He could see the red-faced man lying on the jail floor with blood oozing out of the corners of his mouth. After a long quiet spell the rocker began to squeak, and it made the boy jump, but his mother didn't notice. She began to rock as she picked out walnut kernels. She hummed for a while, and then she began to sing like she was almost whispering for no one to hear but herself:

You've gotta walk that lonesome valley,
You've gotta walk it by yourself,
Ain't nobody else gonna walk it for you . . .

In bed, the pressure of the bed slats through the straw tick felt good against the boy's body. His pillow smelled fresh, and it was smooth and soft. He was tired, but he lay awake for a long time. He thought of the store windows full of so many things. He thought of the beautiful candles in windows. He dreamed his father's hands were chained against the prison bars and he was still standing there with his head down. He dreamed that a wonderful man had come up to him as he was trying to read the store signs aloud and had said, "Child, you want to learn, don't you?"

In the morning the boy lay listening to his

mother as she opened and closed the stove door. He heard the damper squeak in the stovepipe as she adjusted it. She was singing softly to herself. Then the boy thought he heard another familiar sound, a faint whine on the cabin porch. He listened. No, it couldn't be. Sounder always scratched before he whined, and the scratching was always louder than the whine. Besides, it was now almost two months later, and the boy's mother had said he might be back in a week. No, he was not dreaming. He heard it again. He had been sleeping in his shirt to keep warm, so he only had to pull on his overalls as he went. His mother had stopped singing and was listening.

There on the cabin porch, on three legs, stood the living skeleton of what had been a mighty coon hound. The tail began to wag, and the hide made little ripples back and forth over the ribs. One side of the head and shoulders was reddish brown and hairless; the acid of the oak leaves had tanned the surface of the wound the color of leather. One front foot dangled above the floor. The stub of an ear stuck out on one side, and there was no eye on that side, only a dark socket with a splinter of bone showing above it. The dog raised his good ear and whined. His one eye looked up at the lantern and the possum sack where they hung against the wall. The eye looked past the boy and his mother. Where was his master? "Poor creature. Poor creature," said the mother and turned away to get him food. The boy felt sick and wanted to cry, but he touched Sounder on the good side of his head. The tail wagged faster, and he licked the boy's hand.

The shattered shoulder never grew together enough to carry weight, so the great hunter with the single eye, his head held to one side so he could see, never hopped much farther from the cabin than the spot in the road where he had tried to jump on the wagon with his master. Whether he lay in the sun on the cabin porch or by the side of the road, the one eye was always turned in the direction his master had gone.

The boy got used to the way the great dog looked. The stub of ear didn't bother him, and the one eye that looked up at him was warm and questioning. But why couldn't he bark? "He wasn't hit in the neck" the boy would say to his mother. "He eats all right, his throat ain't scarred." But day after day when the boy snapped his fingers and said "Sounder, good Sounder," no excited bark burst from the great throat. When something moved at night, the whine was louder, but it was still just a whine.

Before Sounder was shot, the boy's mother always said "Get the pan, child" or "Feed your dog, child." Now she sometimes got the pan herself and took food out to Sounder. The boy noticed that sometimes his mother would stop singing when she put the food pan down at the edge of the porch. Sometimes she would stand and look at the hunting lantern and possum sack where they hung, unused, against the cabin wall. . . .

*   *   *

The town and the jail seemed to become more remote and the distance greater as each day passed. If his father hadn't said "Don't come again," it wouldn't seem so far, the boy thought. Uncertainty made the days of waiting longer too.

The boy waited for the visiting preacher to come and bring word of his father. He thought the people for whom his mother washed the soft curtains could certainly write and would write a letter for his mother. But would someone in the jail read it for his father? Perhaps none of the people in jail could read, and the big man with the red face would just tear it up and swear. The visiting preacher might write a letter for the boy's father. But how would it get to the cabin since no mailman passed and there was no mailbox like the boy had seen on the wider road nearer the town?

The boy wanted to go to the town to find out what had happened to his father. His mother always said "Wait, child, wait." When his mother returned laundry to the big houses, she asked the people to read her the court news from their newspapers. One night she came home with word of the boy's father; it had been read to her from the court news. When the younger children had gone to bed, she said to the boy, "Court's over." And then there was one of those long quiet spells that always made the boy feel numb and weak.

"You won't have to fret for a while about seein' him in jail. He's gone to hard labor."

"For how long?" the boy asked.

"It won't be as long as it might. Folks has always said he could do two men's work in a day. He'll get time off for hard work and good behavior. The court news had about good behavior in it. The judge said it."

"Where's he gonna be at?" the boy asked after he had swallowed the great lump that filled up his throat and choked him.

"Didn't say. The people that has the paper says

it don't ever say wher' they gonna be at. But it's the county or the state. Ain't never outside the state, the people says."

"He'll send word," the boy said.

VI

NOW THE CABIN was even quieter than it had been before loneliness put its stamp on everything. Sounder rolled his one eye in lonely dreaming. The boy's mother had longer periods of just humming without drifting into soft singing. The boy helped her stretch longer clotheslines from the cabin to the cottonwood trees at the edge of the fields. In the spring the boy went to the fields to work. He was younger than the other workers.

He was afraid and lonely. He heard them talking quietly about his father. He went to do yard work at the big houses where he had gathered weeds behind his father. "How old are you?" a man asked once when he was paying the boy his wages. "You're a hard worker for your age."

The boy did not remember his age. He knew he had lived a long, long time.

And the long days and months and seasons built a powerful restlessness into the boy. "Don't fret" his mother would say when he first began to talk of going to find his father. "Time's passin'. Won't be much longer now."

To the end of the county might be a far journey, and out of the county would be a far, far journey, but I'll go, the boy thought.

"Why are you so feared for me to go?" he would ask, for now he was old enough to argue with his mother. "In Bible stories everybody's always goin' on a long journey. Abraham goes on a long journey. Jacob goes into a strange land where his uncle lives, and he don't know where he lives, but he finds him easy. Joseph goes on the longest journey of all and has more troubles, but the Lord watches over him. And in Bible-story journeys, ain't no journey hopeless. Everybody finds what they suppose to find."

The state had many road camps which moved from place to place. There were also prison farms and stone quarries. Usually the boy would go searching in autumn when work in the fields was finished. One year he heard "Yes, the man you speak of was here, but I heard he was moved to the quarry in Gilmer County." One year it had been "Yes, he was in the quarry, but he was sick in the winter and was moved to the bean farm in Bartow County." More often a guard would chase him away from the gate or from standing near the high fence with the barbed wire along the top of it. And the guard would laugh and say "I don't know no names; I only know numbers. Besides, you can't visit here, you can only visit in jail." Another would sneer "You wouldn't know your old man if you saw him, he's been gone so long. You sure you know who your pa is, kid?"

The men in striped convict suits, riding in the mule-drawn wagons with big wooden frames resembling large pig crates, yelled as they rode past the watching boy, "Hey, boy, looking for your big brother? What you doing, kid, seeing how you gonna like it when you grow up?" And still the boy would look through the slats of the crate for a familiar face. He would watch men walking in line, dragging chains on their feet, to see if he

could recognize his father's step as he had known it along the road, coming from the fields to the cabin. Once he listened outside the gate on a Sunday afternoon and heard a preacher telling about the Lord loosening the chains of Peter when he had been thrown into prison. Once he stood at the guardhouse door of a quarry, and some ladies dressed in warm heavy coats and boots came and sang Christmas songs.

In his wandering the boy learned that the words men use most are "Get!" "Get out!" and "Keep moving!" Sometimes he followed the roads from one town to another, but if he could, he would follow railroad tracks. On the roads there were people, and they frightened the boy. The railroads usually ran through the flat silent countryside where the boy could walk alone with his terrifying thoughts. He learned that railroad stations, post offices, courthouses, and churches were places to escape from the cold for a few hours in the late night.

His journeys in search of his father accomplished one wonderful thing. In the towns he found that people threw newspapers and magazines into trash barrels, so he could always find something with which to practice his reading. When he was tired, or when he waited at some high wire gate, hoping his father would pass in the line, he would read the big-lettered words first and then practice the small-lettered words.

In his lonely journeying, the boy had learned to tell himself the stories his mother had told him at night in the cabin. He liked the way they always ended with the right thing happening. And people in stories were never feared of anything. Sometimes he tried to put together things he had read in the newspapers he found and make new stories. But the ends never came out right, and they made him more afraid. The people he tried to put in stories from the papers always seemed like strangers. Some story people he wouldn't be afraid of if he met them on the road. He thought he liked the David and Joseph stories best of all. "Why you want 'em told over'n over?" his mother had asked so many times. Now, alone on a bed of pine needles, he remembered that he could never answer his mother. He would just wait, and if his mother wasn't sad, with her lips stretched thin, she would stop humming and tell about David the boy, or King David. If she felt good and started long enough before bedtime, he would hear about Joseph the slave-boy, Joseph in prison, Joseph the dreamer, and Joseph the Big Man in Egypt. And when she had finished all about Joseph, she would say "Ain't no earthly power can make a story end as pretty as Joseph's; 'twas the Lord."

The boy listened to the wind passing through the tops of the tall pines; he thought they moved like giant brooms sweeping the sky. The moonlight raced down through the broken spaces of swaying trees and sent bright shafts of light along the ground and over him. The voice of the wind in the pines reminded him of one of the stories his mother had told him about King David. The Lord had said to David that when he heard the wind moving in the tops of the cedar trees, he would know that the Lord was fighting on his side and he would win. When David moved his army around into the hills to attack his enemy, he heard the mighty roar of the wind moving in the tops of the trees, and he cried out to his men that the Lord was moving above them into battle.

The boy listened to the wind. He could hear the mighty roaring. He thought he heard the voice of David and the tramping of many feet. He wasn't afraid with David near. He thought he saw a lantern moving far off in the woods, and as he fell asleep he thought he heard the deep, ringing voice of Sounder rising out of his great throat, riding the mist of the lowlands.

VII

WHEN THE BOY came home after each long trip in search of his father, the crippled coon hound would hobble far down the road to meet him, wag his tail, stand on his hind legs, and paw the boy with his good front paw. But never a sound beyond a deep whine came from him. The bits of news he might bring home his mother received in silence. Someone had heard that his father was moved. Someone had been in the same work gang with his father for four months last summer on the Walker county road. When she had heard all he had heard, she would say "There's patience, child, and waitin' that's got to be."

Word drifted back that there had been a terrible dynamite blast in one of the quarries that had killed twelve convicts and wounded several others. His mother had had the people read her the story from their newspapers when she carried the laundry. None of the prisoners killed was the boy's father.

The months and seasons of searching dragged into years. The boy helped his mother carry more and more baskets of laundry to and from the big houses; the clotheslines grew longer and longer. The other children, except for the littlest, could fetch and tote too, but they didn't like to go by themselves.

"Time is passing" the woman would say. "I wish you wouldn't go lookin', child." But when one of the field hands had heard something or when somebody said that a road camp was moving, she would wrap a piece of bread and meat for the boy to eat on the way and say nothing. Looking back from far down the road, the boy would see her watching at the edge of the porch. She seemed to understand the compulsion that started him on each long, fruitless journey with new hope.

Once the boy waited outside the tall wire fence of a road camp. Some convicts were whitewashing stones along the edge of a pathway that came toward the gate near where he stood. One might be his father, he thought. He could not tell until they got closer, for they crawled on their hands and knees as they bent over the stones. He leaned against the fence and hooked his fingers through the wire. If none of them was his father, they might know something anyway, he thought. He wished they would stand up and walk from one stone to the next. Then he would know his father easily by his walk. He could still remember the sound of his footsteps approaching the cabin after dark, the easy roll of the never-hurrying step that was the same when he went to work in the morning and when he came home from the long day in the fields. The boy had even been able to tell his father's walk by the swing of the lantern at his side. But none of the men whitewashing the round rocks that lined the path stood up and walked. They crawled the few feet from stone to stone, and crawling, they all looked the same.

Suddenly something crashed against the fence in front of the boy's face. A jagged piece of iron tore open the skin and crushed the fingers of one of his hands against the fence. Lost in thought and watching the convicts, the boy had not seen the guard, who had been sitting under a tree with a shotgun across his knees, get up and come to a toolbox filled with picks and crowbars which stood near the fence.

The piece of iron lay on the inside of the fence at the boy's feet. Drops of blood from his fingers dripped down the fence from wire to wire and fell on the ground. The boy pulled his fingers away from the wire mesh and began to suck on them to stop the throbbing. Tears ran down over his face and mixed with the blood on his hand. Little rivulets of blood and water ran down his arm and dropped off the end of his elbow.

The guard was swaying back and forth with laughter. His gun lay on the lid of the open toolbox. His arms swung in apelike gyrations of glee, and he held another piece of iron in one hand and his cap in the other. A white strip of forehead, where his uniform cap kept off the sun, shone between his brown hair and his sunburned face. His laughter had burst the button from his tieless shirt collar, and a white strip outlined his gaunt neck. For a second he reminded the boy of a garden scarecrow blowing in the wind, body and head of brown burlap stuffed with straw, the head tied on with a white rag just like the white band around the guard's neck, the head tilting from side to side, inviting a well-placed stone to send it bouncing along a bean row.

The men whitewashing the rocks made no sounds. No one among them suddenly raised himself to the height of a man almost as tall as a cabin porch post.

"He ain't there," the boy murmured to himself. If he was, the boy knew, by now he would be holding the scarecrow of a man in the air with one hand clamped all the way around the white strip on the skinny neck, the way he had seen Sounder clamp his great jaws on a weasel once, with the head stuck out one side of the jaws and the body the other. And the man would wheeze and squirm like the weasel had. His legs would paw the air in circles like his hands, then he would go limp, and the boy's father would loosen his grip, and the man in the brown uniform would fall in a heap, like when somebody untied the white rag that held the scarecrow to the stake. And the heap would roll down the slope and lodge against the fence, like the scarecrow rolled along a bean row until it caught in the brambles at the edge of the garden.

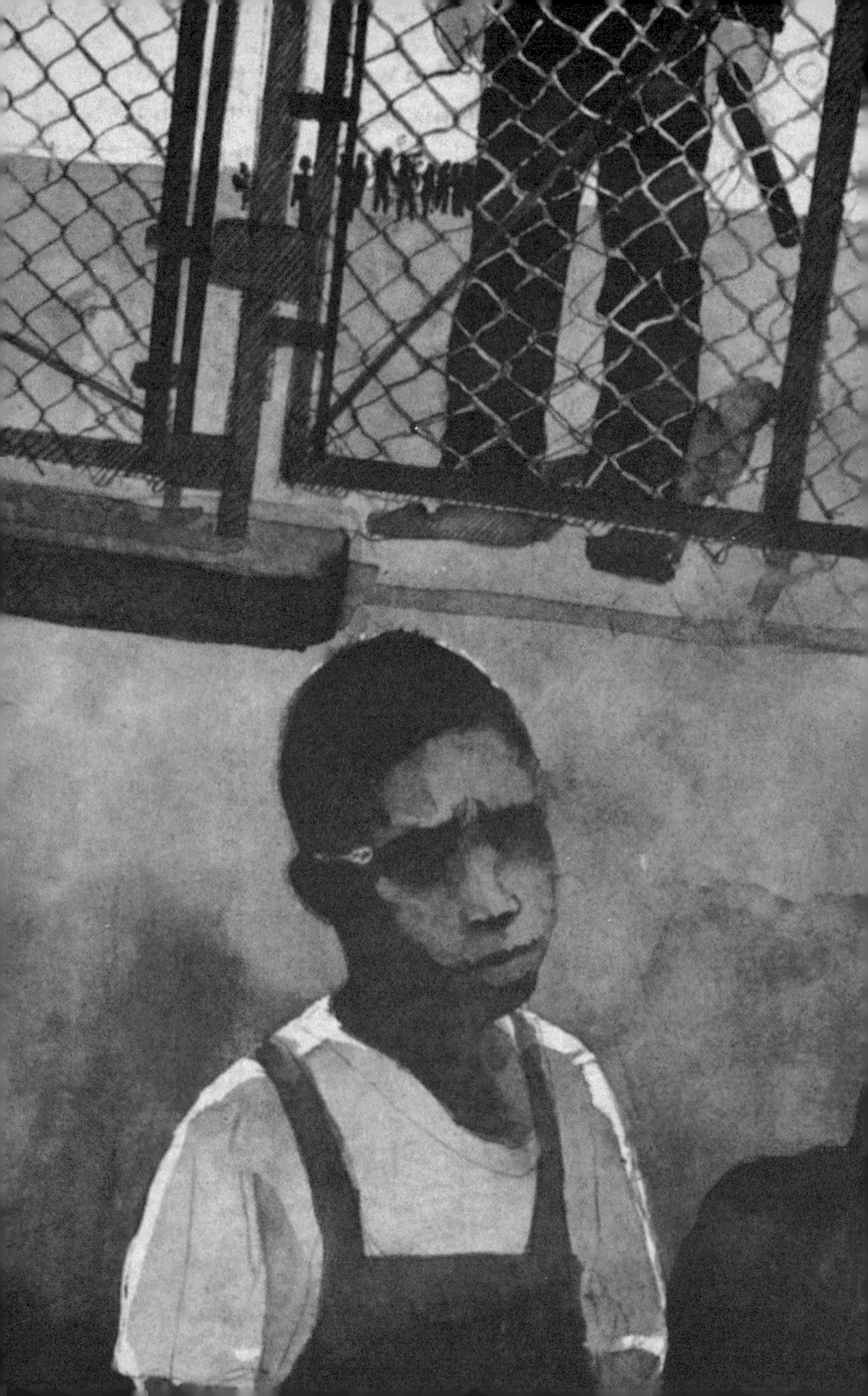

Feeling defeat in the midst of his glee because the boy had not run but stood still and defiant, sucking the blood from his bruised fingers, the guard stopped laughing and yelled at him, "That'll show you, boy! Git! And git fast!" The boy turned and, without looking back, began to walk slowly away. The guard began to laugh again and threw the scrap of iron over the fence. It landed a few feet from the boy. He looked at the iron and he looked at the man. The white spot between his hair and his eyes was the spot. The iron would split it open with a wide gash, and blood would darken the white spot and make it the color of the man's sunburned face. And the stone that David slung struck Goliath on his forehead; the stone sank into his forehead, and he fell on his face on the ground, the boy thought. But he left the iron on the ground.

Still sucking his fingers, the boy looked once more at the men whitewashing the stones. They were almost at the gate. He didn't need to wait and ask. His father was not crawling among them.

* * *

Later that day, passing along a street in a strange and lonely town, he saw a man dump a box of trash into a barrel. He noticed that a large brown-backed book went in with the trash. He waited until the man went back into the building and then took the book from the barrel. It was a book of stories about what people think. There were titles such as Cruelty, Excellent Men, Education, Cripples, Justice, and many others. The boy sat down, leaned back against the barrel, and began to read from the story called Cruelty.

> I have often heard it said that cowardice is the mother of cruelty, and I have found by experience that malicious and inhuman animosity and fierceness are usually accompanied by weakness. Wolves and filthy bears, and all the baser beasts, fall upon the dying.

The boy was trying to read aloud, for he could understand better if he heard the words. But now he stopped. He did not understand what it said; the words were too new and strange. He was sad. He thought books would have words like the ones he had learned to read in the store signs, words like his mother used when she told him stories of the Lord and Joseph and David. All his life he had wanted a book. Now he held one in his hands, and it was only making his bruised fingers hurt more. He would carry it with him anyway.

He passed a large brick schoolhouse with big windows and children climbing on little ladders and swinging on swings. No one jeered at him or noticed him because he had crossed the street and was walking close up against the hedge on the other side. Soon the painted houses ran out, and he was walking past unpainted cabins. He always felt better on his travels when he came to the part of town where the unpainted cabins were. Sometimes people came out on the porch when he passed and talked to him. Sometimes they gave him a piece to eat on the way. Now he thought they might laugh and say "What you carryin', child? A book?" So he held it close up against him.

"That's a school too," the boy said to himself as he stood facing a small unpainted building with its door at the end instead of the side, the way cabin doors were. Besides, he could always tell a school because it had more windows than a cabin.

At the side of the building two children were sloshing water out of a tin pail near a hand pump. One threw a dipper of water on a dog that came from underneath to bark at the boy. The school was built on posts, and a stovepipe came through the wall and stuck up above the rafters. A rusty tin pipe ran from the corner of the roof down to the cistern where the children were playing.

The dog had gone back under the building, so the boy entered the yard and moved toward the children. If one of them would work the pump handle, he could wash the dried blood off his hand. Just when he reached the cistern, a wild commotion of barking burst from under the floor of the school. Half a dozen dogs, which followed children to school and waited patiently for lunch-time scraps and for school to be over, burst from under the building in pursuit of a pig that had wandered onto the lot. In the wild chase around the building the biggest dog struck the tin drain-pipe, and it clattered down the wall and bounced on the cement top of the cistern. With a pig under the building and the dogs barking and racing in and out, the school day ended.

Two dozen or more children raced out the door, few of them touching the three steps that led from the stoop to the ground. Some were calling the names of dogs and looking under the building. The boy found himself surrounded by strange inquiring eyes. Questions came too fast to answer. "You new here?" "Where you moved to?" "That your book?" "You comin' here to school?" "Kin you read that big a book?" The boy had put his bruised hand into his pocket so no one could see it. Some of the children carried books too, but none were as big as the one he held close against his side.

Just when the commotion was quieting down, a man appeared at the schoolhouse door. The children scattered across the lot in four directions. "Tell your pa that he must keep his pig in the pen," he called to one child.

Then it was quiet. The boy looked at the man in the doorway. They were alone now. The dogs had followed the children. And the pig, hearing a familiar call from the corner of the lot, had come grunting from his sanctuary and gone in the direction of the call.

In his many journeyings among strangers the boy had learned to sniff out danger and spot orneriness quickly. Now, for the first time in his life away from home, he wasn't feared. The lean elderly man with snow-white hair, wearing Sunday clothes, came down the steps. "This pipe is always falling," he said as he picked it up and put it back in place. "I need to wire it up."

"I just wanted to wash my hand. It's got dried blood on it where I hurt my fingers."

"You should have run home."

"I don't live in these parts."

"Here, I'll hold your book, and I'll pump for you." And the mellow eyes of the man began to search the boy for answers, answers that could be found without asking questions.

"We need warm soapy water," the teacher said. "I live right close. Wait 'til I get my papers and lock the door, and I'll take you home and fix it."

The boy wanted to follow the man into the schoolhouse and see what it was like inside, but by the time he got to the steps the man was back again, locking the door. "I usually put the school in order after the children leave," he said, "but I'll do it in the morning before they get here."

At the edge of the school lot the man took the road that led away from the town. They walked without much talk, and the boy began to wish the man would ask him a lot of questions. When they had passed several cabins, each farther from the other as they went, the man turned off the road and said, "We're home. I live here alone. Have lived alone for a long time." Fingering the small wire hook on the neatly whitewashed gate which led into a yard that was green, the teacher stopped talking.

A cabin with a gate and green grass in the yard is almost a big house, the boy thought as he followed the man.

Inside the gate the man went along the fence,

studying some plants tied up to stakes. He began to talk again, not to the boy, but to a plant that was smaller than the others. "You'll make it, little one, but it'll take time to get your roots set again."

The boy looked at the white-haired old man leaning over like he was listening for the plant to answer him. "He's conjured," the boy whispered to himself. "Lots of old folks is conjured or addled." He moved backward to the gate, thinking he'd better run away. "Conjured folks can conjure you," the boy's mother always said, "if you get yourself plain carried off by their soft spell-talk."

But before the boy could trouble his mind anymore, the man straightened up and began talking to him. "Some animal dug under the roots and tore them loose from the earth. It was wilted badly and might have died. But I reset it, and I water it every day. It's hard to reset a plant if it's wilted too much; the life has gone out of it. But this one will be all right. I see new leaves startin'."

"What grows on it?" the boy asked, thinking it must be something good to eat if somebody cared that much about a plant.

"It's only a flower," the man said. "I'll water it when the earth has cooled a little. If you water a plant when the earth is too warm, it shocks the roots."

Inside the cabin the man started a fire in the cookstove and heated water. As he washed the boy's hand with a soft white rag he said, "You musta slammed these fingers in a awful heavy door or gate." Before the boy could answer, the teacher began to talk about the plant he must remember to water.

He don't wanta know nothin' about me, the boy thought.

"When I saw your book, I thought you were coming to enroll for school. But you don't live in these parts, you say."

"I found the book in a trash barrel. It has words like I ain't used to readin'. I can read store-sign words and some newspaper words."

"This is a wonderful book," said the teacher. "It was written by a man named Montaigne, who was a soldier. But he grew tired of being a soldier and spent his time studying and writing. He also liked to walk on country roads."

The teacher lit two lamps. The boy had never seen two lamps burning in the same room. They made the room as bright as daylight.

"People should read his writings," the man continued. "But few do. He is all but forgotten." But the boy did not hear. He was thinking of a cabin that had two lamps, both lit at the same time, and two stoves, one to cook on and one to warm by.

The man sat in a chair between two tables that held the lamps. There were books on the tables too, and there were shelves filled not with pans and dishes, but with books. The mellow eyes of the man followed the boy's puzzled glances as they studied the strange warm world in which he had suddenly found himself.

"I will read you a little story from your book." The boy watched as the fingers of the man turned the pages one way and then the other until he found what he wanted to read.

"This is a very short story about a king named Cyrus, who wanted to buy the prize horse that belonged to one of his soldiers. Cyrus asked him how much he would sell the horse for, or whether he would exchange him for a kingdom. The soldier said he would not sell his prize horse and he would not exchange him for a kingdom, but that he would willingly give up his horse to gain a friend. . . . But now I have told you the whole story so there's no use for me to read it."

"You've been a powerful good friend to take me in like this," the boy said at last. "My fingers don't hurt no more."

"I am your friend," said the man. "So while I heat some water to soak your hand and make your cot for the night, you tell me all about yourself."

"I had a father and a dog named Sounder," the boy began. . . .

VIII

"WHO'S BEEN KINDLY to your hurts?" the boy's mother asked as she looked down at the clean white rags that bandaged the boy's fingers. Rocking on the porch, she had seen the white dot swinging back and forth in the sun when the boy wasn't much more than a moving spot far down the road. "For a while I wasn't sure it was you," she said. "Why you walkin' fast? You done found him? Is your hand hurt bad? Is that a Bible somebody's done mistreated?" The woman's eyes had come to rest on the book the boy held in his good hand.

"No. It's a book. I found it in a trash can."

"Be careful what you carry off, child," his mother said. "It can cause a heap o' trouble."

"I got somethin' to tell," the boy said as he sat down on the edge of the porch and ran his bandaged fingers over the head of the great coon dog who had stopped his jumping and whining and lay at the boy's feet with his head cocked to the side, looking up with his one eye. The younger children sat in a line beside the boy, waiting to hear.

"Is he poorly?" the woman asked slowly. "Is he far?"

"It's about somethin' else," the boy said after a long spell of quiet. "I ain't found him yet."

The boy told his mother and the children about his night in the teacher's cabin. The teacher wanted him to come back and go to school. He had been asked to live in the teacher's cabin and do his chores. The children's eyes widened when they heard the cabin had two lamps, two stoves, and grass growing in a yard with a fence and a gate. He told how the teacher could read and that there were lots of books on shelves in the cabin.

"Maybe he will write letters to the road camps for you," the mother said, " 'cause you'll be so busy with schoolin' and cleanin' the schoolhouse for him that you can't go searchin' no more."

"Maybe I'd have time," the boy said. "But he says like you, 'Better not to go. Just be patient and time will pass.' "

"It's all powerful puzzlin' and aggravatin', but it's the Lord's will." The boy noticed that his mother had stopped rocking; the loose boards did not rattle as the chair moved on them.

"The teacher said he'd walk all the way and reason about it if you didn't want me to come to him. You don't want me to go, but I'll come home often as I can. And sometime I might bring word."

"It's a sign; I believes in signs." The rocker began to move back and forth, rattling the loose boards in the porch floor. "Go child. The Lord has come to you."

* * *

When he returned to the cabin with books on the shelves and the kind man with the white hair and the gentle voice, all the boy carried was his book with one cover missing—the book that he couldn't understand. In the summers he came home to take his father's place in the fields, for cabin rent had to be paid with field work. In the winter he seldom came because it took "more'n a day's walkin' and sleepin' on the ground."

"Ain't worth it" his mother would say.

Each year, after he had been gone for a whole winter and returned, the faithful Sounder would come hobbling on three legs far down the road to meet him. The great dog would wag his tail and whine. He never barked. The boy sang at his work in the fields, and his mother rocked in her chair and sang on the porch of the cabin. Sometimes when Sounder scratched fleas under the porch, she would look at the hunting lantern and the empty possum sack hanging against the wall. Six crops of persimmons and wild grapes had ripened. The possums and raccoons had gathered them unmolested. The lantern and possum sack hung untouched. "No use to nobody no more," the woman said.

The boy read to his brother and sisters when he had finished his day in the fields. He read the story of Joseph over and over and never wearied of it. "In all the books in the teacher's cabin, there's no story as good as Joseph's story" he would say to them.

The woman, listening and rocking, would say "The Lord has come to you, child. The Lord has certainly come to you."

Late one August afternoon the boy and his mother sat on the shaded corner of the porch. The heat and drought of dog days had parched the earth, and the crops had been laid by. The boy had come home early because there was nothing to do in the fields.

"Dog days is a terrible time," the woman said. "It's when the heat is so bad the dogs go mad." The boy would not tell her that the teacher had told him that dog days got their name from the Dog Star because it rose and set with the sun during that period. She had her own feeling for the earth, he thought, and he would not confuse it.

"It sure is hot," he said instead. "Lucky to come from the fields early." He watched the heat waves as they made the earth look like it was moving in little ripples.

Sounder came around the corner of the cabin from somewhere, hobbled back and forth as far as the road several times, and then went to his cool spot under the porch. "That's what I say about dog days," the woman said. "Poor creature's been addled with the heat for three days. Can't find no place to quiet down. Been down the road nearly out o' sight a second time today, and now he musta come from the fencerows. Whines all the time. A mad dog is a fearful sight. Slobberin' at the mouth and runnin' every which way 'cause they're blind. Have to shoot 'em 'fore they bite some child. It's awful hard."

"Sounder won't go mad," the boy said. "He's lookin' for a cooler spot, I reckon."

A lone figure came on the landscape as a speck and slowly grew into a ripply form through the heat waves. "Scorchin' to be walkin' and totin' far today," she said as she pointed to the figure on the road.

A catbird fussed in the wilted lilac at the corner of the cabin. "Why's that bird fussin' when no cat's prowlin? Old folks has a sayin' that if a catbird fusses 'bout nothin', somethin' bad is comin'. It's a bad sign."

"Sounder, I reckon," the boy said. "He just passed her bush when he came around the cabin."

In the tall locust at the edge of the fence, its top leaves yellowed from lack of water, a mockingbird mimicked the catbird with half a dozen notes, decided it was too hot to sing, and disappeared. The great coon dog, whose rhythmic panting came through the porch floor, came from under the house and began to whine.

As the figure on the road drew near, it took shape and grew indistinct again in the wavering heat. Sometimes it seemed to be a person dragging something, for little puffs of red dust rose in sulfurous clouds at every other step. Once or twice they thought it might be a brown cow or mule, dragging its hooves in the sand and raising and lowering its weary head.

Sounder panted faster, wagged his tail, whined, moved from the dooryard to the porch and back to the dooryard.

The figure came closer. Now it appeared to be a child carrying something on its back and limping.

"The children still at the creek?" she asked.

"Yes, but it's about dry."

Suddenly the voice of the great coon hound broke the sultry August deadness. The dog dashed along the road, leaving three-pointed clouds of red dust to settle back to earth behind him. The mighty voice rolled out upon the valley, each flutelike bark echoing from slope to slope.

"Lord's mercy! Dog days done made him mad." And the rocker was still.

Sounder was a young dog again. His voice was the same mellow sound that had ridden the November breeze from the lowlands to the hills. The boy and his mother looked at each other. The catbird stopped her fussing in the wilted lilac bush. On three legs, the dog moved with the same lightning speed that had carried him to the throat of a grounded raccoon.

Sounder's master had come home. Taking what might have been measured as a halting half step and then pulling a stiff, dead leg forward, dragging a foot turned sideways in the dust, the man limped into the yard. Sounder seemed to understand that to jump up and put his paw against his master's breast would topple him into the dust, so the great dog smelled and whined and wagged his tail and licked the limp hand dangling at his master's side. He hopped wildly around his master in a circle that almost brought head and tail together.

The head of the man was pulled to the side where a limp arm dangled and where the foot pointed outward as it was dragged through the dust. What had been a shoulder was now pushed up and back to make a one-sided hump so high that the leaning head seemed to rest upon it. The mouth was askew too, and the voice came out of the part farthest away from the withered, wrinkled, lifeless side.

The woman in the still rocker said, "Lord, Lord," and sat suffocated in shock.

"Sounder knew it was you just like you was comin' home from work," the boy said in a clear voice.

Half the voice of the man was gone too, so in slow, measured, stuttering he told how he had been caught in a dynamite blast in the prison quarry, how the dead side had been crushed under an avalanche of limestone, and how he had been missed for a whole night in the search for dead and wounded. He told how the pain of the crushing stone had stopped in the night, how doctors had pushed and pulled and encased the numb side of his body in a cast, how they had spoken kindly to him and told him he would die. But he resolved he would not die, even with a half-dead body, because he wanted to come home again.

"For being hurt, they let me have time off my sentence," the man said, "and since I couldn't work, I guess they was glad to."

"The Lord has brought you home," the woman said.

The boy heard faint laughter somewhere behind the cabin. The children were coming home from the creek. He went around the cabin slowly, then hurried to meet them.

"Pa's home," he said and grabbed his sister,

who had started to run toward the cabin. "Wait. He's mighty crippled up, so behave like nothin' has happened."

"Can he walk?" the youngest child asked.

"Yes! And don't you ask no questions."

"You been mighty natural and considerate," the mother said to the younger children later when she went to the woodpile and called them to pick dry kindling for a quick fire. When she came back to the porch she said, "We was gonna just have a cold piece 'cause it's so sultry, but now I think I'll cook."

Everything don't change much, the boy thought. There's eatin' and sleepin' and talkin' and settin' that goes on. One day might be different from another, but there ain't much difference when they're put together.

Sometimes there were long quiet spells. Once or twice the boy's mother said to the boy, "He's powerful proud of your learnin'. Read somethin' from the Scriptures." But mostly they just talked about heat and cold, and wind and clouds, and what's gonna be done, and time passing.

As the days of August passed and September brought signs of autumn, the crippled man sat on the porch step and leaned the paralyzed, deformed side of his body against a porch post. This was the only comfortable sitting position he could find. The old coon dog would lie facing his master, with his one eye fixed and his one ear raised. Sometimes he would tap his tail against the earth. Sometimes the ear would droop and the eye would close. Then the great muscles would flex in dreams of the hunt, and the mighty chest would give off the muffled whisper of a bark. Sometimes the two limped together to the edge of the fields, or wandered off into the pine woods. They never went along the road. Perhaps they knew how strange a picture they made when they walked together.

About the middle of September the boy left to go back to his teacher. "It's the most important thing," his mother said.

And the crippled man said, "We're fine. We won't need nothin'."

"I'll come for a few days before it's cold to help gather wood and walnuts."

The broken body of the old man withered more and more, but when the smell of harvest and the hunt came with October, his spirit seemed to quicken his dragging step. One day he cleaned the dusty lantern globe, and the old dog, remembering, bounced on his three legs and wagged his tail as if to say "I'm ready."

The boy had come home. To gather the felled trees and chop the standing dead ones was part of the field pay too. He had been cutting and dragging timber all day.

Sometimes he had looked longingly at the lantern and possum sack, but something inside him had said "Wait. Wait and go together." But the boy did not want to go hunting anymore. And without his saying anything, his father had said, "You're too tired, child. We ain't goin' far, no way."

In the early darkness the halting, hesitant swing of the lantern marked the slow path from fields to pine woods toward the lowlands. The boy stood on the porch, watching until the light was lost behind pine branches. Then he went and sat by the stove. His mother rocked as the mound of kernels grew in the fold of her apron. "He been mighty peart," she said. "I hope he don't fall in the dark. Maybe he'll be happy now he can go hunting again." And she took up her singing where she had left off.

Ain't nobody else gonna walk it for you,
You gotta walk it by yourself.

* * *

Sounder's scratching at the door awakened the boy. It was still night, but the first red glow of dawn was rising in a faint crescent over the pine woods.

"Sounder just couldn't poke slow enough for your father," the mother said to the boy as they stood in the doorway, straining and sifting the dark for some movement.

"Lantern wouldn't burn out in this time," the boy said. "No sign of light. He must have fallen or got tired. Sounder will show me."

Sounder was already across the road into the stalk land, whining, moving his head from one side to the other, looking back to be sure that the boy was following.

Across the stalk land, into the pine woods, into the climbing, brightening glow of the dawn, the boy followed the dog, whose anxious pace slowed from age as they went. "By a dog's age, Sounder is past dying time," the boy said half aloud. Fear had always prompted him to talk to himself.

Deep in the pine woods, along a deserted logging road, the boy and dog came to a small open space where there had once been a log ramp. The sun was just beginning to drive its first splinters of light through the pines, bouncing against tree trunks and earth. At the foot of one of the trees the boy's father sat, the lantern still burning by his side.

"So tuckered out he fell asleep," the boy said to himself.

But the figure did not move when Sounder licked his hand. The boy put his hand on his father's good shoulder and shook ever so gently. The chin did not lift itself; no eyes turned up to meet the boy. "Tired, so tired."

When the boy returned to the cabin and told his mother, her lips grew long and thin and pale. But when she finally spoke, they were warm and soft as when she sang. "When life is so tiresome, there ain't no peace like the greatest peace—the peace of the Lord's hand holding you. And he'll have a store-bought box for burial 'cause all these years I paid close attention to his burial insurance."

They buried the boy's father in the unfenced lot behind the meetin' house. The preacher stood amid the sumac and running briars before the mound of fresh red earth and read:

> The Lord is my shepherd; I shall not want,
> He maketh me to lie down in green pastures.

* * *

"There's plenty of wood, and I must go back to school," the boy told his mother several days after they had buried his father. "Sounder ain't got no spirit left for living. He hasn't gone with me to the woods to chop since Pa died. He doesn't even whine anymore. He just lies on his coffee sacks under the cabin steps. I've dug a grave for him under the big jack oak tree in the stalk land by the fencerow. It'll be ready if the ground freezes. You can carry him on his coffee sacks and bury him. He'll be gone before I come home again."

And the boy was right. Two weeks before he came home for Christmas, Sounder crawled under the cabin and died. The boy's mother told him all there was to tell.

"He just crawled up under the house and died," she said.

The boy was glad. He had learned to read his book with the torn cover better now. He had read in it: "Only the unwise think that what has changed is dead." He had asked the teacher what it meant, and the teacher had said that if a flower blooms once, it goes on blooming somewhere forever. It blooms on for whoever has seen it blooming. It was not quite clear to the boy then, but it was now.

Years later, walking the earth as a man, it would all sweep back over him, again and again, like an echo on the wind.

The pine trees would look down forever on a lantern burning out of oil but not going out. A harvest moon would cast shadows forever of a man walking upright, his dog bouncing after him. And the quiet of the night would fill and echo again with the deep voice of Sounder, the great coon dog.